DUNGEONS OF STRATA

Deepest Dungeon #1

G.D. PENMAN

Contents

ONE

Dissolution in the Midnight Sanctum

Blue-hot flames boiled out from between the yellowed bones of the dragon's jaws. Two tiny lights flickered into being within its eye sockets – pinpricks of cold in the darkness.

Martin stood back and watched as Jericho and the other juggernauts clanked ahead, bellowing the guild's name.

"Iron Riot!"

An answering roar from the ranged fighters behind them was so loud Martin almost snatched off his headset.

"Iron Riot!"

The undead dragon Ulkanthrax rose from the massive pile of bones, head swaying towards the roof of the Midnight Sanctum as sinuously as a cobra's.

Martin readied his weapon, but the boss was invulnerable as it rambled through its usual script of threats and insults. All around Martin, the other players were preparing themselves, drinking potions, gathering mana and using abilities to boost their damage in the first crucial phase of the fight.

He felt a swell of pride as they all rattled through their tasks seamlessly, as they had a dozen times before. There was a reason Iron Riot was one of the greatest raiding guilds in the history of Dracolich Online. He'd trust any one of these raiders to perform their task perfectly, even in the hardest raid of the game. With a smirk, he aimed his bow and cast his own *Hunter's Mark* just as the juggernauts charged.

Hunter's Mark 426 mana
Increases ranged attack damage by 12.7% for 20 seconds.
Increases critical chance by 31.4% for an additional 10 seconds.
Prevents targets from entering stealth for the duration of both effects.

A solid mass of arrows, bullets and spells hammered into Ulkanthrax as it spread its wings and belched flames that coated half the room. The healers on that side were forced to scatter, but Martin and his team had been lucky this time. They'd get a chance to rattle through another rotation of attacks before the flames died down and they had to make a run for it themselves.

Adriel yelped out from the midst of the scorched healers in her helium-high voice, "Bloodmages, cast *Vigor*. Shamans, don't stand in the fire!"

The shamans leapt away, but it was too late for one of them; distracted by casting healing spells on everyone else, Dante hadn't noticed his own health plummeting. Martin groaned. That was clumsy, especially so early in the fight.

He caught a brief glimpse of Lindsay's character in the midst of the melee, hacking away at the dragon's side with both swords a blur of motion. She was the guild's leader, but Martin wasn't sure she had even noticed they'd lost a healer yet.

Ulkanthrax was losing its own health fast; it was down to 75% by the time it turned to breathe fire on Martin's side of the room and the ranged attackers had to make a run for it. He cast *Arcane Accuracy* as he sprinted to help keep the damage up.

Arcane Accuracy 699 mana
Increases hit chance for party members by 62% for 5 seconds.
Increases critical chance for party members by 13% for 10 seconds.

He fired off a barrage of arrows as he sprinted to his new position, each of them arcing around to strike into the tangled heart of dark magic inside Ulkanthrax's ribcage, no matter how wild Martin's aim. The monster's health bar continued to shrink.

Jericho tossed a grappling hook into its face to drag the dragon's attention his way, protecting the other melee attackers.

It was entirely accidental that Martin came to a halt standing on top of the crisp-fried remains of Dante, but he wasn't exactly upset about it. They had been raiding the Midnight Sanctum every week since it was released. If someone couldn't remember the first phase of the last boss in the game by now, they deserved to be burned. And stamped on.

Ulkanthrax lunged forward, dragging its massive body free of the heap of bones. The first phase had been the easy part, but now the chaos really started. With its bare-boned wings tucked in against its sides, the dragon launched itself forward towards Martin's group, fire trailing from its gaping maw and leaving a trail of blue death behind it.

Gritting his teeth, Martin loosed arrow after arrow into Ulkanthrax's face. He would get in one last bit of damage before he dodged away. He saw the warmages and the ironsights up ahead of him leaping out of the dragon's path, but he held on till the last moment, hammering it with ensorcelled arrows.

At the very last moment he leapt aside, rolling across the broken and scattered bones of the raiders who had come before him. He bounced back to his feet and readied his bow once again—

—and the whole world went dark.

Martin blinked. Then he cursed and yanked his headset off, reality reasserting itself in a horrid rush. He was sitting in his chair in front of his desk, the VR controls strapped to his hands and the shouts of his guild-mates and the wailing of the dragon fading away into the background. There was a baby crying next door, setting his teeth on edge. His view, once a riot of colors, was now replaced by the peeling plaster of his bedroom wall. Real life was ugly.

He fumbled one of the gloves off and grabbed a tiny screwdriver from a drawer. His VR rig was so ancient that Martin suspected parts of it were fossilized; so old that he couldn't even get replacement parts, even if he could afford them. Which he couldn't.

He yanked the front panel off his headset and felt around inside until he found the loose connection. The tiny spark that shocked his finger helped track it down. He jammed the screwdriver inside, forcing the connector back into place, then slapped the whole contraption – still trailing loose wires – back onto his head.

It couldn't have been more than twenty seconds, but somehow everything had gone to hell. Lines of blue fire crisscrossed the room. Five of his guild were down, including two of their healers.

Lindsay was bellowing orders that nobody seemed to be following. Ulkanthrax still had the same amount of health as before. Martin groaned. Why hadn't Lindsay just called it a failure and started the whole fight over again?

He opened his mouth to suggest it when he spotted the clock at the bottom corner of his field of vision. It was two in the morning. If they gave up now, half the guild would just go to bed. They were probably running on nothing but adrenaline as it was.

Ulkanthrax spun at the end of the cavernous room and lowered its horned head at Martin, ready for another charge. They were down three of their five healers, and Martin knew there was no way they could push through the amount of damage Ulkanthrax was dealing out. It was time to switch gears. Martin thumbed on his voice-chat.

"I need all the ranged attackers to switch target. Now."

He set his *Hunter's Mark* on the massive stalactite dangling from the roof of the cavern, and with a level of trust that he probably would have found heart-warming if he hadn't worked so hard to earn it, the guild opened fire on the spike of rock above them.

"It won't come down," Lindsay yelled in his ear. "We already tried that, remember?"

"We tried it back when we first started raiding here," Martin shot back. "Not with all the top-tier gear equipped. We've got the damage we need this time."

He hoped he sounded more confident than he felt.

"And if we don't?" Lindsay's words were strained.

Martin forced a smile, though nobody could see it. "We'll all be dead anyway if it charges again."

There was a long moment of silence before Lindsay answered.

"All right. Do it."

"You're both idiots," Jericho growled. "Some glorious day, I'm going to stand back and let you both die of your own idiocy."

"But not today?" Lindsay laughed.

"Not today."

Martin watched as Jericho and his juggernauts threw their grappling hooks onto Ulkanthrax, dragging themselves behind it and slowing the gargantuan beast's charge to a crawl.

Martin and the other ranged attackers kept up their barrage, launching everything they had into the stalactite. Then, to his delight, it began to wobble.

With a silent prayer to whatever gods protected MMO players, Martin cast the spell he'd been saving for the end of the fight.

Worldbreaker 9,876 mana.
Deals 32,800 spell damage to immobile targets.
Mobile targets are immune.

The arrow left his bow as nothing but wood and steel, but by the time it reached the ceiling it was surrounded by a near-blinding glow. It hit the stone just as Ulkanthrax broke its bonds and lurched forward.

With a crack, the stalactite came loose and plummeted down. For a single, heart-stopping moment, it looked like it would miss. But their timing was perfect.

The spear of rock hit home, pinning the dracolich to the cavern floor like a needle through a gigantic undead butterfly. Smoke belched out, obscuring Martin's view, even as attacks from his allies whipped into the maelstrom.

As the smoke cleared, the full payoff of their success came into view. Blue flames still boiled up out of the monster's maw, but the lethal charging was over. It was trapped in place, skewered to the ground between the rows of monstrous ribs.

The whole guild started whooping with delight in voice chat, even the dead ones. The survivors unleashed hell, hacking and blasting the trapped beast with abandon.

Soon enough, the fight entered the final phase. The skull of Ulkanthrax drifted loose, surrounded by a nimbus of crackling power. By now, the guild was usually reduced to a fraction of its number. But not today.

With the last phase turned into a cakewalk, momentum carried the guild through. They didn't falter for a second. Every living member of the guild was like a moving part in a complex machine. And like a machine, they performed their roles seamlessly. Martin couldn't have been more proud of them.

Lindsay landed the final blow, setting off the long animation of the skull exploding in a shower of flames, but their victory had been certain from the moment the stalactite fell. Lindsay's voice cut through the tail end of the ranting dragon's death scene.

"All right folks, that is a wrap. Bring out your dead and come grab some loot."

Adriel, the leader of their healers, brought her own people and then the rest of their fallen friends back to life, and in the midst of the chatter someone touched the remains of Ulkan-thrax, bringing up the loot table in front of everyone's faces.

Martin was about to wave it away without a second thought – he had the best gear in the game already – when he spotted the *Heroic Bladedancer's Cuirass* on the list. It was the last item they needed from the Midnight Sanctum. The last excuse they'd had to keep coming back here week after week. It was over.

Lindsay selected it from the list as her reward, and nobody challenged it. As they watched, her character's outfit changed into the full matching set and she took on a purple glow as the armor's passive effects took hold.

The reality of the situation fell into Martin's gut like a lead weight. Dracolich Online was really over. Sure, the servers might go on running for a few more years, but the developers had announced that there would be no new content and no future expansions. Lesser guilds might take that time to dawdle through all of the end-game content they hadn't reached yet, but Iron Riot was finished.

If he was being honest, they could have quit after beating the hardcore heroic version of the Midnight Sanctum for the first time, but there was a streak of completionism in Lindsay. She wasn't ready to give up the game until there was nothing left.

Iron Riot gathered around the crumbling heap of bones at the center of the cavern to listen as Lindsay said a few words, just like every other night.

"All right, folks. We had one hell of a run. First to clear Anguish Keep. The fastest Forest of Flickering Flames run in history. First to clear the Midnight Sanctum, too. Iron Riot have done it all, we've done it first and we've done it the best."

"Hear, hear," Jericho rumbled.

Lindsay turned in a slow circle, looking at the assembled guild in all its bloodstained glory.

"Listen. It's late, and we don't need to make any hasty deci-sions about what we want to do next. What do you say we take a day off, then have ourselves a think about where Iron Riot should go from here?"

There were a few mumbled agreements, but the same sadness that had hit Martin as the boss died seemed to have taken root in all of them too. One by one, they began to blink out of existence. Jericho came over and patted Martin on the shoulder.

"It's the end of an era."

Then he was gone too. All at once, the rest of the raiders were snuffed out like the candles on a birthday cake.

Lindsay mimed a salute as she vanished. Adriel blew a shy kiss. Martin tried to open his mouth and say something. Anything. But the words had escaped him.

Without another sound, he opened up his menu and logged out.

TWO

Exile in the Lifeless Kingdom

Martin stared at the screen and let the numbers blur together into a meaningless gray smudge. Everything had felt drab and pointless since the moment he woke up, and it was still too early in the day for him to be feeling the impact of his 3 a.m. bedtime. He had to assume that he was depressed.

Work wasn't the happiest part of Martin's life even at the best of times, and the last few months had become increasingly unpleasant. If his new boss had treated him with the same level of general malevolence that she inflicted on everyone else in the office, he probably could have tolerated it, but there was something about Martin in particular that seemed to bother Gillian.

The fact that he did not make mistakes, show up late to work or break the rules in any quantifiable way seemed to indicate to Gillian that he was getting one over on her, rather than being a sign that he was a model employee. He could feel the loathing radiating off her, even when she wasn't hovering around looking for some fault to exploit.

To Martin's mind, middle managers were necessary to a business in the same way that mosquitos were necessary to a functional ecosystem. They would both have no noticeable impact if they were removed. And they both sucked. He blinked and focused on the screen again, hands moving of their own volition to work through the orders.

Since Gillian's arrival, he had taken the time to read through the employee evaluation materials carefully. Martin and his colleagues were judged on their productivity in two ways: on a bell-curve with the other employees, and on a year-to-year analysis.

The year-to-year part was what concerned Martin. A little over a year back, in response to the inexplicable hatred of his boss, he had coded an automated macro to handle all of the simple orders, pushing his productivity through the roof compared to his colleagues.

That had been great for denying her ammunition last year, but now he had to compete with his own numbers, and it was going to be difficult to show significant improvement – especially now that he had shared out the program with the rest of the staff. A reasonable boss would have been delighted with him taking initiative. Gillian was not reasonable.

After a long miserable morning of forcing himself through the motions, he clocked out for lunch at precisely the correct time then slumped back into his seat to play with his phone. By force of habit, he went to open up DracolichNews.org. He paused, fingers hovering above the screen.

This was the problem. Not his awful boss. Not his mindless job processing orders for an internet service provider. Not even his absent social life. It was the game. He'd lost the only thing in his life that he had to look forward to. He set his phone face down on the desk with a sigh.

Even as he did, Gillian stopped by his cubicle and stared at him. He could feel her eyes boring into the side of his head. He silently counted to ten, then swiveled his chair to face her.

"Can I help you with something?" he asked.

"You're meant to be on your lunch break."

He forced a smile. "I am."

"You're sitting at your desk." She smiled back.

He took a deep breath. *Calm. Friendly. Accommodating.*

"Do you need me to go somewhere else?" he asked.

"Don't you have somewhere else you need to go? Don't you need to eat?"

"Got to watch my figure." He smiled back, patting his stomach.

Gillian's eyes narrowed. Despite eating nothing but garbage and leading a life characterized by a series of seats and desks, his body still refused to take on the spherical shape he was clearly destined for.

Gillian did not share his metabolism. She was starting to look a little round at the edges, despite her daily trips to the gym, and she was known to be touchy about it. *Damn.*

There was a definite edge to her voice when she replied, "Proper nutrition and rest are important to living your best life, Martin."

"Thanks for caring, Gillian."

He didn't let his smile slip for a moment, and after another long glowering moment, she moved on. Once he was sure that she was gone, he shuddered.

His life might be sad, and he was in pieces over finishing a video game, but at least he wasn't Gillian.

Now that he had acknowledged why he was feeling miserable, the afternoon went by a little easier. Long ago he'd made a game out of processing the orders and finding new ways to tweak the system to make the process faster.

It wasn't exactly mentally stimulating work – except when something went horribly wrong and he got roped into trying to fix everyone else's problems. Then it made him feel like his brain was burning as he tried to puzzle it all through.

Today, there was no helpful crisis to keep him occupied, so his mind kept drifting back to the quiet death of Iron Riot. Lindsay had asked them to go their separate ways. He supposed that meant picking a new game to play, but what could ever compare to Dracolich?

He'd dabbled in other VRMMOs over the years, even hitting the level cap in a few of the better ones, but Dracolich and the guild had always been the center that he orbited around. He supposed he could just vote to stay put – to linger in the world they had conquered for a little bit longer – but without the challenge he wondered if he would get anything out of it beyond nostalgia. No matter how distasteful it might be, he was going to have to look for a new game.

He'd jump online when he got home, browse around and talk it out with Lindsay. There were plenty of new games out there that would already have her attention. All he had to do was convince her to pick one that was old enough for his rickety old gear to operate, then switch to an all-ramen diet for the rest of the month so he would be able to afford the software. He could have just picked a new game for himself, he supposed, but letting go of Dracolich and Iron Riot at the same time seemed like too much to bear.

He hit the power switch exactly as the clock ticked past five and hurried past Gillian so she couldn't drag him into another pointless conversation about pointless things. Some other poor sap had the full weight of her attention as Martin ducked into the elevator.

Much like his work life, Martin had optimized the trip home. A brisk walk to the subway station with a stop at a convenience store on the corner if he was trying to save money, or one of the innumerable fast-food joints if time was more valuable that day.

With the purchase of a new game on the horizon, he opted to buy a pack of instant ramen for dinner and browsed the net on his phone as he walked, hoping to see which old VRMMOs were still being updated. Unfortunately, the moment he tapped "VRMMO" into the search engine he was flooded with people gushing about the newest, hottest one around: Strata Online. He skipped right past it without even looking.

The hype around that game – and the brand new "NIH" VR rig that you needed to play it – was ridiculous. Nothing could be as good as people were claiming Strata was. The fact that you couldn't get any footage from inside the game just made his disdain for it deepen. All that hype and nothing to show for it sounded like the latest industry scam to him.

Normally he jogged from the subway station to his block, but tonight he strolled. There was nothing waiting for him in his crappy little apartment, so what was the point of rushing?

Dead trees lined the boulevard, their leafless branches abstract against the backdrop of brutalist concrete. The streets were clogged with trash this far out from the center of town, but nobody in this neighborhood could afford a car anyway, so it didn't make much difference except when he had to crunch across a road.

The elevator from the street to his apartment had been out of order for somewhere in the region of six years, so Martin took the rusty utility access stairs in the alleyway instead.

Behind every door he passed on his way up the building were people living their lives, cooking their meals, or screaming at each other for one mundane reason or another. Martin drifted by them all like a ghost.

He was so lost in his thoughts that he didn't notice the box dumped outside his apartment until he tripped over it, mashing his forehead into the plywood of his door and leaving a dent. That would probably come out of his security deposit if the land-lord ever swung by.

The box wasn't huge, but it felt like it was filled with bricks when he tried to lift it. He hadn't ordered anything. He wouldn't order anything unless he was sure it would be delivered when he was here. He was lucky this package hadn't already been stolen. Yet here this mystery parcel sat.

Flipping it over showed his address printed very clearly on the front, right beside the "This way up" stamp that the delivery guy had completely ignored. Martin picked it up and was halfway through unlocking the door before a sense of something being not quite right made him re-read the label. The address was correct, but the name was Ake Stormbringer – the gnome juggernaut he had once made as an April Fool's joke.

Only one person in the world knew both his address and that name. Lindsay. Even more intrigued than before, Martin rushed the package straight to his desk and cut it open with the point of his tiny screwdriver. The cardboard split, and Martin hissed, "No way."

A plastic card bore the words "Strata Online" on its front, along with an alphanumeric code. But the real prize was what lay beneath: a brand-new, pristine NIH VR rig.

Martin clapped a hand over his mouth to stop a squeal from escaping. She couldn't have. She wouldn't. He knew Lindsay had a decent job compared to his own entry-level hell, but there was no way she could have dropped this kind of cash just for fun. The Neural Interface Headset alone cost more than a month of his rent.

This was insane. While he had frequently accused Lindsay of madness before, he never suspected she would actually do something like this.

Lindsay. He needed to speak to her immediately. He had to get her to return the NIH and the game. She could still get her money back if he was quick enough.

He doubled back to lock the door and put the ramen on the boil while the computer booted up, then jumped right into chat. Lindsay was online, of course, but next to her name there was the damning little note: *In game - Strata Online.*

He stared at the words until the pot started to boil over, then ran back to rescue his noodles before it was too late. Scooping a pair of chopsticks from the sink, he slurped his dinner down and returned to staring at his screen.

If Lindsay was playing – and playing on the same schedule they usually did – she would be online for another six hours or more before she got any messages he sent her. She was notorious for sealing herself off from all distractions.

He glanced at the returns policy and the date on the blacked-out receipt inside the box; it would have to be sent back before the night was out. But he couldn't do that himself. He needed Lindsay's details.

If he installed the NIH and the game to get in touch with her, she would lose her money on the game, but the NIH could still be returned.

A traitorous little voice in the back of his head added, *and you will get a chance to see what all the fuss is about with Strata.* He tossed the pot and sticks into the sink and came back to the computer with excitement bubbling just beneath the surface.

Even if he didn't keep Strata, he would get to see all of the character creation options, not to mention test out the next generation of VR before he saved up for the rest of his adult life trying to afford his own set. He could play for just one night. He had enough self-control to pack this all back up in the box later after he found Lindsay and sorted all this out.

With reverence, he lifted the thin metal band of the NIH out of the box and connected it to the computer to start installing. Tapping in the Strata code to activate his account was easy. He jumped back online while he waited for both hardware and software to get their act together. There was so little information about Strata it was almost impressive.

All he could really find online were auction listings for in-game items, but from those he was able to get the first hints at some of the classes and stats involved. The number of items that were actually on sale was miniscule compared to most MMOs, and the prices were much higher as a result.

It made him wonder just how exclusive a club Lindsay had dragged him into. He was just starting to compare the listed stats across the different items when a notification went off and on-screen instructions talked him through adjusting the NIH to fit his head. It didn't pinch exactly, but there was definitely pressure where it ran over the fresh bruise on his forehead, pressure that amped up to a throbbing when the countdown to activation appeared onscreen.

He hurried to lie down before the VR kicked in. He didn't know much about NIH, but he'd heard all the horror stories about people falling and hurting themselves when it activated unexpectedly. Even as he scrambled blindly towards his bed, he started hearing the countdown.

Three.

Two.

One.

Darkness.

THREE

Decisions in the Darkness

For an awful moment, Martin thought he was dead; that something had gone wrong with the neural interface, and it had accidentally shut down his heart along with his voluntary motor functions. He was blind.

Panic strangled him, the encroaching darkness growing colder. Then, from nowhere, words coalesced like gathering mist.

*Welcome to **Strata Online**.*
Would you like to create a new character?

There were other options drifting beneath those words but they were nebulous and dark; choices he couldn't make yet. Martin tried to reach out, but with a lurch in his stomach, he realized he had no hands, no arms, no body.

Looking down, he couldn't see anything at all. He tried to bring his hands up to touch his face but there was simply nothing there. Closing his eyes did nothing without eyelids to block his sight. The same words were still hovering in front of his non-existent face.

Martin groaned, and the sound echoed through the boundless void. Okay, he could at least make noise.

"Yes," Martin said.

From out of the darkness, a ring of people stepped forward, materializing from the same smoky nothingness. Each wore different armor and sported different weapons, but their faces were the same – a blank white mask. He might have shuddered if he still had a body.

He examined the closest form It bore a suit of intricate full-plate armor, coupled with a sword and shield in its hands. As he stared, it evaporated into a mass of words.

*The questing **Knight** is a bastion of martial might. Wielding the heaviest armor and armaments, they make up the bulk of the Crusade's fighting force.*

Strength: 6 Agility: 4
Endurance: 8 Willpower: 4
Health: 40 Stamina: 30 Sin: -10

The words vanished as Martin read them, replaced by a mass of other statistics and sample abilities. *Armor Proficiency. Lancing Strike. Shield Slam.*

Martin let his gaze unfocus, and the words resolved themselves back into the shape of a man. His brief bout of fear had faded away – this was at least familiar. He looked around the circle, reading off the class names.

After the **Knight** came the **Knave**, clad in light armor and wielding daggers. Next, the **Invoker,** draped in a robe with a staff clutched in one hand and a glowing fireball in the other.

Those were all easy enough to understand; the fighter, thief and mage had parallels in every fantasy game going. The rest were a little harder to understand.

The *Exorcist* had some armor on, but nowhere near as much as the knight, with a sword in one fist and a golden light emanating from its counterpart. Maybe it was some sort of paladin?

The next one along, the **Hierophant**, wore robes and carried a staff just like the other caster, but instead of elemental magic, that golden glow surrounded its form too. *Probably the healer class.*

The last one in the circle was strangest of all. The **Martyr** had a few pieces of armor strapped onto its featureless body, but huge expanses of skin were bare. And instead of weapons, its empty hands were held out. Some sort of monk, or unarmed combatant? Martin looked closer.

Drawn to the Dungeon of Strata by strange dreams and omens, the Martyr is one of the chosen of Aten. Imbued by the god of light with holy powers, and a ceaseless desire to protect others, even at the expense of their own lives.

Strength: 4 Agility: 4
Endurance: 6 Willpower: 8
Health: 50 Stamina: 30 Sin: -30

Sufferance – You suffer 10% of the damage that would otherwise be dealt to your allies within a 20ft radius.

Penance – Increases the effect of *Sufferance* to 50% of your allies' damage for 20 seconds.
[1-minute cooldown]

Celestial Body – You regenerate 1% of your health per second at all times.

Martin grinned. The language might have been different, but the meaning was the same: martyrs were some sort of masochistic tank class. Martin assumed the self-healing scaled up with time to make up for the lack of armor.

It was a neat change from the usual man-in-a-can set-up, but he had no interest in playing a tank ever again. He'd learned from his last attempt in Dracolich that it wasn't for him. When you spent the whole battle face to face with the enemy, there was no chance to read the battlefield or to plan out your strategy. You couldn't see the woods for the trees, or the dungeon for the dragon.

The big problem in choosing a class was that he didn't know what Lindsay would have chosen. It was hard to complement her choice without knowing. She would never have picked the martyr – because she hated tanking as much as Martin did – but beyond that he had no idea which direction she would have jumped.

He'd seen her take on every other role over the years, although he doubted she'd have picked a healer if she was the only one playing. Still, he couldn't pick the healer class in case she was an invoker, because then they would be stuck without any melee fighters at all.

He wasn't a huge fan of healing, if he was being honest. It felt like it all came down to churning out raw numbers, and that just wasn't terribly satisfying. Still, with no inherent healing at all, their progress would always be limited, and even if the game had healing items, they usually weren't very economical. Martin stopped in front of the exorcist and peered closer.

A foot-soldier of the Crusade and a mortal instrument of Aten's will, the **Exorcist** *seeks out darkness wherever it takes root, using every tool at their disposal, from steel to the holy light itself to drive it back.*

That wasn't a particularly useful description, but the sample abilities helped a lot more.

Strength: 6 Agility: 4
Endurance: 6 Willpower: 6
Health: 30 Stamina: 40 Sin: -20

Celestial Strike – Deals combined physical and light damage equal to the user's weapon damage.

[10-second cooldown]

Healing Touch – Restores 33% of a target ally's health on physical contact.
[60-second cooldown]

Rite of Retribution – Increases all allies' critical hit chance by 33% for 1 minute.
[60-minute cooldown]

Healing abilities, melee combat, and buffs too – it seemed exorcists had a good spread of abilities, and hopefully he'd be able to build his character more in one direction or the other as they leveled up. That way, he could fill whatever gaps there were in the party.

That was, if he planned to keep the game and the NIH. Which he definitely didn't. He was only here to talk to Lindsay. It didn't matter which class he picked. He was just here to talk.

Martin said, "Exorcist," and the other class mannequins took a step backwards into the darkness once more.

To his surprise, four new figures stepped forward. Each of them was clad in the exorcist's light armor, but the bodies inside were wildly different. It seemed Strata Online didn't have any of the usual generic fantasy races to play.

There was a lizard-man, a wolf-man, a bird-person and a rat-man to choose from, with any other options still to come drifting in the maelstrom of shadows just beyond Martin's field of vision. He drifted closer to the wolf man to marvel at the detail on its fur.

It looked real. The faint breeze passing through the darkness was ruffling the individual hairs. But how was his computer managing to render all of that detail without melting through the desk?

A sudden block of text appeared, and he was startled out of his admiration.

*The proud and powerful **Wulvan** are the undisputed masters of the northern steppes. While even the name of their race has always been synonymous with warfare, they have come to the Dungeon of Strata on a mission of peace, to prevent the darkness within it from spilling out and consuming the world.*

Strength: +3 Agility: +2
Endurance: +2 Willpower: -2 Sin: 0

Scent of Blood – Damage dealt increased by 15% when you are below 25% health.

Cullthe Weak – Damage increased by 5% when facing only a single enemy.

Thick Fur – 10% resistance to cold damage, 10% increased vulnerability to waterlogged status.

Next came a flood of statistics that grew more and more complicated the longer Martin stared at them. *Strength, Agility, Endurance* and *Willpower* all seemed straightforward enough, and both *Health* and *Stamina* were determined from a combination of those stats and the chosen class, but everything that came afterwards meant practically nothing.

There were rows upon rows of status effect resistances that Martin couldn't even begin to grasp, as well as something called *Sin*, which seemed to start off in the double-digit negatives for the exorcist class. And it could take him forever to puzzle through all the intricacies of how willpower related to both spell damage and magic resistance.

It was too much. He didn't have the time to work through it all right now; he was just going to trust to the racial bonuses to decide it. After all, he could always reroll if Lindsay somehow managed to convince him to keep the game. Which she wouldn't, because he was definitely returning it.

Looming to his immediate right was the lizard-person, which the game helpfully informed him was called a Sythvan. They were resistant to fire damage, susceptible to cold, could breathe underwater and could choose to play dead when their health dipped under 10%. All helpful traits, but nothing mind-blowing.

The bird-person, the Corvan, was up next. The Corvan's racial traits were a lot more flavorful. *Shiny Things* made it easier to spot treasure, *Hollow Bones* gave a 50% reduction in falling speed in exchange for a 1% increased susceptibility to all other damage, and *Bird Brain* gave them a 50/50 chance to resist stun effects. They had a natural bonus to *Perception* too, which sent Martin flicking down through the swathes of stats in search of more information on what *Perception* covered.

He tried to wet his lips when he found it nestled amongst *Throwing Weapon Proficiency* and *Alchemy* only to discover he had neither the lips nor tongue required. Being disembodied was really confusing, but it did nothing to detract from his excitement.

There was just so much hidden away in this game already. He could spend days and days just puzzling through it all and he hadn't even started playing yet.

He should have chosen quickly, but the completionist in him wouldn't let him move on without at least considering all the options, so he turned to the last one: a rather miserable-looking rat-man.

The Wulvan were imposing, the Sythvan and Corvan had special traits that could change the gameplay experience, but this thing felt like it was going to be a joke. Moving closer, the racial traits rolled down into his field of vision.

*The timid **Murovan** were the first to discover the Dungeon of Strata and the first to succumb to the temptations that the darkness within it breeds. Making their dwellings mostly in the sewers of the cities built by greater races, the Murovan have been carried along with the tide of the Crusade unwillingly.*

Strength: -2 Agility: +3
Endurance: +1 Sin: 20

Cowardice – You move 20% faster when your health is reduced below 30%.

That wasn't a great start. With descriptions like that, it was as if the developers didn't want people to play as Murovan.

Night Vision – Your *Perception* is not reduced by low-light conditions.

Not much to write home about there either. It seemed like the game was going to be taking place mainly in this "Dungeon of Strata," but it wasn't like all the other players were just going to be left to stumble about in the dark; there would be torches or lanterns for sale. The *Night Vision* trait would only be useful for knaves, and being a sneaky rat-man kind of felt like stereotyping.

Greasy Fur – 10% resistance to water damage and waterlogged status, 10% increased vulnerability to burning status.

All in all, the Murovan seemed like the obvious worst choice. They were underpowered when it came to racial traits, and the statistical bonuses that came with selecting them were marginally lower than for the other races.

When Martin dug down into the sheets of stats a little bit, he discovered that being a rat-man actually negated some of the benefits of choosing an exorcist, resetting the Sin score to 0. Not that he knew what that even meant. With a sigh, he stepped away from the rat-man to turn his attention back to his viable options.

He was burrowing through the miniscule stat differences between the Corvan and the Sythvan races when a niggling doubt at the back of his mind made him turn back around. He looked from the looming Wulvan to the other three and paused. He had immediately discounted the Wulvan; head-on attacks weren't his style, and the bulk of the thing had put him off. But there was a flip side to that.

This wasn't just an MMO; it was a VRMMO, so the attacks that monsters and players made on each other would hit or miss based on the actual movements made, not on some random number generation. That meant that something big was easier to hit, and something small would be harder.

The Murovan might not look like much, but the scrawny, stunted species would be twice as hard to hit compared to the Wulvan. He zipped in closer to examine the actual proportions of the character models.

The Wulvan and Sythvan had a big advantage when it came to reach compared to the other two, but Strata was set in a dungeon, which meant tunnel fighting. Being bigger could actually be a disadvantage when you were in close quarters. That extra reach might mean not being able to take a full swing with the sword.

Martin couldn't work out why the Murovan seemed so underpowered compared to the other three, but with the hidden advantages that came with the way VRMMOs were played, they might actually be the best choice.

He took another look through the stats and realized that the reduced strength and endurance were loosely proportional to the size difference. The Murovan *was* the best choice. He could feel it in his gut. Not that he currently had a gut. Without another thought he said, "Murovan."

Darkness swooped back in and the other models fell away. Martin was surrounded instead with walls upon walls of customization options to change his avatar's appearance. With no small amount of relief, he realized that he could finally reach out and touch them, despite anything like limbs still being hidden from his sight.

After a few slaps of the randomizer button, he went into fine detail, tweaking a few features to look a little less ridiculous before finally turning his attention to the empty box that demanded a name. He'd used so many names throughout his gaming career that he didn't really have a "go-to".

Besides, he wasn't sure that the vaguely Norse-sounding names that he'd picked to fit in with the setting of Dracolich were going to suit Strata, or that they'd be a good fit for a grumpy little gray rat-man either. He dredged a name from the recesses of his memory.

"Skaife."

That had been the name of his very first character back in Dracolich, so Lindsay would find it easier to recognize him. The fact that it sounded shady enough to suit a rat-man was just a bonus.

The moment he confirmed his choice, the rat-man avatar abruptly shed its fancy gear, leaving nothing but ragged clothes and a rusted dagger tucked through its belt. Then, with the irresistible drag of gravity, the Murovan he had just created came closer.

Martin wasn't sure if he was moving or the rat-man was, but either way, they were being dragged together. His incorporeal self passed through the fur and flesh without any sensation. Then, suddenly, he could feel his body once more… or rather, *a* body.

He blinked. He breathed. He looked down at his furry little hands, each finger tipped with a pointed claw. A stranger's voice, nasal and grating, came out of his mouth when he opened it.

"Wow."

This was completely different from the VR games he had played before. He could feel things as if they were *real*. When he ran his fingers over his fur, it tickled. When he nipped at his lip with the pointed Murovan teeth, it stung. He could feel the wind flowing past his character, hear the whistling of the air as it passed him by. Even the breeze had a faint taste of mildew.

The last sensation to arrive was a sick lurch in his belly that told him he was falling. Martin yelped as he tumbled end over end, his vision a dark blur as he fell towards a tiny circle of light beneath him.

The opening at the bottom of the shaft grew larger and larger, the spot of white becoming a gray expanse of torchlit cobblestones.

With a whimper, Martin closed his eyes.

FOUR

Ill Met in Beachhead

It didn't hurt when Martin hit the stone floor but he still felt it – like he would feel a dentist digging around in his gums despite the novocaine.

The sensation was distant, but some animal part of his brain knew that it should be hurting. He struggled to draw in a breath, eyes out of focus, a red tint around the edges of his vision shading the blurry sight of stone right in front of his face.

If he didn't move, the next character to spawn was going to land right on top of him, and if the game had knocked the air out of his lungs just from falling he really didn't want to see how the physics engine would treat him if one of the much bigger races landed on his head.

His claws made little scrabbling noises as he tried to get them underneath him. It took a herculean effort to roll himself over, but when he did a whole new world passed by him in a kaleidoscope.

Martin was left staring up at water-smoothed stone above him, a single gaping hole the only thing breaking up its uniformity.

After a moment, he could breathe again and suddenly he was completely overwhelmed by all of the sensory input. Up close, he could hear the braziers of coals around him crackling, but beyond that there was a hubbub of voices.

But that was nothing compared to his shock when he realized that he could smell the distant damp of the cave, layered over with a sharp tang of wood, the sourness of sweat, spices and the iron tinge of blood.

In real life, he did his best to ignore everything that he smelled, but here even the sickly-sweet aroma of rot seemed rich and lush. The pain might have been distant, but now he could feel the grainy texture of the stone beneath his paws, the ridges and striations pressing into the soft pads on his fingers.

Pressing his eyes shut gave him the moment of respite that he needed. This all felt too real now that he had a body. Now, it was easy to understand why everyone was losing their mind over Strata. This didn't feel like a game. It felt more real than reality.

Despite having his eyes closed, Martin was still being bombarded with information.

His health and stamina were displayed on the periphery of his vision when his eyes were shut. The impact on the floor had knocked a solid 50% off his health, but as he watched, it gradually ticked back towards a full red bar, one point at a time.

Health regenerated outside of combat; that was good to know. He'd have to check back in during a fight to see if the martyr class were the only ones whose health regenerated all the time.

Beyond the bars at the side, there was even more information to be found when he had his eyes closed.

The darkness here was like the darkness of the character generation sequence, filled with mist that would readily coil into words if he concentrated. No matter where he looked, his health and stamina followed, but at the bottom of his field of vision he realized that two words also persisted. **Deep One.**

He could worry about what that meant later. By thinking about it, he discovered he was able to pull up his sparse inventory, containing nothing more than *Tattered Rags [0 armor]* and a

Rusty Knife [1-3 damage]. That was just depressing, so he let his attention lapse and found himself back in the dark.

There was a thump that shook the ground beneath Martin's head. His eyes snapped open and he startled to his feet. A massive golden-furred Wulvan had just fallen from the hole in the roof and was lying in the middle of the circle of braziers, groaning.

Martin backed away quickly. This other new player seemed just as overwhelmed as Martin had been. He lay face down, alternating between moaning and growling. As Martin stared with his mouth hanging open, words sprang into being above the Wulvan's head, coalescing out of nothing the same way things had appeared in the darkness up above.

Dogmeat McBone Level 1 Wulvan Knight

The words reminded him that this was all just a game, and a switch in Martin's head flicked from panic to observation. Now that his brain had stopped screaming, Martin looked around and took it all in.

Someone had built a town in this huge cavern, not all at once, but in stages, layering one heap of garbage on top of another until it started to take on the shape of a building. There were strewn pieces of masonry, dragged in from who knew where; planks of wood that all seemed to end in splinters; and raw green branches and logs that seemed likely to have been pulled straight from a tree's roots.

Interspersed among those faintly logical pieces were other things that had no place being parts of buildings. Vines had been grown in place of mortar. A full suit of armor had been beaten flat and formed the roof of the nearest lean-to. There were even bright-colored animal hides stretched over the many holes in the walls, a consequence of this slapdash approach to construction. Not that they'd need to be watertight down in a cave with no rain.

The overall appearance was of a chaotic mess, but that was probably contributed to by the swarms of people moving just beyond the circle of flames.

While Martin had been spinning around, trying to take it all in, the knight had pulled himself up onto his hands and knees, a long line of drool trailing from his muzzle to the cold stone. He looked up at Martin with dull fury in his eyes. When he growled, it took Martin a moment to remember that this was only a game. That was when the Sythvan fell onto the Wulvan, head first.

By all rights it should have killed both of them, but Martin understood that you had to give game developers a little creative license to keep things fun. The new arrival survived. The Wulvan most certainly did not.

As the Sythvan moaned and flopped around, Martin decided that discretion was the better part of valor. He strolled away before the stunned serpent could start asking him questions he didn't have the answers to.

Beyond the circle of torches, the crowd was like an ocean just waiting to sweep him off in the tide. He let it, slipping into the stream of traffic and letting the press of bodies carry him along to the marketplace.

The vast majority of the people around him were other players, and giving them a moment's attention led to their names, classes and levels popping up above their heads. Doing the same to NPCs gave him their job title more often than an actual name. He turned his attention away from the nearest *Marketplace Merchant* to look at their actual wares.

From the brief glimpse at his inventory Martin knew he had no money to spend, but it was still fascinating to study all the objects spread out on the stalls and try to work out which ones would be useful and what was just pointless filler.

He found that if he stared at some items for long enough a little tooltip would pop up, but for others they just remained objects. He closed his eyes for a moment, pulling up his character sheet with a thought.

Skaife Murovan Exorcist
Strength: 4 Agility: 7
Endurance: 7 Willpower: 6
Health: 35 Stamina: 45
Level: 1 Sin: 0
Standard Attack Damage [Rusty Knife]: 5-7

The longer he looked, the more information presented itself: *Carrying Weight, Lifting Weight, Throwing Range, Movement Speed, Jumping Distance, Poison Resistance, Disease Resistance, Curse Resistance.* As he shuffled down through the endless complexities of the sheet he eventually found what he was looking for:

Appraise: 7

Appraise determines your ability to identify the function and value of items within Strata. It is calculated based on your class, level, exposure to materials and crafting skill levels.

Grinning felt strange when his mouth was a completely different shape, but Martin couldn't help it. He was a complexity addict; he loved this stuff. This game had stats tracking absolutely everything and they all interacted together.

He could spend months digging into it all before he would really understand everything. There was so much to see, and he hadn't even gotten into the actual game yet, just the starting area. There was a bounce in his step when he spotted a barbecue pit set up in the middle of the market with a chubby Corvan hawking her wares. He wondered if *Appraise* or an as-yet undiscovered cooking skill would tell him about the benefits of food in-game.

An elbow caught Martin in the side of the head.

[Skaife suffers 1 bludgeoning damage]

That same strange lack of pain spread through his skull as he tumbled into the dirt.

"Out of my way, rat."

Martin was up with his *Rusty Knife* in hand without even thinking, but whoever had hit him was already lost in the crowd. There were a few guards dotted around the marketplace, but if he had thought to appeal to them for help, he was badly mistaken. They glowered at him until he slipped the knife back into its sheath, but even once it was hidden he could still feel their glares on him.

Had they been staring at him like that the whole time? He glanced around furtively and noticed that the stall owners kept turning his way too.

There was no way they had programmed the NPCs to be racist against rat-men. That was just crazy.

Martin made his way to the nearest guard to help drive off his suspicions, but as he looked up at the sneer plastered beneath the Sythvan guard's half-helm, he realized he had been right.

"What do you want, filth-fur?"

Resisting the urge to snap back was difficult, but picking a fight with some random town guard wasn't part of his plans for the day.

"I just arrived in Strata. Can you tell me where I need to go?"

The guard rolled his eyes.

"Dumb as you are ugly. Go look for Lord Exorcist Khargen. He'll find some use for your idle hands before they turn to picking pockets. And remember to keep your nose clean. We've got our eyes on you."

With a false smile locked firmly in place, Martin sidled away into the crowd and did everything he could not to look back. There were no maps pinned up around the bustling marketplace, so Martin struck off away from the crowds to try to work things out on his own.

The town seemed to have grown organically outwards from

the central hole where all the new arrivals dropped in, with the majority of the larger buildings arrayed around it and the quality and quantity of structures dropping off the further he ventured out. Eventually Martin ran into a fence that encircled town – constructed in the same haphazard way as the rest – and followed it around until he found a gate.

He'd hoped that if he caught a Murovan guard he could ask for directions without a side order of abuse, but most of the guards seemed to be Wulvan, with the odd Sythvan sprinkled in for variety.

As a matter of fact, he couldn't recall seeing any other Murovan in town at all. The description in character creation hadn't exactly been flattering, but he'd assumed there would be some rat-lovers who'd choose them anyway. It was strange.

Strolling up to the gate as casually as he could manage did nothing to alleviate the stares of the guards. Beyond them, the truth about the town's location became clear: there was a wide-open expanse of bare cavern floor, fading into darkness beyond the light of the town's torches.

With his low-light vision, Martin could see past the edge of the torchlight better than most. He could make out the nearest wall of the cavern, looming up to encompass them. Good thing he wasn't claustrophobic. He took a step forward, still peering out at what looked like tunnel openings on the cave wall.

"Good riddance."

Martin blinked, then turned to look at the guard. "Excuse me?"

The Wulvan sneered. "Good luck out there with the rest of your kind. Hope you're very happy with all your little rat friends. When you get there, tell them that if they try raiding here again, we're going to burn out the guts of their whole filthy warren."

"I'm not going anywhere." Martin would have squared his shoulders, but Murovan didn't seem to be capable of it.

The other guard snorted.

"Of course not. Haven't gone to mooch your free gear from

the crusade quartermaster yet, have you? Can't stab us in the back by running off to join forces with the rats if you haven't got a blade to stab us in the back with."

Martin bit back his answer again. He was getting sick of this treatment and he'd only been on the receiving end of it for half an hour.

"Where is this quartermaster? And where is Lord Khargen, while you are at it?"

The guards glanced at each other nervously over the top of Martin's head. "What do you want with that maniac?"

They were nervous. Good.

"We're both exorcists. Seems like we'll have a lot to talk about."

"You? You're meant to be an exorcist? Stop pulling my tail."

Martin smirked. That was an expression that worked well on his new face. At least there was one.

"Where is he?"

The first guard sighed and pointed with his spear. "He'll be in the Temple of Aten if he's anywhere. Over in the east quarter."

Martin gave them a curt bow, then stalked off without another word in what he hoped was the right direction.

This Khargen character could give him whatever starter quest he needed and point him in the direction of the quartermaster. It wasn't a good idea to be roaming around in rags, after all. With that done, he could then see about finding Lindsay somewhere in this chaotic mess of a starter town.

Whatever preconceptions Martin had about what a temple looked like were wiped away when he finally found the place.

Aten's holy symbol was a rising sun. Someone had daubed that half circle onto a tattered rag of animal hide and stretched it out into something like a banner above the door of an otherwise nondescript wooden shack.

He probably would have strolled right past it, the banner lost amidst all the other colors and scraps of the town, if it hadn't been for the singing inside. It was like a dirge, the drone vibrating through the stone floor and up into Martin's bare feet.

Inside, there was very little to distinguish the temple from any other building in town. It had a ceiling so low that the Wulvan in the crowd were scraping their heads on the exposed beams, leaving tufts of fur amidst the splinters.

There was something like an altar up at the front with a golden statue of that same half-sun icon cast large enough that the people at the back could make it out.

Martin glanced around for Lord Khargen, only for his eyes to be inevitably drawn to the Wulvan who sat perched on a stool near the back of the room. His armor bore traces of golden filigree around its edges, a hint of wealth in this otherwise impoverished place, but his clothes did a lot less to convince Martin than the faint golden glow about him.

Being careful not to attract any attention, Martin crept along the back wall of the temple as the dirge droned on. Khargen's eyes followed him the whole way, but unlike every other pair that had tracked his progress around town, Martin didn't feel any judgment there.

"Lord Khargen?" he asked.

The Wulvan bared his teeth in what was probably meant to be a smile. "Welcome to Beachhead, young exorcist. Have you been made welcome?"

Martin scoffed. "Hardly."

Khargen's smile faded. "Then let me do what I can to remedy your poor greeting. I am Lord Exorcist Khargen, the master of the Crusade's forces here in Beachhead. It is to me that you shall report until such time as you catch up to our soldiers further down into the dungeon."

He rose to his feet, startling Martin back a step.

"Come, let us get you a weapon in your hand and armor on your back before you venture forth. The first deep of the dungeon is mostly safe after long months of strife to make it so.

But once you have passed through the first Deep Gate, you will be alone with the monsters."

The next few minutes passed in a blur. The crowds that would have trampled Martin without a second thought parted around the towering Wulvan, and whatever contempt the other people of the town might have felt for him was masked in their awe of the Lord Exorcist.

The Corvan quartermaster handed over a *Copper Shortsword [7-12 damage]* and a full set of *Piecemeal Leather Armor [10 armor]* that Martin equipped in the blink of an eye. Literally.

"Now that you have a sword in hand, shall we see what you can do, little one?" Khargen grinned.

There was a patch of bare stone close by, where the buildings had never been allowed to spread. Dotted around it were dummies that looked something like scarecrows designed by people who had never seen a scarecrow before.

The mash-up of features from the different races made for some interesting combinations, although Martin noticed almost immediately that the smaller, rat-sized dummies seemed to be a lot worse for wear than the more substantial ones.

A couple of Wulvan in armor that looked as shiny and new as Martin's were swinging away at one of the Murovan-sized dummies with some passion. They eyed Martin as he approached but did not dare to say anything with Khargen so close by.

With a little swagger in his step, Martin strode up to the largest dummy he could find and swung his sword. It whacked off the side of the dummy's body with a satisfying clang, but then Martin had to take a step back, perplexed.

He had felt the blow make contact, but there was no sign that he had dealt any damage. Pressing his eyes shut, he pulled up the menu and scanned quickly through all of the interface options until he found *Combat Feedback*. It was currently set to *Realism*.

Realism might have been great for a casual player, but he needed to know how all these numbers fit together. The next option was *Balanced*, but he skipped right over that to *Technical*. That sounded more his speed.

He rolled his sloped shoulders and readied his sword again. A quick prod at the dummy produced the results he was looking for.

[Dummy suffers 11 piercing damage.
Weak Hit - Minimum weapon damage dealt]

It tracked how hard he was swinging. That was another interesting detail. This time, Martin put the full strength of his wiry little frame into a clumsy swing and it rebounded off the giant tortoise shell that had been strapped onto the dummy as a shield.

[Dummy BLOCKS 16 damage]

Once again that strange numbness that should have been pain spread up Martin's arm. With a grunt that sounded less human and more rodent, he swung again from the other side and felt the sword bite into the dummy with some satisfaction.

[Dummy suffers 14 slashing damage]

This wasn't like the usual MMOs where he could just swing away. He actually needed to land his hits to deal damage.

Maybe he should have just picked an invoker; he'd never been the most athletic guy and he wasn't sure how far the hand-eye coordination he'd developed in all his years of gaming would translate into actual mortal combat.

Of course, if he'd picked a spellcaster, the fact that he had no idea how to use any of his abilities would likely have been more of a concern.

As if he were reading Martin's mind, Khargen called out, "Now, show me the power of your *Celestial Strike.*"

"How… uh… how would I do that again?"

Khargen barked with laughter. "Simply focus on the gifts Aten has given you when you wish to use them."

If that actually worked, then it wasn't much different from the way Martin had focused on things at the marketplace stalls.

Closing his eyes, he concentrated on the name of the ability, repeating it in his mind. And like clockwork, the tooltip for *Celestial Strike* popped into his periphery.

Celestial Strike - Deals 6 physical and 6 light damage to a single target on a successful hit. *[10-second cooldown]*

Holding that thought in his mind, Martin readied his sword. Even though he was planning for it to work, he was still startled when the blade suddenly lit up like a halogen bulb. He snorted with delight and it came out as an embarrassingly high-pitched sound; a little like a mouse's squeak. He swung, the light blinking out as the blade hit home.

[Dummy suffers 6 slashing damage and 6 light damage]

It was less than a usual sword swing in total, as it didn't account for his strength score like a regular attack, but Martin guessed that deeper in the dungeon there would be a lot of creatures susceptible to the light.

He tried to call up his Celestial Strike ability again but discovered that he couldn't even bring up the tooltip until the ten seconds had passed.

There was clapping from the side of the field and Martin padded over to Khargen with a wry smile.

"All right, so I'm not completely worthless."

Khargen cupped Martin's furry cheek in one massive paw and rumbled, "Oh, but you are. We are all worthless. Powerless but for the might that glorious Aten allows us to wield in his name. You are just an instrument of his will. Do not think for a moment that this power is yours. If you sin, it will be stripped from you in an instant."

That explained a little something about that particular statistic.

"All right. So, I'm just another hammer in your god's tool-box? Then put me to work."

"Our god. The effervescent Aten." Khargen's rumble was more of a growl now. The Wulvan duo messing around with the training dummies started to back away nervously.

"Yeah, that guy. What can I do to help him out?"

Khargen hovered on the verge of apoplectic rage for a moment before slipping on his mask of sanity and formality.

"There will be many here who doubt your devotion. Many who will look at you Murovan, riddled with *Sin*, and think that you come to the Dungeon of Strata not to purge it of the dark-ness but to indulge in it."

The Wulvan exorcist gripped Martin's shoulder and stared into his eyes.

"Where all others will be trusted solely on the weight of their virtues, you will need evidence of your commitment to the cause above all else. You must prove beyond all doubt that your sympathies lie with the Crusade."

"And how would I do that?" Martin asked.

The quest tooltip sprang up in front of his eyes so suddenly it startled him.

Level 1 Quest: Rabid Ratmen

The settlement of Beachhead is constantly being raided by a nearby colony of Murovan Deserters. Before you can proceed deeper into the Dungeon of Strata, you must defend your supply lines by ending this threat.
Victory Conditions: Slay 10 Murovan Deserters.

Martin blinked. As far as starter quests went, this should have been on par with killing bears and bringing back their asses, but after a day of being treated like he was subhuman by the people of Beachhead, it was hard not to get emotional about it.

If all the Murovan were treated like him, it was no wonder so many of them deserted.

Martin accepted the quest with a curt nod, and the Lord Exorcist dismissed him with a wave of his hand.

It was time to see what this game was really like.

FIVE

Rebirth of a Riot

This time, Martin didn't even slow as he approached the guards. He had heard enough last time. There was some muttering as he went on his way, but when you only came up to someone's crotch, it was easy to keep your head down.

From the outside, Beachhead looked even more ramshackle than he had previously suspected. The fence was held together with string and hope in most places. Martin didn't claim to be an expert, but he had a suspicion that it was for show more than it was for defense. Given a running start he was pretty sure even he could break through it, and he was a four-foot-tall rat in starter gear.

The top of the cavern wasn't actually much higher than the roofs of the two-story buildings. Everything looked much higher than it really was because Martin was still getting used to his new perspective.

The cavern itself was like an upturned dome over the little town, the ceiling starting to curve down the moment Martin was outside of Beachhead. That was another advantage of being Murovan: he was a lot less likely to bump his head on the roof.

With no guidance about the direction of the *Rabid Rats* even when he pulled up his quest log, Martin just headed off towards the nearest tunnel entrance to start exploring.

He eventually managed to conjure a map out of the menu that appeared when he closed his eyes, but it only showed him the places he had already been, and even those seemed to be fading away gradually. Far from annoying him, he was actually quite pleased about that.

As much as he had loved Dracolich Online, the chance to discover something completely new was gone almost the instant that new content was added to the game. He could have avoided the information other people had gathered, but that would have put the guild at a disadvantage, and he couldn't have that.

At the back of his mind, he had been pondering why Strata wasn't the same, but he suspected it was because of the neural interface. It was easy enough to data-mine information from a graphics engine or a database but a lot more difficult to harvest it from simulated brainwaves.

If someone wanted to carry information out of Strata then they would have to memorize it, and while he was pretty sure he could retain a fair chunk of statistics at a time, there was just so much in Strata that he wasn't surprised it put people off trying.

The technology was probably why there were no Strata streamers either; you couldn't show yourself playing this game because there was no video feed to show.

Someone would probably crack the mechanics of it eventually and flood the whole web with every scrap of information that could be found inside Strata. All of the mystery would vanish and it would become nothing more than another game amidst millions, but until then there was a whole new world to discover.

It occurred to Martin that he probably should have been afraid as he stalked off down a pitch-black tunnel looking for monsters, but the whole scenario was just so familiar to him. He had been delving in dungeons for as long as there had been dungeons to delve in. There had been other video games over the years, and aliens sometimes took the place of goblins, but at the end of the day he always came back to fantasy. It felt like home.

Up ahead of him in the tunnel, there was a snuffling sound. Martin's hand drifted down to the sword at his hip and he tried to creep forward quietly. It had to be a monster. He was a few minutes out of the starter town, and he had just ambled through the tutorial. It was monster time.

The snuffling grew louder and more guttural the closer he got. There was a flicker of light around the corner, just enough for long shadows to be cast across the tunnel wall.

He drew his sword as swiftly as he dared. He had no idea what would be waiting for him. In most of the games he'd loved, the first monsters were usually animals, or animal people, but in Strata, the players were the animal people.

As he came around the bend, several things happened in quick succession: a huge pig caught sight of Martin and reared up on its hind legs.

Martin, panicking, swung his sword at the beast but instead scraped the tunnel wall, showering them both in sparks.

The last, and most significant, event was that the copse of smoldering mushrooms that the pig had been delicately nibbling let out a gout of flame, searing its hindquarters and flooding the tunnel with the smell of crispy bacon.

[Savage Swine suffers 17 fire damage]

The hog squealed in pain and terror, still dancing back on its rear legs. With such an obvious opening, Martin rushed forward, sword held out in front of him.

The blade buried into the pig's stomach, even as the hilt rammed Martin's gut, knocking the wind out of him.

[Skaife suffers 3 bludgeoning damage]

[Savage Swine suffers 18 piercing damage]
Savage Swine has died.
Skaife gains 120 experience.

The pig collapsed, its great weight toppling forward, pinning Martin to the ground. There hadn't even been enough time to find out the pig's health before the whole thing was over.

Hot blood poured down Martin's arm, soaking his fur and washing over his armor.

Martin had to wrestle and roll to get out from under the pig, but once he'd found his feet, he felt surprisingly good. In real life, even being near to violence had always left him shaking, but here, all he felt was proud.

With no sign of a bigger, angrier pig lurking nearby, he shuffled over to examine the mushrooms.

Unknown Plant *[Requires* Herbalism*]*
A strange gray fungus that reacts oddly to heat.

The lack of information was a bit annoying, but what he had seen of the combustible mushrooms was enough to make him pluck what he could find and send them off to his inventory for further study. He would really have to find some trainers – that weren't completely obnoxious to the Murovan race – to help him dig into the mechanics of the crafting systems.

With that brief foray into botany over, he returned to the corpse and crouched down to examine the spoils of war.

Savage Swine
This feral pig escaped from the Crusade's food stocks early in the campaign, fleeing to the nearby tunnels to make a new life for itself.
Loot: *Tiny Tusks, Mystery Meat, Trotters*
Requires Leatherworking *to harvest: Light Leather Scraps*

He had just started transferring the presumably useless items into his inventory when another tooltip suddenly popped into his line of sight. Martin let out another embarrassing squeak. He was really going to have to work out how to turn those off before he got into a proper fight.

*You have been invited to join the **Iron Riot** guild by its founder,*
Tesra Stormcrow.

He *definitely* hadn't forgotten about Lindsay in the excitement of playing a new game. That would have been ridiculous. With another nod, he accepted the guild invitation.

Suddenly, he heard a whisper from behind his left ear.

"Nice of you to finally show up."

He could practically hear Lindsay grinning.

Martin whipped around to look for her, but there was nothing behind him but echoing darkness and an undercooked portion of pulled pork.

"Uh, hello?" His voice echoed off down the tunnel.

"Still haven't worked out how to talk back, eh? Maybe it is better like this. I've always said I could do with a lot less chatter from you." Lindsay was practically cackling.

Martin concentrated on her character's name. He repeated the words in his head. Tesra Stormcrow. Almost immediately, an abridged version of her character sheet appeared.

Tesra
Corvan Knave Level: 1 Sin: -5

He focused on that sheet and said, "Lindsay?"

There was a startled gasp, then:

"Did you just whisper to me directly? How do you do that? I'm just touching my guild crest when I want to talk to you."

Martin glanced down and discovered that the bristling swords of the guild's old logo were now embossed on the chest of his armor. He let Tesra's sheet fall away and laid a hand on the icon.

"That is a lot easier. Where are you?"

"I'm just outside of Beachhead on a quest to kill some grubby little rat-men. What about you?"

Martin flinched at that but pressed on regardless. "Me too. Can we meet up?"

His map called for attention, like an itch that needed scratching, so he closed his eyes and pulled it up. There was a little black feather lying on an unexplored patch of the map a little further around the curve of the main cavern's wall.

"Perfect. I'll catch up to you in two minutes. Don't go anywhere."

Knowing what he did about her attention span, Martin ran. His stamina bar drained startlingly quickly, but at least his health had filled back up after all the time wandering around town.

As his stamina bottomed out, he actually started to feel tired. In real life he knew from his brief sprints to catch the train that he could push through tired and keep on moving, but here in Strata it seemed to be a real limitation. He slowed to a walk as the green bar refilled.

Tesra was perched on a ridge above the tunnel entrance when he arrived. He had only seen a few Corvan NPCs in town and they had all trended towards the old and portly. Tesra was anything but.

Her feathers were black and shiny, with a strangely lithe body beneath the dark leather of her armor. Her eyes sparkled lilac when she hopped down to greet him.

"Oh, no – it *is* one of the grubby little rat-men! What possessed you to pick that when you could have been a lizard? I thought you were all about those dragons?"

Martin couldn't help but smile. Lindsay's enthusiasm was as infectious as it was boundless. That reminded him of why he was here.

"Listen, Lindsay, I really appreciate you getting this game for me, but it's just too much. You've got to return the NIH and get your money back."

She cocked her head to one side.

"Rubbish. It's my money. I'll do what I want with it. What's the point of spending all your time working if you can't blow all your money on something fun?"

"Lindsay, it is far too much money for you to waste on me."

He wondered if she could see him blushing through his fur. She pointed a pinfeather at him.

"That's where you're getting it twisted, though. Me buying you a headset and a game – that isn't a waste, that's an investment. Other games have got downloadable content so that folks can throw more money at them to make them easier. You're my launch-day DLC. I spent a little bit of extra money that I didn't really need anyway and got the best strategist money can buy."

Flattery wasn't completely lost on Martin, but he still had a few tricks up his sleeve.

"If you just return the NIH, I'll buy one myself in a couple of months when I've saved up for it."

"No can do, my fuzzy little friend. I need you now, not months from now when some other guild has already gotten the drop on us. This is a race to the finish, same as always, and you are my rocket-booster powerup."

"You want to be the first one to finish Strata?" he asked her flatly.

"Wait." She cocked her head the other way. "Do you seriously not know?"

"Know what?" Martin sighed.

She hopped a little closer.

"You really don't know?"

That was enough.

"Will you just tell me what I don't know!"

Lindsay was giggling but it came out in a weird cacophony of croaks through her beak.

"How am I meant to know what you don't know?"

He took hold of her shoulders, feeling the hollow bones shifting in his grip. "Lindsay, will you stop dicking around and just tell me whatever it is?"

She shoved him off.

"All right, all right, all right. Uh, okay, you know Strata is a big dungeon, right? Well, they have it split up into different levels they call Deeps, so that we don't get them mixed up with character levels. Anyway, there are a hundred deeps in the whole thing, with a boss every ten. Nobody has gotten below Deep Fifty yet."

Martin scratched his chin. "But the game has been out for months."

"Yeah, but it is hard as hell. Anyway, the reason everybody is in such a mad rush to be the first to the bottom is, first off, eternal bragging rights."

She began counting the reasons off on the five feathered fingers at the end of her wing. Martin nodded. "Of course."

"The developers will add our characters to the game as NPCs."

"Okay, very cool."

"And you get every game they have ever made and will ever make from now on until the heat death of the universe for free."

He shrugged. "Icing on the cake."

It was her turn to grab him by the shoulders.

"I want to be the first one to the end, Martin. I want Iron Riot's name to go down in gaming history. I want them to put us in history books. Like, really weirdly specific history books about MMOs."

He tried to shrug again but her grip kept his shoulders pinned in place. "Who wouldn't want that?"

She was practically vibrating with excitement. "So, you're on board?"

He grinned. "You had me at 'eternal bragging rights.'"

She bumped her forehead against his, just hard enough that

the numbness started up and then died out again. It was what they had always done. The same gesture they'd been repeating over and over since they first started playing VRMMOs, but this time he actually felt it.

He couldn't even remember the last time he had touched another person in real life, at least not deliberately. It was like she was right here with him. Like they were friends in real life instead of having the vast expanse of cyberspace stretched out between them. He could hardly believe it.

"Awesome, dude. Want to go kill some rats?"

"I mean, we're first-level adventurers. I guess we've got to."

She was croaking with amusement again.

"Iron Riot?"

They bumped heads again, more forcefully this time.

"Iron Riot."

SIX

The First Sin

Even with their skills and maps combined, it took the two of them an hour of aimless wandering through the tunnels of Deep One before they got even a hint of the Murovan deserters.

There *was* one more pig roaming the tunnels, browsing the variety of odd mushrooms on display. Martin stood back and let Lindsay brutalize it with her daggers while he prodded at the various mineral deposits that provided no more helpful information than *[Requires Blacksmithing]* when he peered at them.

There were definite signs of mining in some of these tunnels. Deliberate attempts had been made to shore up the ceilings and there were distinct patterns of scratching that he would have associated with pickaxes.

In a normal fantasy game, you had dwarves messing around in mines. Here in Strata, the vaguely anti-Semitic merchant-race traits of the dwarves seemed to have been foisted off onto Corvan characters, but making birds into miners didn't seem like a good fit. The Wulvan would have been scraping their heads along every one of the wooden frames above their heads, eliminating them from the running too.

Martin's bet was that the Crusade used the Murovan contingent as miners. After all, mining was dangerous, thankless work, and the Murovan intro text had described them as living in tunnels. It made perfect sense.

When he told Lindsay, she nodded along. "You think they're down here?"

"They would know the terrain here better than anyone else, and if this was where they spent all their time, it might be where they felt safest?"

She tossed aside her torch, drew her daggers and stretched her arms out until the blades were touching both sides of the passage.

"So, if we're getting close, I should probably start using stealth, scouting ahead, right?"

It was the right move, but Martin felt strange about letting her go on alone without him.

"First sign of trouble, you head back."

She scoffed. "First sign of trouble, you charge in and find me."

"Don't I always?"

He sighed down the suddenly empty tunnel. Apparently, stealth worked on allies too. Good to know.

He crept forward along the tunnel with his hand resting on the hilt of his sword. The passage had dozens of side-branches, enough that you could probably get lost in the tangled warren of stone for days, but knowing Lindsay, she would have sprinted straight down the main one for as long as she could.

He paused for a moment. He didn't need to rely on guesswork. The guild crest felt odd beneath his finger pads, like it was charged with static.

"Straight down the main tunnel?"

"Obviously," she hissed back.

He grinned. "Any trouble?"

"Not yet, but the night is young."

He picked up the pace a little. If she was actually in trouble, he was relatively confident that she would let him know, but it wouldn't matter if he was too far away to do anything. That jogged his memory. He closed his eyes and pulled up a list of his exorcist abilities to find a healing spell.

Celestial Strike [10-second cooldown]
Healing Touch [60-second cooldown]
Rite of Retribution [60-minute cooldown]

He concentrated on the words *Healing Touch* but nothing happened. He had to swing his sword to get *Celestial Strike* working, so he gave the blade a few practice waves, to no avail.

Then he realized. It was so obvious he could kick himself. Exorcists couldn't use shields, they didn't dual wield and they didn't use two-handed weapons. They needed a hand free. He thrust his empty paw forward and a golden glow surrounded it. Perfect. He touched it to his chest and felt warmth spreading through his body. A blink confirmed that whatever health he'd chipped off during his misadventures with the pig were now fully restored.

"You'd better hurry if you want to get this quest finished today," Lindsay's voice whispered in his ear.

"You've found them?"

"Yeah, but we're late to the party." Lindsay groaned. "You'd better run."

Without another word, Martin sprinted down the corridor as fast as his little furry legs would carry him.

When he burst out of the tunnel into a wider cave, he skidded to a halt, overwhelmed yet again by his senses being overrun with too much information. The Murovan had built a little shanty town in the cave out of their mining supplies, even more ramshackle than Beachhead and quite a bit smaller. Everywhere Martin looked was covered in blood and clumps of fur.

"What—"

Lindsay burst out from between a pair of shacks with her daggers in hand, chasing after an unarmed Murovan girl who was squealing for mercy. Without thinking, he stepped in between them and Lindsay skidded to a halt. "What do you think you're doing? We need ten of them between us and half of ruddy Beachhead got here before us."

He moved back into Lindsay's path as she tried to duck around him.

"Something isn't right."

"Oh, don't be a bleeding heart," she groaned. "Just because they're rats and you're a rat doesn't mean anything. They're NPCs! They aren't people. How many elves do you think I killed back in Dracolich?"

"You aren't listening to me. Something isn't right. If the designers wanted us to kill these things, why would they make them scared and defenseless? Why would they try and make us feel sympathy for them?"

His brain felt like it was whirring, trying to decipher this new puzzle.

"It has to be some sort of morality system? They are testing us to see if we'll just follow orders, or if we'll do what is right in spite of the orders. 'Can you kill ten rats?' isn't any sort of question at all. Should you kill them? That is a real question."

Lindsay stopped trying to chase the rat girl as she scampered out of sight.

"So, what, you think we just go back and say we aren't doing it?"

"They made them look like scared kids. What kind of psychopath could kill scared kids?"

As if on cue, a Wulvan in full chainmail burst out of one of the shacks, blood crusted in every crevice.

Dmitri Blackpaw Level 2 Wulvan Knight

The axe in his hands was dripping with gore.

"That one's mine," the Wulvan called. "I've only got one to go."

Martin rolled his eyes. "I'm with you. I'm a player."

Dmitri's pace didn't slow, even as Lindsay called out, "He's with us. He isn't a monster."

"Looks like a little rat bastard to me." He hefted the axe in his hands. "Tell you what: if it doesn't count towards my ten, I'll send him an apology."

The knight leapt and Martin only just got his sword up in time to deflect the razor edge of the descending axe.

[Skaife BLOCKS 18 damage]
[Skaife suffers 18 stamina loss]

The time for talk was done. The black-furred knight spun, putting more force into the next sweeping blow, knocking Martin's feeble guard wide open.

[Skaife BLOCKS 12 damage]
[Skaife suffers 12 stamina loss]

Martin backed away. The next swing missed him by a hair's breadth and forced his heel into the slippery innards of a dead Murovan. With a yelp, he fell on his back.

A sweep of the axe brushed past the tips of his pointed ears as he went down.

Lindsay rushed at the Wulvan, daggers ready and any doubts forgotten, but the towering mass of fur and iron just batted her aside with the flat of his axe.

[Tesra suffers 16 bludgeoning damage]

She smashed right through the paper-thin wall of the nearest hovel before falling out of sight.

[Tesra suffers 4 bludgeoning environmental damage]

Martin barely had time to stand before the Wulvan's fury

came raining back down on him. He scrambled back, deflecting each blow as it fell. His stamina dwindled with each parry. Each strike got closer and closer to finding its mark. Martin's stomach turned when he realized the knight was laughing.

The frantic crab-walk forced him further and further from the paltry torchlight of the settlement, back into a dark alleyway between two pathetic heaps of splinters that some poor Murovan must have called home.

The low-light vision of Martin's race kicked in, showing the world around him in dull shades of gray, but Dmitri must have been swinging blindly at shapes in the shadows.

Martin needed to stop reacting and start thinking. This wasn't a brawl, it was a game, and he was good at games. The next time the Wulvan hefted his axe, Martin called his *Celestial Strike* and his sword burst into light. There was only one moment when the wolf-man was blinded, but in a fight, a moment was all it took.

Martin didn't even try for a killing blow. Instead, he leapt between the knight's legs. He rolled over the bloodied stone and came back up to thrust his sword into the wolf-man's backside.

[CRITICAL HIT]
[Dmitri suffers 28 piercing damage]

The Wulvan threw back his head and howled. Apparently, the situation wasn't funny anymore. Martin yanked his sword back out of the knight's armor-free rump then took a step back.

"Are you ready to talk now?"

Evidently the answer was no. With a roar, the next flurry of attacks came, but what Martin had not realized in his initial panic was that the attacks were clumsy.

[MISS]
[MISS]
[Skaife BLOCKS 12 damage]

[MISS]

This was a new player, and the longer Martin observed him, the more he realized how badly this Dmitri was actually playing.

Martin ducked forward instead of backwards when the next swing came, inside the circle of the Wulvan's arms and inside his defenses. He thrust his *Copper Shortsword* right into the Wulvan's guts, then watched as the idiot's health trickled away. It felt warm as it ran over his hand.

[Dmitri suffers 15 piercing damage]

Martin smirked as the less-than-noble knight toppled to the ground in a groaning heap.

Dmitri has died.

For a moment Martin lingered, considering trying to steal some of the knight's gear, but on examination there didn't seem to be any way for him to move things from dead players into his inventory. That was probably for the best; he wouldn't want somebody murdering him and stealing his stuff, either.

With a shrug, Martin hurried back to dig Lindsay out of the wreckage, only to find her already staggering around the muddied and bloodied street, looking miserable.

"There you are! I thought dog-boy had buried some of you for later."

"I'm afraid not. Neither of you were that lucky."

She took another staggering step forward, then paused. "You ain't got a healing spell or something handy, do you?"

Martin shook his head ruefully. "As a matter of fact, I figured I'd end up spending half my time in this game patching you up, so I picked one out especially for you."

"You're a gentleman."

He concentrated on *Healing Touch* and lifted his hand towards her, but nothing happened.

"Huh. Hang on a second."

He closed his eyes and opened up his abilities menu again, wondering if he'd remembered the name wrong.

Void Strike [10-second cooldown]
Withering Touch [60-second cooldown]
Unjust Curse [60-minute cooldown]

Martin froze for a moment. That was all wrong. What had happened? He pulled up his character sheet.

Skaife Murovan Shadow Templar
Strength: 4 Agility: 7
Endurance: 7 Willpower: 6
Health: 33/35 Stamina: 36/45
Level: 1 Sin: 1
Standard Attack Damage [Copper Shortsword]: 11-16

What was a shadow templar? That hadn't even been an option in character creation. He opened his eyes only to see Lindsay peering at him with a concerned look on her face, which must have been hard to convey with a beak and no eyebrows.

"Sorry, the healing spell isn't working just now. And... my class has just changed."

"You can do that?" Lindsay cawed. "I didn't know you could change mid-game. Show me how to do it. What did you change to?"

She seemed to forget all about her injuries as soon as there was something new to get excited about. A race of magpies was a perfect fit for Lindsay.

Martin sheepishly wiped blood off his sword onto his thigh. "I'm a shadow templar now, whatever that means."

Lindsay was bouncing on the spot.

"So, what, have you got evil powers now?"

Martin concentrated, and an eerie red glow formed around his empty hand. His *Withering Touch.*

"Uh… yeah, it kind of looks that way."

Lindsay was staring at his hand, wide-eyed. "Well, that is cool as hell."

He stared into the blood-red light gathered around his little gray paw, marveling as it flickered and coiled around his fingers.

"I think it might be because I killed another player. Maybe this is the PvP version of my class?"

Lindsay had stopped bouncing. For the first time that Martin could remember, she was staying completely still.

"Well, I hope it works on monsters too."

He turned around as slowly as he could manage. The Murovan deserters were back in force, and this time they looked neither pathetic nor defenseless.

Those that didn't have pickaxes in their hands had armed themselves with wicked looking cleavers. Every last one of them was staring at Martin and Lindsay as if they were the ones who had just stomped into their home and slaughtered all of their friends.

Martin flexed his glowing fingers.

"Okay. Maybe we are meant to fight."

SEVEN

Wrath of the Ratmen

The Murovan horde swept forward with their weapons held high. Martin was fairly confident that the lit torches near the back of the pack would have been accompanied by pitchforks if they weren't so impractical for tunnel fighting.

Lindsay whispered, "What's the plan?"

"Run!"

Martin turned tail and fled into the ramshackle town, dragging Lindsay along by a sleeve until she got her stumbling feet beneath her.

He didn't look back, not when he could hear the chorus of squeaks and squeals right at their heels. They rounded a bend and almost plowed into the back of another posse of furious furballs.

With one hand trailing red light like it was smoke and the other clenched tight around the hilt of his sword, Martin spun, trying to take it all in. If they had both been in fighting form, he might have risked charging, trying to break through to escape and regroup, but there were just so many of them, and Lindsay already looked like a strong breeze would be enough to drop her. They needed an advantage.

He slapped the flat of his blade into the palm of his glowing hand.

"Up."

"What?" Lindsay's confusion only lasted a second before she sprang into action, putting a foot on his sword as he hefted her higher.

There was a brief, uncomfortable scramble as she moved her clawed feet from Martin's sword to his head, and then launched herself up onto the roof behind him.

That was Lindsay out of harm's way for now. Outside of combat, her health should regenerate; he just had to keep the heaving mass of enraged Murovan miners distracted long enough for it to make a difference.

He stood nose to nose with the other ratmen, feeling like he was on even footing for the first time since he'd fallen into Strata, and while they had filled the street on both sides of him, they were eyeing him warily instead of charging in. They were cowards; that was what the character creation text had said. Now he just needed to use that information.

"Who wants to be first?" he yelled.

It was hard to be intimidating when your voice came out in a wheezy squeak, but he was doing his best.

The crowd swayed, keeping their distance, eyes darting from side to side. That was fine; the longer they waited, the healthier Lindsay got. There was a bit of pushing and shoving among the squabbling mass, then one of them got ejected into the street in front of him.

It was a white-furred runt with a dagger in each hand, a dagger in its teeth and a dagger wrapped in the tip of its tail. A knave. Or the NPC equivalent.

Knaves were designed to fight from an ambush, or at range. The best plan here was to meet it head-on. Martin tried for a grin, but his bared teeth probably looked more queasy than smug.

"Come on, then," he snarled. "Let's see what this thing can do."

He dashed forward, leading with his blade, and the poor Murovan actually flinched, bringing every weapon at its disposal around to block Martin's feigned sword thrust. His glowing hand darted in past its defenses.

[Tunnel Rat suffers 2 strength drain, 2 agility drain, 2 endurance drain]

The Murovan shriveled up under his touch, already-scant muscles wasting away as the vicious red light rushed over its pale fur in a wave. The daggers trembled right out of its paws and jaws as Martin sucked the life out of it and it became too weak to hold them anymore. He took a step back and swung with all his strength.

[Tunnel Rat suffers 15 slashing damage]
Tunnel Rat has died.
Skaife gains 180 experience.

Rabid Ratmen.
1/10 Murovan Deserters slain.

He flicked the blood from his sword, spattering it in the faces of the nearest Murovan and allowing himself to feel the beginnings of confidence despite the swarms of enemies just waiting to leap at his throat. This was just a game. He could do this.

"Who's next?"

For one long silent moment, nobody moved. Then suddenly the tension in the air broke and the ratmen came pouring forward, wailing and squealing. The press of emboldened bodies in the back ranks drove the terrified-looking Murovan at the front towards Martin like a solid wall.

He probably would have felt some disgust about "his people"

using each other as living shields, but he would probably have done the same thing.

They had the advantage of numbers, but they couldn't press that advantage if they were worried about losing a couple of grunts. If they closed in on him, it would all be over. He needed more time.

When he darted forward, it wasn't to kill, it was to maim. The closest Murovan squealed in terror at his approach and he swung low under their meagre defenses, scoring a line across their shins.

[Warren Warden suffers 3 slashing damage]
[Tunnel Rat suffers 4 slashing damage]
[Warren Warden suffers 3 slashing damage]

It wasn't enough to do them any serious injury, but it was enough to trip them, and when the rank behind them kept on pushing forward, one whole side of the battle line collapsed into a complaining pile-up. Martin let out a little squeak of triumph.

[Skaife suffers 12 piercing damage]

That terrible numbness spread out from one sharp point in the middle of his back. Twelve damage was more than a third of his health, gone in a single hit. He spun around and managed to deflect the next pickaxe swing with a clumsy parry.

[Skaife BLOCKS 16 damage]
[Skaife suffers 16 stamina loss]

He had wondered why his abilities just had cooldowns and no resource costs. Most games would have made him pay stamina or mana to use every special ability, but all that Strata seemed to demand was time. Now he understood why.

The fighting here wasn't some slow slog of grinding damage. It was brief and brutal.

Before he lost it in the class change, his *Healing Touch* might have restored all his lost health in an instant. But it would have seemed like an eternity before he could use it again when people died so quickly.

The black-furred miner who had been searching for minerals near Martin's spine ducked back into the crowd before he had a chance to hit back, but there were plenty more enemies where that one had come from.

Two of them swung at Martin at the same time. Their picks hooked over the blade of his sword when he brought it up to parry.

[Skaife BLOCKS 12 damage]
[Skaife BLOCKS 14 damage]
[Skaife suffers 26 stamina loss]
[Skaife suffers 2 exhaustion damage]

Apparently, you could push your body past its limits here, but it would kill you. Martin wrestled to pull his weapon free before some opportunist hacked into his ribs, but the rat-men were nothing if not persistent, pulling back just as hard.

He reared back with all his strength, and suddenly the pressure was gone. Both pickaxes clattered to the ground at his feet as he stumbled back. In the place of his attackers there was a blood-streaked blur of feathers and steel.

[SNEAK ATTACK for double damage]
[Warren Warden suffers 38 piercing damage]
Warren Warden has died.
[SNEAK ATTACK for double damage]
[Warren Warden suffers 36 piercing damage]
Warren Warden has died.

Rabid Ratmen
3/10 Murovan deserters slain.

[Tesra suffers 2 environmental damage]

Lindsay rose to her feet amidst the carnage, cawing in victory with her bloodstained daggers held aloft.

"Iron Riot!"

She was going to get herself killed. Martin charged in, slashing wildly at the Murovan rushing into the gap behind her.

[MISS]
[MISS]

It was enough to give her a moment to jump clear. But Martin wasn't sure how much more favorable their situation was when it was just the two of them, back to back in an ever-tightening circle of enraged Murovan deserters.

Whatever temporary distractions Martin had managed were forgotten, and the horde's bravery seemed to be returning. Lindsay was a comforting weight at his back.

"Have knaves got any tricks up their sleeves for situations like this?"

She scoffed. "If you turn out the lights then I might be able to sneak attack again?"

Martin's eyes narrowed. *Celestial Strike* had been bright enough to light the whole cave; what would its dark counterpart do? He held his sword up above his head and called on *Void Strike*.

Void Strike - Deals 6 physical and 6 dark damage to a single target on a successful hit. *[10-second cooldown]*

A tiny sliver of a black hole took the place of Martin's sword, a black so dark that no light could escape it. A hole in the world.

The Murovan torches guttered and spat as the flames streamed towards him. It wasn't enough to put the fires out, but it was enough to bring back the fear.

He heard the nearest rat-man squeal in terror, "Gods below!"

Hefting the weightless blade of darkness, Martin took a step forward and watched his enemies scatter before him. The Murovan, so brave just a moment before, went scampering for their burrows in the face of a little bit of magic. He slashed at the back of the closest one as it turned to run.

[Warren Warden suffers 6 slashing damage]
[Warren Warden suffers 6 dark damage]

It collapsed in a heap at his feet, but some fevered energy still drove it to scramble away. Martin kicked it over onto its back as it grunted and squealed. He could smell its blood, rich and cloying as a butcher's shop.

"Why? You should help us, not killing us!" it wailed.

Martin paused, blade held ready to plunge into the rodent's unprotected stomach.

"Why? Because I'm Murovan like you?"

"Because we both belong to Strata."

Lindsay let out a yelp of distress behind him, so Martin hammered his sword down into the Murovan and spun away to help her.

[Warren Warden suffers 14 piercing damage]
Warren Warden has died.
Skaife gains 220 experience.

Rabid Ratmen
6/10 Murovan deserters slain.

Lindsay had been busy while he was distracted. She'd cut

down a pair of the panicking rats before they'd made it more than a few feet, but now the rest were standing their ground.

It would be another few seconds before Martin could call on *Void Strike* to scare them off again, so it looked like they were back to fighting, on slightly more even terms.

In the midst of the crowd of Murovan, Lindsay moved like a blur of feathers, daggers flashing red in the torchlight.

[Warren Warden suffers 3 piercing damage]
[Tunnel Rat suffers 2 piercing damage]
[Pack Rat suffers 3 piercing damage]
[Warren Warden suffers 4 piercing damage]

Martin couldn't even keep up with how fast she was going, but despite the flurry of strikes darting out from the knave, none of them seemed to be doing much more than stinging and startling the Murovan. Without the element of surprise, she couldn't make the lethal sneak attacks that seemed to be her most powerful ability.

The Pack Rat's heavy backpack of wares made him easy to pick out. It also made him too top-heavy. Martin grabbed him by the tail and yanked as hard as he could. The merchant's pointed face hit the stone floor with a crunch.

[Pack Rat suffers 3 bludgeoning environmental damage]

A quick thrust finished the prone rat-man off.

[Pack Rat suffers 16 piercing damage]
Pack Rat has died.
Skaife gains 180 experience.

Rabid Ratmen
7/10 Murovan deserters slain

His first mistake had been treating Strata like it was real – and acting like he was really in danger – but his second mistake was in treating it like any other game. Swinging away constantly with his weapon, using every ability the moment it came off cooldown; those might have worked in other games, but Strata demanded more.

Strategy paid off here. It wasn't like other MMOs where he had to wait until the endgame before his talents actually became useful. It was like this game had been made for him.

Stepping right over the skewered corpse of the Pack Rat, Martin knocked a descending pickaxe off course so that it narrowly avoided Lindsay's exposed back.

[Skaife BLOCKS 6 damage]
[Skaife suffers 6 stamina loss]

"Took you long enough," she called. He could hear the laughter in her voice, almost on the edge of hysteria.

The blade of his sword was notched and bloodied, but there was still enough of its surface clear for him to see movement behind him. He spun and thrust it forward in the same motion, hammering the blade into a Tunnel Rat's guts, right to the hilt.

He was used to the sight of blood. That was normal video game fare. The smells were something else.

[Tunnel Rat suffers 14 piercing damage]
Tunnel Rat has died.
Skaife gains 180 experience.

Rabid Ratmen
8/10 Murovan deserters slain

"Sorry," he grunted in response to Lindsay's comment. "I didn't want to interrupt before you got your hits in. It's like having a dog. You've got to give it plenty of exercise or it turns weird on you."

She ducked a swinging pick that would have created a mine-shaft right out the back of her head and cackled. "Did you just call me a bitch?"

[MISS]

"No. I just called you a hyperactive puppy."

Martin threw himself onto the back of the Warren Warden, wrapping his free arm around its neck and leaving it reeling – wide open to Lindsay's attacks.

[CRITICAL HIT]
[Warren Warden suffers 22 piercing damage]
Warren Warden has died.

Rabid Ratmen
9/10 Murovan deserters slain

She flicked blood from her knives onto the last surviving Murovan. "Puppies are cute. I can live with being a puppy."

The rat backed away into the side of a building. Now that he had time to slow, Martin couldn't help but notice how amazing the graphics were. He could actually see the Warren Warden's throat moving as it gulped.

"Mercy?"

Lindsay glanced from the monster to Martin, eyes dancing over the corpses littering the village all around them, then back at the last thing between them and completing their quest. Lindsay answered.

"Bit late for that, ain't it?"

[Warren Warden suffers 11 piercing damage]
[Warren Warden suffers 14 piercing damage]

Warren Warden has died.
Skaife gains 90 experience.

Rabid Ratmen
10/10 Murovan deserters slain. Quest complete.

They both stood very still for a long moment; the only sounds were the crackling of dropped torches and the heaving of their breath. Martin was startled when another message popped up.

Your Sin has been purged and you have returned to Aten's grace.

He blinked open his character sheet. His class had returned to exorcist, his *Sin* now resting comfortably at -3. So... the change of class had been because his Sin had drifted into the positives. He was going to have to find someone to ask about that mechanic.

Sin definitely increased when you killed other players, but did it go down when you killed monsters? Was it tied into some sort of faction system? He really needed to find someone who wasn't part of the crusade. And who wasn't likely to set him on fire just for asking.

He called up his *Healing Touch* and patted Lindsay on the head, restoring her feathers to their original sheen and closing up the more obvious wounds on display.

[Tesra recovers 9 health]

She rustled those newly-shined feathers in appreciation. "Better late than never. You switched teams again?"

Martin shrugged. "Apparently killing rat-men isn't as sinful as killing douchebags who are trying to murder you."

"Who knew?"

Picking over the corpses revealed 19 silver pieces and a lot of vendor trash weapons that did comparable damage to what they already had equipped. It was their first quest; hardly surprising the game wasn't showering them with riches.

They beat a hasty retreat out of the Murovan settlement before the remaining rat-men could rediscover their courage. The tunnels that had seemed so dangerous on their approach passed them in a blur.

Martin had never understood the visceral rush Lindsay got from games – his enjoyment had always been more about the satisfaction of solving a particularly tricky problem – but now he got it.

He was buzzing with energy. Joyful.

They burst out into the open air of the main cavern, still buoyed along in a cloud of their own contentment. Martin was halfway across to Beachhead before he realized Lindsay had fallen behind. He backtracked.

"What's up?

Her eyes were closed.

"My notification just pinged," she said. "I've got to call it a night."

"Wait, what time is it?"

Martin briefly shut his own eyes and searched around for a clock, but there was nothing of the sort.

Lindsay's eyes opened.

"Like, three or something? I set the reminder to the maximum it would let me."

"You can set a reminder?"

Martin went back to searching through the menus.

"You're meant to. Didn't you get the health and safety spiel?"

Now it was his turn to snap his eyes open.

"Uh… no," he said.

"The whole thing about overuse causing brain damage, and dreams about the game being a warning sign you're playing too much?" She shrugged.

"Maybe I skipped it?" he said.

"Well, uh, don't play too long or you'll get a headache or something." She started walking again, calling back over her shoulder, "I'll keep you right, don't worry."

His brain was finally catching up to their conversation. Three in the morning. He had to be up for work in four hours.

"Do you still have time to hand the quest in?" he asked.

"Yeah, of course. Not like ten more minutes is going to hurt, right?"

They strode into town with their heads held high, but the residual pride only lasted for a moment before one of the guards hissed. "Decided to come back then, did you? That's a pity."

Lindsay spun on the lizard-man, hands going for her daggers. "The hell did you just say?"

Martin already had a grip on her wrist. "Don't. It isn't worth it." He dragged her deeper into the town as she grumbled.

Lindsay had been given the quest by the captain of the guard, and since Martin didn't fancy listening to another lecture about how meaningless he was compared to some made-up god, he went along with her to hand it in instead.

Captain Culvair was a Sythvan knight from the looks of him, with armor inlaid with ivory and scales to match. Like the other Sythvan, his eyes were vertically slit and strangely lifeless. The only clue Martin had that the immobile reptile was even alive and not a statue was the way his tongue kept flicking out to taste the air.

As usual, he let Lindsay do the talking.

"We killed ten Murovan deserters, as requested."

Culvair didn't move from his place. They'd found him at the top of the rickety central tower looking out over Beachhead. Much like the Lord Exorcist, he only had a few regular haunts, apparently.

"Tales of your triumph precede you. You did well, both of you, though I know it pained one of you to do it. You will go far in this crusade with commitment like that."

Rabid Ratmen *completed.*
Skaife gains 900 experience.
LEVEL UP!

Lindsay mumbled, "Thanks" to the captain, but her attention had obviously been drawn to her iteration of that little golden notification too. Martin kept his mouth shut, but he was already desperate to get away from this place and look at what he'd earned.

"There is another task for you, now that you have proved your value—"

Lindsay cut him off.

"Maybe in the morning, eh? Catch you later."

They clattered back down the rickety stairs of the tower and burst out onto the street, their glee from earlier returning. Lindsay's eyes were already pressed shut.

"Okay, let's do this," she said.

Skaife Murovan Exorcist
Strength: 4 Agility: 7
Endurance: 7 Willpower: 6
LEVEL 2

You have 3 points to assign.

Obviously, *Strength* translated directly into how much damage his weapon attacks did.

Agility covered a lot of his mobility within the world, which now seemed to be a lot more important than he'd originally assumed. Higher agility could have gotten him up onto the roof out of harm's way earlier.

Endurance determined both health and stamina, which were proving to be absolutely vital now that he understood how the combat actually worked.

As far as he could tell, stamina regenerated at a flat

percentile rate, probably based on the class – he'd have to experiment with other options to be sure. If it was a percentile, a bigger stamina pool meant faster regeneration too.

He still hadn't seen *Willpower* in action. From the way it impacted the other derived statistics it seemed to improve resistance to magic, and it seemed to increase the power of more mystical abilities too.

All of them had value, but at this point, when he was still getting used to the combat, he didn't think making himself into a glass cannon was a good plan. Once he was more confident in his skills with his sword and spells, he could dump everything into strength or willpower as his preference demanded, but for now, making himself durable enough to survive to higher levels seemed like a better idea.

*Strength: 4. Agility: **8***
*Endurance: **9** Willpower: 6*
*Health: **45** Stamina: **58***

Martin strained to do the math in his head, but it all seemed to add up. That extra stamina was going to be particularly useful if combat went on being so technical.

You may select 1 new ability.

Trinity Strike – Activates after two successful *Celestial Strikes*.
Shares a cooldown with *Celestial Strike*.
Deals 12 light damage.
Increases critical chance for all allies by 33% for 30 seconds.
[30-second cooldown]

Rebuke – Repulses a target creature by 5ft.
[60-second cooldown]

Halo – Blinds all hostile creatures looking in your direction within 20ft for 5 seconds.
Increased effect on targets with light-weakness.
[60-second cooldown]

All of them were pretty tempting. If this had been a regular MMO, Martin would have been all over *Trinity Strike* the moment he saw it, but here in Strata without a whole guild at his back, the other two seemed more immediately useful.

Halo was the first area of effect ability he'd come across so far, so that called out to him, but this game had fall damage, which meant that being able to give monsters a five-foot nudge could become incredibly useful in a lot of situations.

He selected *Rebuke* with a firm nod, then opened his eyes to see Lindsay bouncing up and down on the spot in front of him.

"I know we have to go to sleep, but this is amazing. Right?"

"Better than I could have imagined." Martin grinned. It was starting to feel more familiar now. This body was starting to feel like it was his.

Lindsay rubbed at the back of her neck, not quite making eye contact.

"So I did the right thing, bringing you along?"

With some effort, he swallowed his pride.

"I… Yes. Thank you so much. And I will totally pay you back for the rig and the game and… everything. I promise. It might take me a little—"

Lindsay wrapped her hands around his snout.

"Stop. Stop. Honey, I don't care about money. If you really want to pay me back, then you get me down to the end of this dungeon before everybody else. You use that juicy little brain of yours to puzzle it out and get us through to the end before everyone else. Then we're even. Deal?"

He tried to answer, but she was still holding his mouth shut, so he was forced to nod. Lindsay crowed with victory.

"All right. Sleep tight. See you tomorrow!"

She closed her eyes and a pillar of light shot down from above to consume her. By the time Martin had blinked the after-images away, she'd vanished, back into the real world.

With a heavy sigh, he opened up the menu and found the logout button himself. He knew that he had to sleep. He knew that he was going to be an absolute wreck in the morning regardless.

But choosing to leave Strata was still difficult, even if he had a million reasons to do so.

Martin didn't see some shining light when he logged out. Only the darkness of his empty apartment.

EIGHT

Bane of the Beholder

If it wasn't for caffeine, Martin was sure the whole world would come apart at the seams. Coffee might not have had the most delicious flavor, it might not even be a pleasant experience, but you could rely on it to pull you through when all your friends and family had abandoned you. There was no problem in life enough caffeine couldn't fix. Well, maybe some heart conditions.

Today's minor problem was having had only three hours' sleep after being dumped unceremoniously back into an aching and exhausted body that barely felt like his own. The solution? One can of room-temperature coffee from the stockpile beside the computer, one "36-Hour Energy" from a vending machine at the subway station and one gut-wrenching serving of the slop from the office coffee machine.

Enough caffeine to give a bull elephant palpitations was just about enough to keep Martin in motion.

There was a tremor in his hands, but as long as Gillian kept out of his personal space nobody was likely to notice something that minor.

He'd remembered his clothes and ID badge, and patted his hair down into something resembling a hairstyle when he caught a glimpse of his haunted looking face reflected back at him from the subway train's window. Nobody needed to know that anything was out of the ordinary.

But somehow, Gillian did.

Every time he glanced away from the screen she was there, hovering at the periphery of his vision like some deranged moth being drawn to the flame of his misery. She'd give him a scrunched-up little smile that reminded him of a sick dog and then he'd turn back to the screen because anything was better than looking at her faux pity, knowing she was just waiting for the opportunity to pounce on him and tear him to pieces.

By lunchtime he had been more productive than half the office combined, outstripping his usual score of orders processed by a frankly ridiculous amount, particularly considering that he felt like the front of his head was slowly collapsing inwards.

The tremors ground to a halt at about 1 p.m., and his productivity nosedived about ten minutes later. He stared down at his keyboard for a long moment, his headache gradually building in intensity until he was giving serious consideration to hiding under his desk.

"Martin, are you feeling all right?" Gillian's voice drifted over from behind him. "You don't look well."

It felt like his tongue had swollen up to twice its size.

"Just a little headache."

"I hope you weren't out partying all night," she tittered.

Why won't she just go away?

"Nope," he said. "Quiet night in as always."

"Well, you can always use one of your sick days if this is a genuine medical problem and not self-inflicted."

It was her voice. Just on the wrong side of shrill. He pressed his eyes closed, bathing in the hot darkness throbbing away in there.

"Just a headache, Gillian. It will pass soon enough."

"Hmm."

She had an amazing ability to make innocuous noises sound like pointed accusations. He kept his eyes shut until he was sure she wasn't going to say anything else. A moment later he heard her across the office, hovering over someone else for a change. Finally.

Martin had blown through his break, trying to keep going while his energy lasted, and Gillian's sympathetic noises would not extend to letting him take his break outside of the scheduled time.

Still, he was technically entitled to fifteen minutes of toilet breaks throughout the day. Most people portioned those precious moments of company time out into five-minute segments, just long enough for a brief run out onto the plaza to catch up on their vaping.

The trip to the bathroom by the elevators was under a minute. He could always go hide in the toilet for thirteen minutes. That would leave just three hours until the end of the day. Three hours in this state sounded like hell.

A six-minute detour to the coffee machine on the way back would still give him seven minutes to hide in a bathroom stall. Was seven minutes too long for a trip to the bathroom?

If he took too long, would they assume he was being sick and send him home? He didn't want to have any sick days on his record, and if he was going to blow through one of his four allotted sick days for the year he certainly didn't want to waste one of them on a mere three hours when he could take a whole day off.

He started to drift into a daydream about what a whole day off might look like. A quick trip down to the store for supplies, then settling in for a solid twelve hours of Strata.

He'd always been good at portioning out resources in games; he'd always known when to use a potion and when to wait. It wasn't time to use up a sick day yet. When they were deeper into Strata and they were getting close to the finish line he could take all four days, play for six full days in a row if he scheduled it next to a weekend. But it wasn't time for that yet. He was just getting started.

Regardless, he needed to do something to get through *this* day, so he lurched to his feet and made a beeline for the bathroom. He could feel Gillian's eyes on him every step that he took until he was finally out of sight.

In the sanctuary of the bathroom cubicle, he pulled out his smartphone and started searching around for information about Strata. There were a few forums dedicated to the game, but they seemed to be sparsely populated. He'd seen more players in Beachhead last night than seemed to be posting regularly.

The only website he found that seemed to be showing just how many people were actually playing Strata was an auction site.

There were no images, just descriptions. He had a quick glance through the listings to see if there was anything that might be helpful, and his eyes almost bulged out of their sockets.

Items from just a few deeps down were going for hundreds of dollars – not even magical items, just regular equipment. The few magic items that were listed cost more than his rent.

Martin stared down at the numbers for a long moment before something clicked in his exhausted brain. In a normal MMO, not everyone was racing for some finish line. They were exploring, they were completing quests, they were crafting.

Equipment in Strata must have all come from the crafting systems, and everybody was ignoring those in favor of rushing ahead as fast as they could. No wonder people hadn't made it to the end of the game yet; they were trying to face nuclear bombs with peashooters.

It was a self-fulfilling prophecy. The more of a rush people were in to get to the last deep, the less likely they were to be equipped to deal with it.

The more people failed, the more it encouraged others to keep barreling forward at full speed, because that carrot on a stick was still dangling right in front of their faces. The grand prize was still there for anyone to take, just out of reach.

He filed that little titbit of information away and went hunting for stat blocks again. On some obscure blog a dozen pages through his search results he found what he was looking for: somebody else doing the bare minimum of statistical comparison between the different race and class combinations.

Whoever it was hadn't taken the size differential into account, so Murovan of all classes were ranked at the bottom across the board, but it didn't take long for Martin to do the math himself.

None of the other combinations were better. It didn't matter how he calculated it; the stats were the same. He'd have to dig into the specific abilities of the – still tempting – invoker to be completely certain, but stats-wise they all seemed to be on par. Except Murovan, who had the same comparative stats, but were harder to hit.

If he restarted as something else, not only would he lose the level he had gained last night, but he'd lose the mechanically best race.

The pre-alarm warning popped onto his screen and he thumbed it off. Time to grab a caffeine top-up and get back to the grind.

The coffee must have made some difference to his pallor, because apart from one more appraising look from Gillian, he was left in peace on his return to his desk. Without her hovering, he was able to split his attention between the order processing program and a hastily assembled spreadsheet where he input the different stats from memory, adding in his own percentage adjustments based on size and the value of their racial abilities.

Given how easy player-versus-player combat was to initiate – and how well put-together the game seemed to be – he was sure that the classes would be balanced. Changing class wasn't important anyway. Changing race was what this was all about.

One night as a Murovan had been enough to convince him that he didn't want to be treated that way again. It was bad enough being treated like garbage in real life; he didn't want to endure it in his free time too.

"What are you working on there?"

Gillian was right behind him. Close enough that her breath tickled the small hairs on the back of Martin's neck. He jumped involuntarily, one flailing hand slapping the dregs of his coffee across the desk. There was nothing on the screen but numbers. She didn't know he wasn't working. He could lie. He just had to think.

The brown sludge started creeping across towards his keyboard until he slapped his arm down and let the worst of it soak into his shirt sleeve. Damaging company property would have been just the pretext Gillian needed to initiate disciplinary procedures and finally get rid of him. The coffee was lukewarm by the time it reached his skin, and he rolled up his sleeves without thinking.

"Sorry, Gillian. Just trying to work out an improved algorithm for the automatic order queue."

It was the perfect combination of jargon and reminder that he'd upped office productivity.

She smiled tightly at him, eyes darting down to his bare forearm.

"No need for that. Just worry about what's in front of you. I'm sure the tech support guys can handle that back-office stuff."

What was she looking at? Martin glanced down and spotted the shimmer of metallic ink on his skin. The tattoo. She was trying not to stare at it. He had forgotten all about it; it was as familiar as a birthmark by now and the metallic sheen was starting to fade.

Lindsay had drawn the Iron Riot guild crest back when they were just starting out in Dracolich Online, and after they'd finished the world's first successful Anguish Keep raid, all the senior guild members had gone out to get their allegiance branded onto their skin.

Martin didn't know if any of the others had actually gone

through with it – the slight downside of having friends that you never physically met – but ultimately, he didn't need to know because that tattoo was about his commitment to the guild, not anyone else's.

Gillian obviously wanted to say something about it, some comment about the dress code or some simpering invasive personal question. He had to fend it off before it came. There was no way he was going to spend the rest of his day trying to explain VRMMOs to his boss.

"Sorry, Gillian, you're completely right. I shouldn't let improving the process that handles hundreds of orders a day distract me from my work. I know how important productivity is to you."

The tight smile got even more pinched. They both knew he'd carried the whole department through the last annual review with his little process automation widget. It didn't matter how much she hated him. She had to tolerate him because of his results.

He smiled right back at her, much more genuinely. There was something perversely enjoyable about being trapped in this office with both of them painfully aware of how much better he was at his job than her.

Without looking, he deleted his worksheet and turned back to the order processing UI. Gillian made a little huffing noise, but the conversation seemed to be over. There was still an hour left in the day and spite was a powerful motivator.

Despite the mid-afternoon slump he was still going to beat everyone in the office. It was like they weren't even trying to be the best.

Martin didn't even recognize his own reflection when he was riding the train home that night, in no small part because a smile was still hovering on his lips. Anticipation of the night ahead was finally outweighing his exhaustion.

Every time they blasted past the bright lights of a station and his face reappeared Martin did a little double-take. He was half expecting to see Skaife's ratty little face reflected back at him.

He flicked through the general news feeds, searching for anything about Strata, but beyond the impressive number of players it boasted and its position on the bestseller charts there was nothing at all. Usually every MMO had some bad press by now, some luddite screaming that gaming was dangerous and holding it up as an example, but on Strata they were silent. Even the usual poop-socking stories about people staying online for days at a time were absent. Weird.

Usually when he was this tired, he would load up on sugar and buzz through until a crash at about midnight, but tonight he found himself craving protein. He stopped in at the station convenience store on his way out and surfaced with more decent food than he'd normally eat in a month.

With no need to budget for a game or an upgrade to his computer, eating like a human being had become a viable option again; that was kind of exciting in a sad, grown-up kind of way.

By the time he'd wandered up to his apartment, Martin had already devoured half a roasted chicken, well aware that the moment the NIH came into sight, he was going to want to put it on.

He forced himself to go through the motions of putting his groceries away and washing up as best he could before turning on his computer.

Lindsay was already in the game. Whatever thoughts he'd been entertaining about restarting vanished in an instant when the prospect of getting back into the game was in front of him.

So the whole town of Beachhead hated him just for existing. So what? All he had to do was what he always did. Outshine them all.

NINE

The Key of Culvair

It felt like falling again the second time that Martin came to Strata, but this time it was just a sensation before he slammed down into Skaife's wiry rodent frame. It was already waiting for him in the same spot he'd left it.

He opened his eyes and grinned. The bustle of the town around him was full of purpose and energy, not like the aimlessly drifting strangers he had just passed by out in the real world. How could it already feel like coming home?

"Oi, tourist. Stop gawking. You ain't here to take in the view. You're here to quest."

He spun around looking for Tesra before realizing the guild crest on his chest was glowing again. She must have been somewhere nearby.

He touched the crest to reply to her, still wondering where she was, when suddenly a speck of silvery light appeared at the periphery of his vision. When he released the crest, the glow vanished.

Interesting.

With his paw flattened on the guild sign once more he turned in a slow circle until he spotted the light outlining a figure lurking on a rooftop just outside of the torches' reach.

"Aren't you a little short to be Batman?"

The dark figure popped up from its crouch.

"Cheeky. What took you so long? I've been waiting ten minutes."

"Waiting, or...?"

Martin was entirely too familiar with his brave leader's deficit attention span. He could see her bouncing on her heels, even from this distance.

"All right, so maybe I already picked up the next quest from Culvair. We have to go hunt some dark rabbit or whatever."

"A dark rabbit," he replied flatly.

Lindsay paced back and forth along the roof.

"Dark rabbit? Night rabbit? I don't know. Some bunny monster or other."

Martin scratched his head. "Is it some kind of rabbit-man?"

She dropped down off the roof, out of sight, and her outline was replaced with a spark of light to mark her position.

"Oh, I don't know. Will you just get your ass in gear? I've got places to be and people to see."

Martin rolled his eyes. "Yeah... I'm going to go see Culvair. Maybe he'll know what the hell you're talking about."

"Ugh, come on," she wheedled. "Let's go kill something. It's been a crappy day. I want to get my murder on."

He was entirely too used to Lindsay for her complaining to have any impact.

"Five minutes. You can go check the marketplace for new weapons or food or something."

"But... but... murder." She sounded despondent.

"Soon. I promise. All the murder you can eat. I just need to find out what kind of rabbit we're after."

He was smiling again. This was the most fun he'd had all day, and all they were doing was arguing.

Was it possible to pout with a beak? If it was, Lindsay was almost certainly doing it.

"Fine, but if you take a minute longer, I'm trading you in for a younger, prettier rat-man."

"Five minutes," Martin sighed.

"Five minutes. Or else."

The watchtower where Captain Culvair lingered was still right beside him, so Martin scrambled up the stairs as fast as he could. It was a funny little detail, but the steps were just slightly too high for him, like they'd been made with longer legs in mind. What would have been a stroll for any other race cost him stamina.

Culvair was still in his place atop the tower, staring out into the endless darkness beyond the reach of the town's torches. Blind to everything that Martin's Murovan vision could make out easily.

Here in town, everything had been designed with Wulvan, Sythvan and Corvan in mind, but in the other parts of the dungeon – the natural parts that the Crusade hadn't colonized yet – he was starting to suspect that those places were made with Murovan like him in mind.

"Your associate has already passed through here," Culvair said, his back still turned to Martin. Martin could have sworn he'd been quiet coming up the stairs and that the strange reptile hadn't even cast a backwards glance.

Culvair's tongue darted out again. Tasting the air. Martin grinned; he'd assumed it was just an idle animation. It hadn't even crossed his mind that the NPCs could smell things too.

"Well, I don't know if you've noticed, but she can be a little… flighty. I just wanted to check what sort of pest you have us chasing after this time."

"Pest?" Culvair's head snapped around, his dead eyes boring into Martin. "Did that fool tell you nothing at all?"

Martin rubbed his temples, wondering if it was possible to get a headache inside a game. "Let's just assume that she didn't and start over."

"For the past month, I have been losing patrols. At first it was just a stray guard here or there. It was assumed that they were deserters, or that they had pressed on to deeper settlements."

Culvair leaned against the waist-high balustrade and stared back out into the darkness. He paused for a moment, gathering his thoughts.

"I did not assume this. I know my men. Eventually, they returned to us from beyond the veil of death. Cast back down into Beachhead. Each one of them terrified and broken."

Martin stepped up next to Culvair, resting his chin on the barrier. "They came back from the dead?"

Culvair scoffed.

"I forget how fresh you are to this hell. I forget how little they tell you before you descend. Once you have entered the Dungeon of Strata, you cannot leave until the evil at its root has been defeated. We are all prisoners here. Even in death we cannot escape. The dark magic of this place will not let our souls ascend to Aten."

Martin tried to look up at Culvair's face without moving.

"Well, that's a good thing, right? They can't deplete our numbers."

"It is another of Strata's wicked tricks. Another means of corruption. How can the crusaders fight with all their passion when they know that the only reason they live is thanks to Strata? That the evil in the heart of the darkness is the well-spring of their existence?"

The fine leather of the captain's gauntlets creaked as his hands curled into fists. For someone cold-blooded, he certainly seemed to have a temper.

"Okay, I guess I can understand why that might make you feel a little... conflicted."

Culvair moved, twisting and craning his long neck until he was nose to nose with Martin.

"You understand nothing," he hissed. "Standing there with your fur still warmed by the touch of holy Aten's glorious sun.

Some of us have been here for years. Some of us have fought and died for this crusade a dozen times over."

Martin edged away slowly. "I'm sorry. That sounds awful."

"We endured. Just as you shall endure. All of us safe in the knowledge that someday the Crusade will end." Culvair's dead eyes turned back to the shadowy void of the cavern. "Someday we will be able to return to the surface, with the darkness here defeated once and for all."

Changing the subject seemed like a good way to keep the knight away from the screaming edge of madness.

"So... something was picking fights with your patrols?"

"There was no fighting. Only slaughter." Culvair's tongue flicked out, like he was still tasting the blood on the air. "My guards are good men, brave enough in their own way, but there is a reason they linger here as close to the surface as possible. They have delved deeper into Strata, faced the darkness beneath us and found themselves to be wanting."

He reached out with one weary hand to pat Martin on the head. Like he was a pet.

"There is no shame in knowing your limitations," Culvair continued. "They did not fall to corruption and turn on their own. They did not try to shirk their duties to the Crusade. They merely recognized that the things that dwell in the deeper dark are beyond their ability to best. With that recognition, they returned here, where they can defend our supply lines in relative peace. Once you have defeated the first Archduke, Strata will no longer return you here. If you face him and defeat him, you will return in his place, just as slaying the next Archduke will deliver you back to life even deeper into the darkness. You may not find being swallowed into Strata to your liking. You may wish to stay here once you have seen what is beneath us."

That lit some tiny spark of defiance in Martin. He wasn't like these losers. It didn't matter if he was a detested Murovan or a detested office worker. He was never going to be like them. Clenching his jaw, he bit back the worst of his reply.

"I doubt it."

Culvair's ability to sneer without lips was fairly impressive.

"You are all so brave when you first arrive. Before Strata breaks you."

Martin resisted the urge to roll his eyes at all the dramatics. Time for another nudge in the right direction.

"What was killing your guards?"

"A Night Ravager. A demon of the darkness." A shudder ran down the length of Culvair's body. "You won't see it until it is already upon you. They are twice the size of a Wulvan and three times as strong. Their claws rend armor like it is paper. It should not be here. They are lone hunters, stalkers of the lower deeps. They have never come so close to the light before. Never."

There had to be more to this.

"If it's so dangerous, why are you sending two brand-new players out to face it?" Martin asked.

"If not you, then who? My broken guards? That zealot Khargen and his wild-eyed disciples? Someone must slay the creature if Beachhead is to survive." Culvair's head snapped around again, his words coming faster and faster. "Your companion came to me, desperate to gain access to the deeps below. I told her that she was not ready. I warned her that her strength would falter in the face of the foes that will meet you. She would not believe me either. So I offered her this poisoned chalice. If she can defeat the Night Ravager, I will give her my blessing and turn over the Deep Key that you require to delve further into Strata."

That was the moment Lindsay chose to stroll up the stairs. She squawked at him.

"Come on! You must be done jabbering now. Can we please get going?"

She grabbed Martin's tail and started dragging him away. Holding onto the barrier with both hands, he squeaked out, "Just one last question. Why is this Ravager up here if it usually sticks to the lower levels?"

Culvair had turned his back on them once more.

"Who can say for certain? The ecosystem of Strata is complex. Perhaps some larger and more fearsome monster has laid claim to its hunting grounds. Perhaps it is simply seeking out easier prey. The Deep Gates only prevent passage when you are descending. It could have strolled up through forty deeps to get here and we would never know why."

Martin lost his grip. Scrambling to stay in place, he called back to Lindsay, "Hold on. Did he just say ecosystem?"

Lindsay just kept on tugging. "Nope. Don't care. Boring. Murder time. Come on. Let's go, move it."

He managed to rescue his tail from her feathered grasp by the time they reached the marketplace. Then he spitefully delayed her for just long enough to exchange the junk items he'd harvested from the pig for some silver. Probably less than he would have gotten if he wasn't Murovan, but he certainly wasn't going to trust Lindsay to handle the money. They didn't need a repeat of the pink dye incident.

Without any means of identifying the smoldering mushrooms – or, more importantly, appraising their value – he tucked them back into his empty inventory and forgot about them all over again.

Judging by the prices of the few weapons for sale in town, he had made very little money. That, or the in-game economy was just as skewed as the real world one that had grown up around the game. But there wasn't much time to consider it. Lindsay was on the verge of bodily dragging him out of town.

Whatever jibes the guards at the gate flung his way went right over Martin's head, both because he was lost in thought and because now there was an edge of pity to his feelings towards them.

These were the crusaders who were too afraid to crusade. It was hard to take their insults to heart when he knew how pathetic they were.

The word 'ecosystem' wasn't something Martin had ever

expected to hear coming out of any NPC's mouth in a fantasy game. It had a lot of implications attached to it.

If this game had its own internal ecology, with the different monsters all interacting with each other, moving into territory when it was abandoned or brutalizing weaker monsters to take their prime real estate, that would explain why there was no information online about the different deeps of Strata.

They would be constantly changing. Higher-level enemies would constantly be moving upwards to the easier prey of the low-level players. It was like players and monsters were spawning at opposite ends of the dungeon and racing each other to get to the other end first. No wonder nobody could make it past the middle deeps; they must have been a warzone of mid-level players and mid-level monsters both trying to get by.

Martin was only drawn out of his reverie when Lindsay patted him on the top of the head. He'd been so lost in thought that he'd just followed her through the twists and turns of unmapped tunnels without a second thought.

Lindsay was bouncing up and down on the spot.

"Dude. This is it."

He stared at it for a moment before answering.

"What... what am I looking at here?"

Set into the raw stone of the cave floor was a perfect circle of solid steel, polished until it reflected Lindsay's torchlight. Around the outside of the circle was a raised rim, once again burnished completely smooth with the exception of one keyhole, set right by their feet.

"This is the Deep Gate. Every deep has one. They're all locked until you get that specific deep's key. How are you not up to speed on this already?"

He grumbled, "Because someone drags me away by the tail every time I try to talk to an NPC to find out what's going on?"

Lindsay leaned her head on his shoulder and cackled. "You love it."

Crouching down to look at the keyhole more closely, he asked, "So where do we get these keys?"

"Uh, I think it's different in different places, but normally we just have to complete a special quest or beat some sort of boss monster. You know, business as usual. Oh, and I think there are meant to be some special gates that will jump you more than one level? Everyone was pretty vague on that part."

He stood up again and met her smirk with a smile of his own.

"All right, then. Let's go find the monster that makes Captain Cobra crap himself."

TEN

Blacker Than Night

———————————————

The hunt for the Night Ravager was never going to be simple. It had evaded the guards of Beachhead for weeks already, and the terrain was very much in favor of a creature trying to hide.

The endless warren of tunnels stretching out from the central cavern twisted and turned, full of dead ends and false trails, and the constant clatter of other players ruined any chance at the element of surprise.

Beyond the bustling town and the encounter in the Murovan camp they hadn't encountered too many other players so far, and those they did pass in the tunnels seemed too intent on their own quests to give the two of them much more than a cursory glance.

Most of them were a couple of levels above Martin; people who had been lingering here despite the call of the deeps below. It seemed unlikely that literally everyone was a coward, or that they hadn't heard about the prize at the end, so he concluded that finding Deep Keys really wasn't as straightforward as Lindsay was making it out to be.

It would be so like her to find an NPC and badger them so hard that they gave her an impossible quest just to get rid of her. Martin already had concerns about rushing through the game too quickly and never having time to upgrade their equipment or achieve the proper level.

Maybe they should have hunted around town for alternate quest givers. Judging by all the dead pigs and pillaged mushrooms they came across in their travels, there was definitely at least one other starter quest out there.

At one point, Martin caught sight of a black-furred Wulvan that he was quite sure was Dmitri, born back into the world to be a nuisance all over again. But like all the other adventurers out here in the tunnels, he was gone without a word, hurried along by the rest of his group before Martin could say a word.

Time slipped away from them as they roamed up and down tunnel after tunnel, slowly filling out their map but losing precious moments of game-time with each step. Lindsay's eyes roamed over every surface, desperate for a clue.

Meanwhile, Martin's attentions had turned inward. This Night Ravager was an apex predator, from the way that Culvair had so briefly described it. Perfectly adapted to stalking and hunting prey through the maze of tunnels that made up a dungeon. There was no way they were going to find it just by traipsing back and forth all night.

"We need to split up."

Martin didn't even realize he was speaking until the words were already out of his mouth.

"What? Have you never seen a horror movie? You never split up. Don't split the party. Rule number one." Lindsay prodded at a pig corpse that had been kicked into the corner, hoping for claw marks on its hide instead of the usual sword slashes.

Martin snapped his fingers. He relished the soft leathery feel of his new skin.

"Exactly. Monsters don't like crowds. They like easy pickings. Lost and lonely wanderers. I'm not crazy. I'm not proposing that you actually go anywhere. You've got stealth; you should be using it."

"Wait." Lindsay glanced back at him. "You want to be bait?"

Martin shrugged. "I'm the one clunking around in armor. I'm the one who's snack-sized. It makes sense to me."

"Okay, first off, 'Snack-size' is now your new nickname. Second, this isn't even close to your worst plan."

There was a hint of musical laughter in her voice. Just a little touch of amusement that told Martin there wasn't going to be any further argument.

Lindsay soon faded out of sight as they rounded the next bend, and before long he had almost forgotten she was there at all. It was entirely possible that she wasn't. For all he knew, she'd got distracted by something shiny down some side-branch of the tunnel and abandoned him immediately. She wasn't exactly known for her attention span.

He could really have been alone in the dark with whatever was lurking just out of sight. The monsters they'd encountered so far in Strata hadn't exactly been terrifying, and for all he knew, this Night Ravager wasn't going to make much of an impression either, but an active imagination was a terrible thing.

Pitch-black tunnels provided nothing to distract him. The echo of every footstep had him twitching. The sound of his own breathing seemed almost deafening when he was straining every sense for even the slightest hint of the monster in the dark.

He caught the scent of it first. Before he heard a sound or saw any sign, there was a metallic tinge to the air. A coppery tang that reminded him of the raw meat his mother used to buy from the store.

Blood.

He lingered in the tunnel, unwilling to move his feet, but eventually curiosity overcame dread and he followed his nose.

It did not take long for him to find the smell's source. There were gore-sticky feathers scattered all around the little volcanic bubble of a cave that he'd arrived at. For a brief, terrifying second, he thought it was Lindsay. It was only on closer examination that he realized these feathers were gray and white rather than Lindsay's black. A Corvan, but not *his* Corvan.

He slipped his sword out of its sheath and crept further out from the dubious safety of the tunnel mouth. The other player's body lay in a broken heap against the far wall, mauled beyond recognition.

There were two other tunnels leading away. With a tremor in his hand, he reached down to touch the corpse. It was still warm. The blood was still oozing out under his fingertips. Whatever killed this guy was likely still nearby.

"Lindsay. Keep your eyes open." Martin had tried to shout, but it came out barely louder than a whisper from his dry mouth. "I really hope you're still here."

The dark tunnels ahead took on a new, sinister cast as Martin crept his way forward. Before, he had been on edge, but now the fur felt like it was trying to climb off his skin. Every echo of his own footsteps had him jerking his head around.

Yawning open like some great mouth, the tunnel spread out into another cave just as suddenly as it had the last. There was no decorative arrangement of feathers this time. Just the constant encroaching darkness everywhere Martin looked.

A dozen more tunnels branched out from this hub, an endless maze that could have hidden any number of monsters.

Damn it.

Martin was starting to suspect that he wasn't the delicious treat he'd thought he was. Maybe even Night Ravagers turned their noses up at rat-men. He rolled his eyes and then tried to decide on another tunnel to follow.

There was no warning growl. No announcement that the fight had started. One moment Martin was staring out at the empty tunnels and the next the Ravager was coming.

Nothing so big should have moved that fast. It didn't just run, it hooked into the tunnel walls with all four of its arms and flung itself forward, metallic claws shrieking and scarring the stone. Martin let out a little bleat of terror and dove to one side as the titanic mass of muscle plowed right past him into the wall.

[MISS]

Whatever his imagination had conjured up couldn't match the thing in front of him. He could barely make out the shape of it in the darkness and the cramped conditions. Beyond its body having four arms and passing for vaguely humanoid, most of the bigger picture was lost on Martin.

Only fine details stood out to him in his panic. The sinews and exposed muscles rippling across the creature's surface. Rich black oil seemed to be leaking from the crevasses between those wiry bundles, coating the whole surface in a solid slick coating.

Now that they were close enough to touch, the creature's stench washed over Martin. Sharp and acrid, cloying and strangely normal. Martin couldn't quite place it, but it was intimately familiar.

When it turned, the jagged, chaotic tangle of metallic-tinted tusks and fangs hanging out of the Ravager's mouth swept right past Martin's face.

That mouth was not made for eating. The rust-tinted teeth would have gotten in the way. It was a weapon. The whole creature was a living weapon.

Arrayed around that awful mouth like a strange constellation were six glowing green eyes. They narrowed as the Ravager focused on him.

It closed the distance and spread its arms wide, like it was welcoming Martin in for a hug. He was almost drawn into its embrace before Lindsay's voice cut through the darkness.

"Hit it!"

Martin snapped out of his paralyzed terror, and with all the poise of a toddler being pursued by a wasp, he hit it.

[Night Ravager suffers 4 slashing damage]

Black oil flooded in to the scratch on its hide, closing over it before Martin had more than a glimpse of the raw red flesh below. He hoped that was just a visual effect and this thing wasn't going to just regenerate whatever damage he dealt it.

The Ravager's jaws opened wide as it reared back, those horrific teeth spreading open like a blossoming flower of death. The stupid joke about being bite-sized ran through Martin's mind, now turning his guts to water instead of being vaguely unamusing.

When it lunged for him again, he leapt backwards, crashing off a wall and tumbling into the waiting mouth of a tunnel.

[Skaife suffers 2 blunt environmental damage]

Lindsay leapt onto the Ravager's back the moment it turned to chase Martin. Both daggers hammered home with wet thuds that reverberated around the strangely silent cave.

[SNEAK ATTACK FOR DOUBLE DAMAGE]
[Night Ravager suffers 38 piercing damage]

It didn't even flinch. It barely even seemed to notice her. The Night Ravager was single-minded in its pursuit.

Martin managed to find his feet and hold out his sword in both shaking hands. Time seemed to slow as the Ravager bounded towards him. His brain was finally starting to spin into action. It was a Night Ravager. A demon of darkness, according to Culvair. Everything he needed to know was right there. Martin concentrated on *Celestial Strike*.

His sword lit up, illuminating the whole chamber and giving him an entirely too-clear view of the hideous Ravager, and Lindsay still dangling off its back. It flinched away from the light, the charge faltering. With a savage bark of joy, Martin plunged the glowing sword into the center of the Ravager's mass.

[Night Ravager suffers 6 piercing damage]
[ELEMENTAL WEAKNESS: DOUBLE DAMAGE]

[Night Ravager suffers 12 light damage]

The oil bubbled away from the light and there was the first hint of real red blood. But as soon as the damage was dealt, the light within the sword faded away and the oil came roiling back to cover the wound. It was all Martin could do to wrench his sword free before it was enveloped too.

He'd expected a scream, a roar of pain, anything to make this inhuman monstrosity seem more human, more mortal, but it didn't make a sound. There wasn't even a grunt of effort when it swung its claws and batted him to the ground like he was nothing.

[Skaife suffers 31 slashing damage]

For one moment that seemed to stretch on forever, all he could feel was numb. There should have been pain. He had heard the dreadful claws rattling across the bones in his chest and he was slick with blood.

How was he still moving? How was he even conscious? He slipped in his own blood as he tried to find his footing again. Two thirds of his health gone in a single casual swipe of its claws. They really were outclassed here.

[Night Ravager suffers 19 piercing damage]

That wasn't stopping Lindsay. She wouldn't go down without a fight, even if it was a hopeless waste of time and resources. In the midst of everything else, she'd managed to scramble forward on the Ravager's slick hide and hammer her daggers back down into what might have been considered its neck, if it were only a little thinner.

That determination was contagious. All they needed was a little more time. The creature was completely ignoring Lindsay, and as long as it kept underestimating her, she'd keep whittling away at its health. It didn't matter how deep the Ravager's health pool was, eventually she'd empty it. All Martin had to do was keep it busy.

He quickly cast *Healing Touch* on himself as he wobbled to his feet in the tunnel mouth.

[Skaife recovers 9 health]

It wasn't much, but the brief flare of golden light from his hand was enough to make the Ravager flinch again. Every moment it wasn't ripping him to pieces was a win. Martin rolled his little sloped shoulders, feeling the bones grating together inside him where the healing magic hadn't quite reached. They could still win.

Lindsay was a blur of motion on the Ravager's back, blades shimmering and dancing in the dim gray of Martin's night vision.

[Night Ravager suffers 4 slashing damage]
[Night Ravager suffers 5 slashing damage]
[Night Ravager suffers 6 slashing damage]

It finally took notice of her, twisting its head around to snap at her wrist. Martin wasn't standing for that. He tried to call up his *Celestial Strike* again, but it was still on cooldown, so he hacked at the Ravager with all his strength.

[Night Ravager suffers 9 slashing damage]

Nine damage was just a drop in the ocean, but where he'd hit the Ravager, close to one of its four wrists, the oil seemed to seep back a little slower. They were wearing it down.

He raised the sword to hack at the same spot again, but when he tried to bring it down, the blade jerked right out of his grip. Martin looked up. The sword was ensnared in the twisted mess of jagged teeth above him, looking no more out of place than any of the other metal protruding from the Ravager's mouth.

The Night Ravager reared up to its full height, its arms spread wide like the jaws of some great bear-trap. Its claws opened out, each one half the length of his shortsword. Martin would be lucky if they found little meaty cubes of him.

The trap snapped shut, but Martin's tiny paw was already outstretched and the swirl of his magic was already coiling around it. With every ounce of his concentration he thought the word *Rebuke.*

If he'd hoped to knock the Ravager off its feet, he was sorely mistaken. It slipped backwards as its claws snapped shut on empty air. It had balance like a cat. A skinned cat that someone had dunked in crude oil, but still a cat.

Lindsay's balance wasn't so good. With only her feet in contact with the slippery surface of the beast, she tumbled forward as it was flung back. The jumble of spikes around its mouth tore ribbons of flesh from her back as she fell past it.

[Tesra suffers 9 slashing damage]

The air was suddenly full of feathers, but through the cloud Martin saw his sword fall to the ground. Darting past Lindsay's prone body, he snatched it up the moment it hit the stone and drove it up into the Ravager's guts with all the momentum of that wild sprint behind him.

[Night Ravager suffers 12 piercing damage]

He tried to tug it clear, but the oil had slurped back into the wound and held the blade in place, like the proverbial sword in the stone. Martin let out a little hysterical laugh, then Lindsay leapt past him into the melee again. She twirled as she slashed at the Ravager, shedding blood and feathers in a spiral.

[Night Ravager suffers 5 slashing damage]
[Night Ravager suffers 6 slashing damage]

Those lethal claws swept down at her, but Lindsay was ready, diving through the Ravager's legs and popping right up behind it again.

When it tried to turn and follow her, it found Martin straining against it with all his strength. He wasn't strong enough to stop it, or even slow it. But he was gripping it hard enough that it had to take notice.

Martin closed his eyes for just long enough to pull up his list of abilities. Each one lay darkened, and had a tiny hourglass pouring out sand beside it.

All except for *Rite of Retribution,* which he triggered now as an afterthought. An extra critical hit or two might come in handy, after all.

The Ravager shifted above him. He could imagine those jagged claws even now rearing up like striking cobras, ready to sweep in and dice him up. Still, he kept his eyes closed and watched the last few grains of sand trickling down until *Celestial Strike* lit up once more.

His sword burst into radiant light inside the Ravager. All the sinews across its torso lit up from the inside, burning bright and red for one glorious moment. The oil leapt back from the blade and Martin was able to draw it free as if it were nothing.

With a roar that came out like a scream, he stared up into the void between the nightmarish bramble of jagged metal teeth and thrust the sword inside and into the roof of its mouth.

[CRITICAL HIT]
[Night Ravager suffers 12 piercing damage]
[ELEMENTAL WEAKNESS: DOUBLE DAMAGE]
[Night Ravager suffers 24 light damage]

The light blinked out inside the Ravager, and before Martin could pull back, its jaws crunched shut around his arm.

[Skaife suffers 21 piercing damage]

He could feel its teeth grinding together inside of him, the vibrations rattling up his bones as the Ravager tried to chew through. He should have been in agony, but the game protected him from everything but the spreading feeling of cold.

Two health left. The next attack would kill him. All the Ravager had to do was open its jaws and the fall back to the floor would probably finish him off.

It didn't. It played with its food, flicking him from side to side with a turn of its head. It was mocking him. It had just been playing with them all along.

Martin was dimly aware that Lindsay was still slashing away at the back of the Ravager. The damage notifications were still popping up.

[Night Ravager suffers 4 slashing damage]
[Night Ravager suffers 6 slashing damage]

It wasn't going to be enough. He could accept that now. It was the nature of the game. Some battles were just beyond the power of a pair of second-level characters, and this nightmarish thing from the depths of whatever hell lay beneath their feet was one of them.

His heels brushed the ceiling as the Ravager flicked him up and down.

"Lindsay. You've got to run."

She danced away from another swipe of the Ravager's claws. "If we die, we die together. Nobody ever won by running away."

Lindsay had to get lucky every time it took a swipe at her. It only had to get lucky once. Martin fumbled for a lie.

"This time, that is exactly how we win. One of us has to survive. If neither of us make it, killing this thing won't matter."

He couldn't see her through the bulk of the monster, but he could picture the incredulous look on her face perfectly.

"What are you going to do? Choke it when it tries to swallow you?"

"Will you just run?"

The teeth latched onto his arm seemed to be spinning like a food processor, grinding faster and faster through the bone.

When the bone broke, he would fall, and he would die. That was inevitable. There were only a few moments left to make a difference.

All around the wound, he was slick, not only with blood, but with the oil oozing from the beast's head. It was slowly coating him.

The scent of the Ravager filled his nose and Martin finally recognized it. A mixture of tar and petrol. The creature's skin looked like it was covered in crude oil… because it was.

With a blink, Martin summoned the mushrooms from his inventory. The heap tumbled out of his free hand to scatter on the floor below as he was flung from side to side for the Ravager's amusement. Just a spark had been enough to set them off before – enough to douse a pig in flames, and the pig hadn't even been coated in accelerants.

With a start, Martin realized that Lindsay must have finally listened. The Ravager had stopped whipping him from side to side and was now standing stock still. The only movement in the room was the strange slow motion of its spinning lamprey teeth grinding on his arm.

The electric-green neon eyes narrowed as it focused all of its eerily sentient attention on him.

Martin gasped, "I don't suppose you can be reasoned with?"

It cocked its head to one side, flicking him around like a ragdoll. It was so tall that Martin was almost brushing the roof.

He closed his eyes and pulled the *Rusty Dagger* that he'd started the game with from his inventory.

From the moment it appeared, the monster's attention was locked onto the dagger, but the Ravager made no effort to stop him. If anything, Martin would have said it was curious. He supposed it had no reason to be afraid; it wasn't like his puny little weapon was going to bother it.

Drawing in a deep breath of the fume-clogged air, Martin slashed at the stone above his head, scoring a line right across it and sending a shower of sparks falling down around him. Over and over he swept the dagger back and forth.

Tiny motes of heat and light showered down, only to be swallowed up into the pitch darkness of the Night Ravager or to die out on their own long before they reached the explosive fungi.

With a scream of frustration Martin slammed the dagger into the Ravager's face. The blade broke in two, barely piercing the hardened flesh.

[Night Ravager suffers 1 piercing damage]

It was surprised enough to drop him. He tumbled to the ground to land in a broken heap by its hooves.

[Skaife suffers 1 bludgeoning environmental damage]

The numbness was everywhere now. His night vision began to falter. Martin could swear that he was starting to hallucinate too. It looked for a moment like those merciless green eyes were looking down on him in pity. Like the silent terror of the Night Ravager was whispering, *"Come to me."*

The cave grew darker and darker, but with raw willpower Martin was able to move his paw forward and drag the snapped remains of his Rusty Dagger across the stone floor. It was feeble, but it was enough to throw one spark onto the crackling mushrooms.

For one glorious second, the darkness was pushed back. A gout of flame burst out of the mushroom, setting off all the rest in a chain reaction.

With a distant whoosh, Martin saw the Night Ravager enveloped in fire. The oil on its skin caught instantly. A towering inferno. The only light in Martin's world.

[CRITICAL HIT: DOUBLE DAMAGE]
[ELEMENTAL WEAKNESS: TRIPLE DAMAGE]
[Night Ravager suffers 102 fire damage]
Night Ravager has died.
Skaife earns 3080 experience.
LEVEL UP x 2

That last gasp of victory was short-lived. The oil that still clung to Martin's already oily fur caught light, and he was so very glad for the numbness and oblivion that followed a moment after.

[Skaife suffers 21 fire damage]
Skaife has died.

ELEVEN

The Master and the Murovan

Martin didn't know what to expect when he died. He supposed nobody really did. His current predicament was probably a lot like being a ghost.

The cave where he had died had already been dark, but now it was like he was looking at it through a thick black fog, the antithesis of the pale light that text coalesced out of when he was looking at the game menus.

Looking down, he realized he was disembodied again. The broken and charred remains of his character lay by his feet, the only thing that wasn't shrouded by the damned fog. If he had a stomach, the sight probably would have made him feel queasy. As it was, he just felt a little uncomfortable.

After a moment of staring, one of the little hourglasses that appeared next to abilities on cooldown formed above the corpse. The grains of sand were falling quite rapidly. He had wondered how the game could stay balanced if people just sprang back to life again every time they were struck down, but just like everything else in Strata, it was all about timing.

[30 minutes until rebirth]

That wasn't so bad. It was longer than any other game would have dared to slap on a player, but at the end of the day, Martin was willing to wait through nine hours of work to get back into Strata. Half an hour was small change by comparison. A slap on the wrist, really.

Martin had no eyes to close, but he found the shadows and mist around him reacting as if they were already shut. The menu appeared easily with just a little bit of concentration on his part. He was just about to log out when movement at the periphery of his vision caught his attention, and that distraction allowed the white text to fade away.

Lindsay had come creeping back into the room. He couldn't hear what she was saying but he saw her beak moving as she took in the scene. She picked her way carefully past the Ravager's scorched remains to give Skaife's body a prod with one clawed toe. So disrespectful. Once she was sure he was dead, she started rummaging through the monster's remains. Business as usual.

"Now, what were you doing all the way up here, my lost little darling? You aren't meant to come wandering higher than deep thirty."

If Martin had a body, he would have jumped. As it was, all he could do was swivel his field of view around to look for the source of the strange, soft voice.

A hooded figure was hanging immobile in the air above the corpses. Whatever features were beneath its cowl were lost in deep shadows. If it had limbs, they didn't extend beyond the edges of the robes. The only hint of motion was the rippling of that tattered gray cloth, set in motion by some unfelt wind.

"Uh, hello?"

The hood snapped up and Martin saw for certain that there was nothing but darkness within.

"What? You? You did this? You laid this mighty creature low?"

There was a tiny bubble of pride in Martin's chest that even the robed figure's contemptuous tone couldn't puncture.

"Yep. That was me. I mean, Lindsay… uh, Tesra… helped, obviously, but I'd say the majority of it was probably me."

It drifted around to face him. The softness of the voice belied the venom in the words.

"But how could this be so? You are barely even arrived. This makes no sense. I had expected some veteran recalled from the lower deeps by the wailing of the victims. Not some noob— uh, newborn."

If he'd had eyelids in that moment, Martin would have blinked. "Wait, you're human? Who are you?"

The figure began to drift in a slow circle around Martin's disembodied presence.

"Did you think that this dungeon sprang into existence fully formed? Or that it changes of its own volition? We are the Masters of Strata. The creators and the caretakers."

That made sense. There was so much going on in Strata, it was no wonder it needed constant attention to keep everything running smoothly.

"Oh, you're one of the game developers. Cool. I love Strata. You've done an amazing job."

"Our beloved dungeon is a masterwork, is it not? Which is why we must work so tirelessly to correct any faults that we find within it before they can be exploited."

The Master lunged forward suddenly, the darkness within its empty cowl suddenly filling the whole of Martin's vision. It spoke once more, a voice drifting from the black void.

"We must prevent impossible challenges like this monster from being encountered by crusaders too weak to face them, and to ensure that the impossible cannot happen. So, you must tell me. How did you defeat the Night Ravager?"

Martin could just picture some douchebag neckbeard sitting in a customer service cubicle with a NIH strapped to his head, talking down to Martin like he was the grand high wizard in a fantasy novel. That image helped shake off the confusion.

Realization struck Martin just before he opened his mouth. If he told the game developers about the mushrooms, they'd probably be patched out of the game and he wouldn't be able to use the same trick again.

Even if the Night Ravager had killed him, the experience had pushed him up two levels. He was level four. With a bag full of fungus firebombs, he might be able to dive right down a dozen deeps and power-level by exploding high-level monsters. Those stupid little mushrooms might have been the shortcut they needed to catch up with the rest of the pack in the race to the bottom.

Assuming that every monster they met was weak against fire attacks and willing to stand still for a few minutes while he scattered mushrooms around its feet. And assuming Martin landed a critical hit every time. Honestly, they probably weren't all that useful at all. But now Martin's curiosity had been piqued for other reasons.

He drifted away from the Master, watching out of the corner of his eye as Lindsay escaped back into the tunnels.

"If you're a developer, can't you just scroll back through the combat logs and see what happened?"

The robes stopped flapping for an instant, then resumed their animation as if nothing had happened.

"It is better for you to explain things in your own words so that we can be sure nothing… untoward happened. If you are co-operative, then there will be no reason to suspect that you have tampered with Strata in a way that might lead to your banishment."

"Wait, you think I hacked the game?"

They couldn't be serious.

"When something impossible happens that breaks the rules of the reality we have created here, we are forced to consider that someone has gone outside of those rules." The cave had slowly faded away while they were speaking; now they were floating in the black void of the menu screens. "And of course, when the rules are broken, there must be punishment. So that there is fairness to those who were obedient."

In the total darkness, the dusky gray of the Master's robes became the only light, the only real thing in a pit of nothingness.

"I wouldn't even know how to hack this game, or any game really. Even if I could, I wouldn't do it. What's the point of winning by cheating? Where's the victory in that?"

There was a strange singsong quality to the Master's voice now.

"If you haven't broken any of the rules, then why are you so reluctant to tell me what you did?"

Martin didn't consider himself to be particularly stubborn, but after a day of being slyly bullied by coworkers, he'd had enough.

"I didn't use anything you didn't put into Strata to beat your monster. If you really care that much, just go and check the logs."

"It isn't that simple. There are too many variables at work. Too much of the information I would need to piece this together is… decentralized." The master crept closer and closer. "Now tell me what you did."

That was actually an interesting little detail that he'd hold onto for later. Even the creators of the game couldn't keep track of everything. It made sense that there was no central server, given how quickly everything in the game responded, but the fact that they couldn't even access all the cloud storage?

"You're telling me you designed this game, and you don't know what is happening in it?"

"I am telling you that if you do not comply, you will suffer."

They couldn't bully him into talking. He held all the cards. "If you ban me, you'll never find out what happened."

The Master laughed. A flat, emotionless undulation.

"You sweet fool. You think that banishment is the worst fate

I can concoct? This whole world can be shaped to my whims. Every door that you open will lead to a pit. Every monster that you face will be summoned up from the darkest depths. I will dog your every step. Whatever you most desire in Strata, I will snatch from your grasping hands. That is… if you do not tell me what you did."

It was probably for the best that Martin's smug grin had no face to manifest itself on. It was known to infuriate people.

"Wouldn't that just break the game even more?"

The Master snapped, "Tell me what you did!"

"No."

[The Masters of Strata have intervened]

[Skaife lost 1 level]

"Hey! What the hell? I earned that!" Martin growled.

"Tell me what you did or I will strip you of every level. I will block every ability. You will be left with nothing but a rusty dagger and no hope. Tell me what you did!" There was a cold edge in the Master's barked demands that completely negated all the other softness.

"All right!" Martin yelped. "The mushrooms, the exploding mushrooms."

"The embercaps?" The Master's hood cocked to one side. Pondering. "They can't do that sort of damage. They're just environmental decoration. Potion ingredients."

"If you pile enough of them up, and the monster is weak to fire, and you get a critical hit, then you do this sort of damage."

The Master began to drift away.

"Overlapping effects. Interesting. The issue will be attended to when we next restructure the dungeon. Thank you for your… eventual… co-operation."

Martin floated after the robed figure as it drifted up into the void. "Always happy to, uh, co-operate. Could I have my level back now?"

The Master paused.

"No… I think not. Let this be a practical lesson for you. If you cross the Masters of Strata, there are consequences."

"That isn't fair!" Martin's dismayed shout was muted by the dark mists coiling all around them.

"What have you ever seen that could possibly convince you that anything in life is fair?" The empty sleeve of the robe was raised towards him and some invisible pressure began driving him backwards. "Now shoo. The grown-ups have work to do."

Pressure kept on building up until Martin was straining with all of his will just to stay in place.

"Give me my level back!"

The hood tilted to the side and Martin had the distinct impression that eyes were being rolled. The Master flicked its arm at him again and he dropped back into his own body with all the force of a car crash.

His crappy little apartment spun around him and his stomach heaved. Coming out of Strata the normal way didn't feel like this, and the sudden lurch from having no body to being back in his own horrible little meat prison was awful.

Balance gradually returned, but as he became more aware of his body again the contrast between nothingness and all the niggling aches and pains became more apparent.

He felt like he'd just run a marathon. His whole body was still trembling, but it had nothing to do with leaving the game and everything to do with this so-called Master of Strata being a complete bastard.

He'd died to earn that level and they snatched it away from him for nothing. No wonder nobody was able to get to the end of Strata if they were slapping the levels off people for no reason.

With a heavy sigh, he pulled himself up off the bed and stumbled over to land in his desk chair. It took two attempts to pry the neural inducer off his head, his hands were shaking so hard with fury.

It took him twice as many attempts to get his old VR helmet

strapped onto his head instead. Anything was better than looking at his real life. Whether it was Strata, Dracolich or something else, he didn't care. He just didn't want to be here anymore.

He didn't want to be Martin for one minute longer than he had to be.

TWELVE

Those Who Were Abandoned

Because he'd last logged out of Dracolich in a raid, Martin found himself bounced back to the Iron Riot guild hall when he logged in. He had always felt like it was a sacred place. A home, in the way that a half-dozen rented apartments over the years had never been. Apparently, he was the only one who felt that way.

All of the trophies and rare treasures had been pillaged off the walls by the other members of the guild. When Martin popped open the banking tab, he discovered that their vaults had been annihilated too.

The other guild members had sensed that Iron Riot's lifespan in Dracolich had come to its end, and while Martin's response had been sadness, theirs had been to pounce on the corpse like scavenging dogs.

Everything that was in the guild that could be sold along for easy gold had been taken. Everything that wasn't nailed down.

Martin had thought of these people as his friends – as a replacement family for the biological one that had let him down so badly in his early years – and this was how they repaid that trust and devotion. By robbing him blind.

Technically, everything here had belonged to the guild as a whole, and if any one of his fellow guild members had asked for anything Martin would have given it to them without qualms, but looking around the empty spaces that lined the hall, he could remember the wonders that had once filled them.

Some had taken days, weeks or even months of careful planning and preparation to craft or retrieve from the dungeons of Dracolich, and now they'd be tossed up onto the auction house to scrape together whatever gold could be sold off at a discounted rate to the remaining dregs before the whole world of Dracolich went dark forever.

Lindsay had told them they'd reconvene to make a decision on the future of the guild tonight. It seemed the decision had been made for them. Iron Riot was over, at least in this world.

As he looked around at what had once been the pinnacle of achievement in Dracolich, Martin couldn't believe how ugly everything was. He knew it was a silly thought, considering everything else that was going on, but compared to the graphics of Strata this place looked blocky and old.

Most of the time when you were playing Strata you didn't even realize that it was a game. The new NIH technology lit up all your senses directly. This place still had polygons and background music on loop to drown out the fact that nothing you interacted with actually made sounds.

He was almost relieved that the new headset only worked with Strata; he didn't think he'd want this jagged ugliness projected into his brain.

The guild message board was part of the game's infrastructure, so nobody had managed to haul it off the wall and sell it along. Martin summoned a keyboard and typed up a message to any of the guild that were still active.

Iron Riot are relocating to Strata Online. We had a great run here in Dracolich, and the challenges we faced here have made us all better players. Come and join us for the next great challenge. Come to Strata and send a message to Tesra Stormcrow.

With that done, there didn't seem to be much else to do. He supposed he could join in the frantic pillaging of all Dracolich's resources before this month's subscription ran out, but he didn't really have the stomach for it at the moment.

He took a glance at the clock in the upper corner of the screen and let out a sigh of relief. His half hour of death was almost over.

After he'd removed his glitchy old VR headset, Martin had to blink a few times to see if his eyes weren't adjusting properly. He hadn't noticed how dark it was when he'd made the scramble from Strata to Dracolich, . While his attention had been exclusively focused on the ticking minutes on the clocks he had seen, the hour now stood out to him just as clearly. It was after midnight.

Damn.

They'd wasted the whole night hunting after the Ravager, and he'd nothing to show for it but a charred corpse and one measly level after that Master had their way with him.

He pushed those thoughts aside. He'd managed today – or rather, yesterday – with just a few hours of sleep, and he certainly wasn't going to give up his time in Strata just because of something as paltry as exhaustion.

It wasn't like he was doing hard labor, anyway. He was just lying in bed the whole time that he played Strata. That was practically sleeping anyway. No reason to worry at all.

A sigh of relief escaped his lips as he fell back into the familiar darkness of the game, like he was a fish that had been hauled up out of the water and was only now getting back to its natural element. He could breathe again.

The darkness enveloped him, and for one long awful moment he thought that the spiteful Master had deleted his character or banned him, but then he caught sight of the glowing hourglass hanging in the air, the last few grains of sand finally trickling through it.

The hourglass blinked out, and all of a sudden Martin felt

himself falling. He let out a groan when he saw the circle of torchlight opening up beneath him. This hadn't been fun the first time around, and now he didn't even have shock to distract him from the inevitable crunch when he landed back in Beachhead.

Some things never changed; the numbness spreading throughout his body, the cold stone against his face and the hubbub of the town were just the way they were when he was born into this world the first time. Despite the landing, Martin still found himself grinning as he scrambled to his feet.

Culvair's tower was a handy landmark for navigation in the bustle, and now that Martin was used to the hostility of the townsfolk he found it easy enough to duck the elbows and dodge "accidental" kicks sent his way.

It was a little bit sad that when they were confronted with a magical fantasy world everyone reverted to behaving like school-yard bullies, but it was hardly surprising. In Martin's experience of working life, the only difference was that you got pantsed figuratively rather than literally.

There was a glint up by the guardrail that told Martin that Culvair was still in position, so he bounded up the stairs two at a time. It wasn't easy with his stubby little legs. The serpent's head snapped around when Martin cleared the top step.

"Why have you returned to me? I would have thought the valiant slayer of the Night Ravager would have already pressed on to the next deep and beyond."

Martin gave him a rueful smile.

"I got a little bit... ravaged. This is me just coming back from the dead now."

"I welcome you back to the land of the living and entreat you to remember the gift of true life comes from the sun," Culvair intoned. "Strata may be able to produce a mockery of true life, but eternity can only be truly found through radiant Aten."

Martin wasn't used to having Culvair's undivided attention. He supposed that slaying the Night Ravager had earned him enough respect for the snake to finally turn his head around, but the dead black eyes were disconcerting. Despite the unnerving gaze, Martin had one question to ask.

"As for pressing on to the next deep, that's why I came to see you. I'd like the key you promised us, please."

Culvair cocked his head. Martin realized that familiar tilt was like raising an eyebrow for creatures without eyebrows; a question, and a challenge.

"The key to the second deep? Do you think that I have an infinite supply of such treasures? How could you possibly have lost it already? Please tell me you didn't sell it off to some unready buffoon at the market?"

"Wait. Slow down." Martin held up his paws. "You already gave me the key?"

The serpent's head bobbed up and down. "The leader of your guild claimed the key and has opened the way for all members of Iron Riot."

Martin's stomach dropped.

"Oh no." He darted towards the stairs, then skidded to a halt. "When did she get the key?"

Culvair looked bemused. "It could not have been more than fifteen minutes ago."

"Oh no."

Martin was off and running before the captain had even finished speaking.

"Oh no."

He dashed through the crowds and ducked past the guardsmen who felt obliged to grab at any Murovan that they saw running.

"Oh no."

Fifteen minutes was a hell of a long time for Lindsay to be roaming around unattended. She could already be in an almost infinite number of impossible situations, and that was before taking malevolent Masters into account.

Martin tried to shake that thought out of his head. She was a grown woman. One who'd proven herself more than capable over the years. The only trouble was that she was the kind of person who, when confronted with a sign that said "bottomless pit," would jump in to see how deep it really was.

When he was talking about their leader to the other Iron Riot guild members, he'd always done his best to describe her as "bold" rather than "overconfident" or "suicidal." That boldness had carried them through in a lot of situations where he had flinched away to look for a better angle of approach. He would spend his time trying to work out how to get around a circle of fire while she'd jump right through it.

Neither of their approaches worked perfectly in every situation, but that was why they complemented each other so well. That was why she'd chosen him to come with her to Strata. Even she could recognize the value of having someone who could yell at her when it was time to stop, just like Martin understood that he needed someone to yell at him when it was time to go.

He was well clear of Beachhead before he thought to give it a backwards glance. If everything went well, he might never be back here again. In other MMOs he would have spent months or even years coming back to the same town over and over, learning all of the backstreets and secrets. In Strata, he had no time to look back. The only way was down.

The Deep Gate loomed open ahead of him just as his stamina ran dry, so he stopped beside the gaping hole to let it regenerate for a moment. It seemed to go up at a much better rate when he wasn't moving, but he hadn't had time to experiment yet. He closed his eyes to make sure his health was fully restored from the drop into Beachhead and was greeted by a little reminder.

[Level Up]

The Master might have snatched one of the levels he'd earned away, but not both of them. He pulled open the screen.

***Skaife** Murovan Exorcist*
Strength: 4 Agility: 8
Endurance: 9 Willpower: 6
LEVEL 3

You have 3 points to assign.

Endurance had served him well last time, but now that he'd seen the sort of monsters they were going to be dealing with in the lower deeps of Strata, Martin decided he needed a little more raw power to deal with them. Stamina was great when he was dealing with threats on the same level as him, but with something like the Night Ravager, being able to knock off big lumps of its health bar before it could completely annihilate him would have been better.

So, the question became: strength or willpower? Strength had a lot of handy knock-on effects, like increased carrying weight and reduced stamina drain when he was climbing or swimming; but buffing up his magic, such as it was, might be more helpful when confronted with giant monsters, since it seemed to have the same effects regardless of the enemy's toughness.

There was also a nagging worry at the back of Martin's mind that he'd be running into an enemy with magic before long, and if he kept neglecting willpower he'd have no defenses against whatever lightning bolts were being flung his way.

In the end, he came to a compromise.

*Strength: **6** Agility: 8*
*Endurance: 9 Willpower: **7***
*Health: **45** Stamina: **58***

Adding a little bit to both wasn't optimal, but at this point, Martin still had to cover his bases. He might have to commit hard to either magic or good old-fashioned violence later in the game, but for now, marginal improvements to both meant that both paths were still open to him.

You may select 1 new ability.

Trinity Strike – Activates after two successful *Celestial Strikes*.
Shares a cooldown with *Celestial Strike.*
Deals 12 light damage.
Increases critical chance for all allies by 33% for 30 seconds.
[30-second cooldown]

Halo – Blinds all hostile creatures looking in your direction within 20ft for 5 seconds.
Increased effect on targets with light-weakness.
[60-second cooldown]

Lay on Hands – Restores 100% of an ally's health. Reduces your stamina and stamina regeneration by 10% for 5 minutes.
[60-minute cooldown]

That new addition to the selection was immediately appealing. His healing touch was handy, but it couldn't really compare to bringing someone back from the brink of death.

The cooldown of an hour was nightmarish, though. He could understand why it was necessary, but it took a lot of the shine off the ability.

Trinity Strike was still tempting, but it would probably be more valuable once they'd pulled together a larger group. Particularly since he was doing reduced damage with each hit when he was using *Celestial Strike,* compared to a normal attack that got the benefit of his strength score.

He quickly selected *Halo* before he could second-guess himself, then opened his eyes.

The hole to the next deep still hung open before him. The

drop was just far enough that a torch wouldn't cast a light to the bottom.

Murovan night vision came to the rescue again. There was a shallow covering of water across the next level's floor, murky enough that he might have mistaken it for the surface itself if he couldn't see the sheen and ripples. Arching tree roots reared up out of the water here and there, and more trailed and looped out from the muddy walls.

Martin probably would have jumped down to splash in the giant puddle without a second thought if he hadn't seen a poor Sythvan flailing as they sank into the swamp just underneath the entrance hole.

Taking a careful grip on the roots by the Deep Gate, he swung himself down, hoping yet again that Lindsay hadn't gone charging in head-first.

THIRTEEN

The Moss on the Morass

Martin's stamina bar began to shrink. The longer he was hanging from the roof of the damp tunnel he'd just found himself in, the faster it seemed to decline.

In a panic, he fumbled his way across to the nearest wall and worked his way down that concave surface until he reached the water. He dipped a toe in, tentatively, watching ripples spread out in every direction at his touch. Then he lowered his foot in to check the surface below.

His foot sank into the cold mud and he was startled to feel it pressing up between his toes. A few tentative presses later, he let go of the wall and stood up.

"Will you stop messing around and help me? I've been stuck here for hours. Please. Dude. Help!"

Martin had sincerely hoped that the other player had been too distracted to notice him, but now he plodded back towards the entrance, carefully testing the ground with each step.

He worked his way in a slow circle around the partially submerged Sythvan, testing the ground to find the limits of whatever quicksand or bog was hidden beneath the placid water.

A tooltip popped up informing him that this new companion was a level four knave named... Snekboi. Martin loathed him already, just for the name. His constant prattling didn't help either.

"Dude. What are you doing? Dude. Help me? Dude! Say something! Come on, dude."

Martin sighed, "I am trying to think of a way to get you out without getting myself stuck too. Will you just stop for a second?"

Snekboi let out an obnoxious bark of laughter.

"I jumped right in, dude. There were no warnings, no nothing. This game is brutal. It's totally awesome, but… man, it's really out to get you, you know? Like, everything is a trap. You got to be cunning, dude. Got to outthink it."

"I'm trying to outthink it." Martin fixed him with a stare. "Just give me a second to outthink it, yeah?"

The knave looked away first.

"Right. Sorry, dude. Take your time. I mean, I've been here for like, three hours with nobody to talk to, but whatever. You have your me-time."

There was no way Martin could reach Snekboi, not with his stubby little rat limbs. He might have been light enough to creep out onto the soft mud without breaking the surface tension, but the moment he tried to pull on the heavier Sythvan, he would just lever himself down into the same slowly sinking fate.

He could try to head back to town and get some long poles or rope to drag Snekboi out. He might even be able to round up some low-level players with a bit more strength than him to help out, but that would take time. At least an hour to organize everything. He couldn't spare an hour, not when Lindsay was down in these fog-clogged tunnels by herself. There was a faster solution.

Martin crouched down to look out over the surface of the water. "What happens when you try to swim to the side?"

"Dude, every time I move, I start sinking again. It is totally sinister and stuff. It is trying to make me kill myself."

Snekboi was straining to look at Martin, while also trying not to move his body. It was kind of funny, in a tragic sort of way.

It was like this sometimes with his coworkers. When there was a really obvious solution they'd get annoyed at him for pointing out, he had to lead them to it step by step.

"And you've been stuck here for three hours?"

"Yeah, dude. It sucks. I even tried logging out and back in again and I just ended up right back in the mud."

Snekboi's straining had caused him to sink down another inch or so, although he didn't seem to have noticed. Martin had wasted enough time on this stranger already.

"Have you thought about maybe just dying?" he asked.

"Dude, what? No? I'm not going to die just because of some mud. Come on, help me out."

Without being too obvious, Martin strolled around the edges of the sinking mud. It forced Snekboi to keep turning. Corkscrewing himself deeper into the mud.

"If you die, you'll be back in the game in half an hour. That's much quicker than I could put together a rescue."

"I don't care. I don't want to die!" Snekboi was shouting now, drawing the attention of whatever might be lurking out in the cloudy tunnels. "I heard somebody say that if you die then the dungeon takes you over and makes you evil and hunt other players or some junk. I don't want to do that. I hate PvP games."

Martin started climbing up the roots at the side of the tunnel, glancing back at Snekboi. Calculating the angles. "Sometimes having PvP in a game can actually be a really helpful tool. It can give you solutions that you might not normally have."

Snekboi was straining his neck back to look right up where Martin was dangling above him, swinging by his sword hand.

"Like what?"

"Like this."

Martin cast *Rebuke*.

Snekboi vanished under the water's surface with a loud pop, like the cork coming out of a bottle in reverse. The bog had stopped toying with its food and finally swallowed the morsel whole.

[Snekboi suffers 1 water environmental damage]
[Snekboi suffers 1 water environmental damage]
[Snekboi suffers 1 water environmental damage]
[Snekboi suffers 1 water environmental damage]

Every sixth of a second the same message popped up, flooding Martin's screen, over and over.

[Snekboi suffers 1 water environmental damage]
[Snekboi suffers 1 water environmental damage]

That was enough wasted time. He swung himself well clear of the drowning Sythvan and set off along the tunnel in what seemed to be the most promising of the two directions it might lead.

With a little bit of distance, the notifications slowed and stopped. He had already saved Snekboi from another wasted hour; he didn't feel the need to hang around to see the last bubble rise.

But still, despite all the justifications Martin had created for his actions, he couldn't deny that there was some dark satisfaction when he got the message:

[Your Sin has increased by 1]

A quick glance confirmed that he was still, just barely, above the watermark as far as *Sin* went and that his class hadn't changed on him again. Then Martin went sloshing off down the tunnel once more.

Given what he now knew about the way Strata was put together, and the malevolence of the people running things, Martin made slow progress through the flooded tunnels of Deep Two.

Somewhat predictably, there were several more patches of quicksand – or, more accurately, quick-mud – hidden beneath the stagnant waters. Martin soon got into the habit of trailing along the side of the tunnel with one arm already raised to grab a root when he inevitably started sinking.

Even with those precautions, he still couldn't shake the feeling that there was probably something evil lurking just under the water's murky surface; some fantasy version of a crocodile just waiting to snap onto his leg, or some noxiously venomous fish covered in lethal spines.

The anticipation was probably worse than the fright was going to be when something finally happened, but knowing that did nothing to ease the tension. If anything, waiting for the other shoe to drop added another layer of irritation. This was what the game was designed to do to him, and he was falling for it like every other rube. He understood the trick and he was still falling for it.

The simmer of anger was useful. It helped to drive the paralyzing chill of fear away. It was fuel to keep his brain churning.

Stonework showed in patches behind the muddy walls of the tunnels: intricate carvings, smeared with muck. It was like the whole deep had once been carefully constructed before flooding and overgrowth filled in the corners. If the stone had still been bare, the echoed shouts from up ahead probably would have reached him sooner. Someone was fighting.

Lindsay.

Martin threw caution to the wind and ran. If there was a fight going on, the odds were good that Lindsay was right in the middle of it. He couldn't recall drawing his sword, but there it was in his hand when he glanced down. It was strange to have new instincts slotting into place so easily.

The tunnel opened up into a partially-submerged chamber, a great spherical room almost the size of the Beachhead cave, with the entrances arrayed around the equator and heaped mud within the stone confines providing a ramp down to the swamp at the bottom.

Across the curve of the roof, roots were bursting through the cracks just as they had in the mud-walled tunnels. Martin took it all in with a glance then skidded down the slippery slope towards the brawl.

Aquatic monstrosities were what Martin had been expecting, but Strata had managed to surprise him again. At the center of the melee there stood a creature somewhere between moss and man; a giant construct of swamp-weed, half-rotten root tangles, caked mud and vine-wrapped hunks of stone. Faceless and furious, it swung its huge blunt arms at Lindsay as she ducked away.

[MISS]

There were two other players arrayed around the beast, up to their knees in the troubled waters. One was a Wulvan, towering almost as tall as the gargantuan plant-creature's shoulders. The Wulvan was surrounded by a nimbus of golden light and his hands were empty, so Martin marked him as a martyr.

The other one, a Sythvan, was a little harder to place. She was wearing robes over her golden scales, but they were neither the flamboyant starter robes of the invoker or the white ones of the hierophant. They looked like leather at this distance, but he didn't have the time to go prodding at them. Until she cast something – or he found a moment when they weren't in the middle of a fight to prompt her character details to appear – Martin couldn't be certain.

Lindsay tripped over a hidden root as she danced around the *Faceless Morass* and splashed face-down into the water.

[Tesra suffers 2 environmental bludgeoning damage]

That was all the opening the brutal vegetation needed. It raised both arms above its head and was about to smash her to pieces when Martin bellowed, "Hey, swamp thing! Over here!"

It looked up in surprise as he skidded down the slope and he laughed as he cast *Halo* with a thought and a flick of his wrist.

The sudden blast of light illuminated every dark corner of the room. Martin was just glad that the light exploded out from behind him or he'd be just as blind as everyone else.

[Faceless Morass is blinded]

The Morass rocked backwards, letting out a wail that sounded like the grating of stones and clapping the fingerless stumps of its arms over the bland topology of its mossy face. Apparently, it did have something like eyes somewhere in there.

Lindsay was back on her feet and moving again, coughing up a beak's worth of water as she ran around behind the Morass to use her backstabbing abilities again.

The other two had been taken by surprise by Martin's *Halo* but they seemed to be recovering well. Martin had no idea what the martyr would look like in the game, but his assumption of some sort of bare-fisted monk seemed to have been in error. The Wulvan's clawed hands never raised from his sides, but that golden aura lashed out like a flurry of fists, pummeling the Morass with blow after blow.

[Faceless Morass suffers 5 light damage]
[Faceless Morass suffers 4 light damage]
[Faceless Morass suffers 6 light damage]

If they were going to be landing lots of small hits, then Martin's *Rite of Retribution* was going to come in handy to give them a boost. He activated it just before he got into striking distance and made his own clumsy hack into the writhing central mass of the Morass.

[Faceless Morass suffers 16 slashing damage]

That extra strength was really going to make a difference

going forward, even if he hadn't gotten the critical hit he was hoping for.

Martin hefted his sword again, ready to take another swing before the shifting tendrils of half-rotten plant matter reformed its stony armor, but the wounded Morass swatted him away with a suddenness that surprised them all.

[Skaife suffers 28 bludgeoning damage]

Numbness slammed through his body. Martin went flying across the dank water and for one awful moment he wondered if he was just going to skip across the surface like a tossed stone until he hit the wall. It was almost a relief when he sliced through the surface to land on a cloying, soft cushion of thick mud.

By the time Martin had resurfaced and scooped the slime from his eyes, the Morass' sight had returned too. It was trading blows with the martyr, who barely seemed to flinch as the mighty trunks of its arms swung down. He held up his hands in supplication and trusted to that golden glow to keep the brutal blows from connecting.

[Jericho BLOCKS 24 bludgeoning damage]
[Jericho BLOCKS 26 bludgeoning damage]

Martin spat mud and charged back in, relieved to find he still had his sword in a white-knuckled grip. In pursuit of Jericho, the Morass had spun away, and Martin found himself running up alongside Lindsay at the beast's stony backside. Her daggers lashed out, drawing nothing but sparks and echoed grunts of frustration from its armored hide.

"Can I offer you a lift?" Martin smirked.

"Finally!" Lindsay cackled. "What took you so long?"

She splashed back a few feet, then ran at Martin. He dropped to one knee and held up his empty paw like it was a step. As she leapt, he cast *Rebuke,* and she was flung up to the same level as the Morass' head.

With a screech of triumph, Lindsay hammered her daggers down into the soft moss and tangled vines of its neck.

[CRITICAL HIT: DOUBLE DAMAGE]
[Faceless Morass suffers 36 piercing damage]

Martin waited for a moment, expecting her to fall down, but both daggers seemed to be lodged in the Morass pretty solidly. With her safely out of the way, and the Morass' attention turned towards Jericho, Martin renewed his attacks.

[BLOCKED]
[BLOCKED]
[BLOCKED]

The stone armor that had thwarted Lindsay was turning aside his sword just as easily. Damage just wasn't cutting it – figuratively and literally. Martin cast *Celestial Strike,* waited a moment to see his sword light up, then hammered it home in one lunging thrust.

[CRITICAL HIT]
[Faceless Morass suffers 16 light damage]
[Faceless Morass suffers 16 piercing damage]

The monster let out a mournful wail that sounded like it was gargling pebbles. It arched in agony as Martin dragged his sword out of its back with a shriek of steel on stone, like some cock-eyed Arthurian legend. The once and future rat king.

Good old *Celestial Strike* wasn't as useless as it had first appeared; the light damage let him bypass armor and physical resistance. He might not get the full whack of damage each time, but the deeper they went into Strata and the more resilient monsters became, the more useful just being able to get basic weapon damage through an enemy's defenses was going to get.

With the welcome distraction of Martin's backstab, the other two went to work on the front side of the Morass. From the lack of spells being flung around, Martin had guessed that the Sythvan wasn't an invoker. The steady pulses of light she was pouring into Jericho confirmed his suspicions.

Serene was an expression Martin had never thought would be applicable to a wolf's face, but Jericho looked completely at peace as the golden glow around him coiled and lashed out according to his will.

[Faceless Morass suffers 4 light damage]
[CRITICAL HIT]
[Faceless Morass suffers 12 light damage]
[Faceless Morass suffers 5 light damage]

Each impact knocked another hunk of the seething Morass loose. Every blow kept it off balance, unable to fight back. Lindsay was still on top of it, lost amongst the flashing light and chaos, but still moving with purpose despite all the distractions.

She dug her daggers into the Morass' neck, slicing up, dragging the sharp edges through whatever connective tissues and dirt were hidden beneath the surface. With a heave, she made the "Faceless" part of the monster's name even more true.

[Faceless Morass suffers 18 slashing damage]
Faceless Morass has died.
Skaife gains 420 experience.

Pieces began to tumble off the Morass, spattering in the water around it in a shower. Fragments of stone. Clumps of sod. Withering coils of roots and vine. It all rained down on them as the monster died.

Lindsay leapt down from its shoulders, crowing out their victory.

"Iron Riot!"

"Iron Riot!" echoed back without a thought from Martin, Jericho and the Sythvan.

It only took him an instant to recognize their voices. Jericho had been their main tank when they were raiding in Dracolich. It was handy that he had kept the same name so that they didn't have to learn a new one, since Jericho was more than a little reluctant to share details about his real life with his gaming buddies.

Martin now finally had time to look at the Sythvan for more than a moment, so he did just that until the tooltip popped up showing her character's name as Adriel, the usual alias of Julia.

Julia had been one of their best healers, with a great sense of timing and the kind of upbeat attitude that could carry the whole guild through a night of failure with a smile. On the downside, she was more than a little flaky, often missing crucial raids with vague excuses about work, family or forgetting.

If he'd been given the option to hand-pick the best of the best to carry over with them to their new game, those two would have been at the top of the list. Well, in the top ten, certainly.

He strode over to the towering Wulvan and tried to slap him on the back in greeting, but he could barely reach above Jericho's ass, so he aborted that plan at the last moment.

"I am so glad to see you two," he said.

Julia wrapped him in a hug from behind, scales scraping over his fur and making it stand on end. "Was being alone with Lindsay driving you crazy?"

"Are you kidding? He's already blown himself up to prove how much he loves me!" Lindsay guffawed. "Thank god you guys are here to save me from this creepy little stalker!"

She glanced around conspiratorially then added in a stage whisper, "He keeps trying to make me call him snack-size."

Martin threw his sword at her, and she ducked away cackling.

Jericho's voice was always deep, but with the addition of his new Wulvan features, it had the unmistakable bass tones of a growl. "It is good to see that no matter which game we play, some things never change. The two of you are still idiots."

As he waded around looking for his sword, Martin asked, "So how did you guys get to Deep Two so quickly?"

When he glanced back, the two newcomers were looking at each other guiltily while Lindsay pretended to be extremely interested in her own feet in the water. Martin sighed.

"How long have you two been playing Strata?"

Julia had the good grace to look embarrassed about it. "Probably around about a week, on and off?"

Martin stubbed his toe on the hilt of his sword. "Because Lindsay had already told you both that we were moving here. A week ago. Before she even spoke to me."

Jericho nodded. "Guilds here can only have ten members to limit sharing of the Deep Gate keys. Lindsay picked only the best to come with us. Very hush-hush."

That explained the lack of an official announcement. Like the one he'd just posted in Dracolich. Whoops. Martin turned to Lindsay, who was still staring at her feet.

"So, what happened? Did someone else turn you down? Is that why you came to me a week after everyone else had already started?"

She sloshed the water back and forth.

"You're a bit... I mean... you can be a little... resistant to change."

"She said it would be better to surprise you with it," Julia blurted out.

Martin closed his eyes, took a deep breath and crouched to retrieve his sword from the silty water. By the time he stood up again, he had bitten back all the bitter replies and his smile was fixed back in place. "She was probably right."

Moments ago, they had been locked in a life-and-death struggle with an overly aggressive shrub, their virtual lives hanging in the balance and their purpose in danger of being subverted, yet it wasn't until now that the tension finally left the echoing chamber.

Julia practically melted on the spot. Lindsay's beaky grin seemed a little less fragile than it had a moment ago. Even Jericho's massive shoulders seemed to slump in relief.

"It is good that we are all here together. You are idiots, yes, but… not the worst I have played with," he rumbled.

Lindsay punched Jericho, ineffectually, in the arm. "Love you too, meat-face."

Julia had both sets of eyelids closed over eyes just as golden as her scales, her concentration directed inward to the menu screens. "So, same time again tomorrow?"

That was enough to crack Martin's mask of civility.

"What? I just got here. We've got so much to catch up on."

Lindsay was trying to subtly massage some life back into her hand. "Dude, tomorrow is Friday, we've got the whole weekend to catch up. Go get some sleep. You'll be trashed for tomorrow if you don't."

He wasn't going to beg. He couldn't, not when his ego was already fragile after Lindsay's little deception.

"Don't you want to explore just a little bit further? Find somewhere secure to log back into? I only just got here. I'd like to get the lay of the land before we—"

"Sleep time now." Jericho patted him on the head. "See you tomorrow."

A pillar of light enveloped the wolf, and he blinked out of sight. Julia shrugged apologetically.

"I've got a morning meeting. Sorry, Martin."

With a flash, she was gone too, leaving Martin alone with Lindsay again. She eyed him warily.

"You're still going to yell at me, aren't you?"

"You didn't want to give me the chance to say no or to delay you until I could afford the game. I get it." He sighed. "I probably would have argued with you if you'd come to me earlier instead of waiting until I was feeling… vulnerable after Dracolich ended. I should probably be impressed that you out-maneuvered me, right?"

"Dude, I didn't want to trick you, I just… I really wanted you to come along."

Martin stared off over her shoulder at the tunnels arrayed around them. "Because I'm your winning edge?"

"Because we're friends. You ass."

He couldn't help but laugh, despite the sting of betrayal. "Yeah, I guess we are."

"Which makes me paying you feel a bit weird. Maybe I should keep the loot from the Ravager? Since we're friends?"

"Anything useful?"

"Just some silver. It was like there was other loot there but I couldn't touch it? Like a glitch or something."

"A glitch, or one of the moderators deliberately screwing us over."

She seemed to catch that negativity and take it as a personal challenge to be more bubbly. "So, you'll be here tomorrow? Right?" Same time as usual?"

She wasn't just looking at him, she was studying him. Maybe they were spending too much time together.

"Yes Lindsay, I'll be here, same time tomorrow."

She sidled a little bit closer.

"You know I'm going to message you about a million times tomorrow to make sure you don't change your mind?"

"That is a pretty much guaranteed way to make me change my mind." Martin snorted.

She danced back, eyes sparkling with amusement. "Too late. Can't take it back now. It'd be a pinkie promise if we both had pinkies."

"See you tomorrow, Lindsay."

She blew him a kiss. "Catch you later, Snack-size."

He threw his sword at her again, but before it made contact, she vanished into a pillar of light. Her cackling persisted until the light blinked out and Martin was left alone in the dark once more.

With his weapon retrieved, Martin was trapped in a moment of indecision. The others had been right. Sleep was definitely the smarter option at this point in time.

Of course, knowing that did nothing to make the temptation of the tunnels disgorging their steady streams of water into the chamber any less intense.

The monster crumbled apart a little more at his feet, revealing something glinting inside.

Martin was no fool. He knew all that glittered wasn't gold, and that something shiny to attract your attention in this game was probably more likely to be an anglerfish's lure than treasure, but he also knew that nobody had looted the Morass after they fought it, and most enemies so far had dropped something at least.

He crept carefully towards the already moldering heap. The looting window appeared in front of him the moment his toe nudged a lump beneath the water.

Faceless Morass
These lumbering giants lurk in jungle rivers and overgrown sewers, accumulating biomass from the moving water until they have become large enough to serve as formidable guardians and their sentience ignites.
Loot: *14 silver, Whetstone Bracers, Rain Tear Crystal.*
Requires Herbalism *to harvest:* **Unknown Plant, Unknown Plant, Unknown Plant, Unknown Plant,** *Fertile Substrate.*

He really was going to have to pick up a trade skill soon; there was a whole world of items that he couldn't even comprehend yet. He dumped everything into his empty backpack just to be on the safe side. No way of knowing which plants would actually be useful until he found an herbalist, and it wasn't like he had a lot to carry at the moment.

The new wrist-guards were interesting at least. He equipped them and then closed his eyes to read the tooltip.

Whetstone Bracers (16 Armor)
Once the property of a master swordsman, these stone-bound greaves do little to protect the wearer, but instead provide them with ample opportunity to sharpen their weapons. After all, the best defense is a good offense.

He tried them out, dragging his sword over the silvery stone and enduring the awful scraping until the *Sharpened* property attached itself to his old Copper Shortsword, granting it a 3% increased critical chance for an hour.

That wasn't too shabby, and the bracers didn't seem to have any limitation on how many times they could be used in a day. He couldn't believe they had forgotten to loot the body and nearly missed these. What an amateur-hour mistake. They really must be overtired.

Five more minutes. Just five more minutes to check if the rest of this deep was going to be as nerve-racking as the entrance area.

Then he would definitely log out, get a reasonable amount of sleep and pass himself off as a functioning member of society tomorrow without any more incidents with Gillian.

Five minutes. Easy.

FOURTEEN

Hero of the Quagmire

Applying real world logic to Deep Two did not seem to help with navigation. All of the tunnel water seemed to be slowly pooling in spherical chambers like the first one, yet there wasn't a single dry tunnel anywhere to be found, regardless of their elevation.

The persistent fog might have explained it if the water was being restored through condensation, but that would have required some part of the tunnel system to be warmer, and so far there was no indication that there was anything but clammy mist everywhere that Martin went.

In some places, the mud was splattered in a thinner smear across the walls and the graven patterns stood out more clearly. There was something about them that felt intimately familiar to Martin. He was certain they didn't match any ancient hiero-glyphics or language he'd ever read about, but nonetheless he felt like he knew them, like their meaning was just out of reach.

Maybe the Masters had reused some old assets from another game that Martin had played, or maybe he was just going insane from sleep deprivation. Also a distinct possibility.

Sphere after sphere opened up in front of Martin as he roamed through the deep, slowly but surely filling out his map. In some of the chambers the water rose almost to the level of the tunnels that fed them and he didn't dare to go swimming out for all of the imagined crocodiles beneath the surface.

In some of the others, he found more *Faceless Morass*, standing completely immobile in a way that had to be a deliberate attempt at camouflage. These chambers he backed away from quietly until he reached another crossroads.

A pattern soon emerged: each spherical chamber was evenly spaced from the last, arrayed in a grid that stretched out in every direction except where he'd come from. Martin remained certain that there had to be a hot part of the dungeon to explain the water cycle, and the complete absence of any change in the spheres did nothing to convince him otherwise.

The Masters might have been assholes, but they were smart assholes. They'd applied logic and physics to every other part of the world they'd made; why would this be different?

He diligently moved on, slowly filling in his mental map, counting as he went. There seemed to be a near infinite number of these chambers. He felt like he had been creeping through them for hours. That was when he noticed the footprints.

Cutting through the edge of the mud by the waterside in this latest sphere, he could see the three-toed tracks of a clawed creature. With a cold weight settling in his stomach, he put his own foot down inside the print. It was a perfect fit.

There was no way he'd gotten backtracked or turned around. He had been going in a straight run through this line of chambers for a dozen of them already. He hadn't made any turns. He hadn't made any mistakes.

Time seemed to slow and the trickle of water fell silent. As he watched, the room he was in spun with the soft sound of grinding stone, realigning itself to the next exit around. If he walked straight on, he was now making a right-angle turn.

There were no signs of a mechanical reason for these balls to spin. There was no logic to it. By all appearances, these chambers were literally set in stone.

"What the hell?" he groaned.

A voice came from behind him, soft as a whisper.

"I can't believe it took you so long to notice."

Martin jumped away from the voice on pure instinct, spinning and drawing his sword in one fluid motion. The blade lashed out through the gray hooded figure behind him but left no mark. It swung through the space the Master occupied as if there was nothing there at all.

"You again?" Martin growled. "What am I supposed to have done this time?"

The Master held up their empty sleeves in false supplication.

"Nothing at all, dear crusader. We conduct regular maintenance and adjustment of the dungeon to ensure everything runs smoothly. It was just an unfortunate accident that you happened to be caught up in the middle of some reconstruction."

"An accident. Right. Of course. Silly me, thinking this was harassment."

The Master drifted closer to him. Martin was certain it was the same one as before. Their appearance was nondescript, but the attitude was identical.

"Harassment is a very strong word. You would seem quite mad if you were to use it. This is merely maintenance. And you are merely in the wrong place at the wrong time, yet again. I have no control over your actions, any more than I have control over your luck."

"My luck? You're the reason no decent equipment is dropping?"

"It is a minor thing to tweak certain probabilities. As we discussed before, there are certain rules that cannot be broken. The laws that keep this whole world ticking over correctly." The Master spun the room again, flinging Martin around like a ball in a roulette wheel. "If I break those rules, then I am no better than the likes of you. The whole construct of reality will fall apart and this world of ours, this Strata, it will fall to chaos."

Spitting out the swampy water, Martin scrambled back to his feet.

"You've spun me around and wasted my time. You've stolen a level from me. What more do you want?"

"What could any Master want? I want you to succeed despite the challenges laid at your feet." Sarcasm was oozing from every word. "The name of Iron Riot is well remembered by the Masters. Many of us have crossed your path before in other worlds. We recall your great victories."

The Master darted forward, and Martin stumbled to land on his backside in the puddle yet again.

"Do not think that Strata will be such a simple task. We will not see our lives' work slaughtered on the altar of your petty ambition. Strata will defeat you. It will crush you. You will fall to this dungeon as surely as the rising of the sun."

With that last word of encouragement, the Master vanished. The air seemed to thin; the water began to trickle once more. Martin should have been furious – he should have been gnashing his teeth and screaming about how unfair it all was – but instead he was filled with a building satisfaction.

The Masters knew him, and they were running so scared that they were trying to toss extra hurdles in his path. They thought he could beat their game, based on his reputation alone, and he had always been underestimated.

His lips split into a grin. Every time they tried to set him back, they just told him more about the game and how to beat it. There were unbreakable rules, rules that would destroy their game if they were tampered with – and that was why this Master didn't simply kill him or de-level him over and over.

The Masters were as powerless as a player inside the net of rules they had forged for this game. That was probably why they had to ask for information instead of having a log, too. They'd made a game so complex that not even they could get around it.

Martin picked himself up and then backtracked – with constant references to his map – to the only place he was certain couldn't be interfered with so easily. The entrance to the deep had been one long, winding tunnel, and only luck – and his recollection that Lindsay always turned right when confronted with two options – had brought him in this direction at all.

Lindsay. He was trying not to think too hard about Lindsay at the moment. He knew he liked to have a routine, but knowing he'd become predictable was another thing entirely.

Lindsay was his friend – inasmuch as anyone using him to serve their own purposes could be a friend – so the idea that she understood him well enough to manipulate him shouldn't have been this troubling.

He emerged back into the first sphere, carefully peering around the edge of the tunnel to make sure that the Morass hadn't respawned.

From what he'd been able to gather so far, respawning didn't seem to be a feature of any of the monsters. If the ecosystem of the dungeon actually shifted with the players' actions, then presumably the Morass would eventually be replaced by something else. The chamber was as abandoned as when he'd last seen it.

It was resolved now. He would just have to keep his head in the game in the future. With a shrug he started splashing back along into the first tunnel and pressing ever onwards towards the dark fuzzy patch on his map, hoping all the while that he wouldn't bump into Snekboi or any of the other morons that seemed to populate the playerbase on his way past the trap at the entrance.

Luck was not on his side. Snekboi was back in the tunnel up ahead, prodding at the quicksand with his tail, and a looming black-furred Wulvan was with him. Dmitri. Martin groaned. What were the odds that the two players he had killed so far in this game would just happen to get together?

Either he was interrupting the Iron Riot survivors support group, or this was a vengeful ambush. He didn't feel good about either option. It didn't take long to do the math here. Two of them, one of him, and both of them a level above him.

He couldn't even rely on the tunnel as a chokepoint; it was

easily wide enough for two people to fight side by side. They had every advantage. Still, Martin strode forward without ever letting them see him flinch.

Snekboi spotted him and reached for his daggers. Dmitri rolled his shoulders and stepped forward to meet him head-on.

"I want to talk to you!"

"Then talk," Martin quipped. They still weren't moving. Snekboi should have dropped into stealth and tried to circle him, but he was too lost in his own drama.

"You know what they call player killers in this game? Sinners." Dmitri growled, patting an empty palm with the haft of his axe. It was still the starter weapon.

"You're a sinner," he went on. "And we're here to spank you for it."

Keep poking at them. Keep them too angry to think.

"Sorry, I'm not into that kind of role-play. But I'm glad you've found a little friend who is."

"Oi," Snekboi bellowed, but Dmitri just ignored the noise with another display of the callous disregard that had made Martin fight him to begin with.

Dmitri hefted his axe and growled again. "You're going down."

"All the way down, eventually," Martin said. "But right now, I'm going that way."

Martin lifted up his hand to point past Dmitri. Then cast *Rebuke.*

The knight was clad in full plate armor that probably would have turned Martin's sword away like it was made of rubber, but it was heavy, and thanks to the Wulvan build, it was particularly top-heavy.

Dmitri didn't just move backwards; he flipped right over, landing face down in the quicksand that had claimed his little friend earlier. He squirmed and roared uselessly into the thick mud.

[Dmitri Blackpool suffers 1 water environmental damage]

Martin kept on walking, right over the fallen idiot. How did these people expect to get through the dungeon with no awareness of their surroundings?

Snekboi was still standing to one side, his mouth hanging open in dismay. Martin looked him up and down and scoffed.

"Don't try something like this again. You won't get lucky twice. The only reason you're alive is that you aren't worth my time."

It was a calculated risk, walking away. There was a chance that Snekboi would come after him and stab him in the back before he rounded the next corner, but Martin didn't think he was that competent, or that focused.

Just as likely, Snekboi would remember this display of foolish bravado as a sign that Martin was beyond reach, and he'd never have to deal with him again.

From the lack of a death notification and his unchanged Sin score, he assumed that Snekboi's attentions had been diverted to saving his friend. The only good thing about the two idiots sticking together was that they'd slow each other down even more. Once Martin was a few deeps down, he'd never see them again.

Heading in the other direction from the entrance to the deep, the tunnel got muddier and more overgrown, but the water was shallower as a result and he was able to walk without checking whether every footstep was going to be lethal.

Without that danger to focus on, and with a growing certainty that Snekboi wouldn't be coming after him any time soon, his mind began to wander.

He summoned the Rain Tear Crystal out of his backpack and toyed with it as he walked along. It seemed to exude water with the slightest touch of pressure, like ice at room temperature. Maybe these gems were the source of all the moisture down here?

Magic was always a useful handwave solution to world-building problems, but Martin had thought better of the people who had made Strata – at least until he'd met them. They'd put so much effort into realistic physics, and the NPCs paid lip-service to ideas of ecosystems; why wouldn't they take the extra step and have the environments make sense?

The sound of splashing up ahead drew Martin out of his reverie and he let the gem vanish back into his bag without a second thought. Splashing meant movement. Movement meant something alive.

His hand drifted down to his sword, but he didn't draw it just yet, not when the noise might be another player who didn't share Lindsay's fixation on always going right.

One case of mistaken identity had been enough for one life-time. He didn't need to encourage random players to attack him by charging at them with his weapon drawn.

The tunnel opened out abruptly into a vast mud-roofed cavern, all traces of the stonework that had defined the other half of the deep lost beneath the overgrowth of vines, mosses and fungi

The only constant from the rest of Martin's explorations seemed to be the water pooling on the floor, but while it had been in constant motion elsewhere – even in the stone cisterns – here it was stagnant and reeking of decay.

As before, Martin waded out into the murky water cautiously, but unlike before, his caution was well-founded. He was up to his waist after only a few steps and the next one was likely to put him up to his neck.

He shuddered as something squishy wriggled out from under his feet. This place was definitely inhabited, but it remained to be seen whether all the local wildlife was hostile.

[ANNOUNCEMENT: *The Brotherhood in Exile* have defeated **Carnifex, Tenth Archduke of Strata**]

Martin blinked the message away. Every time he started to enjoy the solitude in Strata, another reminder that he wasn't alone in this world seemed to intrude. It wasn't that he didn't like playing with other people – the experience of being on a properly organized raid team was a special kind of bliss – it was just that the majority of the other people he encountered in games seemed to be intellectually stunted frat-boys in wolf's clothing.

Lily pads and pond scum drifted ever closer to his face as he pushed his way forward through the uncomfortably thick water. He was making more noise than he would have liked, but that only served to reinforce the idea that whoever or whatever he had heard in here couldn't have gotten far.

Once the water was tickling his chin, Martin realized it wasn't getting any deeper. He wouldn't have to swim, but he would still be almost entirely useless in these deep expanses at the center of the cavern. Even turning around to make his escape seemed to take forever with the murky water dragging at him.

When he came back with the rest of the guild tomorrow, he was going to have to come up with some sort of solution to this. Maybe they could pool their gold and buy something like a canoe back in Beachhead, or steal one of the raggedy gates and use it as a raft.

Halfway back to the entrance, there was another splash. He spun around, looking for the source and sending a low wave out in a spiral all around him.

"Who's there?"

There was no reply; just the gentle bobbing of the detritus and vegetation on the surface of the water. Despite the lack of any evidence, Martin was sure that somebody was watching him. The few patches of fur on his body that weren't sodden were trying to stand up on end.

He drew his sword and held it up out of the water. *Celestial Strike* lit up the blade, setting the dull green-tinged water shimmering and reflecting the haunting bright spots of eyeshine from just a little further out.

He didn't run; he didn't panic; he just kept on moving slowly backwards towards the entrance. He could count more than a dozen eyes out there, just barely breaking the surface of the water, the bodies they were attached to concealed by natural camouflage or a layer of pond scum thick enough to trick his vision.

The spacing was just about right for alligators, and there was a definite reptilian flavor to those big round eyes and their yellow glow.

They blinked at him in unison. He gave up on trying to walk over the mud-slick floor and started paddling for safety as fast as his stubby legs and one free arm would carry him. The splashing behind him started up again and his own noisy attempts at movement swiftly drowned it out as he grew more and more frantic.

He crashed headlong into some thick hidden root and the breath he hadn't realized he was holding was forced out of him in a yelp.

The hidden structure was thick enough that it might support his weight, and now that he'd been stopped, the splashes approaching from behind were unbearably close.

He hauled himself up onto the woven bridge of roots that he now realized he'd crashed into, ready to make a last stand against whatever fresh nightmare was bubbling up behind him.

Weapon blazing with light and eyes bulging out of his head, Martin turned to face his pursuers and froze.

The monsters he had been expecting were nowhere to be seen. There were creatures arrayed in a semicircle, but they were far from the mass of scales and teeth he'd been expecting. The closest one had its massive eyes locked on his sword, and it was cowering back slightly from the light.

They were humanoid, in the same sense that Murovan or Corvan were humanoid. They had the same basic torso, but that was when the amphibian traits came in. Those huge yellow eyes swiveled on the sides of a distinctly frog-like face, and from what Martin could see of the webbed hands and patterned, slimy skin, that resemblance continued throughout the creature.

The light flickered and died. He had spent too long without using his *Celestial Strike*. Even when darkness swept back over the water, the frog-things didn't come rushing forward. They were staring at him. Almost...expectantly?

"Hello there... uh... frog people?"

More heads popped up out of the water like jack-in-the-boxes. The coloration of each different frog-man seemed to be a unique pattern, so Martin was just about able to tell them apart.

In a predictably croaky voice, one of them spoke.

"You make hurt?"

"No. No." Martin let out a sigh of relief. "I come in peace."

The speckled spokesman cringed and some of the closer frogmen dove back under the surface.

"You make us pieces?"

"What? No! Sorry, no. I am not going to..." Martin paused, sheathed his sword, and recalculated. "Me no hurt?"

Speckles came forward.

"You welcome, dry-friend. We Anurvan. What you?"

Martin did not feel particularly dry at the moment, but on the sliding scale of comparison he supposed that he lacked the slime coating of a frog, and that made him drier than them.

"I'm hu... uh... Murovan."

"We welcome Hu'Uh'Murovan. We be good friends." Speckles and a few of the smaller, braver Anurvan paddled closer, with a couple of them popping up out of the water onto the walkway. "How make sword shiny?"

"Oh, I, uh, I'm an exorcist. That's just something we can do."

"You teach?"

They crept closer and closer along the walkway, more details becoming apparent as the pond scum slithered off. They were skinnier than Martin would have expected, their bones clearly visible where the skin was stretched thin. Their state of near starvation was apparent because they didn't have much in the way of clothes; mostly just little patches of rank-smelling fish-scales and some bones strapped on as decoration.

Their weapons were similarly lackluster; little axes and a few spears here and there, topped with barely sharpened bone. These were not the apex predators of the dungeon. They were the bottom-feeders.

Martin blinked, backtracked to the last thing said and quickly answered Speckles.

"I wouldn't know how. Sorry."

The Anurvan seemed to weigh Martin's words every time he spoke, as if he was imparting some great wisdom. When Speckles was close enough to touch, he croaked softly.

"Others come, they hurt us. Send us down to dark water. I think you like them, but you not like them too?"

Martin could only imagine what the arrival of a regular group of players would look like to these frail creatures. These little frog-men didn't even have a few layers of fearsome monsters between them and the first wave of bloodthirsty crusaders.

It would be a genocide. An endlessly repeating genocide, as the dungeon brought them back. If the ecosystem of the dungeon worked the way he suspected it did, with weaker monsters respawning along with all the rest and being driven up through the layers by the horrors of the lower deeps, he was amazed they hadn't ambushed him while he was still in the water when they had the chance.

He couldn't even conceive of living through all that and still being trusting enough to answer when somebody shouted hello on your doorstep.

Martin shuddered.

"No. I'm not like them. I don't kill for fun. Just when it is necessary. Like you and your fish."

All of the Anurvan nodded solemnly at that. Maybe the bobbing heads were just some sort of acknowledgement that another person was speaking, but they seemed to understand him clearly enough.

"You come with us?"

Martin found himself nodding back, until they were all bobbing their heads up and down. Speckles reached out a three-fingered hand.

Despite everything Martin knew about contact poisons and toad secretions, he decided to trust the Anurvan. He clasped Speckles' hand, and then they were off.

Without a guide, Martin would never have been able to make his way across the hidden tracks beneath the water's surface, but trailing so close behind his amphibian assistant, he didn't even have a chance to misstep and fall into the murk.

His low-light vision had helped him a lot, but he soon realized that here it served only to confuse him. He could see what looked like a solid surface under the waters, but that was just the depth that his limited vision could make out. Anything could be beyond it.

He had no idea just how deep the water had become as they moved out towards the center of the cavern. All he knew was that in some places, even the Anurvan chose to hop up out of the water rather than risk swimming over the top.

"Why you no hurt?" Speckles was close enough that he could be heard over the soft splashing of their movement without the other frog-folk listening in. "All from above hurt. Kill. Take. What you come for if not hurt?"

Martin had to think about his answer. Then, when he remembered that this was all just a game, he had to think it through all over again while also worrying about the fact he'd forgotten that this was just a game.

His first, gut instinct was that it was wrong. That the Anurvan were people, just the same as anyone else. But they weren't. This was a video game, and these were just characters in a story – characters so minor that they didn't even warrant names.

By all rights he should have slaughtered them all, taken anything of value and moved on. They were just walking chunks of experience. Probably not much experience, but all together they'd probably be enough to replenish all that the Master had stolen from him.

Yet he'd been talking to them as if they were people, and they'd honestly behaved more like people than most of the other players he'd met so far. He had learned to trust his gut, but years in a guild had taught him how to justify his intuition too.

"I told you before. I'm an exorcist. We're meant to hunt down evil things. I've met some of those evil things since I came to Strata, and I'm pretty sure I can recognize them when I see them. You guys aren't evil. You're just unlucky enough to be born in the wrong place at the wrong time."

Speckles blinked its transparent eyelids.

"Less… words?"

Martin tried to parse it down to the bare minimum.

"I hurt bad things. You not bad."

Speckles bobbed its head, seemingly satisfied with his answer yet again. Who knew peace was so easy?

Peering ahead, Martin could make out the shape of what might have been a village on stilts, hanging above the surface of the swamp, but the shape was bizarre, like the cone-roofed structures had poured down from the ceiling rather than being built.

As they got closer, he realized that each little hut was made from a single root, teased down out of the ceiling and trained to coil into the required shape over years. The wood was still alive. With a start, Martin realized that the hidden walkways beneath them had been grown out in the same way.

As they got closer to the village, the walkways spread out and split, with different Anurvan scattering across the complex web of paths, following them by memory back to the different huts and halls dotted around the periphery of the central mass of roots.

It was like a mirror of Beachhead above it: a thriving little town balanced on the surface of unknowable depths.

Despite the size of the place, Martin couldn't see many Anurvan about. The little scouting party that had picked him up had contained almost as many frog-folk as he could spot arrayed around the fishing holes and darting between huts. This place was a piece of art, generations in the making, and it should have been thriving. Instead, it was a ghost town.

Here and there, he could make out hints at why. A charred root dangling dead from the roof where a building had once been. Glimpses of green wood where axes or swords had scarred the roots. One whole walkway was twisted up out of the water, struck by some massive force powerful enough to overpower the decades it had spent growing into its current form.

That last one didn't seem likely to be the work of the crusaders. The Anurvan were stuck between the hammer and the anvil, powerful monsters preying on them from below and invading crusaders crashing down from above.

Words didn't seem to be sufficient, but Martin mumbled them out anyway.

"I'm sorry this has happened to you."

Speckles looked genuinely surprised. Martin was more than a little surprised at himself too. The story and setting in games had always been secondary to him; useful information to help hone his tactics, but never an emotional burden.

He really hadn't started his day expecting to end up feeling bad for a bunch of made-up frog-people. When he was rational about it, it seemed ridiculous.

A hush fell over the village. The Anurvan peered out from behind their doorframes. Speckles was letting out reverberating croaks as they walked, calling out to the others in their own tongue. It didn't seem to be sufficient to draw them out of hiding, but it was enough to keep Martin safe from a last-minute pitchfork-and-torch panic.

An enormous Anurvan, almost twice the size of Speckles and

the rest, sloughed out of the central hut. The smooth skin of the other frog-folk was cracked and weeping on its humped back. Its cataract-coated eyes were almost as big as Martin's hands.

When it finally spoke, its voice was deep enough that Martin would have worried about it vibrating out his fillings in the real world.

"Gods below! Why you bring to us?"

They were speaking in the player language for his benefit. This was showmanship. They wanted him to know what was being said.

Speckles stepped up. "This one no hurt. This one dry-friend. Fight bad."

Martin assumed that was a comment on his ethics rather than his combat skills. "I mean you no harm. I'm just passing through."

"Mean no harm," the ancient Anurvan wheezed. "What you mean, no matter. You come, bring more from above. Much hurt."

This pidgin language stuff was starting to get on Martin's nerves. He added learning in-game languages to his long list of tasks for the next friendly settlement they reached.

"I promise I will do my best to shield you from any harm that I might have brought with me."

"You know nothing. You carry hurt. Call out to hurt."

Was this frog trying to psychoanalyze him? "What?"

The Anurvan leader lurched forward, throwing out its spindly arms to keep it from falling on its face.

"You take Tear. You bring hurt!"

The Rain Tear Crystal? Martin called it out of his inventory. It was still exuding a trickle of clear water, but now it was also pulsing slowly with a dull blue glow. Like a homing beacon.

In the distance, Anurvan started screaming. Beneath the lattice of the village, waves were rolling as something huge and moving ever closer displaced the still water.

Speckles stared at the stone in horror, frozen in place with its head bobbling up and down as the other Anurvan in the village began scattering and fleeing, diving right off the edge and into the murky depths.

"No. You say you no hurt. You say you fight bad."

"I do." He drew his sword. "I will."

A tooltip popped up.

Level 5 Rare Quest: Defender of the Frogs
The Anurvan of the Second Deep have suffered greatly at the hands of the Morasses and their creators. Defend their village from one of the daily assaults.
Victory conditions: Slay 1 Invading Morass.

Speckles couldn't be convinced to head in the direction of the coming doom, but it did reach out to smear some strangely floral-smelling slime over Martin's eyelids when he tried. Martin was so shocked that he just stood there for a moment before the green-tinted jelly evaporated away.

[New Ability: Swamproot Sight]

Just as his *Night Vision* allowed him to see into the darkest corners of the dungeon, so did this new green filter on his sight allow him to make out the root paths and walkways beneath the surface of the swamp.

They weren't exactly glowing, but they were clear enough to manage. Martin patted Speckles on the back with what he hoped was a reassuring grin and then strode off in the direction of trouble.

Without his Anurvan honor-guard, the swamp had taken on a darker aspect again. The sweeping waves heralded something huge and monstrous, and while Martin was pretty sure what form it was going to take, the waiting was still hellish.

The walkways began to thin the further he got from the town, and the fewer walkways there were, the more his mobility was going to be impaired.

He could wait, lure the thing closer in to the village and try to tackle it there, but if he failed then that would leave the frog-folk with no chance to flee. It was a balance between what he knew was the best tactical sense and this newfound urge to play the hero.

Water sloshed up to batter across his shins as he waited. Games had never brought this out in him before. They'd been puzzles to solve, or more frequently a grind to endure before he could get to the challenges that he savored, but this was more like something Lindsay would do. Charging off to fight because she cared about some NPC. It was crazy. Yet he was here, doing it.

The Invading Morass wasn't any bigger than the last one Martin had faced. If anything, it looked smaller, since it was up to its waist in water, but he could still feel the hair on his back standing up in fear, or anticipation. When there had been four of them against a Morass, it had been a challenge. Now he was alone.

He told himself that it was only a game, but it felt like a lie. All his senses were telling him that he was really here, that he was really facing off with something huge, ancient and powerful.

He conjured the Rain Tear Crystal out of his bag and held it up. The dull blue pulse of it lit up the water's surface and made the Morass seem even more primordial with just its upper half exposed. The eyeless face turned towards the light like a flower tracking the sun.

"You want this?"

In reply, the monster let out a rumbling tectonic groan.

Martin blinked the stone away and then roared right back. "Come and get it!"

The Morass surged forward, throwing a wave ahead of it that nearly cost Martin his footing. He did not want to end up in the water. The moment he left the walkway was the moment he lost the fight. Getting sloppy wasn't an option.

He let the Morass take the first swing – a huge over-armed

thump that set the whole root-path vibrating beneath the surface and nearly bucked him off his feet when he dodged aside.

[MISS]

Those huge trunk-like arms were coated thoroughly in stone fragments, so he didn't bother blunting his sword on them. Instead, he cast *Halo*. This close up, the Morass took the full blast in its featureless face.

[Invading Morass is blinded]

Martin didn't even need to dodge the next swing, or the one after that. All he had to do was keep his balance, scrape his sword over the back of his bracers for an extra buff and stab into the mossy center of the beast.

[Invading Morass suffers 14 piercing damage]

He hauled his sword back – he'd learned his lesson from the Night Ravager about weapons getting stuck – and he almost overbalanced in the process. The walkway bounced again as the blinded Morass hammered in futile fury at the space where he'd been.

[MISS]

This was working. Martin could hardly believe it. He was going to win. He cast *Rite of Retribution* as he found his balance, then he started swinging.

[Invading Morass suffers 12 slashing damage]
[Invading Morass suffers 8 slashing damage]

Precious moments of blindness were ticking away. Any

moment now, the Morass was going to see him, and it was going to hit him. He needed to be ready. With a grunt of effort, he took one last swipe at the Morass' defenseless chest.

[CRITICAL HIT: DOUBLE DAMAGE]
[Invading Morass suffers 24 slashing damage]

The next sweep of its arms was right on target. It abandoned its attempts to crush him in a single blow, aiming instead to knock him from his perch. Martin was ready. He didn't try to duck or dodge the pillars of stone swinging at him, choosing instead to dive right up and over them, casting *Rebuke* down at them as they scraped under his belly.

[MISS]

Martin hadn't been sure that would work, but as he scrambled back to his feet amidst the massive splash that he'd created, he saw it had worked too well. The force of his *Rebuke* had toppled the Morass forward on top of the walkway, and now, instead of righting itself, it was hauling its mass up onto the straining roots. If it couldn't knock him off, it was going to drag the whole structure underwater instead.

With a roar, he charged forward, hacking at the stony arms, desperate to loosen its grip.

[Faceless Morass suffers 1 slashing damage]

The stone armor was too resilient. The water was almost up to his chest. *Celestial Strike* set his sword ablaze and he swept that glowing blade down again. Hacking straight into the Morass' mammoth shoulder. Snapping vines like sinews.

[CRITICAL HIT]
[Invading Morass suffers 16 light damage]

[Invading Morass suffers 16 damage]

One whole arm came away from the central core of the Morass, vines and lichens straining out to each other across the gap and catching at Martin's armor instead. They hooked into it, pressing through the gaps to tangle in his fur below. He had to leap back before it got a grip on him, and even then he could still feel some stray strings of vine wriggling against his skin.

Denied the opportunity to add a rat-man arm, the tendrils struck downwards instead, plunging into the fertile water. Martin blinked to check his cooldowns then readied his sword for his next attack. If the Morass got some distance, it could destroy him with its superior reach. Staying close was his only hope.

He'd only made it two steps forward when suddenly the walkway lurched beneath him. Flexing. As if it had suddenly come alive.

The Morass had turned its blank face towards him. How could something with no features beyond moss look like it was smirking? The vines from its wounded shoulder now hung beneath the surface of the water, and they were starting to thicken and grow darker. This monster added biological matter to its mass. That was what the description said. Only…it was trying to add the whole root system.

This time, when the walkway flexed, it wasn't just the spasm of a new-found muscle; it had malice. It flicked Martin right up into the air, tumbling him head over tail until he landed with a sickening crunch right on the Morass' waiting fist.

[Skaife suffers 31 bludgeoning damage]

It didn't hurt. It was amazing just how much it didn't hurt as all the life was hammered out of his body. He tried to draw breath, to speak or curse, but nothing was forthcoming. The

Morass let him slide from atop its craggy fist back onto the walkway.

His broken body was so numbed that even the cool lapping of the water couldn't penetrate it. He couldn't believe he had still held onto his sword.

Darkness pressed in around the edges of his vision. One more hit was all it would take. He pressed his eyes shut and spotted the one ability that he hadn't used yet. *Healing Touch.*

[Skaife regained 15 health]

Life seemed to flow back into him from that glowing touch, bringing motion back to his limbs and pushing the numbness away. With a gasp, he flung himself to one side. The Morass brought its trunk-arm down so hard that it tore right through the roots where Martin had been lying just a moment ago.

Bouncing and rolling with all hope of footing long lost, Martin plunged into the water. He choked as it rushed into his open mouth. Pain might have been withheld by the game but drowning came with a whole host of other awful sensations. He could feel the water in his lungs, and while there was no burning, there was no air either.

[Skaife suffers 1 water environmental damage]
[Skaife suffers 1 water environmental damage]

It was just luck that brought his flailing fingertips in contact with the walkway, and only sheer willpower that let him drag himself back up into the air. He coughed out the foul tepid water and gulped in air that didn't taste much better. He never wanted to do that again.

Behind him, the Morass reared up, one arm fused hopelessly into the walkway and the other upraised, ready to smite him back down into the drowning deeps.

Time seemed to slow as the stone-capped fist came rushing

down towards Martin. It was as if he had all the time in the world to wrap both hands around his sword hilt and swing it up so that the blade pointed straight at the landslide punch that was headed his way. *Celestial Strike* lit up his blade just an instant before the blow fell.

[Faceless Morass suffers 16 light damage]
[Faceless Morass suffers 16 piercing damage]
[Skaife suffers 32 stamina loss]
[Skaife suffers 4 EXHAUSTION damage]

With a grating scream, the Morass jerked away, cradling its wounded arm against its chest.

Martin's sword was sticky and green with sap and algae. His mind buzzed with numbers. He wasn't sure exactly how much health these creatures had, but he knew he was close to its limit.

The only variable that he didn't have from the fight earlier was how much damage the others had dealt to their Morass before he arrived. It couldn't have been much. They couldn't have been engaged with it for long, or Lindsay would have either found some way to catastrophically injure herself or to do something heroic to the lumbering creature that would have rendered Martin's involvement moot.

One more hit. That was all it would take. One way or the other. He wouldn't survive another hit and neither could the Morass. He wondered, briefly, if whatever intelligence drove the monster understood that. If it would behave differently now that its end was in sight.

He staggered to his feet and hefted his sword once more. *Celestial Strike* took 10 seconds to refresh. There wasn't a chance he'd survive that long. He couldn't rely on it to penetrate the Morass' armor. If he wanted to hit it somewhere soft, he was going to have to do it the old-fashioned way.

Running was practically impossible, and the water seemed to

suck at his feet when he tried to jump, but with the Morass teth-
ered to the walkway, it wasn't like he had far to go.

Martin sailed through the air in a crooked arc and slammed
right into the Faceless Morass' namesake. He hammered his
sword down into it before he could fall.

[Invading Morass suffers 14 piercing damage]
[Invading Morass has died]
Skaife gains 480 experience.
Defender of the Frogs
1/1 Invading Morass Slain. Return to Quest Giver.

A little bark of laughter escaped Martin's lips. He'd done it.
He'd won. The Morass began to tumble apart beneath him, the
coils of vines releasing lumps of moss, hunks of stone and a
bounty of seeds and dried-out mud into the swamp.

Martin started to sink into the decaying creature. The dying
vines which had been lashing about aimlessly suddenly seemed
to regain their purpose. They coiled around him, tightening as
the whole hulk sank down into the water.

Martin couldn't bring his sword to bear. He couldn't get free.
Down and down he went, the chill of the swamp creeping higher
and higher up his legs as he gasped in panicked breaths.

He was going to die, and not in the painless way that he'd
chosen to sacrifice himself last time. The water and the dragging
vines crept ever higher as he tried to close his eyes and stay
calm.

This was a good death. He was dying for something that
mattered. Maybe not out in the world beyond Strata, maybe not
even to the other people playing Strata, but to him this victory
mattered, and if this was the end of his playing for the night
then so be it.

The water closed over the top of his head. His whole world
turned murky and brown. He opened his mouth and took a deep
breath.

[Skaife suffers 1 water environmental damage]
[Skaife suffers 1 water environmental damage]
[Skaife suffers 1 water environmental damage]
[Skaife suffers 1 water environmental damage]

The sensations of drowning set his whole body convulsing. There was no pain here in Strata, but that didn't mean suffering wasn't on the cards.

[Skaife suffers 1 water environmental damage]
[Skaife suffers 1 water environmental damage]
[Skaife suffers 1 water environmental damage]
[Skaife suffers 1 water environmental damage]

His wretched little rodent body involuntarily jerked and pulled against the vines. Every instinct he had – man or rat – was screaming at him that he had to find air. That he was dying. The numbness might have been worse than pain. At least with pain he would have felt something instead of this absence.

He closed his eyes against the encroaching darkness and watched his health bar shrink. It was only a game. It was only a game. This wasn't death. He couldn't feel water pressing inside his real lungs. This wasn't the real world. It was only a game.

Finally, when panic had almost broken through that mantra, the notification he had been waiting for appeared.

Skaife has died.

When he opened his eyes, he was floating on the surface of the water, the light all around him dimming towards darkness and the pale hourglass hovering above his sodden grave.

[60 minutes until rebirth]

An hour instead of half an hour. The punishment grew with

each death. It was over. He'd go to bed. It was probably long past due anyway. Normally, frustration would have kept him up another hour, but this had been a good death. Satisfying. Like he had earned his rest. If he had a mouth at that moment, he would have smiled.

He probably would have slunk off to bed completely contented if he hadn't heard the whispering just on the edge of his perception as he navigated to the logout screen. The awful soft voice of that same Master of Strata encroached on his thoughts from every direction at once.

"It seems I was right. You aren't special at all."

FIFTEEN

The Tear in the Veil

It was only 2 a.m. when Martin got to his bed, and despite the slight tremor of rage that still shook him even as he was drifting off, exhaustion won out quickly.

He woke with his first alarm feeling surprisingly well rested. The tension headache that had haunted him all day yesterday was gone and he had the strangest feeling that he'd had a good dream, even though he couldn't quite remember it beyond a distant whisper that still lingered in his mind.

"Come to me," it had said.

Weird.

Logically, five hours of sleep should not have been enough, but Martin was hopeful that he could make it through the whole day before logic caught up to him.

Even if today went badly, it hardly mattered. He had the whole weekend stretched out in front of him after just one short shift of being stuck out here.

He went through the motions of a normal morning like he was in a dream, eyes locked onto his smartphone, still mining through comment boards and half-hearted fan projects to gather whatever information he could about the road ahead.

The way Martin saw it, there were two options: The people playing Strata were so obsessed with it that they never did anything else in their free time, abandoning all of their previous hobbies and interests and choosing not even to talk about the game when they could be playing it.

Or there was a high level of data-discipline on display, a degree of organization that went far beyond what Martin would usually have expected from gaming guilds.

Here and there he would come across a question about a specific monster on a fan forum, but ninety percent of the time those questions went unanswered. Either the spread of information was being deliberately suppressed by the guilds, or every single individual who was playing Strata had their eyes firmly on the prize and nobody wanted to give away the slightest advantage.

If this was what the Masters of Strata were up against every time they asked someone how a monster was defeated, it wasn't surprising that they were getting a little draconian in their methods of extracting information. Still, what kind of game developer couldn't see the contents of their own game? And what kind of asshole stalked a player around so that they could make snide comments when they died?

Martin would have filed a complaint if there was any way to contact the company, but it seemed like the developers were even more mysterious than the game content. He couldn't even find the name of the company online, and raking through the game industry news sites showed a level of confusion on par with his own. The game had been released through a smaller publisher that was mostly known for mid-budget indie productions that looked promising and went nowhere.

They were a dead end. Every attempt to pry information about the developers had been met with an almost eerie silence in an industry that was usually so loud you couldn't hear yourself think.

As far as marketing went there was practically nothing. The

NIH headsets had been showcased online with very little fanfare alongside basic information about the game, and both the tech and the game had been announced with nothing beyond the press-release statement about Strata's grand prize.

Three weeks later, Strata hit the shelves and interest in the game had spread almost entirely through word of mouth. It was possible that all this mystery was some sort of marketing ploy in itself.

Now that he was digging into articles about the game, there was a sort of manic fascination starting to emerge in the language of the reviewers and pundits, but if it was a deliberately manufactured mystery, why wouldn't they have dropped something mysterious to keep that passion burning instead of staying quiet all this time? It didn't add up.

The NIH seemed like the easiest path to pursuing the developers. New technology like that, particularly technology that was such a leap from the previous generation of VR, had surely left a paper trail somewhere. Research and development couldn't happen in a vacuum. Someone had to have applied for patents. Someone had to have gotten the device through health and safety checks. Even if software could be secretly coded and dumped out onto the web, hardware was trackable.

Martin was in the middle of digging through patent records when a polite cough made him look up from his phone. Gillian. Shit. He'd made it all the way to the office without noticing. A quick glance down confirmed that he had at least dressed himself before leaving the house. That was a small comfort.

"Your shift started five minutes ago. You arrived here in plenty of time, but you've just been standing there staring at your phone. Has something happened? Is everything all right?"

Martin could feel the flush of embarrassment creeping up his neck, heading for his cheeks. He took that rush of shame and he used it for all it was worth. "I am so sorry, Gillian. I was completely lost in thought."

"Lost in thought?" Gillian raised an eyebrow. Martin had missed eyebrows. They were so expressive.

"For ten minutes?" she added.

He groaned internally. "It was a particularly large thought?"

Gillian clasped her hands.

"Okay, let's just pretend that I'm not your boss. I am just a concerned friend right now. Are you sure you are all right? These last few days... you've looked ill. You've been distracted. You haven't been at all like your usual self."

Martin didn't growl. That would have been unprofessional. "Has my productivity been down?"

"No, Martin. This isn't about your work. I'm concerned about you."

It was a trap. Every time a boss told Martin that they were friends, that the office was a family, it was the preface to asking him to work for free. Every time he shared any personal details, they used it as leverage to try to get him to do something he didn't want to do.

There was a reason he kept to himself. There was a reason he didn't try to "make friends" at the office. If something wasn't about work, then why the hell was Gillian talking to him about it?

He smiled. "Nothing to worry about, Gillian."

She wasn't buying it. Every line of her face and her body was screaming that he was a liar, but there was nothing that she could do about it. At the end of the day, his work was still getting done, and he was doing it better than everyone else.

"All right. Well, if you need anything, you know that you can always come to me."

"Come give me the rope to hang you with," she meant. No thanks. If she decided to drop the "let's all be friends" nonsense and actually write him up, he had memorized the disciplinary procedures.

He was entitled to one verbal warning, one written warning and then a meeting with HR before she could touch him, and that was for tardiness only. Any other issues had to be handled separately. Even if this hippy intervention nonsense could be considered a verbal warning, he still had plenty of second chances, and the warnings reset every year.

This didn't matter. It wasn't a loss. It wasn't even a setback. Even if Gillian pulled him up in front of HR, he had his numbers to back him up. She'd never convince them to get rid of the most productive member of the team. Never.

Martin slumped into his seat and booted up the computer with the same automatic movements that he did every day. He could probably have gotten away with continuing his hunt through the patents on his phone, but he didn't want to take any chances.

Gillian was definitely going to be watching him today, and while she'd have to start down a separate branch of the disciplinary tree if he was messing around at his desk instead of working, it still would have felt like too much all at once.

Her obsession with him and his behavior would just be exacerbated. The specific disciplinary procedures might have been on separate cooldowns, but her fixation got ramped up by anything that he did outside of the routine.

The next few weeks would have to be exemplary. He would have to act as normal as she wanted. He might even have to sit with someone at lunch and pretend he cared about their inane conversations about nothing so that she wouldn't pester him to be "part of the team" as she usually did when there was nothing else for her to latch onto. That would be a smart move to keep her settled until she'd forgotten about this. With a shake of his head, he started work, almost fifteen minutes late.

He took a glance at the "Team Screen" where everyone could compare their productivity. The highest score on the board was still in single digits. Martin scoffed, then his hands started to move and he forgot about everything else except the orders on his screen.

When he came out of his processing fugue, the numbers had

tilted back in his favor. Drastically back in his favor. The fifteen-minute head-start that the others had picked up must have been burned away within the first hour. He was absolutely killing it today.

It took him a couple of blinks to realize that he hadn't stopped because of the regular lunch break alert that he'd set up; that was still almost an hour away. Something else had snapped him out of work mode.

A quick glance around showed Gillian hovering over someone else's desk, pointing at something on the woman's screen as if she had a clue about any of the actual work that was done in this office. If it wasn't Gillian, then what the hell had distracted him? His phone buzzed again, silently against his leg. That would do it.

Double-checking that Gillian hadn't moved, he slipped the phone out of his pocket. It was a message from Lindsay.

Dude. You'd better be there tonight. Not kidding. Will leave your ass behind. Not really. Please show up. We can go all night long. Like students or joyfully unemployed slackers. No work tomorrow. Usual time tonight. Already missing you, Snack-size.

Martin rolled his eyes, then shot a quick message back.

Will be there. On time. As usual.

She responded with an animated clip of a breakdancing kitten, which he took to be a positive thing. He turned his attention back to the computer, only to be interrupted again by another buzz on his leg, then another and another as Lindsay bombarded him with dancing cats of all shapes and sizes.

He gritted his teeth and tapped out.

Please stop. Trying to work.

There was a long silence, during which he almost reached for his keyboard again, but some sixth sense warned him that this wasn't over. Lo and behold, his phone buzzed again.

You love it.

He sighed and turned his phone off. There were still three-quarters of an hour left before lunch and he was damned if he was going to fall behind just because Lindsay had nothing better to do than stuff cats into every electronic device she could access.

At some point he was really going to have to pick one of the cliques in the office to linger next to during his lunch break, but now wasn't the time. He slunk off to the bathroom where he was sure no eyes would be on him and turned his phone back on to receive the inevitable avalanche of cats. He should not have let Lindsay know she was getting to him.

Before Gillian interrupted him at the start of the day, he had been on the tail of something important. The patents. At some point between home and work, the hunt had stopped being about reporting the abusive Master and turned into a new challenge for him.

Little indie productions could come out of nowhere but the idea that something this cutting-edge could do the same was ridiculous. A big company would have been needed to make something like Strata, which meant that same big company was being hidden deliberately.

Why would a studio hide when their game was being hailed

as the greatest thing that had ever been made on every message board Martin came across?

If it was a flaming trashcan of a game then Martin could understand quietly sloping off, but this made no sense. If something made no sense, it was a clue.

The patents database was easy enough to find, but narrowing the search down to the specific date was a lot harder. Martin knew the date that Strata had launched four months back, but the patent could have been any time before that, and searching through VR gaming patents when the industry was in a massive boom was less than fruitful.

He searched for "neural interface." Nothing. He searched for "VR headset." Nothing useful. In desperation he even searched for "NIH" which brought up about a million patents to do with the National Institute of Health. He flicked the screen off and stared at the cubicle door for a few seconds, mind buzzing, looking for angles of attack.

Maybe this other "NIH" was a hint in the right direction. Maybe the patents weren't in video games at all. Maybe they were in healthcare. "Neural interface" did not scream "smart tech-bro marketing" to Martin. It sounded like a medical device.

With only a few minutes left before he had to be back at his desk, Martin dove into the medical patents, filtering everything out that didn't have the world "neural" in the name and then scanning through them as fast as he could, trying to cut through the jargon.

There were more than he could count, and he was running out of time. His eyes darted back and forth between the complex legalese of the patents, the dense medical information and the tiny clock at the top right of his screen. Two minutes left. He cursed and tabbed the patents away for later.

His fingers hovered for a moment over the latest cat picture. Apparently, this particular kitten was in desperate need of grammar lessons as well as a cheeseburger.

The classics never went out of fashion for Lindsay. Not when she had a whole folder on her desktop called The Classics, where she had been stockpiling miscellaneous images from the internet for a decade. Before he could regret it, he typed:

We need to make some serious plans.

There was only a moment's pause before Lindsay started typing a reply. Where the hell did she work that she could mess around on her phone all day?

If you are asking me to marry you, I should let you know, I will be forced to cheat on you a lot since in my mind you are a giant bipedal rat dude.

One minute left. He really needed to head back to his desk.

Ha. Ha. Ha.

The reply came back quickly.

Creepy.

He washed his hands out of well-ingrained habit before typing back.

We have a solid 48 hours of prime Strata time. Do you have any other commitments? Do the rest of the guild?

More dancing cats.

Nope. We are playing all weekend. AAAAAALLLL WEEEE-KEEEENDDD.

When he glanced up, he was back in the office, Gillian's eyes already burning into him.

And the other two are fine with that?

Another soft buzz on his palm as he ducked into his cubicle.

EVERYBODY. ALL WEEKEND. CAN'T STOP THE RIOT. CHOO CHOO.

He let out a little snort of amusement.

All right. See you tonight.

Lindsay couldn't help getting the last word in.

Where would I find a tux to fit a giant rat anyway? #TailProblems.

Martin rolled his eyes and turned off his phone again before she could get him into any more trouble.

The rest of the day was almost suspiciously painless. Gillian got dragged into one of the seemingly endless meetings that she had to attend, leaving the whole office a little more upbeat and energetic than usual.

It wasn't that she harassed any of the other workers the way she dogged Martin's every step; it was just the usual general camaraderie and positivity that appeared in a workplace when there was no boss. Even Martin found himself getting caught up in it. Smiling in the office felt vaguely wrong, but he still found himself doing it.

A quick check of the productivity scoreboard confirmed Martin's suspicions that everything was gradually grinding to a halt, but it did that every Friday afternoon anyway. Even if everyone else was working at full pelt, they wouldn't come close to his numbers for the day. He could afford to slack off a little.

He went back to his patent hunt with one hand while clicking slowly through the automated order queue with the other. If anything was wrong with the order, he glanced up for the half second it took him to diagnose it, then turned back to the phone.

The general buzz in the office was a good enough alarm system in case of Gillian's return and there were too many patents and not enough hours in the day; even less once you took the time that he planned on playing Strata into account. Practically none, as a matter of fact.

Practice made perfect. Before long he could dance through the patent applications as easily as he managed an order or guided a raid group through a boss, checking in just the vital areas to find the gist of what he was looking for before jumping on to the next one.

It was a process of elimination, working backwards from Strata's release date and raking through each individual "neural" patent from there back towards the dawn of time.

The trouble with patents was that they could be filed long, long before a product was actually being made. The underlying technology could have been invented a decade ago and quietly patented with no practical applications in sight.

Gillian didn't return before the end of the day and Martin found that he almost missed their usual bout of fake smiling while wishing death on each other. Almost, but not quite. He slipped back into autopilot as he headed for home, diving further and further back into the records, growing more and more determined with every passing moment to find whoever it was who had made Strata. To work out why they were hiding. What they were hiding.

He might not have found the developers yet, but the repetitive actions of the patent hunt had at least given him the clarity of mind to understand why he was chasing after them so hard. It was because he liked to have all of the information available to inform his decisions, even the things that other people would overlook.

When they had just started to play Dracolich, the heavy metal steampunk aesthetic had distracted him from the naming scheme. It had taken him until he was level 50 to realize that underneath the armor plating and cogs, the whole setting was based on Norse mythology. That in itself hadn't helped to inform his decisions all that much since so much of fantasy was rooted in the Norse stuff, but once he'd researched the writers and realized that they were from Scandinavia, he had started to understand that he wasn't dealing with the pop-culture Norse mythology, he was dealing with the real stuff.

He'd read through all of the textbooks he could stand, memorized every myth and legend that had been passed down through the ages, and when they finally got to the Anguish Keep raid it had all paid off.

In the game's lore, the Svartclankers had been torturing the last surviving Baldragon there for decades. The Baldragon had been cursed with immortality, so no matter what they did to it, it couldn't die.

In mechanical terms, the raid had to keep fighting off waves of Clanker Torture Engines or the Baldragon would explode, killing them all.

Only Martin had known that the Mistletoe Poison they'd recovered from the Forest of Flickering Flames the month before was meant to end the dragon's suffering before it nuked the whole raid, and it was only once that little titbit had been leaked to the other guilds after they'd poached one of his healers that anyone else managed to clear the dungeon.

Martin didn't play games to beat other players; he played them to beat the creators, and knowing who they were was part and parcel of that.

Martin couldn't help but feel like this was another piece of the puzzle. That something about the studio that created Strata was going to be the clue that would help him to beat the game and win this latest victory for the guild. If he could just find them…

The next time he looked up, it was because somebody had nudged his elbow as they got off the train, just hard enough that the screen moved out of his field of vision. He was really going to have to stop phasing out like that. It was going to get him into trouble.

The phone was hot when he tucked it into his pocket, the battery down to its last dregs. It wasn't usually used this much. Hell, Martin didn't think it had *ever* been used this much.

At his station, he made a detour to the mini-mart to stock up on supplies for the weekend. He had absolutely no intention of leaving his apartment again until he left for work on Monday. As Lindsay was fond of saying: "Outside is for losers."

Some sort of jerky formed the protein backbone of his evening meal as he headed for home. Peppery and leathery in equal measure, he barely even tasted it. His phone was back in front of his face and the patents were starting to thin.

He had been tweaking his search terms as he went, adding more and more filters until all of the medicines and frankly terrifying skull drills vanished. It wasn't until he was on the stairs up to his apartment and a red warning was blinking 2% charge that he found what he was looking for.

Four years back, someone named Edwin Klimpt had patented a theoretical device that could be used to induce hallucinations and read brainwave feedback.

Four years wasn't a ridiculously short development cycle for a game, even for something as colossal as an MMO. Martin wet his lips, savoring the lack of fur for now.

"Edwin Klimpt, who the hell are you?"

SIXTEEN

The Aquatic Engines

Martin managed to get logged in ahead of Lindsay for a change, taking the long, painful dive into Beachhead in his stride.

He could have run ahead and tried to discover the boss of Deep Two before everyone arrived, but instead he detoured to the loathsome marketplace.

The calls of the vendors were loud enough to drown out the slurs being slung his way, and he managed to sell the Rain Tear Crystal for considerably less than he thought it was worth to a Corvan who looked down her beak at him the whole time they were speaking.

700 silver and change was all that he had acquired so far and normally he wouldn't even think of squandering it on new equipment at this stage, but if the Masters were set on denying him item drops, he would need to take whatever edge he could get.

He discounted new, heavier armor immediately. Fighting in the swamp was hard enough with what he already had weighing him down. There were no players selling equipment on this plaza, but the unmistakable plinking of hammer on anvil drew Martin out into the back alleys. The selection was pathetic; starter gear for the most part with a few vendor trash items in amongst them. The only vaguely interesting weapon – a little axe with a faint glow about it – was so far out of his price range that the Wulvan behind the counter wouldn't even let him touch it. After a few minutes of haggling, he managed to acquire a fragile looking Obsidian Gladius [9-16 damage] for the low, low price of only all his savings.

With the little change he had left over, he managed to snag a hunk of roast pig from one of the spits on his way out of town. He hadn't been sure what eating in Strata was going to be like, but it proved to be just as immersive an experience as everything else.

Compared to the crap that he ate in real life, it was probably the single most delicious thing he'd ever tasted, and a quick blink confirmed his suspicion that it had given him a minor buff to stamina regeneration. That was something to keep an eye on for later.

There was definitely some sort of cooking skill available to players judging by the number of vendors with ridiculous names and classes hovering over their heads in the marketplace, and with the heavy reliance on stamina, being able to up its regeneration rate could prove to be absolutely invaluable.

[ANNOUNCEMENT: *Poke It With A Stick* have defeated **Carnifex, Tenth Archduke of Strata**]

Based on how often he was seeing that announcement, Martin guessed that Carnifex was the first of the Archdukes that you came across in Strata. The one that reset your spawn point to further in the dungeon when you beat it. The first real milestone towards victory.

He hadn't been able to find any information about the Archdukes except in the gear being auctioned off online. Even that hadn't told him much beyond a few names. He'd seen a couple of items belonging to Carnifex showing up, but the other Archdukes were either stingy with their drops or gave items too valuable to trade away. The names Tortor and Barathrum had also been mentioned on old, closed auctions, but none of them said anything about what deep those individual Archdukes could be found on.

The journey back to the Deep Gate was uneventful, and without any distractions, Martin made it into the stone chambers again before there was any sign of his guild-mates. Despite the strange moral satisfaction of last night, his extra wandering hadn't actually provided Martin with either of the two things that he needed. Both the Deep Gate and its key still evaded him, and he desperately wanted either one or the other to present to the rest of Iron Riot whenever they deigned to join him.

The swamp was vast and wide-reaching, though; it would be much easier to search it with a group spreading out. It was still tempting, because he really wanted to hand in his quest, but it wasn't going anywhere and he doubted the Anurvan would have run off before he got there.

The clogged cisterns were another story entirely. Travelling in a big – almost inevitably chattering – group was certain to attract the attention of the other Morasses that were still lurking about, whereas Martin could move with some degree of stealth on his own. Not much, but some.

With a vague estimate of half an hour before everyone else appeared, Martin set off to methodically fill in any blank spaces on the grid of circles on his map. Most of the spheres he hadn't visited before were either completely blocked by massed tangles of roots erupting through fractures in their ceilings or held one of the many Morasses that he didn't much fancy facing off against alone again.

The dark patches on his map continued to deplete, until eventually the only part left was the most distant corner of the deep: a perfectly spherical chamber that was almost devoid of the detritus and muck that characterized the rest.

The engravings stood out in stark relief on the stone with no mud to mask them, and not one but two of the lumbering guardians stood watch over the tunnel leading out the other way. That was looking more promising.

At some point he had lost track of time, and he really didn't want Lindsay making a beeline right to him and dragging a train of all the enemies he'd snuck around, so he turned tail and hiked back to the chamber where they'd logged out the night before.

It seemed he was just in the nick of time. Julia and Jericho appeared moments after his return, the pillars of light staggered by only a few seconds. Julia gave him a lipless smile and a nod. "Good evening."

Jericho was less polite, electing to pick Martin up bodily and start swinging him around. "What do you think? Fast-ball special?"

Martin sighed as he hung boneless in the Wulvan's massive paws. "You'd probably get better distance with Lindsay. Corvan have hollow bones. She might be bigger than me, but she weighs about half as much."

Jericho dropped him, and Martin just barely got his feet under him before he hit the murky puddle at the bottom of the cistern. Jericho nodded.

"Solid advice. Where is she, anyway?"

Lindsay appeared in a pillar of light, bellowing at the top of her lungs, "What's up, minions!"

Martin rolled his eyes. "Nice of you to join us." Why had she chosen a character that relied on stealth?

Lindsay took a bow, and despite the beak Martin was almost entirely certain that she was smirking.

"You still bitter I turned down your proposal? I don't know what to tell you, Martin, I'm just not the marrying type."

Jericho let out a little huff of laughter and opened his mouth to make some snide comment before he was cut off.

"Good evening," Julia repeated in an almost identical intonation to the way she'd said it mere seconds before.

When Martin glanced over, her eyes were shut, but they were

also moving beneath those translucent reptilian eyelids. She must have been raking through menus, completely oblivious.

"I think I know where we need to head next," said Martin. "I've been scouting ahead a little and there's a passageway out of these cisterns being guarded by two of the golems."

"Scouting ahead a little?" Lindsay scoffed. "Do you ever sleep?"

Martin shrugged. "I sleep. I just got logged in early."

"What about eating? Did you eat something before you—"

This was starting to verge on Gillian's concern-trolling. Martin cut her off. "What are you, my mother now?"

Anyone else would have recognized the edge in his voice. Even a stranger would have backed down. Lindsay didn't. She didn't seem to know how to.

"I don't know, I got around a lot when I was a toddler... were you adopted?"

Martin bit back an angry retort, took a deep breath of the humid air and started over.

"Two guards, probably guarding something. Or there's a massive swampy area at the other end of the tunnel we came in through initially. The odds are the key is in one direction, the gate in the other."

Jericho and Julia nodded along to that, but Lindsay was on a roll. "All right, son, we'll try your plan, but if it doesn't work, you're grounded."

Martin groaned. "Please stop."

"Sorry, son, it's dad jokes from now until the end of time. You've unleashed my final form. Big Daddy Lindsay."

Jericho just walked away from her. Martin and Julia looked at each other for an instant and then hurried off after. Lindsay was left to cackle alone for almost a whole minute before she realized she'd been abandoned and rushed after them.

Guiding the other three members of the guild through the grid of cisterns was a little like herding cats, particularly when they were passing by chambers with Faceless Morasses inside.

Lindsay was of the opinion that every monster needed to die on the altar of experience points. Martin didn't want to squander their time or their resources.

The other two were incredibly focused on pushing forward – hardly surprising given that they'd just seen Martin and Lindsay jump past a week's worth of progress to catch up to the two of them – and they had served as the tiebreaker every time the argument came up, falling in line with Martin's plan to push on.

Lindsay barged into the middle of the group, mumbling, "This isn't a democracy, you know. I am in charge."

Jericho reached down to pet her on her feathered head. "Yes, you are. You're the boss."

Her mumbling turned to louder grumbling. "I am the boss."

Julia chimed in. "Nobody would deny that you are the boss."

She received one of Lindsay's patented death-glares. "Then why are you following him and ignoring me?"

Julia and Jericho both answered at the same time, talking over one another but both fairly distinct thanks to her voice being helium high and his being deep enough to be mistaken for roadworks.

She chirped, "Because he knows where we are going?"

He rumbled, "Because his plan isn't completely stupid."

Martin pretended he couldn't hear the conversation going on behind him. This was far from the first time they'd had this discussion, and Lindsay wasn't actually a megalomaniac, no matter what her cackling and jokes about world domination might otherwise indicate.

Lindsay was feigning a sulk, trying to lean on one of the curved chamber walls when she found the glitch. With so many rotations the night before, some part of the game world hadn't properly aligned in the exact spot where she was leaning. It looked like a solid wall, but she passed through it like air. It was pure luck that Jericho was looking in the right direction when it happened, and pure instinct that had him leaping to catch her ankle before she vanished through the wall entirely. When he hauled her back in, she was rasping and gasping. "I want to go again!"

Martin approached the wall and felt his way along carefully until it gave way beneath his finger pads. It wasn't cold on the other side. There was no breeze; it was as though he was feeling nothing at all, like when they were disembodied during character creation or death. Nervously, he poked his head through the hole in the wall and looked out.

On the other side of the wall was a darkness richer and more all-consuming than anything Martin had ever experienced. Not just the absence of light, but something darker still. His eyes couldn't adjust to it; it was like he had gone blind, until he looked down and saw the whole dungeon of Strata arrayed beneath them. From the outside it was like a great puzzle, with no hint beyond the color of the stone as to what each deep held, but there they were, slowly being shifted and shuffled around by the Masters who hung immobile in the darkness.

Looking out to the sides, Martin could see the deep that they were in along with a half-dozen others, great caverns up next to where the surface of the earth should be, identical Beachheads all funneling people from all around the world down into the lower levels where they would mingle. There was no sign of the world aboveground. The dungeon was all that Strata comprised.

Lindsay yanked him back and tried to squeeze by him before he caught her by the collar. "Oh, no. None of that."

"Come on, dude. We could hop out there, climb down a few floors, pop back in. They can't blame us for exploiting a glitch they put in."

"They can and they will. You try that crap and they're going to ban us all."

Lindsay's beak snapped shut but there was a glimmer of rebellion in her eyes. She wasn't going to let this go. She let them draw her away, but the idea had already taken root in her head. She was going to throw herself out of the game world as soon as she got the opportunity.

The chambers on either side of the one they were heading to had been completely blocked by collapse and root incursions. It was a bottleneck that they were going to have to pass through if they wanted to go any further. The designers were smart enough to make it seem coincidental while still putting in a really obvious trap. Now he just had to work out how to turn it against them.

A toe-to-toe fight with a pair of Morasses was likely to drag on for quite some time, and while Martin was certain they would be able to slog it out, that solution seemed inelegant. He thought back to his battle with the Morass the previous night.

If he'd just held onto the Rain Tear Crystal, he probably could have used it as bait to draw one of the guardians out. As it was, they were both standing side by side, blocking access to the far door and facelessly facing towards the only entrance. No way to pull one out and fight it alone; no way to get the drop on them.

His stomach flipped as he remembered the way that just one morass had been able to toss him around, the sickly sensation of the ground beneath his feet suddenly obeying his enemy. Martin smoothed down his whiskers and grinned.

"I've got a plan, but Lindsay, you're not going to like it."

It took a minute to explain his idea and Lindsay did not like it. Still, they lined up at the chamber's entrance. Martin diplomatically allowed Lindsay to give the signal.

"Now!"

All four of them charged in, shouting out battle-cries – and in Julia's case, letting out a squeal so high-pitched that only Wulvan could hear it. The Faceless Morasses were happy to oblige, lumbering forward to meet them in the middle of the room and breaking into a charge that should have rolled right over Iron Riot like a truck.

Martin bellowed, "Split!" and the group leapt in two, with the Morasses plowing right through the gap between them. Martin and Julia backed towards one of the blocked exits, Lindsay and Jericho the other.

They could have made a run for the exit, but that left them open to attack from the rear or getting trapped between a living rock monster and a hard place. They might have been in a hurry, but they weren't stupid.

Divide and conquer only worked if you could bring enough destructive force to bear on one half of your enemy to quickly defeat them before they could regroup, and Martin had no illusions about his combat prowess when it came to these creatures.

He wasn't looking for a glorious victory. Just a win. Julia slunk behind him as the Morasses split up and lumbered after their respective targets, just like he'd hoped. When he scraped his sword over the bracers this time, the Obsidian let out a reverberating shriek that set his teeth on edge. That seemed to draw the Morass after him too.

He stepped forward from the wall and *Celestial Strike* ignited his blade. Everything was going to plan. The Morass swung its colossal fist at him and he stepped forward to meet it, hacking at that stony fist for all he was worth.

[Faceless Morass suffers 9 light damage]
[Faceless Morass suffers 9 damage]
[Skaife suffers 28 bludgeoning damage]

As predicted, meeting them head-on was suicide, but even as Martin battered off the tangle of roots behind him, he could feel the sap running down his sword to tickle over his knuckles. That fist was a big open wound now.

Julia rushed over and began to cast a healing spell on him as he staggered to his feet. The healing would have been nice, but the light drew the monster's attention. He cast *Rebuke* on Julia and sent her stumbling back across the room and out of the Morass' path as it charged in for another swing.

Martin stood still as the Morass turned its face towards him. The tangle of protruding vines hanging out of the wounded fist came straight for his head. He didn't flinch until the last possible moment, then he dove to the side.

[MISS]

The blow would have turned Martin into a furry chowder if it had connected. Instead it was driven right into the tightly woven roots behind him. Splinters showered across his side as he scrambled back to his feet. Julia seemed to have remembered the plan now; she was getting some distance from the Morass, and Martin now scrambled to do the same.

It turned its blank face towards him and tried to resume its pursuit, but it couldn't. The vines of its arm had gone seeking biomass to repair its injury, and they had found the root structure of a tree so massive that it reached all the way down here. It tugged helplessly against the tree, bound by its own ever-adapting nature to something immutable. Julia let out a little sigh.

"I can't believe that worked."

Lindsay shouted over, "I can't believe it worked twice!"

The second Morass was trapped in a similar entanglement on the other side of the room, bracing its feet against the roots and pulling with all of its considerable strength.

Martin let out a ragged breath. "I'm glad it worked at all."

Lindsay had closed the distance, so her bellowed reply made Martin flinch, for more reasons than one.

"Hi, Glad It Worked At All. I'm Dad."

Jericho let out a moan of anguish and looked up to the heavens. Julia covered her face with her hands and made something that might have been a sob. Only Martin remained untroubled. He was developing an immunity to Lindsay by this point in their lives, and he'd realized that giving her a reaction like that just encouraged her. He did *not* want to encourage her.

Julia cast a healing spell on Martin to top him back off, then they headed on into the next chamber cautiously. Instead of the spheres they had passed through before, this chamber was distinctly angular, and whether by luck or maintenance there was no sign of the silt and muck that had coated every other part of the Deep.

Martin trailed his hand over the graven wall as they crept inside, still surprised to feel the textures shifting beneath his touch despite all the game time he had logged in the last few days. There was definitely some sort of story cut into these stone slabs, but the language that felt like it was on the tip of his tongue still eluded him.

At the far end of the room, the floor reared up into a pair of ramps leading to an elevated walkway made out of what looked like brass, but the truly fascinating thing was between those ramps.

An enormous, rusted apparatus lay there before them. A relic from their own world's history dragged into this one and dumped unceremoniously into place. The pipes and chambers of the thing could be mistaken for a robotic heart if you had a poetic mindset, but Martin recognized it for what it was.

A massive water-pump.

SEVENTEEN

Suffering of the Uprooted

Movement up on the walkway caught Lindsay's eye, and she grabbed Jericho and Martin by their tails to jerk them back towards the entrance. She pointed up at the unaware enemy and hissed, "Anybody know who the hell that is?"

It looked related to the Faceless Morass in the same way that humans looked related to gorillas. It was a fraction of the size, carried barely any of the same bulk, and the sheets of lichen draped around it looked almost like robes or a dress.

There was no mistaking its plant-like nature; tiny buds were blossoming into little yellow flowers down one side of its body, but in the dark, without his specially adapted eyes, it would have been quite possible to mistake it for another person.

"It's a plant-person. Same as the others. Just a bit smaller."

Jericho rumbled softly. "How can you see anything? It is pitch black in there and boss-bird says no torches."

Lindsay tugged on his tail again. "Hush up, meat-head."

They all looked to Martin, as if he had any more of an idea what was going on than the rest of them.

"Okay. It is either a new monster type or a unique enemy. If it's a unique enemy then it is probably the boss of the deep. If we want the key, we have to kill it."

Julia whispered, her split tongue flicking out with every word. "I think we have all worked out that much."

"Right. Sorry." Martin rubbed at the back of his own neck nervously. "It looks like the Faceless Morasses, so it will probably have the same abilities. That means that you want to stay clear of its injuries or it might try to assimilate you into its biomass."

Jericho groaned out a flat, "What?"

"They don't just latch onto other vegetation, so be careful."

Lindsay sniggered. "Martin, did you stay up all night getting assimilated by plants?"

He didn't dignify that with a response.

"Beyond that ability, I'm not sure what we're up against. The big guys were too dumb to use their special abilities very well, but this one is smaller, so they've probably coded it to be a brains-over-brawn kind of enemy."

Lindsay prodded him. "What, the shrub is going to outsmart us?"

"Probably not, but don't assume it's as stupid as the things we faced before." Martin paused, straining his memory for any other clues. "Uh… prehensile vines are probably going to be a thing. Just because you are out of reach, don't assume that you are safe."

Lindsay rolled her eyes. "Can we just go kick her in the bush already?"

Jericho should have known better, but he still laughed at that, muffling his muzzle with one hand and earning another sigh from Julia.

"Okay, let's go for a basic tank and spank. Lindsay can go stealth. We'll draw the monster down. Jericho will keep her attention, the rest of us will chop her up or patch each other up as needed."

Lindsay stepped back and faded out of sight with a whisper of, "Iron Riot."

"Iron Riot!"

Martin hadn't taken his eyes off the figure on the walkway, and when they raised their voices, he saw it freeze in place. They'd been noticed. Good.

Jericho strolled out into the room, clapping his hands together just to be certain.

"Plant-lady, come out to play!"

There was a flicker of movement, then a javelin of raw green wood was suddenly protruding from the martyr's massive shoulder, a few inches above his heart.

[Jericho suffers 14 piercing damage]

Julia rushed over to him, healing at the ready.

"It has ranged attacks!" she cried.

"Then get down!" Martin replied.

He was already sprinting for the nearest walkway, and he assumed Lindsay was doing the same thing. Another javelin whipped past his head, leaving a trail of sap across his fur.

[MISS]

That could have been extremely bad. If he'd just known the composition of the guild team ahead of time, he would have picked a ranged caster again, tunnel fighting be damned. Now they had no options except to run, duck and hope for the best.

From this close he could see the creature's name and the beginning of some of its features. The *Fecund Swamproot* didn't have a feminine shape so much as a liquid one. Where the Morass had been a mess of different materials, this creature was all natural. Vines and fresh green wood tangled around each other into a vaguely human shape, but it was willowy to the point of being ungainly in its height.

It flicked one of its arms in his direction and he dove forward to avoid the next attack, hands scrabbling against the moist tiles of the walkway to keep up his forward momentum.

[MISS]

Lindsay appeared out of a puff of shadow behind the Swamp-root bellowing "Raptor Strike!" at the top of her voice.

The first part of her leap had been hidden by stealth, but the final arc of her descent was all too obvious. The monster's feet stayed firmly planted in place, but its upper body lashed to the side.

[MISS]

Lindsay tumbled past her target and nearly slid right off the edge of the platform to land amongst the machinery. For some reason, dungeons never seemed big on handrails.

A horrid reedy sound started wheezing out of the Swamp-root, a whistling that rose and fell rhythmically as Martin closed on it. It was only at the last moment before he swung that he realized that it was laughter.

[MISS]

Once again, the Swamproot hadn't given an inch, just leaning back out of reach of his blade while staying rooted to the spot.

From so close by Martin could see the Rain Tear Crystals planted amidst the vines of its face in the place of eyes. A nice obvious weak spot if the damned thing would just stay still long enough to be hit.

He felt more than saw Lindsay returning to her feet at his side. He didn't dare look away from the Swamproot, not with the way it kept feigning attacks in his direction. If it could launch those javelins across the room, he had no doubt they left its body with enough explosive force to cause him some serious damage, and he'd rather avoid that if he could.

Lindsay started to circle around behind Martin, putting her back towards the rear wall and all of the burnt-out machinery that loomed there. The Swamproot's gaze followed her every step.

Without any more bombardment, Jericho and Julia were on their way to join the fight, halfway up the far walkway and showing no sign of slowing.

There was no way the Swamproot was just going to stand there and wait for reinforcements to arrive. It had to act now, and the guild had to act first.

"Go for the eyes!" he yelled.

Martin and Lindsay darted forward together in the perfect harmony that was normally reserved for paired dancers, and they were slapped back with the same synchronicity too.

[Skaife suffers 12 bludgeoning damage]
[Tesra suffers 12 bludgeoning damage]

The Swamproot hadn't struck at them so much as it had exploded outwards in every direction, the densely packed coils of its vine system suddenly unravelling and then coiling back the other way to form the same vaguely human shape all over again.

The two of them skidded back, Lindsay catching herself on the consoles and steam-pipes and Martin running on the spot with his claws skittering over the tiles just to avoid being flung off the edge. The smug plant hadn't even moved since it reformed. Just started to flute laughter at them again.

A wave of anger rushed over Martin, but he quashed it as quickly as it arrived. The Swamproot was taunting them, trying to make them act irrationally.

Lindsay let out a croak of frustration and flung herself forward. She was taking the bait. The Swamproot started to lose its cohesion, the twisting coils of live wood preparing to spring out into a new shape. A lethal shape.

Martin didn't have time to watch the trap snap shut. He cast *Rebuke* on Lindsay. She rebounded off the machinery and went tumbling over into Jericho's waiting arms.

Every part of the Swamproot from the knees up shot forward into one terrible impaling spike, slicing through the air where Lindsay had been just a moment before.

[MISS]

The spike blossomed open and curled back towards its source. If Lindsay had been hit, it would have torn her into chunks. What level was this monster, anyway? The quest to fight the generic Morass had been level 5 – already a risk when you were only level 3 – and this thing was *so* much more dangerous.

It seemed like it was making another feign when it launched a quick javelin at Martin. Luck more than skill saved him from it. Some twitchy instinct made him bat at the sudden movement with his sword, and it was just enough to turn the slick spike of wood aside.

[Skaife BLOCKS 16 damage]
[Skaife suffers 16 stamina loss]

By the time he had recovered, the Swamproot had already moved on to another target.

[MISS]

Julia was cowering on the floor with a thick line of sap across her robes showing a near miss. Lindsay had only just found her feet again, eyes blazing with fury. The only one who wasn't off balance was Jericho. The aura that surrounded him had brightened once more and while the Swamproot was lashing at him tentatively, it didn't seem to know how to deal with an enemy that it couldn't hit.

[Jericho BLOCKS 12 bludgeoning damage]
[Jericho BLOCKS 12 bludgeoning damage]

Jericho was too much of a professional to laugh in the monster's face, but there was definitely some satisfaction as he drew his fists down to his sides and unleashed a dazzling flurry of attacks.

[Fecund Swamproot absorbed 6 light damage]

Martin froze. "Wait."

[Fecund Swamproot absorbed 7 light damage]

"Stop!"

[Fecund Swamproot absorbed 5 light damage]

White strobed across the chamber as Jericho pummeled the Swamproot with bolts of light. Each time the monster was lit up, it seemed a little bigger.

It was a plant… and they were feeding it light

Each sinuous vine that made up its body had thickened, and tiny buds were forming across their surfaces. Martin did not want to see what happened when they opened.

The wheezing, fluting laughter had grown along with the monster, now so loud that Martin had to bellow to be heard over it.

"No more! The light is just making it stronger."

"But all my attacks use light!" Jericho roared back, his aura pinging as it deflected another whipping vine.

[Jericho BLOCKS 9 bludgeoning damage]

"Then block for us. Keep its attention!"

Martin stayed stock-still, watching and waiting for the right moment, when the lashing vines had reached their full extension against Jericho's invisible shielding.

[Jericho BLOCKS 14 bludgeoning damage]

They would need to recoil before they could whip out again.

"Lindsay, pincer now!"

Together, they darted in, but even at its most vulnerable, they still couldn't make contact. Martin's swings at the limbs were evaded with a simple undulation, and the central trunk split open when Lindsay launched into another *Raptor Strike*.

[MISS]

She flew through the gap, headed right for Martin. If it wasn't for his new bracers, his panicked parry would have been completely useless. Her daggers raked down over the whetstone with a discordant chime and took on a new sparkle.

"Did you just buff my knives?"

He pushed her away as another javelin of live wood was flung at them.

[MISS]

"Yes! Did you just attack me?"

She looked as sheepish as a crow-person could. "Sorry?"

In the midst of the bulging tendrils, the Rain Tears still shone in Martin's low-light vision like the eyeshine of animals in headlights, distorted from their positions as mockeries of human eyes, but still laid out on the same horizontal line.

The next whipping vine swung past at ankle height and they both had to skip over it.

[MISS]

If he had tentacles like that, Martin would have been trying to go over and under their defenses, attacking from angles that they couldn't protect against.

The plant was thinking in two dimensions.

"You go high, I'll go low."

Laughter crept back into Lindsay's voice. Nothing like an insurmountable enemy to cheer her up.

"Bounce me?"

She flung herself at him, clawed feet flailing in the air until his *Rebuke* hit her and launched her up towards the ceiling.

There was no time to check if her descent was going to be successful. He had to grab the Swamproot's attention now and make it forget all about Lindsay. He had to make this gamble count. With a stray thought, he activated *Rite of Retribution...* and charged.

Throughout it all, the creature's legs had remained immobile. Martin didn't know if it was habit, fighting style or necessity, but he'd happily exploit it either way. He dove forward under the lashing thicket of vines and swiped at its feet.

[MISS]

Both legs retracted up into the central mass as his sword swung close and the whole bulk came thumping down on top of him.

[Skaife suffers 28 bludgeoning damage]
[PENANCE: Jericho suffers 28 bludgeoning damage]

What little breath he had left was driven out of his lungs by the crushing weight of the Swamproot, even though Jericho's penance had absorbed half the damage. He couldn't even cry out as he felt the tendrils begin to probe at his armor, creeping inside, trying to take root in his flesh.

Lindsay slammed into the Swamproot, blades first, and the shock of the impact travelled down through it to grind Martin into the tiles once more.

[CRITICAL HIT]
[Fecund Swamproot suffers 49 piercing damage]
[Skaife suffers 11 bludgeoning damage]
[PENANCE: Jericho suffers 11 bludgeoning damage]

He only had six health left, and even though he had lit his hand up with *Healing Touch,* he couldn't move to touch himself with it. The next time the Swamproot moved, he was going to die from its weight alone.

Up above him, he could hear Lindsay screeching and slashing as she tried to get free of the encompassing vines. Jericho was cussing at the two of them under his breath as he strained, trying to pry their living wooden prison apart with his bare hands.

Then he saw it. In the pitch darkness beneath the tangled woods of the Swamproot, Martin could suddenly see a shape. Just like he'd been able to see the root network beneath the surface of the water.

There was a single corkscrewing root coming down from the center of the creature above him, lit up with that same strange blue glow as the Rain Tear Crystals that seemed to animate all of these monstrous vegetables. It twitched just by Martin's face and wormed down into a crack in the tiles beneath him, spreading out in a fine web under the surface of the tiles into a massive fungal network. No wonder the Swamproot was reluctant to let go of its footing when it was drawing all its strength from the earth.

His sword was too far away, pinned as uselessly as his *Healing Touch,* but Martin wasn't a human here in Strata. He was a rat. And there was nothing rats did better than gnaw.

He'd expected something tough when he bit into the root, but it was soft and spongy, like a mushroom or a tongue. It tasted vile – like burdock, licorice and anise had crossbred and then been left to rot in a bog for a thousand years – but it gave way beneath his sharp incisors easily.

[Fecund Swamproot has been uprooted]

The cohesion of the monster suddenly fell apart. The crushing grip on his arms and legs loosened, and he started to crawl his way out through the chaotic undergrowth. When he managed to pry his glowing hand free, he pressed it to his chest, then kept it close so it wouldn't get ensnared all over again.

[Skaife regains 15 health]

Lindsay seemed like she was finally having some success too, and with a sound like tearing paper, Jericho finally managed to clear a path for her escape. Martin burst out into the dim light of the pump-room and gasped for fresh air.

The second he could speak, he called out, "All clear?"

Lindsay had a quaver in her voice. "Let's not fight any more tentacle monsters, yeah?"

Martin hated hearing fear in her voice. She was meant to be joyful and confident – some might say overconfident. He couldn't stand to think of that unshakeable faith in herself being broken.

"Give me a dragon any day."

She let out a little squawk of laughter. It sounded wetter than he would have liked, but at least it sounded like her again.

"Hey now, whatever happened to good old-fashioned goblins?"

Severed from the fungal network below the tiles, the Swamproot seemed to have lost all reason and semblance of form. Martin was starting to suspect that the parts it had hidden under the floor were the parts it used for thinking.

He could still see that one blue glowing tentacle linking up the Rain Tears on one end and wriggling around wildly on the other, desperately rooting around inside the other stems. Searching. It had literally lost its mind.

This was their chance.

"Get it!" he yelled.

All hesitation was thrown to the wind. Martin could hear Lindsay hacking at the far side of the exploded Swamproot, catching brief glimpses of her through the swaying, writhing cords of green.

[Fecund Swamproot suffers 9 slashing damage]
[Fecund Swamproot suffers 7 slashing damage]
[Fecund Swamproot suffers 8 slashing damage]

His own sweeping blows cut readily through the nearest tendrils in swathes.

[Fecund Swamproot suffers 16 slashing damage]
[CRITICAL HIT]
[Fecund Swamproot suffers 32 slashing damage]

In the midst of it all, suspended on the glowing blue vine, Martin could see the Rain Tear Crystals whipping back and forth on their uncontrolled tether. He was sure that the two of them were all that was still granting this thing life, but he didn't know how to get past the cyclone of vines to get close enough to sever them.

The whole thing was working on instinct now, automatic defenses making it flail around until it could regain sentience. Sensory input was just setting its shoots into action without any intervening logic.

"Guys, I've got an idea that could go extremely wrong."

Jericho groaned as Lindsay yelled back, "Those are the best kind!"

Martin smiled despite himself. "Close your eyes."

This time, Julia was the quickest on the uptake. "But light makes it stronger."

"I know." Martin's grin was getting perilously real now. "But strong doesn't matter when you're dead." He cast *Halo* and all hell broke loose.

The buds along the vines burst open into vicious looking thorns, dripping with some foul ichor that sizzled when it hit the tiles. The vines themselves began to swell once again, getting thicker and extending their reach even further.

All of these things would have terrified Martin if it weren't for the fact that the moment his *Halo* struck the Swamproot, all of the dozen eyes it had been using to track them had been struck blind.

He didn't hesitate, just dove headlong into the venomous thicket of paralyzed vines, hacking his way through to the Rain Tears, ducking and dodging wherever he could.

When the Swamproot came back to life, this place was going to be like standing in an oversized blender. Martin had no intention of ever letting it come back to life.

The blue glow of the Rain Tears shimmered ahead of him and the sword in his hand felt like an extension of his arm. He was already swinging the moment the thought crossed his mind.

[CRITICAL HIT]
[Fecund Swamproot suffers 36 slashing damage]
Fecund Swamproot has died.
Skaife has earned 840 experience.
[LEVEL UP]

The crystals shattered into a shimmering dust and the plant fell limp with a sound like a deflating balloon. All the vines thudded down in a great spiraling blossom around him and he finally saw the rest of the party again.

Jericho was glaring across at him with the very special annoyance that he reserved for situations like this; when everything had gone right despite his warnings and now he didn't even have something to be angry about.

Martin savored those moments; they had come less and less frequently, the more competent he had proven himself to be.

Julia healed Lindsay, who looked across at him with something like admiration in her eyes. Admiration marred by jealousy.

"Next time, maybe you could tell me what is happening so that I can fight too, yeah?"

Martin's pride shrank a little. Maybe he was getting too used to playing by himself. "Sorry, I didn't have much time to think."

"Well, don't leave me standing around with nothing to do again." Lindsay had already been irritated with him for taking the lead earlier. Now he'd stolen the killing blow out of her hands too. She wasn't petty, but she still needed to be in charge. "You know, you got lucky this time, but I could have hit those eyeballs faster than you if you'd just given me the go-ahead. You know?"

Martin should have just let it go. He should have just taken his lumps and moved on, but some treacherous little voice of logic in his head made him ask, "You could see them in there?"

Lindsay set her shoulders, feathers rustling down her back. "I could see them just as well as you."

"Are you sure?" He cocked his head to one side. He really needed to stop talking, because there was no way that this wasn't going to escalate into a full-blown argument if he kept poking at her. "Because I've got Night Vision and Swamproot Sight."

Jericho rumbled, "The hell is Swamproot Sight?"

Martin crouched down and scooped up some of the less poisonous-looking sap from one of the many wounded vines. "Come here, big guy." He smeared it over Jericho's eyelids and then saw the hulking Wulvan blink as the notification appeared.

"So, what, it helps you see plants?"

"I guess? It came in handy in the swamp."

Lindsay and Julia wiped some on themselves. Lindsay's temper was temporarily defused by the new discovery.

"Come on, let's loot this bitch. Get our key and move on!"

Martin turned to the Swamproot's corpse and the looting tooltip appeared.

Fecund Swamproot

The undisputed masters of the fifth deep, the Swamproots are the lethal leaders of the Morasses, Stranglers and Snapjaws of your earlier tribulations. Strangely lucid and cruel for a plant, they will torture their prey for no discernable reason.

Loot: *79 silver, Rain Tear Crystal Dust, Swamproot Sap, Tarnished Censer, Swamproot Stave, Pearlfeather Cloak.*

Requires Herbalism *to Harvest:* **Unknown Plant, Unknown Plant, Unknown Plant, Unknown Venom,** *Fertile Substrate.*

Masters of the fifth deep? This was yet another displaced monster. No wonder it had nearly wiped the floor with them. If it had been a toe-to-toe fight like you'd expect in an MMO then they would have been slaughtered by this thing.

It was really just luck that had put Martin in position to hit it where it was weak. Luck, and the help of his little frog-friends with their handy goop. Otherwise things would have gone very differently.

A second realization followed on the heels of the first. If the Swamproot was a wandering monster from further in the dungeon then it probably wasn't the boss of this level, and it wouldn't have the Deep Key.

He let out a groan, then turned his attention to the loot. The crystal dust would probably sell for even less than the whole crystal had. The Swamproot Sap was incredibly useful in the context of this one deep and would probably be of great benefit to anyone fighting these creatures down in deep five, but they had all gained the buff now, and the lack of any countdown seemed to imply it was permanent.

Anyone they sold the sap along to would have the same advantage that Martin had earned for the guild, and when the competition was as fierce as it seemed to be, he wasn't sure if giving anything away was smart, not unless they could trade it for something better.

The censer, stave and cloak all looked a lot more promising, and he was less conflicted about upgrades that they could use themselves instead of passing on to whoever had the most ready cash.

Tarnished Censer [4-8 damage]

The Crusade stretches ever on into the future, but it began many years ago and for every hero raised up in triumph there have been a hundred laid low by the trial. This relic belonged to one of those forgotten martyrs and has lain rotting in the fetid waters until now.

It looked like a very ineffectual morningstar, a ball of hollow metal at the end of a chain. Once, it had all been filigreed in silver, but now it was clotted with thick verdigris. It wasn't much of a weapon, but closer examination revealed that it was useable by any class, even the usually empty-handed martyrs. He tossed the censer to Jericho.

"Something to use next time we're up against something immune to light."

Jericho dangled it from his meaty fist with a sigh. "Fine."

Swamproot Stave [4-8 damage]

Amidst the tangled wood of the Swamproot, it is rare to find even a single stretch that is straight, yet in your hands you hold a length worthy to be wielded as a stave. Beneath the surface of this still-living wood, the flow of sap can still be felt.

It could only be used by hierophants, and the practical information about what it actually did was hidden from Martin's sight when he tried to read it. With disgust, he tossed it to Julia. She fumbled the catch and had to scoop it up from the floor, but whatever irritation that might have caused vanished as she read through the special effects of the staff. A glint appeared in her eye.

"Thank you very much."

Pearlfeather Cloak

The Pearlfeather Clan of Corvan are few in number, in no small part because of the bounty upon these feathers. Shimmering and iridescent, they shift color to match their surroundings, providing the wearer with a great boon to their stealth.

Martin almost grumbled as he handed the last piece of loot across to Lindsay, who was clapping her hands and rambling something about him being Santa Claus. Another powerful enemy beaten and not a piece of loot for him. It was getting past the point where he could believe it was just bad luck. He was being sabotaged. The Master had been true to their word.

Lindsay flung her new gear on without a second thought.

"Invisibility cloak. Nice! Going to sneak up on all y'all and tickle you. Make you think you're haunted. Woo. I'm a ghost." She froze, realization spreading across her face. "Oh! Oh! I'm the ghost of Christmas past. Rat-boy is Scrooge, handing out presents after seeing us all. Jericho can be the big guy that eats everything. Julia, get your hood up, you can be the spooky skinny one at the end."

Jericho growled – actually growled, like a dog – and Julia gave one of the watery smiles that somehow translated well onto a lizard face. "I would prefer not to."

Lindsay fluttered over in a shimmer of changing colors to drape herself on Martin. That was one of the best things about Lindsay. She got angry quickly, but it vanished just as fast when she found something to amuse herself with.

"Dude, where is your Christmas spirit?"

"Firstly, it is August." He counted off on his fingers. "And secondly, bah humbug."

She gasped in faux horror. "Shame on you, sir. Shame."

Jericho butted in before she could launch into the next round of antics. "You have the key?"

"No. This monster wasn't even supposed to be up here. It's from deep five. The actual boss must be around here somewhere…" Martin trailed off.

If this was an ecosystem, it wasn't likely that the new apex predator would have tolerated the previous one for long.

"It's probably underneath the body. The Swamproot probably killed it when it took over."

Jericho grumbled some more, but it didn't take long for all four of them to work their way across the walkway, dragging the now-limp branches of the Swamproot out of the way. Julia found what they were looking for, eventually: the mostly decayed body of another Sythvan.

It was almost mummified, with all of the moisture dragged out of the corpse to feed the parasitic plant that was sprouting from the top of its head. Closer examination revealed that the hybrid was called a *Sprouting Snapjaw,* and it had been a much more appropriate challenge for their levels.

The Deep Key was all that was left in its decaying inventory, but Julia claimed it without complaint.

Lindsay was bouncing up and down by the time they had the key. "All right. All right. Let's go."

On their way out, Martin eyed the mechanical apparatus that dominated the room with avarice. Technology like that, it was a whole new development on what he had thought was a thinly veiled medieval fantasy world. The developers were laying the groundwork for an almost industrialized society somewhere in the game's history.

Which meant that at some point, almost inevitably, they were going to end up going head to head with the remnants of it. He could hardly wait.

EIGHTEEN

The Deep Rains

As they made their way back out past the trapped Morasses, which seemed to have begun decaying, Martin blinked open the menu and started to level up, eyes flickering open every once in a while to make sure the group were heading the right way.

He wasn't sure if the others had leveled up too, but he didn't want to slow them down or start an awkward conversation about why he was levelling faster than them.

At the same time, there was a terrible temptation to take over, to tell them how they should be assigning their stats and which abilities they should be picking – a temptation that he knew from painful experience that he must not indulge.

People didn't like being told what to do at the best of times. When you were telling them it was for their own good, it was infinitely worse. And when you were telling them how to build their character – essentially telling them who they should be – they really did not like it.

Friendships had been lost over much less, and Martin was already walking a dangerous tightrope with the guild, trying to maximize their efficiency and progress without making them hate him in return.

He put everyone else out of his mind for now and concentrated instead on doing a little bit of personal improvement.

Skaife Murovan Exorcist
Strength: 6 Agility: 8
Endurance: 9 Willpower: 7
LEVEL 4

You have 3 points to assign.

Now that he had seen a little bit of what the lower levels were going to hold, the course he should take became more apparent to Martin. Humanoid enemies that needed to be blocked and parried were giving way to huge monstrosities that had to be dodged, and for some reason that wasn't half the drain on stamina that blocking and parrying had been. Or at least, it was a more gradual drain.

At some point, he was probably going to have to pump up his agility if he wanted to stay ahead of the blows coming his way, but for now the natural advantage of being a smaller target seemed to be carrying him through.

So, neither agility nor endurance were top picks, at least at the moment. Which left him with the dichotomy of willpower and strength yet again.

He really appreciated the utility of his magic, and it had been serving him extremely well in the last few fights, but the whole exorcist fighting style was still built around him hitting things with a sword.

He could blind them, fling them around, heal himself and increase the odds of a critical hit, but none of those things actually killed the monsters he was fighting, and without direct damage the enemies wouldn't go down.

Every time he had to dodge an attack, he had to be lucky, and with the ridiculous power of some of the enemies they were facing, they only had to be lucky once. What he needed wasn't the ability to avoid more attacks, it was to make the monsters stop attacking. Permanently.

He dropped all three points into his strength score, briefly wondering if it would have a visual effect. The idea of a really buff rat-man was intensely appealing to him for some reason; probably because the same diseased bit of his brain that still made him laugh at Lindsay's jokes was at work.

*Strength: **9** Agility: 8*
Endurance: 9 Willpower: 7
Health: 45 Stamina: 58

A bit more health would have been nice, but this was a compromise he was willing to make. Three extra damage on every hit, six on every critical hit. That could make a big difference.

You may select 1 new ability.

Trinity Strike – Activates after two successful *Celestial Strikes*.
Shares a cooldown with *Celestial Strike*.
Deals 16 light damage.
Increases critical chance for all allies by 33% for 30 seconds.
[30-second cooldown]

Lay on Hands – Restores 100% of an ally's health. Reduces your stamina and stamina regeneration by 10% for 5 minutes.
[60-minute cooldown]

Rite of Passage – Unlocks any Gate without requiring the key.
[72-hour cooldown]

That last option nearly stopped him dead in his tracks. The ability to open a Deep Gate without having to deal with the boss of the deep was beyond valuable. Sure, most of them would be guarded by something lethal that you needed to fight your way through anyway, but still. He nearly selected it on the spot, but at the very last moment, he froze.

They already had the key to this deep's gate, and while he was sure that now they were all together they would be plowing through the deeps that followed all weekend, he had another piece of math to fit into the selection equation.

Was he going to level up again before they got to the next gate? So far, he'd been easily clearing one level per deep, and he was about to get a small bounty of experience points for handing his *Defender of the Frogs* quest in. By the time they reached the next Deep Gate, he was willing to gamble that he would have gone up another level and been able to select *Rite of Passage* as his reward, whereas if he chose it now, the new ability would be sitting unused the whole time they were trying to fight their way to the next gate. A wasted pick, at least for this deep. He flicked his tail anxiously then made his selection.

Trinity Strike didn't seem like a particularly powerful ability back when it had first popped up, but now that Martin realized he could use Celestial Strike to bypass armor, he was likely to use it every time it came off cooldown.

The extra critical chance had been a minor boon when it had just been him and Lindsay, but with a party of four, it suddenly multiplied in value, particularly given the way that Jericho's attacks seemed to come in small flurries.

If the wolf-man was making a flurry of three attacks each time, and Trinity Strike gave a 33% chance, Jericho would be making one critical hit every time he attacked. There was still a gamble involved in taking it over the *Rite*, but Martin could be using it twice a minute instead of once per deep. It was the better investment, at least for now.

With the path clear and marked, the guild made record time heading back to the entrance of the deep. Martin knew from years of experience that the bickering would start up the moment there was any confusion, so he did everything he could to make sure their path seemed so obvious that they'd have to be blind to miss it. Even if it was an uphill battle in some cases.

"So, you're saying that these little frog dudes are monsters but we're not meant to kill them," Lindsay said.

She was swinging across the roots on the roof of the tunnel, mainly to amuse herself at this point, since the Swamproot Sight allowed them to navigate hidden pitfalls with surprising ease.

Martin nodded carefully. "Right."

She dangled by one arm, swinging in ponderous circles. "Because they're super dangerous? Like, poison skin and extendable tongue punches?"

"No." Martin could already feel control of the conversation slipping away from him. "Because they aren't hostile and they can help us out, if we play nicely."

"They are just NPCs?" Jericho grumbled.

"More or less," Martin said, "but they might act a little hostile to start with since they don't know you. I don't want you to misunderstand and start chopping them to pieces."

Jericho paused to look down at him. The Wulvan actually had something like eyebrows to raise, big tufts of fur that put Martin in mind of a Schnauzer.

"You want us to let the monsters attack us?"

"I just want you to give me long enough to explain what is happening to them before you start building a throne with their skulls."

Exasperation was climbing up Martin's throat, just dying to get out. Lindsay dropped down with a splash.

"I would absolutely rock a skull-throne. Majestic and murderous. That is a look."

"Well, at least now I know what to get you for Christmas," Martin chuckled.

She pounced forward, her beak inches from Martin's face, her eyes sparkling with barely restrained laughter. "Are you confirming the rumors that you are secretly Santa Claus, rat edition?"

"I… I don't even know how to respond to that."

Jericho's big hand clapped him over the back of the head and Martin nearly went over.

"Keep your eyes forward. Don't let her distract you."

The swamp spread out up ahead of them, somehow even bigger than Martin remembered it now that he had the roots beneath the surface to grant some sense of perspective.

There was no sign of the Anurvan yet, but Martin felt certain they'd have some sentries keeping an eye on what seemed to be the only entrance to their little domain. Apart from the Deep Gate, which Martin felt certain was in this part of the dungeon, somewhere near to their settlement.

From what Martin could understand of the ecology of Strata, the weak monsters that died up here respawned down at the bottom of the dungeon and then had to make a wild dash for the relative safety of the higher floors.

That explained why there were so few of them up here, if attrition in each deep took care of some of them on each floor between the spawn and their final resting place. It also explained the distribution of weaker monsters closer to the surface in the less contested territory.

To Martin – who had been pondering the mechanics of it all day in between his other mental gymnastics – this meant one very important thing: the monsters had to know where every Deep Gate from here to their spawn point was, otherwise they couldn't make the trip.

If he could lay his hands on a monster guide, they would have a map all the way down. All they'd need to search for in each deep would be the key, and while the boss-monsters were pretty imposing, the fights were usually over in a matter of minutes.

In a race to the bottom, time was their biggest enemy. Now all he had to do was convince a frogman to join the cause and they'd be on course for victory.

He didn't dare mention this plan to the others. Not yet. It

was just as likely that they'd try to shanghai some poor sentry-frog and start a war with the whole village if they realized how valuable an ally the Anurvan could prove to be.

Martin just hoped that his heroics were going to be enough to convince one of them before the rest of the guild worked out what he was up to. What could be simpler?

It was almost startling how easy it was to find the Anurvan village now that the Swamproot Sap had taken effect. Last night had been an arduous hike full of trial and error and no small amount of dread, whereas today it was a walk in the park. Assuming the park was quite badly flooded and smelled stagnant. They didn't even have to pick a route, as every single path led back towards that central point.

Martin couldn't shake the feeling that he was walking into an ambush. The entire time they were traversing the roots he kept straining his hearing, trying to find the tell-tale splash of an Anurvan breaking the surface.

He could understand there being some reluctance to surface on their part – Jericho alone was enough to put the fear into anyone with any semblance of sanity – but he refused to believe that they were completely gone. They would not abandon the home it had taken them centuries to grow.

In his mind, he began trying to plot out whatever catastrophe had hit the Anurvan after he'd abandoned them for his watery grave the night before. Another Morass might have come stomping through, or something more sinister might have crawled up out of the Deep Gate, wherever it was hidden. Martin could picture the impact a Night Ravager would have on the poor little Anurvan. Like frogs in a blender.

When the village came into sight, there was no sign of battle damage, or even a hint that it had been populated just a few hours ago. It looked as though it had always been abandoned; every trace of the frog-folk had been stripped away when they went into hiding. Martin sighed. At least he knew they were safe, even if they didn't feel safe with him right now.

"Okay, this is their village. I'm guessing the giant wolf-man maybe scared them off?"

"Tadpoles, come out to play!" Lindsay bellowed.

That was *super* helpful.

"Listen, why don't you guys start scouting out the trails further in, see if you can see any sign of the Deep Gate. I'll hang back and hopefully they'll come out once they see I'm alone."

"Sounds like ambush time," Jericho grumbled, but he still walked off, scooping up Lindsay under one arm before she could screech anything else.

Julia gave Martin an apologetic wince – as if Lindsay's antics were somehow her fault – before scurrying off after them, further into the looming darkness of the underground swamp.

Martin half expected the Anurvan to pop up out of the water the moment the others were out of sight, but he was disappointed. He sat on the edge of the vine cluster, dangling his feet in the rust-colored water and trying to keep his patience as the minutes ticked by.

He couldn't go anywhere until they found the gate anyway. He wasn't really wasting time. Not really. No matter what that edge of desperation in his gut was whispering to him.

[ANNOUNCEMENT: *Nights in Armor* have defeated **Carnifex, Tenth Archduke of Strata**]

The pop-up was like a punch in the gut. Every minute that he was dawdling here, the more their chances of getting to the end of Strata first dwindled.

He bounced back to his feet with a grumble. If the frog-men wanted to hide, let them. He didn't need to hand in the quest. There would be plenty of experience in the lower deeps; he probably had almost enough banked from that Swamproot to hit level five anyway. He turned around and nearly tripped over Speckles.

The noise that came out of his throat had started as a yell, but he tried to strangle it before it could startle the few frightened frog-folk back into the water, resulting in a croaky squeak that set their huge yellow eyes blinking at him.

"Hi."

Speckles' throat inflated a little before he spoke.

"Dry friend. Why bring bad? You fight bad."

Martin patted the frog on his slimy shoulder. "My friends aren't bad. Well, they aren't all exactly good either, but they're not going to hurt you. I've told them about you. They... they're friends to you too. Probably."

"Words," Speckles croaked as the others crept closer. "Not good? Not bad? No hurt?"

Martin sighed. "No hurt. I promise. No hurt."

That seemed to be enough for Speckles, who held out an empty palm towards Martin. "You fight bad. Save us. You good dry friend. We thank."

Martin held up his own hand in the same pose and the pink pads of his furry paw brushed against the weirdly textured amphibian skin.

[Rare Quest: Defender of the Frogs COMPLETED]
Skaife gains 480 experience.

Some of the other Anurvan were doing a little capering dance that kept drawing Martin's attention. It almost made him miss what Speckles said next.

"We gift. You good friend. We gift."

This was going to be the tricky bit. "I don't want a gift."

"You save us." Speckles ambled closer. "We gift. Is our way."

Martin tried to act disinterested. "There is only one thing that I want from my friends, the Anurvan."

"We give! Good friend." Speckles was practically jumping up and down on the spot. Hopping.

Martin sprung his little verbal trap. "I want your company."

"Always welcome here!" Speckles gestured at all the stagnant mess around him with wide arms. "Our swamp, your swamp!"

"Sadly, I cannot stay here." Martin mimed a big sigh. "But I still want to spend more time with you. Would you perhaps consider travelling along with me and my friends? Serving as a guide, perhaps? We'd be happy to compensate you for your time."

His reply was a long silence, then a blink.

"Many words. Less words?"

Martin tried again. "Me good friend. You come with me?"

"Not that good," Speckles croaked.

Martin cocked his head. "But I thought it was your way to give gifts?"

"Me give gift. Love give gift. But me not gift. Me not crazy." Speckles was backing away towards the water's edge once more. "You go down below. Scary bad. No thanks."

"That makes me very sad to hear." Martin pointed a claw towards his own exaggerated sadness and pursued Speckles to the edge.

Speckles patted him on the head. "Sorry sad. Still no."

The same desperation that the surprise return of the Anurvan had interrupted was beginning to flourish in Martin's gut once again. "I'll pay you?"

Speckles shook his head. Since he didn't have a neck, this involved his whole body swinging back and forth. "Not enough fish in world."

"Is there a younger, braver Anurvan who might take me up on my offer? We desperately need a guide if we're to find the Deep Gates that you've already traversed."

Speckles began to really puff up at that comment.

"Gods below! Me bravest. Me youngest. Me say no. Down is bad! No way going down there."

"All right, all right." Martin's shoulders slumped. "I understand."

"You no understand nothing. Down at bottom is Heart of Strata. Darkness. We run. Through hot and dry, through cold and wet, through slick black and stone. We run all our life to get away from it. But you. You want go down there. It call you like fisher tugging on line."

Martin couldn't suppress a shiver. It must have been the damp air in the cave. "We are going down there to destroy it. We're going to end the darkness. You understand? You can't run forever. Eventually someone has to face it or it will never end."

The little frog-man turned his back on Martin, lipless mouth curled up in a sneer.

"No end. Never end. Just dark, forever."

Along with the other Anurvan, Speckles plopped down into the water and immediately faded out of Martin's sight. The last ripples passed under his feet and just like that, the village was abandoned again.

When he was entirely certain that he was alone, Martin cursed loudly and kicked the stupid wicker village. They could have at least given him whatever reward he was due before slinking off in a cloud of ominous statements. Even if it had just been gold it would have been useful.

He shouldn't have pushed so hard. Maybe the NPCs were more locked into their behaviors.

With a grumble he set off towards the tiny specks of light on his map where the rest of Iron Riot had dispersed. At least he had gotten his experience points, even if the taste of heroism had turned bitter in his mouth.

He understood why these little frogs were afraid; he had felt his own guts turn over more than once when faced with the monsters of the lower deeps, but their terror was different. It was more real. This wasn't a game to them; it was their whole world.

He wondered if they could feel pain, if all the monsters they were facing felt every injury that the players could just shrug off with a laugh. If they could, the fear made more sense.

From the brief glimpses of the creatures below, Martin was starting to develop a very clear picture of the designers' intentions. They weren't just dangerous, they were sadistic. If they treated players like that, players who could actually defend themselves and posed a threat, he dreaded to think how something harmless, small and squishy would manage.

The specks marking his guild-mates were dotted around the cavern. Presumably Jericho had finally decided that they weren't at any risk of an ambush after all and they'd dispersed to search faster. Martin broke into a jog, trusting in his Swamproot Sight to guide him safely across the hidden paths.

A wall loomed up out of the brown waters ahead of him long before any sign of his companions; the same dirt as the walls that had marked the entrance to this swamp. He paused when he reached it, trying to make sense of the striations across it.

Different colored mud lay in lines across the wall, marking water levels from different times. He knew that water was constantly trickling down into this cavern from the tunnels and machinery that they'd just cleared out, but what was draining the water away with such regularity that it had created all of these watermarks?

"What's up with the frogs-bodies then?" Lindsay whispered, right in his ear.

Martin almost lost his footing and ended up in the water. He'd forgotten she could do that.

With a shaking hand, he touched his guild crest and answered. "They're scared of you. They're scared of the lower deeps. They're scared of their own shadows. No help at all."

"Oh, no. What a shocking twist." She spoke in a flat monotone. "I am so surprised that the random monsters you made friends with aren't reliable. Tragic."

"They could have been useful," he grumbled back.

He could practically hear Lindsay's grin. "Uh-huh."

"Have you found the gate yet?" he asked, exasperated.

She let out a sigh. "Not a damn thing. Well. A few damn things. Some big fish. A lizard that looked kind of like a little crocodile. Jericho's ass – I walked into that at least fifty times before I sent him off on his own since he keeps stopping in front of me for no reason."

"I am trying not to fall in the water," Jericho's voice rumbled from behind Martin's other shoulder. He was never going to get used to that. "We are not all little floaty birds."

"Call me a duck one more time, you—"

Martin cut her off. "Ladies. Can we focus on the task at hand?"

Julia spoke up before the others could respond. "There is no sign of a gate on any of these walls. I've gone around the whole perimeter. Or as close as I can get."

Her voice seemed to be coming from the opposite side to the other two, Martin wondered if the "whispered" messages were directional.

Regardless, Julia's message was disappointing. If it had been Lindsay or Jericho, Martin would have discounted that as impatience, but Julia was nothing if not methodical. She would have made sure to look everywhere before delivering such doom-and-gloom news.

"Okay," he said. "Let's regroup and think of a new plan."

"I brought you along to do the thinking so I wouldn't have to," Lindsay snapped.

Even Julia couldn't keep herself from laughing at that particular piece of guild-master wit. Jericho's rolling guffaws were loud enough that Martin could hear them echoing across the swamp.

They met up by one of the Anurvan fishing holes. Martin didn't want to go back into the village proper without a plan of action in mind, otherwise Lindsay might just start swinging at anything that looked capable of fighting back.

Martin paced back and forth around the hole.

"The water level tops up constantly, but the cave never floods. So it is being drained somewhere. Water flows down, so it is probably draining to the next deep. Therefore, the gate has to be under the water somewhere."

Lindsay rolled her eyes. "Of course it's under the water, otherwise we would have seen it."

Martin tapped pensively on his protruding front teeth. "Do we know what the deepest point in the swamp is?"

There was a long pause before Julia politely asked, "How would we go about figuring that out?"

"I have no idea, but I'd bet good money that the gate will be at the lowest point to ensure the maximum drainage every time it's opened."

His pacing grew more frantic. The solution was right there. Right on the tip of his tongue. He just had to get his brain to spit it out.

"Up in Beachhead, they called this dungeon an ecosystem. Logic has been applied to every bit of the design."

Without even looking, he casually hopped over the leg Lindsay had extended to trip him up in his well-paced circle.

"They wouldn't want a level that was completely underwater – not so soon in the game – therefore there has to be maximum drainage every time someone does manage to find the Gate, since it probably isn't happening every day now that the bulk of the people racing to the lowest deep are past."

"You have a point?" Jericho groaned.

"I've got something better than a point." Martin pointed at Julia. "I've got a snake girl that can breathe underwater."

She clapped her hands. "That's right! Sythvan can totally do that!"

"So, all we need is for you to take a few quick dives in the places where we suspect the water is deepest."

Lindsay stared at him incredulously. "And, uh, where do we suspect the water is deepest?"

"Well, you don't go fishing in the shallows, Lindsay. You fish in the deepest water you can find, where you think the biggest fish are going to be." He flashed her a long-toothed grin. "The little frog guys are helping us out again, even if they're trying not to."

Julia was a little reluctant to get into the water, despite her usual positive attitude. Martin remembered his initial terror as he splashed and waded his way out into the swamp; the lurking primordial fear that there was something hungry down there.

He caught her by the arm before she slipped into the water.

"Listen, I've been in this water a lot, and, as Lindsay is so fond of reminding us, I'm snack sized. If there was anything down there, it would have taken a bite out of me already. You don't have to worry about a thing."

She pulled her arm free as gracefully as she could. "Thanks for trying, but it isn't that. I am just... not that strong of a swimmer."

"Well, that's all right. All we need you to do is sink. And you can breathe the water so... Yeah. You'll be fine."

Her eyes narrowed. "Thanks. I think?"

The Anurvan had disappeared seamlessly into the water, but Julia seemed to be devoted to doing the exact opposite. She splashed and flailed until eventually Lindsay crouched down and dunked her under the water. Julia hung there for a long moment, then one hand extended up through the surface, led by an upturned thumb.

Martin caught himself holding his breath while Julia was under the water, a weird instinct that he'd picked up from years of gaming when the visual display for oxygen was too often a distraction from the task at hand. He deliberately took a deep breath of the moist air, but his eyes never left the surface of the water.

Time seemed to stretch out as they waited for her to resurface. Every bubble and ripple became an omen. When she did finally pop up, they all jumped. Even Jericho. Which probably made the wait worth it.

Julia spat out a mouthful of water then gargled out, "Nothing but mud and weeds."

Lindsay grumbled, but Martin just held out a hand to the

lizard-woman. "No worries, there are plenty more fishing holes to try."

Patience had never been Lindsay's strong suit. Normally that burning impatience was the fire that kept the engine of the Iron Riot guild turning, but now Martin was starting to grow weary of it.

"Can't you just go shake one of your frog-boys until they tell us where it is?" she crowed.

"No." Martin took a calming breath. "They're still in hiding."

"Hiding, eh?" Jericho grunted.

"Yes. Hiding." It was difficult not to grit his teeth. "Because they're scared of you."

"So, they hide, probably in the last place we'd look?" Jericho asked. "Safest, deepest place under the water, yes?"

Martin opened and shut his mouth a few times before Lindsay let out a hoot.

"Not just a pretty face, are you, Jericho! Watch out Martin, you're going to get replaced if you can't keep up."

She was probably prodding at him for a good reason, to try and force him to rise to his potential or whatever, but at that moment, Martin really could have done without it.

"The Anurvan didn't appear until we got to their village. The gate is probably right underneath it. Damn."

Lindsay didn't waste any time, even once they'd made it back to the village. She started ripping through the huts, searching for anything resembling loot that the Anurvan might have left behind. Martin couldn't even muster the energy to argue with her. He eased Julia down into the water and gestured to the guild-sign emblazoned on her robe.

"If you run into trouble, you should be able to talk to us using that even if you are underwater. Just take a quick dive, see if the gate is there, then come back."

"All right, Dad." She flashed him a nervous smile, then she was gone.

Jericho sat down heavily on what was probably meant to be a

table for the Anurvan. The root structure creaked under his bulk. "She'll be fine. You worry too much. It is only a game."

"Spoken like someone who hasn't drowned yet."

Jericho let out a little hiss. "Unpleasant. Very unpleasant. But she breathes the water. No problems."

Julia's voice passed into his ears. It sounded echoey, as if coming from the bottom of a well.

"There are a lot of frog people down here. The roots go all the way down, and they are hiding in amongst them, and I can't count them because they keep moving, but there are a lot."

"They're pretty peaceful." Martin smiled, hoping that his calm would travel down to her. "I wouldn't worry about it too much."

There was an edge of tension in Julia's voice, something Martin really wasn't used to hearing from her.

"They don't look very peaceful. They've got a lot of spears."

He slipped his hand off the guild-crest.

"Lindsay, get out here! We might need to get down there fast!"

She came skidding out of the farthest hut with her arms full of fish-skins and what looked like bamboo. "Do we finally get to kill some froggos?"

"No," Martin barked. "Yes. Maybe."

Julia's voice bubbled back through to them.

"The gate is here. I can see it down at the bottom. Just the same as the last one."

Jericho slapped his own chest with a meaty thump. "What about the frogs?" he asked.

"They're moving into my path," Julia muttered. " I... I'm going to come back up."

Martin drew his sword with a snarl. "Don't move. We're coming to you."

Lindsay was already at his elbow before he made it more than a step towards the edge.

"Hey dude, is this a good idea?"

"They might not attack if they see me. Either way, we need to get through them. Get the key ready. If we can get past them without fighting, we can get through to the next deep. Even if we still have to fight them after that, it won't be on their turf."

Jericho shrugged. "Makes sense."

"Thanks for the vote of confidence." Martin rolled his eyes. "Let's go."

Water swept over him in a lukewarm rush and it brought all the memories of his drowning flooding back. Time was their enemy. Time was always their enemy in Strata, with every moment they wasted giving their competitors an ever-greater advantage, but down here in the swamp the hostility of the place was amplified threefold.

The water was thick with silt and debris, and only the faint glow of Julia when he brushed his paw over the guild crest convinced him that he was still headed in the right direction.

The impact when Lindsay and Jericho dove in behind him had echoed down to him, but there was no way to see them down here in the swamp water.

Trusting other people did not come naturally to him, and trusting in the competence of other people came even harder, but out of all the people in the world, these three were the ones he knew he could rely on. Jericho and Lindsay would be there for him. They would. He was certain.

Murk and blindness may have interfered with seeing enemies or allies in the water, but his Swamproot Sight laid out his course. The roots of the village stretched down in a great corkscrew spiral to anchor the whole village and they were as clear as day. Clearer than anything else thanks to the thick stew of muck and mulch all around him. All he had to do was swim as hard as he could and let the shape of the trees guide him down.

Gasping would have been a very uncomfortable experience, but Martin still let out a mouthful of startled bubbles when an Anurvan darted across his field of vision, as graceful in the water as they were clumsy on land, gone in an instant.

He was almost as startled when Julia loomed up out of the brown silt ahead of him. She was surrounded by a cyclone of particulate filth, churned up as she spun on the spot trying to keep her eyes on the frog-men as they darted back and forth.

If he could feel pain, Martin suspected that his lungs would be burning by now, and a quick blink confirmed his suspicions. Between the hard swim and holding his breath, his stamina had depleted to just a few points. If he didn't get to air in the next few seconds his health bar would be gobbled up next, then death would follow soon after.

There would be no return to the surface. Either they made it through the gate or they all drowned here in the swamp, in the dark.

He caught Julia's hand and pointed down when her wild eyes finally focused on him. She nodded, but she still wasn't paying attention to him. He could feel the water churn behind him as another Anurvan shot by.

No wonder they got slaughtered all the time, if this was how they harassed every adventurer trying to get through the gate.

What could be so important about keeping Martin out? They'd already declared themselves as allies; why would they keep working against him like this? What could they hope to gain? Unless their personalities were only surface deep, just waiting for their primary programming as defenders of the dungeon to kick back in.

Shimmering in the ever-deepening darkness, Martin could see the Deep Gate beneath them. It looked just the same as the one before, albeit a little bit smeared with swamp mud. They landed on the top of the closed iris of its surface and started to search by touch for the keyhole.

"It's here! I've found it!" Julia called out through the guild crest, just as Jericho descended out of the dark like a falling star, with the tiny, immobile body of Lindsay cradled in one of his arms.

Her knave's stamina must have burned out faster than the

more martial classes. Now that they were close enough, the alerts started appearing in Martin's field of vision.

[Tesra suffers 1 water environmental damage]
[Tesra suffers 1 water environmental damage]
[Tesra suffers 1 water environmental damage]

His own drowning notifications began to flood the screen not a moment later, but he ignored them entirely, prying apart Lindsay's cramped fingers to get the key. It was in the lock and turning when Speckles hit him.

The impact wasn't hard enough to do damage in itself, but in the untethered world down here beneath the water it was enough to send him drifting away.

There weren't many creatures in Strata that a Murovan could expect to wrestle with and win, but these little frogs seemed to weigh nothing at all. Martin tossed Speckles away and swam back towards the gate. The key was still in the lock, glinting behind the flurry of notifications.

[Skaife suffers 1 water environmental damage]
[Tesra suffers 1 water environmental damage]
[Skaife suffers 1 water environmental damage]
[Tesra suffers 1 water environmental damage]

Julia was wrestling off a frog-man of her own, and Jericho swept an entire crowd of them away with just one of his massive arms. Martin's fingertips brushed the key for an instant before Speckles jerked him back by his ankle.

This time, Martin wasn't taking any chances. He took hold of Speckles' rubbery wrist and dragged him forward until they were eye to eye, then flashed a furious grin, feeling the water flooding into his mouth between his jagged teeth. Apparently, he was getting his guide after all.

With one hand locked around the frog's wrist and the other on the key, Martin twisted both.

The gate opened like a drain, dragging every one of them off their feet into the roiling furious white-waters that suddenly surrounded them. He bounced against Jericho, then Julia, then into the silvery rim of the gate. A second later, he was falling through the open air, tumbling down into the pitch darkness. Again.

NINETEEN

The Great Divide

A flat surface caught Martin before he could fall any real distance. Speckles landed with a splat beside him. It shouldn't have been surprising, but somehow it was.

The water from above them was pouring down in a tempestuous waterfall, smashing into the stone beneath them and around on either side.

They were on a rock shelf, protruding from a great waterfall. Beneath was an open expanse, so deep that it turned Martin's stomach just looking down.

Even with his enhanced low-light vision, he couldn't see even a hint of the plunge pool at the bottom. Just the wall of water and the scattered rock sheets jutting out, making a haphazard staircase down into the gloomy depths.

But to his delight, he did see the others on the next rock shelf below. Jericho lay cradling Lindsay and Julia on the spit of protruding rock, reeking of wet dog and glowering up at Martin with unabashed fury in his eyes. He growled, sarcasm dripping from his words.

"'They are friendly', he said. 'Do not hurt them', he said. How friendly were they when they tried to drown all four of us?"

Martin ignored Jericho and cast a glance up to the circle carved into the roof above them, barely visible through the mists and spray that the falling water was conjuring up.

"Hardly surprising they didn't want us to drain their swamp. They do have to live there."

Jericho growled his disagreement. "Slimy runts. Next time I see one, I will –"

Speckles' head popped up over the edge of the stone beside Martin's and the Anurvan blinked down at Jericho with his huge golden eyes. Martin wondered if the patented pathetic puppy stare was an actual racial ability for the Anurvan or if it was a unique talent held by Speckles alone.

"We no want you drain home," Speckled explained. "We no want come back down here. Bad down here."

Lindsay coughed up a lungful of water onto Jericho's chest, eliciting another grumble from him.

"Ugh."

She scrambled to her feet, still hacking and coughing. Meanwhile, Julia seemed quite content to just lie still, nestled under Jericho's arm. Martin filed that little detail away for later contemplation.

From his current step, it might be feasible to jump back up and grab the silver rim of the gate. Now that the waterfall had formed properly, it left the gate more or less clear as it drew the remaining water down from a source above them.

There was no sign of a keyhole on this side of the gate, but Martin seemed to remember someone saying they were a one-way deal. You could go up all you wanted; going down was the tricky bit.

Grabbing Speckles by the back of his string vest of bones, Martin leapt down onto the next platform just as Lindsay's staggering brought her to the edge of the stone shelf.

"Wow. The next step is a big one."

Julia and Jericho chuckled, one high-pitched, the other so

deep Martin could feel it vibrating up through the soles of his feet. Without even thinking about it, he reached out and pulled Lindsay back from the precipice.

The air around them seemed to thicken, and Martin felt like he was moving in slow motion as he turned towards a grinding sound from behind them.

Looming just behind Speckles, the hooded figure of a Master stretched up like a shadow. Its empty sleeves were upstretched and a dance of what looked like code flickered between them in a shimmer of light.

It could have been any one of the Masters in those empty robes, but when the hollowed cowl turned towards him, there was a distinct impression of amused malevolence that told Martin it was the one he had already met.

With a twist of its arms, the step that led back to the last deep slid seamlessly into the waterfall and out of sight.

"You didn't need to backtrack, did you? Someone special like you won't need extra supplies. I'm sure you can make it to the next settlement on Deep Eleven without needing any rest at the speed you are flying through my dungeon."

Martin had only just opened his mouth to answer when, just as suddenly as they had appeared, the Master was gone.

For a long moment Martin couldn't believe the pettiness of it. There was a whole game filled with thousands of players for this Master to persecute, and here they were harassing him because he wouldn't talk about mushrooms.

How many times had this happened? How many times were they on the right track, when parts of the game were shuffled around to spite them? Was this why they kept encountering monsters from the lower deeps?

He opened his mouth to complain about the unfairness of it all but then he stopped himself. The Master could still be here, invisible, untouchable and watching.

Martin had no intention of letting anyone know that they were getting to him. Not now, not ever. Particularly when nobody else seemed to have noticed that anything was happening, or that anything had changed. There were layers to Strata that they couldn't see or touch. The Masters could manipulate everything down here, even time and perception. They were like gods, and he had one of the gods angry at him. Great.

With some effort, he unclenched his jaw and spoke.

"It looks like it's a staircase all the way down. As long as we take it slow and steady, we should be fine."

Lindsay rolled her eyes. "All right, bossy. Boring and boring. We've got it. You two snuggle-bugs ready to move or are you staying there all night?"

Martin would not have expected snake people to be capable of blushing, but Julia managed a good approximation by rustling the scales on her cheeks. "Ready when you are."

Martin turned to Speckles.

"I think you should come with us. There's no way you can get back up to the Second Deep right now, and you'll be a sitting duck for any monster that comes along if you stay here."

A thought occurred to him.

"Plus, more of your people probably fell through too. You should come with us to meet up with them. We'll keep you all safe until you can get home."

Speckles blinked at him. "Words less."

Martin tried to pare it back to as simple as he could manage while still trying to be convincing. "We keep you safe. Come with us. Find other Anurvan."

Speckles tilted his head from side to side, pondering the proposition, but sadly he wasn't the only one with opinions.

"That pond scum tried to kill us. I don't trust him," Jericho growled.

Martin didn't let his welcoming smile slip, so his reply was through near-gritted teeth.

"The Anurvan came up through every Deep Gate in the whole of Strata to get here. They know the way that we need to be going. Or would you rather spend half our time wandering back and forth through an endless maze of tunnels?"

Lucky for him, Lindsay made the decision for them. She stepped up and patted Speckles on the back, then surreptitiously wiped the frog-slime off her hand onto her trousers. "Welcome to the team. You can be our sidekick. Our minion? Mascot. You can be the Iron Riot mascot."

"Me no want go down." Speckles still seemed to be thinking. "But me can not go up."

"You hurt us. Nearly killed us. If you help, we'll all forgive you." Martin leaned in closer and cast a meaningful look across at Jericho. "If you don't help us… he might not."

Speckles may not have understood every word, but he certainly caught Martin's meaning. His gaze darted from Jericho to Martin, his expression from fear to betrayal. "Me come with you. Me show you the way."

Martin almost hugged the stupid little frog-man. There was no way that the situation was going to go well if Speckles had answered any other way.

"Thank you."

Lindsay clapped her hands, startling them all. "All right then, you all ready to make like big wheels of cheese and get rolling?"

Martin started to agree then had to pause and ask, "Why cheese, though?"

Jericho sniffed the air. "I think I know why cheese."

There was certainly an aroma hanging around them after being dragged through the swamp water, but Martin would have placed it closer to the nasty juice that collected at the bottom of garbage bags rather than cheese. Speckles was oblivious; Martin didn't even know if the Anurvan had noses.

Their progress down the steps began after Julia had done the rounds, topping off their health and making sure that their near-brush with drowning hadn't done any permanent harm, but it took only a few moments before arguments started to break out.

[ANNOUNCEMENT: *Wyld Stallynz* have defeated **Carnifex, Tenth Archduke of Strata**]

"Will you hurry it up? Some of us have places to be," Lindsay crowed back over her shoulder.

Jericho was trailing behind the others, his lower agility score and sheer mass slowing him down. Each time he jumped to the next platform he had to take a moment to recover, and after two or three of those jumps Julia insisted on using some feeble flickering spell to top up the health he had lost from fall damage.

Lindsay was already leaping ahead of them. With her hollow bones, she could dance down the layers with barely any effort at all. Martin realized he had to intervene.

"We need to stay together. We don't know what's down here."

"Stay together? Look who's talking, Mister 'explore the whole deep without you,'" Lindsay snapped back.

"I was scouting ahead, and I died for my trouble. We're all in a hurry to get to the bottom. We all want to win this thing, but if you are reckless and get killed then we are going to be waiting around for you to respawn. Slow and steady..."

Lindsay wasn't having it.

"Slow and steady is boring! No wonder you're single. You probably think a hot date involves a library card. Come on, man! Live a little. Take some chances. Jump down some steps. It isn't going to kill you!"

Something burst from the waterfall, colossal pincers clamping around Lindsay and lifting her into the air.

There hadn't even been a shadow. One moment there was a solid wall of water, the next a giant crab had scuttled through.

[Tesra suffers 21 bludgeoning damage]

Martin was already leaping down before he had the time to

think. He could hear the soft litany of, "No, no, no," but it took him a moment to realize that it was his voice.

The monster withdrew into the waterfall, with Lindsay bellowing insults from within its grasp. The crab, which the tooltip helpfully named *Armored Brachyura,* had secured its meal.

The wall of water was solid again by the time Martin got to it, but he had no time to come up with a clever solution. He flung himself forward.

There was no experience in his real life that he could compare to feeling the full weight of the waterfall hammering down on him. It crushed him down to his knees before he'd even moved, bowing his head with the constant torrent of water. Another damage notification popped up for Lindsay, then another, but he couldn't look up to see them.

He had to crawl to move forward, and every inch he gained felt like a mile. Once his forequarters were through the waterfall, he had to drag his tail-end through, claws scrabbling over the slick rock. He only hoped that Jericho had the good sense to shelter Julia and Speckles if they followed.

Solid stone lay on either side of Martin; the waterfall was running directly down the side of this cavern, and only this eroded cave gave the Brachyura someplace to stage its ambushes. There was nowhere for it to hide, no cunningly constructed tunnels for it to scamper off into, just this little chip out of the cliff-face.

It loomed in front of Martin, so big that it filled his vision. He could hardly make sense of it until he realized it was facing away. He swung at its backside, less concerned with damage and more interested in turning it around so that he could check on Lindsay.

[Armored Brachyura suffers 1 slashing damage]

With shell that thick, it certainly lived up to its name. The blow made a hollow noise like a hammer on stone. Still, it must have been enough to garner its attention.

The Brachyura swiveled on the spot to face him. Half of Lindsay's body lay in one of its blood-slicked claws, and the other half dangled out of its chattering wood-chipper of a mouth.

There hadn't been a notification. If she had died, why hadn't the game told him?

That was when he realized the awful truth. Lindsay reached out to him, blood pouring out of her beak as she tried to speak. She still had health left. The game wouldn't let her die.

Martin shuddered. Whatever words of comfort he might have mustered died in his throat as he saw a tangle of her intestines roll out of the clean snip and splatter onto the floor. Bile bit at the back of his throat. He let out a hoarse roar, summoned a *Celestial Strike*, and charged.

There was no question of missing, not with a target so massive trapped in so confined a space, and Martin didn't hesitate to pick a specific target.

[Armored Brachyura suffers 8 light damage]
[Armored Brachyura suffers 8 slashing damage]

His glowing sword slipped through the chitinous hide as if it wasn't there at all, and it came out trailing thick yellow ichor, like the whole thing was an infected wound.

The Brachyura swung for him with its empty claw, but he was ready and ducked.

[MISS]

Lindsay still hadn't died.

[Tesra suffers 3 bleeding damage]
[Tesra suffers 2 bleeding damage]
[Tesra suffers 3 bleeding damage]

There was so much blood he could hardly believe a little bird-woman could hold it all. Could Julia even heal a wound like this? Was a level four hierophant's magic up to the task, or would it be kinder to put Lindsay out of her misery?

He wished he had more time to make these decisions. Wished that the others had shared the information that he needed to choose.

Seconds ticked by, with the Brachyura warily trying to circle around him, its awful little black bug eyes fixed on his sword. It understood pain. That was good. He could use that. If it went on cowering for long enough, his *Celestial Strike* would be off cooldown and he could actually attack again. The obsidian sang as he dragged it over his bracers, and the Brachyura shuddered at the sound. More fear. He needed more fear.

Jericho roared as he burst through the water and took in the horrific scene before him. That was when the Brachyura lashed out. Nothing so huge had any right to move so quickly. It snapped its empty claw a hair's breadth from Jericho, driving him back into the hammering waterfall. Then with a flick of the other claw, it launched the upper half of Lindsay at Martin, bowling him off his feet.

[Skaife suffers 22 bludgeoning damage]
[Tesra suffers 22 bludgeoning damage]
[Tesra has died]

He cradled her broken corpse in his arms for only a moment before he rose to his feet. Martin had always been angry, for as long as he could remember. Everything in the world had made him feel that way, but he had never felt the deep blind fury that now guided his movements.

As it turned to strike at him again, he dove forward under the sweep of the Brachyura's claws.

[MISS]

Suddenly his whole perspective shifted. He was sheltered beneath the armored hulk of the Brachyura, but it couldn't reach him. It spun on the spot above him, the sound of its legs a deafening chatter all around, but no matter how it tried to crush him, he moved with it. Murovan were so short that even when it tried to slam its body down on him, all he had to do was crouch to avoid the impact. He took the brief moment of peace to restore some health with a *Healing Touch*.

[Skaife recovered 15 health]

Jericho returned to the fight with another deafening roar, hammering at the massive crab's turned back with a dazzling strobe of lights.

[Armored Brachyura suffers 6 light damage]
[Armored Brachyura suffers 5 light damage]
[Armored Brachyura suffers 6 light damage]

Martin touched his guild crest and bellowed to be heard over the roar of water and the grinding and chattering of the beast.

"Get it outside!"

Jericho's assault paused for only a moment, but that was all the time that the monster needed to rush him. Martin had to run along underneath it to avoid losing his position. Jericho took one look at the oncoming crab and dove back out through the water.

As they passed under the waterfall, the crab served as an umbrella for Martin, holding the weight of the water off his back. Jericho was sprawled on the ground in the crab's path, but the mist of the waterfall was thick enough that it missed him. Martin grabbed him by the wrist and tried to jerk him to his feet, only to remember that he was a tiny rat-man and Jericho was gigantic.

The three of them took up all of the space on the slate

outcropping, with barely a foot between the rear end of the Brachyura and the torrential downpour. It was all Martin needed.

Celestial Strike reignited his sword and this time he swung it with very clear purpose. He severed one of the crab's rear legs at the weak knee joint level with his head.

[Armored Brachyura suffers 9 light damage]
[Armored Brachyura suffers 9 slashing damage]

The massive beast spun on the spot once more, jerking its wounded hindquarters away from the source of this new pain. The chitinous nub of its leg toppled to the ground in a rush of yellow ichor.

Mustering his courage, Martin stepped out from underneath the Brachyura, right beneath its grinding mouth. The black eyes of the beast were on stalks, and they both swiveled to fix their gaze on him.

It let out a chittering roar and reared up, ready to smash him to paste with those ridiculously oversized claws. With a matching roar of his own, Martin cast *Rebuke*.

The Armored Brachyura's front lifted into the air, not just driven away from Martin by the spell, but by the strength of its rearing legs and the upheld claws.

Even that wouldn't have been enough to topple the crab, if it had its full complement of legs. As it was, its remaining rear legs scrabbled for balance.

For one awful moment it hung in equilibrium, ready to crash back down and kill Martin and Jericho both, but then gravity took over. Its rear legs, scrabbling back, found only the open air of the cavern behind it. It let out a squeal like escaping steam as it fell out of sight.

Martin counted aloud.

"One. Two. Three. Four. Five. Six. Seven. Eight. Nine. Ten. Eleven. Twelve. Thirteen. Fourteen. Fifteen. Sixteen—"

Julia and Speckles peered over the next step up, staring down in blatant confusion. Jericho lay on his back, staring up at the distant roof of the cave and breathing hard.

But Martin had no time to rest. He stared out over the edge, down into the darkness. Hoping to catch any glimpse of the crab as it tumbled to its well-deserved death.

"—Forty. Forty-one. Forty-two. Forty-three. Forty-four—"

Armored Brachyura has died.
Skaife gains 1020 experience.
[LEVEL UP]

He did the math in his head. Forty-four seconds until it hit the ground, falling at an average of about 30ft per second. One thousand, three hundred and twenty feet. A quarter of a mile.

"The bottom of the cave is a quarter of a mile down."

There were probably some more complex calculations that he could do involving the angle and width of the steps that they were taking, but he couldn't quite muster the energy. Not while he was still slick with Lindsay's blood. He padded over to the waterfall and rinsed the worst of it off before turning back to the group.

Jericho and Julia watched him with pity, while Speckles was gawking at him in open admiration.

"You save again! You fight bad! You fight bad real good!"

He tried to smile, but it just wouldn't come. "All right, folks, just hang on here for a minute. I'll log out, talk to Lindsay and find out her respawn schedule."

Julia gave him a tight-lipped smile, and Jericho looked like he was about to say something when Martin blinked to the menu screen and abruptly logged out.

The visual effect of falling upwards into the light was slightly ruined by his apartment being pitch black when he emerged back into the real world. If he were more sensible and less practical, he probably would have switched the lights on before he lay down to play, but the sad truth of the matter was, his apartment was too small and too devoid of furniture to provide any sort of obstacle course when he roamed around it in the dark.

It was only when he tried to move that he realized just how sore he was. He had to rub at his legs before the beginnings of a cramp started to fade away. That made no sense. He was lying perfectly still and relaxed; why would his muscles be tense?

The NIH clearly paralyzed motor function when you were in the game, otherwise he would have been roaming around all over the place, smacking into walls and, most likely, unplugging the headset from the computer. The only explanation was that the NIH was doing something while he was playing. Working the muscles of his resting body so that they didn't atrophy, perhaps?

Another clue, another hint that the NIH had in fact started life as a medical device, just as Martin had suspected. No game developer gave a damn about the physical fitness of their players; if anything, it was in a game company's best interests to keep players unfit so that they wouldn't get distracted by sports, dating or the outside world.

Martin leapt off that train of thought before it stopped at Depression Central and went back to the task at hand. He snatched up his phone, which was down to 3% charge, and sent a message to Lindsay.

Not the practical message that the rest of the guild might have expected of him.

Hey, are you all right?

Drowning had been horrific. Even without pain, people weren't meant to survive having those sensations. They weren't meant to get lost in a memory and start gasping for air.

He couldn't even imagine what it had felt like to be split in two. He would never ask her for details, even though he was incredibly curious. He didn't want to make her relive it.

The experience had clearly shaken Lindsay. All of her usual energy was missing when she messaged him back.

30 minutes until rebirth. Taking a snack break.

So, the respawn timers were likely tied to the number of times you had died, not how far you were into the dungeon. That was good to know, and it also meant that Martin would be a little more reluctant about spending their lives for a short-term victory.

Every death would increase the delay, and if it went on doubling then he could end up locked out of the game for a day or more, plus however long it took them to get back down through the deeps. Even if they didn't have to fight for the Deep Key each time, there were still enemies about. They were only three deeps in; they had to start being more careful.

He sent a message back.

Sorry that happened. Small consolation: we avenged you. Hard.

After that, he waited for a long minute, hoping for a laugh or a vengeful cat picture, but nothing was forthcoming. The NIH had never come off his head throughout the whole exercise, and now all it took was a few keystrokes before he was sinking back into the blissful trance of Strata.

The others startled at his arrival, even though the pillar of light was a pretty clear announcement that somebody was logging in. Martin opened his mouth to speak and was immediately interrupted by the thump of Speckles tackling him around the waist and knocking both of them over.

"You come back!"

He clambered back to his feet with a groan, shoving the little frog-man off him. "She'll be back in half an hour. Call it another half hour to get through the first two deeps. I suggest we wait here for her."

The other two looked pretty imposing, looming at the far end of the step. Martin could understand why Speckles was getting nervous if this was the treatment he'd been receiving while Martin was away. Jericho just shook his head, but Julia was a little more talkative.

"I think she would probably want us to press on... I mean... we want to keep on going."

Martin didn't budge. "You saw what happens when we rush ahead."

"We will move together. We will work together. As we always do. That is not in question," Jericho rumbled. "But we are losing time. Other guilds, they are already fighting Archdukes. It does not matter if Lindsay is with the guild, all that matters is pressing on."

Julia chimed in again. "If we clear the way for her, she can join us much faster, just like you said about the upper levels."

"I don't want to just abandon her."

She had been through too much already. Martin was half tempted to head back up to Beachhead and meet her on arrival, so that she wouldn't have to spend any more time alone.

He still wasn't certain how the instancing in the game worked, although everyone seemed to be seeing the same thing. Maybe for other people the swamp above was still intact? But for Iron Riot, the swamp above would be drained, and there was no telling what fresh horrors had been hidden beneath its surface.

"Why are you pretending that you care? Because you want a balanced party?" Jericho scoffed. "Because you want to minimize risk? This is a race. Every time we wait, the other guilds get further ahead of us. Slow is the risk."

[ANNOUNCEMENT: *OOC Crew* have defeated **Carnifex, Tenth Archduke of Strata**]

Martin bit back his eviscerating reply. This was the face that he'd presented to them, the cold clinical side of his personality.

He couldn't turn around and be angry that they expected him to behave like a robot now.

Logic was unassailable, and he'd wielded it like a weapon throughout the years to prevent any emotional argument from holding sway in the guild. It wasn't surprising that they ascribed him purely tactical motives when he had refused to let any of them see him as anything more or less than a calculating machine.

He forced his jaw to relax.

"We owe it to her to wait. She deserves at least that much."

Sweet, quiet Julia was watching him with a weirdly assessing stare. Like she could see right into his head.

"We don't owe her anything. We like her. She's our friend. But that doesn't mean everything grinds to a halt when she isn't around. Think about it. What do you think you owe her, exactly?"

Everything. He owed her everything. She'd brought him into the guild, the closest thing that he'd ever found to a friendship with others.

Then she'd brought him into Strata, which felt more like home than any of the dozen crappy rented apartments he'd lived in since his mother kicked him out of the house. She had given him a family, she had given him friendship, she had given him this whole world that he vastly preferred to the real one where his entire life felt meaningless.

She'd done all of that for him, and now he couldn't even tell Jericho and Julia any part of it, because he was too embarrassed. Because the idea of admitting that Lindsay had bought him the game and brought him along like a pet or a servant was too shameful.

The hours Martin spent playing these games were the only time that he didn't hate his life and himself, but now that self-loathing was bubbling in his chest.

It was like he was watching the whole thing from a distance. He heard himself say: "Fine. Let's go."

They did not discuss it again, instead beginning the arduous task of making the jumps down the platforms.

Every step took them further away from Lindsay. Away from where he knew in his gut he should remain.

Deeper and deeper into the dark.

TWENTY

The Waters of Strata

Speckles turned out to be the most competent of them all. He had a frog's natural propensity for jumping and only his absolute terror at his surroundings prevented him from bouncing down the whole waterfall-ladder ahead of the group and reaching the bottom within minutes.

Jericho still took the longest, taking a while to wind up and to land on each great platform, but he at least had the decency to jump first in case another ambush predator was lurking behind the waterfall.

It would have been almost too easy for Martin to dwell on his inability to speak out, but he forced himself to keep his eyes on the figurative prize, and to do all he could to make Lindsay's descent easier.

Moving as a group wasn't guaranteed to keep them safe but it was likely to ward off any potential ambushers. That was why he began to linger at the back of the group, making sure everyone else had jumped first before he followed after.

It wasn't that he was using himself as bait – he wasn't suicidal, even if he was having one of his darker moods. And Lindsay's death was delay enough; his own would have stretched out to two hours if they kept escalating at the same rate.

But he had to make sure there were no predators lying in wait for solo travelers.

He was ready for another attack – primed to leap to safety if there was any sign of movement behind the wall of water – but there was none. Either the crab at the top had been a unique enemy or the rest were sensibly remaining hidden rather than trying to pick off stragglers in a larger group.

If it was the former, then Martin would be happy, but if it was the latter then Lindsay was going to be easy prey for every one of them, and the guild was setting her up for another gruesome death.

Just as he didn't want to dwell on his own cowardice, Martin couldn't stomach that thought either. It wouldn't be practical to try and push through the waterfall at every protrusion on the off chance that there was a cave back there. It had been luck as much as favorable placement that had stopped the water pressure from bowling them off these steps before, and even if that risk wasn't there, he didn't think the others would let him slow their progress to a crawl just on the chance that he might be able to lead them into another fight they likely couldn't win.

When they reached one side of the waterfall, the craggy stone of the wall lay exposed ahead of them. Martin gave serious consideration to trying to climb down the wall itself. At first, he thought it was better than having to deal with the stress of a potential ambush lurking just out of sight. But, if he was honest, there were probably giant murderous beetles, land eels or something equally ridiculous hiding in the gaps between the rocks, just waiting for them to choose that path instead.

The whole dungeon was a death-trap and their only mistake so far had been underestimating it. So they continued on in their leapfrogging down, wending back the other way. By Martin's vague estimates, they were almost halfway down before the turnaround, but he could have been wrong.

It didn't take long before his vigilance began to slip. There were so many stairs. It was taking so long. He went a couple without even considering the possibility of another ambush. Then, in a turnabout of anxiety, he realized they were likely reaching a prime spot for a second attack.

He was hyper-aware during the next two jumps, twitching every time the water made so much as an unexpected splash. Then they were down another step, and another, and still the next ambush didn't come. Still the hammer didn't fall. It was torturous, waiting for the monster to pop out. Ingeniously designed to drive a player mad.

After the first attack, he would never be able to shake off the suspicion that every other step could be equally lethal, and that was a trap in itself, designed to heighten the tension of what could otherwise be a boring bit of platforming.

Low-light vision came to the rescue once again, giving him the first glimpse of the cavern floor beneath them. The waterfall was flowing into a huge circular pool at the center of an extensive cavern.

But where Martin had been expecting more of the rough rock that had typified the steps and walls on either side, the material surrounding the pool and beyond was polished and smooth. He couldn't be certain of the color or details at this distance, but he suspected that it was something very like marble.

Classical columns ringed the water, and further in, he thought he could make out more of them, along with worked stone archways. Like they were finally descending into some sort of civilization, or at least the ruins of one.

The second surprise came only a few moments later when he tried to jump to the next platform and nearly mistimed his leap, a movement at the periphery of his vision distracting him.

There was something living and moving around down there. He hit the next step with his shins and tumbled end over end, nearly bowling over Julia and Speckles for his trouble.

[Skaife suffers 2 bludgeoning environmental damage]
[Adriel suffers 1 bludgeoning environmental damage]

[Anurvan Scout suffers 1 bludgeoning environmental damage]

"Be careful," Jericho growled, extricating himself from Julia's armpit.

But Martin wasn't paying the blindest bit of attention. He crawled out of the tangle of limbs and stuck his head out over the edge of the platform.

For a moment Martin thought it was the remnants of the Anurvan population that had somehow survived the quarter-mile fall, before dismissing the idea as a ridiculous fantasy. Even if it were possible, the Anurvan didn't make fires, and they weren't half as tall as some of the figures he saw moving around.

He stared for a long moment, desperately trying to work out what kind of monster they were going to face next, before he realized that they weren't monsters at all.

"There are players down there. A few groups of them. It looks like they've set up a makeshift camp. I guess there isn't another town for a while."

Jericho nodded. "Good. We can trade for food, or potions or whatever."

Martin's experiences of the other players in Strata so far hadn't been all trading and camaraderie, but he supposed that if you were a nine-foot-tall wolf-man then you got special treatment. At least compared to how rat-men were treated. Still, he had the protection of the group now, and the other players didn't have the example of the NPCs treating the Murovan like crap. Maybe things would be better.

They made the final few jumps without incident, and they were almost down to the floor before Martin froze.

"Wait. Wait. What about Speckles?"

Jericho rolled his eyes. "Who is this Speckles?"

Julia was looking at him curiously again, as if he were an unusual fungus instead of a person, but at least she didn't say anything.

Martin grumbled. "He is a frog man, about my height, covered in speckles."

"You named your pet," Jericho rumbled. "How cute."

Martin gave up trying to reason with the humans and turned his attention to the far more sensible frog-person.

"Do you think you can hide? There are other people here. Maybe bad."

Speckles didn't have to be asked twice. He took a quick look around then stepped right under the waterfall, where he vanished instantly in the torrents of water. Simple but effective, assuming a giant crab monster wasn't hiding behind the waterfall, just waiting for a tasty little froggy snack.

"Wait here," Martin said. "We'll get you before we leave."

Silence.

Once again, Martin put it out of his mind and moved forward. There was no point in worrying about what might be when he had enough problems right in front of him just waiting to be navigated.

The Armored Brachyura lay close to the waterfall, the spray doing a poor job of washing away the yellow pus that was seeping from its shattered carapace.

Martin's hand drifted down to his sword as he approached it. He knew it was dead, he'd read the notification himself, but that didn't mean he didn't want to kill it all over again for what it had done.

Armored Brachyura
This monstrous crustacean is a ravenous ambush predator. Brachyura are often employed by more intelligent monsters of the dungeon as guard-dogs.
Loot: *43 silver, Curse-Scarred Kukri, Blue Blood Crystals.*
Requires Blacksmithing *to Harvest: Heavy Chitin Plates.*

The kukri dagger was knave-only, and it would be a good upgrade for Lindsay when she got back – small recompense for the trauma she'd endured, but something at least. When he looked at it on his inventory screen an option appeared to transfer it to another player's inventory directly. That was a handy way to keep everyone in the best gear if they had to split up. He sent the kukri to Lindsay.

The Crystals were strange, presumably something to do with the crafting systems that Martin still hadn't had the chance to touch. None of this was worth the price they'd had to pay for it. Martin gave the crab one last kick for good measure, then wandered back to the group.

The camp was a fair distance away from the waterfall, likely so as to avoid falling players, rocks, or giant crabs. Probably sensible.

Upon arrival, Martin saw it was an all-Sythvan party, which wouldn't have even occurred to him to try. A guild named *Snakes In Your Boots*.

He supposed Strata had been online for long enough now that people could have restarted the whole process with new characters designed to suit the challenges ahead. Presumably a lot more water, if the Sythvan were the race of choice.

He might have been tempted himself if he thought that he'd taken a misstep when building his character. As it was, he still wasn't convinced that exorcist wasn't the best pick overall, despite it being a poor fit for the usual three-pronged party structure of tank, damage and healer.

More importantly, he wasn't convinced that he'd committed so far in any one direction in his build yet that he couldn't recover. Besides, nobody was past the 50th deep yet. No matter how much water this group knew they were going to find in the next few levels, it would almost inevitably be balanced out by dry areas in the deeps they hadn't reached yet.

The one Master that Martin had met seemed to be a raging power-mad asshole, but judging from the quality and depth of the game Martin still found himself trusting that the Masters as a group would design a balanced experience overall. Besides, competence and nicety didn't always go hand in hand. He was living proof of that.

Jericho strode up to the closest campfire and woofed out a loud greeting that made half of the gathered guild flinch.

"How is your run going?"

The nearest Sythvan, a knight called Cobranan, waved to them half-heartedly as they approached. "Not bad so far. What about yourselves?"

If Lindsay were there, she would have been gushing with details of their adventures so far, telling Cobranan every secret that Martin was intent on keeping; exploding mushrooms, roaming monsters, NPCs disguised as monsters and their solution to the problem of the Morasses.

Instead, Martin only had to contend with Jericho, who for all his loudness was normally as communicative as a brick wall. Julia had the sense to keep to herself too, although it was out of respect for Martin's plans rather than any of the antisocial habits the rest of them seemed to cultivate.

The chatter went on, with Martin paying only a little attention as tales were traded and Jericho's rumbling laughter provided percussion. He closed his eyes to a reminder.

[LEVEL UP]

Skaife *Murovan Exorcist*
Strength: 9 Agility: 8
Endurance: 9 Willpower: 7
LEVEL 5

You have 3 points to assign.

It was nice to have committed to a development path; it made life much easier. At least for these few moments there was no indecision to contend with.

*Strength: **12** Agility: 8*
Endurance: 9 Willpower: 7
Health: 45 Stamina: 58

You may select 1 new ability.

Smite – Your next successful melee attack deals an additional 7 light damage.
[20-second cooldown]

Lay on Hands – Restores 100% of an ally's health. Reduces your stamina and stamina regeneration by 10% for 5 minutes.
[60-minute cooldown]

Rite of Passage – Unlocks any Gate without requiring the key.
[72-hour cooldown]

And just like that, the indecision was back again. Not about his ability selection this time – *Rite of Passage* remained by far the most valuable ability – but for his continuing strategy of dumping all his stat points into strength.

It didn't take a genius to work out that the damage *Smite* dealt was tied directly to a character's willpower score. 7 willpower; 7 damage.

Suddenly, willpower became a valuable stat all over again. It converted directly into extra damage, and unlike strength, it wasn't going to be tempered by the enemy's armor score.

Sure, he could only use *Smite* once every twenty seconds, but if he was using *Celestial Strike* every ten and *Trinity Strike* every thirty, it could fill in one of the long gaps in his rotation instead of normal hits.

More importantly, if it was part of the design trend for exorcist abilities it meant that there would be more direct conversion of willpower to damage in the later unlocks. Martin had suspected that the willpower-to-damage conversion abilities had been reserved for the martyrs and invokers; this changed his perspective.

Maybe the exorcist really was going to be a full jack of all trades. Perhaps next he'd unlock a ranged attack, or the ability to sneak, or damage absorption. It would make for a character class without much focus, but when all the bases for a group were already covered, surely having that flexibility to shore up weak spots was the greatest value that could be brought to the table.

He selected *Rite of Passage* for now. Then his eyes snapped open at the sound of his name.

"—this moron, he tried to befriend the little frog people. He even gave them names. Like pets."

Jericho really should have known better. Martin interjected before the fool said too much.

"Shame they turned out to be feral and attacked us in the end. I guess they were just cowards, rather than friendly," he said, as nonchalantly as he could.

The Sythvan invoker, Hespith, made an amused little hiss at that. "Did you think this was a monster ranch game? With cuddles as prizes?"

Martin didn't know how to fake bashful, so he shrugged. "I just thought it would be handy to have someone to carry our stuff."

Jericho laughed, and clapped him on the back so hard he nearly fell into the fire. "Always looking for short-cuts, this one."

Their knave was staring at Martin intently, tapping an elegant finger against the scales where lips would be on a human. "Iron Riot. Iron Riot. Haven't I heard that name before?"

Julia smiled. "We used to raid back in Dracolich. We had a few world firsts."

Hespith's attention snapped her way.

"Oh? So you're the stiff competition, are you? The ones to watch? We used to raid in Dracolich, a while back now. Been playing Strata since launch, you see. Back then, we never got any world firsts, but we made it through everything all right."

Martin tried to be subtle, but talking wasn't his strong point. "And how does Strata compare?"

"This place… this is something else. You've only just stuck your toes in the shallow end, let me tell you. It gets worse every deep you go down. Not just harder but… scarier too. Weirder. We've lost more guildies to the fear than to the fight."

Jericho scoffed. "It is only a game."

Hespith's gaze turned towards the water, but she wasn't really seeing it. Her eyes were unfocused.

"Jezebel is going to be the next to go. You can already see her straining at the edges. She hardly even talks any more. Says she's been dreaming about things before they happen. Says she can hear the Archdukes down below, whispering to her."

Even Jericho's bluster faltered at that. "What do they say to her?"

Hespith didn't even give him a sideways glance. "Why don't you go ask her?" she said.

She nodded over at the pool. There was a Sythvan body lying beside it. Martin had mistaken it for a corpse at first glance, but now he could see the back of her armor rising and falling. She was still breathing, no matter what else had happened to her.

Martin considered it for a moment, then strode off towards the water. If nothing else, this would be a good time waster so that Lindsay had a better chance of catching up to them.

Sane people also had a habit of playing their cards a little close to their chest. A chat with this Jezebel might shake loose some details about what they were going to face in the lower deeps, even if they were part of a ramble about tinfoil hats.

He pondered whether to prod her with his toe or not when she didn't look up at his arrival, but it seemed rude, not to mention counterproductive, so he lay down on his front beside her and looked out over the flat surface of the pool. One of her fingers, claws really, was trailing over the top of the water.

The ripples danced out across the surface, rebounding off the sides, forming complex patterns determined by the movements of the Sythvan's hand.

"The water is what gave it away."

Martin nearly jumped when he heard her speak. He'd expected to spend a few minutes trying to coax her into talking, trying to drag her back to reality from whatever fantasy she was currently occupying.

"Gave what away?"

She sighed.

"No game has ever made water look so real. Even if a game could, would your computer be able to render it so perfectly, with every drop changing the course of all the rest? I know that mine would not. It barely scraped the necessary requirements to run this game at all."

Martin lay as perfectly still as he could. He didn't want to startle her, but he was fighting every instinct to turn from the water and look at her face. It would have sounded completely deranged if he hadn't already been thinking along the same lines. The water right in front of his face just made it worse, rippling at the touch of an unseen breeze, ever shifting, sparkling and impossibly beautiful in the dim firelight.

"If it isn't a game, what is it?"

"Don't you already know the answer? This is real life. We aren't playing a game or sharing a dream. We are travelling to a different world. A world just as real as our own, but different. Distant and strange."

Her voice began to waver the longer she spoke. As if she was not used to speaking anymore.

"There are things that a maker of games just could not know. That they would not consider. There are details here that no rational mind would furnish a game with."

If he challenged this delusion, he was probably going to make her angry, but if he played along, he might make things worse. "You think this is all real?"

"The question isn't what I think, it is what I know to be

true." She dipped her fingers into the water, spreading new hypnotic patterns. "Every one of my senses tells me that this is real life. That this is my own real life, and that the one I have outside of this dungeon is a trick. A distraction. Maybe I never had a real life at all before I came here. Maybe this is all just another of Strata's tricks. It makes us think we are someone else, someone who has not come to kill it."

Martin stood up abruptly. This was all sounding too reasonable. His own real life seemed almost impossibly bland and pointless when he compared it to the grand mission that he had here in Strata. He didn't believe madness was infectious, and he didn't believe that this game was a portal to another world, because both of those ideas were fantasy. But he could follow the train of thought, and it led nowhere good.

There were some good points buried in all that crazy. Nobody had any idea how the NIH technology worked; they had no idea how a world this rich could be emulated using crappy old computers that barely managed to run the last generation's VRMMOs.

Strata might have been a race, but it was even more of a mystery, and he was becoming increasingly convinced that solving that mystery was how he was going to win that race. Nobody understood the first thing about Strata. Even the things that Martin would state as plain fact could have been entirely wrong, shaped by his own extrapolations.

He needed to know who made the game. To find out how it worked. If he couldn't find out, then he might very well end up like the broken mind laid out at his feet.

Jezebel did not look up, but she talked on as though he were still beside her. Just barely loud enough for him to hear.

"You'll see that I am right in time. You'll shake off the lies that the Heart of Strata is feeding you. Then, when you do, you'll hear them. You'll hear them whispering in the deep, in the dark. It is only a matter of time."

He moved away as quietly as he could, but once he was back

at the campfire, Martin still couldn't shake off Jezebel's words. It was like they kept echoing in his head. A frightful mirror held up to his own suspicions, and the places they could take him.

He had no intention of going mad. He wasn't obsessed with Strata. Or if he was, it was just the regular obsession he'd experienced with every game he'd ever played in his life. It wasn't something special. It was just a game. It was only a game. A puzzle for him to solve. A prize for him to win.

He blinked dully when he realized somebody had said his name.

"Huh?"

Cobranan hissed with amusement. "She really creeped you out, nah?"

Martin nodded. "Scary to think that could happen to any of us."

"Nah, she was always a weird one." When the Sythvan shook his head it was sinuous, like the ripples in the water. "Always way too into her games. Played all night instead of sleeping. Lost her job. I don't know the last time she logged out. Every time we come back into the game, she's already there."

Julia frowned. "Do any of you know how to contact her in real life?" she asked.

Cobranan shrugged. Another ripple. "Nah, we're just online friends. I don't even know what country she's in."

"Isn't there some sort of reporting system?"

Martin hated to even suggest involving the Masters, given what he now knew about them, but a life was literally on the line here. If you didn't come out of the game, your body in the real world would die eventually, of starvation if nothing else.

"There has to be something we can do to get her out of here and get her the help she needs," he said.

Jericho rumbled, "You can't help people who won't help themselves. If we force her out, she'll just come right back again."

"And she'll come back alone, where we can't be around to help her," Cobranan added.

Hespith stared over at the limp snake-woman on the ground. "She must be logging out sometimes. If she… it's been weeks. If she wasn't logging out at all then she'd already be… she wouldn't still be here. She must be taking breaks. She must."

"Have you tried killing her?" Martin asked.

They all turned to stare at him in abject horror.

"I don't mean be obvious about it," he blurted, "but you could just put her in the way of harm? If she's dead, she can't play."

"For half an hour," Cobranan grumbled.

Martin waited for someone to contradict him, but they all remained silent. So, despite the depths they'd delved to, they had only died once each. Interesting.

Maybe the game just felt too real for them to risk themselves. No wonder they were struggling to push through the harder deeps if they were too timid to die.

Hespith cocked her head to one side. "It might be enough to snap her out of it?"

"She's fine," Cobranan scoffed. "This guy… he's just trying to screw us up. Sure, Jez has gone a bit cuckoo, but she still fights like crazy. Hell, I'd say she fights better now she thinks this is real life. And it isn't like we're going to be here forever, you know? She just has to keep it together until we win the game. When will that be, a few months? Tops?"

Martin saw Julia's hackles rise, almost literally. She couldn't stand that sort of callous comment at the best of times. Even jokes like that set her teeth on edge. He had seen it in the early days of the guild, when he'd given serious consideration to cutting her from the raid team, before he'd realized that she was enough of an asset to balance out the disruption to the usual gallows humor.

Her eyes narrowed at the other Sythvan. "You seem very confident."

Cobranan didn't even look at her. "Why wouldn't I be? We made it to fifty without breaking a sweat last time, and this time we've got all our progression planned out. Optimized. This isn't like Dracolich. You aren't going to beat us to the endgame this time."

Martin held up his paws.

"We're all just here to have a good time. Whoever wins, wins. I'm not going to shed any tears over it. Not when there's so much game to explore."

Cobranan's head snapped around. "What are you saying? That you're out of the race?"

Jericho's rumbling laugh drew their attention. "We all play the game. We all want to win. No reason we can't get along until the time when we can't."

Hespith smiled up at him and Julia's eyes narrowed all over again. That jealousy could be a very useful lever later on, if Martin ever needed to convince their mild-mannered pacifist that violence was the answer.

He wondered for a moment what the Sin-flipped version of the hierophant would be. Some sort of ranged caster, probably.

The conversation ran dry after that, and Jericho began to eye the exits on the far end of the cavern floor. It seemed Lindsay's time was up. Martin cast one last glance back at Jezebel by the pool and inspiration struck.

"Dinner time."

Julia and Jericho both turned to him in amazement. The big Wulvan's mouth was hanging open, his tongue lolling out.

Julia almost whispered, "You have never suggested that we stop for a break. Not ever. What's wrong? Is your house on fire?"

Martin gave her a half smile.

"We need to remember our real lives if we don't want to end up like..." He trailed off, looking back towards the water.

Jericho nodded. "Yes. Food is a good plan."

"If we just take five minutes, that gives Lindsay time to get logged back in and start heading down. Jumping in and out of the game to talk to her is going to be a nuisance otherwise."

"Hah. I knew you had ulterior motives." Jericho patted him on the head. "Those cogs are always spinning."

"Five minutes," Martin repeated.

The other two nodded, then they vanished in a brief, sudden strobing of white. Martin followed right after them, back up into the light.

TWENTY-ONE

The Awakening

He opened his eyes slowly, savoring the dull ache in his muscles and the momentary peace before his senses caught up to this reality. He smiled and his face felt strange, misshapen and flattened.

Then the noise started. Someone was having sex behind the wall to his left. Below him, someone was screaming at either a pet or a child, although from the tone and volume, Martin hoped like hell it was a pet.

Above him there was silence, interrupted only by the occasional rattle of synthetic gunfire – another gamer winding down after a week of drudgery. The right wall was probably the least disturbing to Martin – there was a family singing together in some language he didn't understand.

Despite the meaningless words, there was warmth in their voices. Joy. They were in the same rat trap as Martin, but they had made it a home.

Dust drifted through the air above his face, lit up intermittently by the red flashing of his phone's death-throes. Real life really did suck. It was hardly a surprise that Jezebel preferred the game.

Whatever Strata did to his body while he was sleeping had

left him ravenous. He didn't look at the time, because that was just asking for trouble. Instead, he went digging through the bags he'd brought home in search of something resembling food.

Protein bars were in order, even if they looked much the same going into his body as coming out. They tasted like nothing, but he shoveled them into his mouth anyway. He needed his energy if they were going to get to the next deep tonight.

There was a gamble involved in pressing on so quickly, but the Night Ravager had proved to him right from the start that it was a fair gamble. They'd face monsters beyond their level, yes, but if they beat them, they'd fly up through the levels so much faster. Besides, he'd never been one to shy away from a challenge.

He couldn't work out if he had brain damage, or if the reality that Strata portrayed was just so much brighter than his real life that it made food seem tasteless.

It was another one of those subjects that it didn't help to dwell on. Much like potential ambushing crabs waiting for Lindsay, or the doubts Jezebel had seeded in his brain.

There was only one way to stop worrying about how Strata did all the things that it did, and that was to find out how it did them. If he could get an understanding of the mechanics of the game on that fundamental level, he would finally have solid foundations on which to lay his guesswork and supposition.

While he chewed his vile meal like a cow chewed cud, he slipped the charger into his phone and resumed his search for Edwin Klimpt.

A quick search produced no results, which Martin was fairly certain was impossible, or at least incredibly unlikely. The name was a little bit unusual, but surely there was an Edwin Klimpt somewhere in the world.

It wasn't like you could move through life without leaving a digital trail. If you'd ever had a home, a job or even an argument online, some of your details were out there.

Two options presented themselves. Klimpt was definitely a

real person, to register a patent, you needed biometric identification, so either this genius was some sort of luddite hermit – despite designing one of the most sophisticated pieces of gaming technology on the planet – or his details were being deliberately hidden. Suppressed, somehow.

Martin flipped back to the tab with the patent. There had to be some information on there, beyond the name of the person who filed. Personal details were absent from the form, hidden away behind personal privacy protections that were probably pretty reasonable, but frustrating in this moment.

All he knew for certain was that the patent had been filed somewhere in America, and even that was only because of the American spelling of words on the document. Everything else had been anonymized.

He closed the tab and went back to his search, feeding in other phrases from the patent application. Technical terms that meant nothing to him, but that might trigger some algorithm to show him some academic paper. A paper with the name Edwin Klimpt at the top. Nothing.

With a beleaguered sigh, and an eye still on the clock, Martin typed in the details to pull up the patent again, but he couldn't find it. He grumbled through some menus to open up his browser history, but while there were literally hundreds of patents there, the last one was not for the NIH.

He backtracked, but it was useless. None of the last ten were for the NIH either. Something weird was going on. He typed Edwin Klimpt into the patent search and it produced nothing.

He stared at the empty expanse of white screen. It was interrupted a moment later by a message from Lindsay.

Heading back in.

There was nothing there. His one lead had run dry. He should never have closed the tab – the moment that he'd suspected something was weird about the search results, he should have dumped everything to the phone memory.

Once there, it would have taken seriously illegal action instead of simple algorithm tampering to take his hard-earned scraps of knowledge back from him.

The patent was a dead end. Edwin Klimpt didn't exist. He was a dead end too.

If he wasn't so broke, Martin might have flung the phone across the room. Instead, he pulled up the auction sites again and started trawling through them for any hints about the gate to Deep Four. The opening to Deep Three had been shaped by the events of Deep Two; it only stood to reason that the next one would be altered by their entrance too.

Very briefly, and with no small degree of guilt, he wondered what his companions' new gear would have been worth at the going market rate. Julia's staff had to be worth something. Lindsay's cloak would have worked for any class, so he could see that selling well too.

If he had been a different person, less set on progress, he supposed he could have hoarded an item from each victory to sell along. Made enough cash to eat real food instead of whatever was currently sitting like a lead weight in his stomach.

He set that thought aside; there was no point dwelling on the minor miseries of this world when there was a whole other one to jump back into. The break was almost over, and he was eager to get back in and check on Speckles before they moved on.

This time, logging in didn't feel like falling. More like slipping into something more comfortable.

Skaife's little ratty hands were starting to feel more familiar than his own. The tail, which had lashed about on its own initially, now seemed to be almost entirely under his control, like another limb. That should have seemed strange. All of this should have.

This was not his body, yet he inhabited it without even the slightest hint of dysphoria. Even the bristles of fur at the periphery of his vision didn't turn his stomach the way he might have expected.

It wasn't like he was being changed. More like he'd been a rat on the inside for his whole life and it was only now escaping.

Speckles had waited dutifully, while the snake posse and the other lingering crusaders seemed to have vanished off into the tunnels.

"Me no like falling water. Feel like my head is drum."

Martin ruffled the frog's head, and instantly regretted it. He wiped the slime on his thigh-fur.

"I'm not a big fan of it myself." he said. "But it was necessary to keep you safe."

"Me like safe. Safe good." Speckles bobbed along. "You keep me safe?"

"I'll do my best." Martin tried for a comforting smile but landed firmly in grimace territory.

He'd had big ideas about a native monster guide, but very few plans as to how to keep that guide safe once the real fighting started. He hoped Speckles wasn't going to become a sad green stain on the floor of the dungeon, but hope was about the only thing that he had to offer to prevent it.

Speckles' huge eyes seemed to take up all of Martin's vision as he leaned in closer.

"Me think your best be good enough. Me think your best is a lot."

With that strange vote of confidence lodged, Martin got down to business.

"Could you guide us to the Deep Gate?"

It was hard to pinpoint what exactly in Speckles' demeanor made him seem uncomfortable when he seemed to be on the verge of wriggling out of his slimy skin at any given moment anyway. Nonetheless, he looked uncomfortable.

"Me could. Yes. If nothing moved."

Martin let out a sigh. He had his suspicions about how regularly the dungeon was re-structured, and here came the confirmation.

"Me came up, many long time ago with other Anurvan. Me think things moved since then."

This was why nobody else was trying to use an NPC guide, and why there were no maps of Strata being shared around online. The dungeon was being reshaped every day by the Masters, tweaked and improved or just rejigged entirely to prevent anyone from learning the way through.

Of course it was. There was no design so perfect that people couldn't think of a way around it, so they just kept on changing the damn design.

He gave Speckles a pat on the back. "Okay. That's all right. We'll find it the old-fashioned way."

Jericho and Julia logged back into the game, arriving in a flash and a giggle. The two of them were definitely in contact outside of the game. They'd spent a week adventuring together to reach the previous deep, without him or Lindsay in tow to act as chaperones.

Martin tried to think back through all of their interactions in Dracolich, to see if this little relationship of theirs had taken root back then, or if it was a new development.

Here in Strata, with such a small group, the fact that they might act as a voting bloc was concerning to say the least. He didn't want to raise it with Lindsay, because she would inevitably just delight in making things awkward for everyone and wouldn't see any harm in it either. If anything, she would give Martin more trouble than Julia and Jericho combined.

He put on his best impression of a socially well-adjusted friend. "Welcome back, you two."

Julia gave him a little wave, but Jericho looked suspicious.

You two.

Great start. Good job, Martin.

"So, I'm thinking we start out searching the deliberately constructed tunnels on the far side. There seems to be a half-dozen of them to choose from. That way, we shouldn't have to deal with too much organic honeycombing or tangled tunnels."

Jericho blinked at him. "I see pretty Roman architecture, you see premonitions of future. Strange brain you have in that little rat head. Very strange."

Julia whacked him ineffectually. "That sounds like a wonderful plan. Thank you."

As one, the guild crests on their chests lit up. Lindsay's voice seemed to echo from all around them.

"Good morning, campers. Sorry I had to split on you!"

Martin groaned and touched his crest. "A whole half hour time out, and that was the best joke you could come up with?"

He could almost hear her eyebrows waggling. "You'll have to forgive me. I'm not half the girl I used to be."

Why had he spent a single moment worrying about her? Nobody bounced back like Lindsay.

Jericho interrupted before another flurry of bisection jokes could start up. "Where are you?"

"Deep One, just heading out of Beachhead." Her beak clattered between each word. She must have been running. "Should I get anything from the shops?"

"Maybe some healing potions?" Julia replied, grinning.

Who knew they had missed their noble leader so much?

"Lindsay, we're going to start scouting for the next gate," Martin said. "I've got an ability to open one up every three days or so, and I think it makes sense to—"

She cut him off with what seemed like a forced laugh.

"Yep. Good plan. Do it. I'll be down as quick as I can. I figure that with my *Hollow Bones* racial, *Acrobatics* passive and *Raptor Strike*, those stairs are going to be a breeze. It's like they designed this deep just for me to show off."

Martin wasn't mistaken; it *was* a forced laugh. She was shaken. Anyone would be after an experience like that. But that made him wonder just how much of her brazen act was a mask over some deeper hurt. Lindsay had always seemed impervious, unflappable in the face of any challenge, and now he found himself questioning how well he knew her at all.

With Jericho taking point, they headed off into the furthest right of the tunnels. Everywhere Martin looked there were signs of the adventurers that had passed through before. The white stonework was scarred by mis-swung blades, and some enterprising crusaders had used the pale expanse as a message board to leave notes to their allies and enemies.

For the most part the graffiti was just a simple statement of existence. "We were here." Scratched and inked into the very stone of the dungeon, demanding acknowledgement and attention.

Martin considered taking the fragments of his first dagger and sinking the Iron Riot sigil into that same stone, making his own statement of existence.

But then, the spiteful Master would probably just come along and wipe it clean. No. He didn't need to leave a scribble, as if Strata was some truck-stop bathroom. His name was going to be set in stone as the rat who beat this dungeon. He was going to be a legend here, just as he'd been in Dracolich.

There were some shattered husks of crab people scattered around the place; looted, dead mobs called *Militant Lithodes*. They were smaller and more humanoid than the monstrous creature up in the waterfall but still substantial enough that Martin wondered how their armor had been so easily cracked.

As it turned out, Martin's worries were entirely unfounded. There wasn't a living specimen to be found anywhere they went.

The tunnel branched and split only twice, leading to dead ends and shell heaps on both occasions, but whatever treasure or experience there was to be gained here had been consumed by the locust hordes of players who'd already been through.

There was no sign of a Deep Gate; not even a hint of it, nor any sign of a monster substantial enough to hold the key.

Once back at the main chamber, the guild began to get restless.

"I thought you were meant to be clever, man," Jericho rumbled. "You said you knew which way to go. What is the point of you?"

Martin bit back the first few replies that came to mind, finally spitting out, "I need more information before I can make an educated guess."

"How much more?" Jericho pressed him. "How many empty tunnels do we walk up and down?"

Martin stopped, the embers of fury in his gut sparking to life. "You want to see behind the curtain? You want to know what I'm thinking? Is that what you want?"

Julia took a hold of his arm, but Jericho didn't stop. He glowered down at Martin with contempt written all over his canine features. "You think you are smarter than everyone. Go on. Prove it."

Martin held up his paw and started to count off points on his claws. "The pool in the central chamber would be the obvious place for the gate. Central, dramatic. But the last gate was under the water and I can't see them repeating the same trick twice. Which makes me think that the pool is going to be some sort of trap."

Jericho grunted in reluctant agreement. Martin was on a roll now.

"There is a narrative convention of hiding good things like treasure behind waterfalls, but the designers of Strata are aware of that. They would invert the expectation and put something bad behind the waterfall."

He pointed at the endless downpour of water.

"The area surrounding the plunge pool is huge. It's the perfect place for a pitched battle with some giant monster. Add in the fact that most people wouldn't trigger the crab attack further up the stairs and you have the perfect recipe for a surprising giant boss monster hidden behind the waterfall. So, we avoid that."

Now even Julia looked impressed.

"The only logical place to put the gate is further down one of these tunnels, so that people couldn't just roll right through into the next deep immediately upon arrival."

He pointed at himself.

"I haven't seen any other exorcists, but the devs still have to take the abilities my class can unlock into account in their design, and the usual levelling curve that would deliver me here with *Rite of Passage* ready to use. Obvious boss monsters, hidden gates. That is the only design strategy that makes sense, at least for the next few deeps, before they can start to subvert expectations again by changing it up."

He stepped up to Jericho and folded all his counted claws into a fist.

"Any questions?"

Jericho was grinning. "Weird brain is doing a great job, but I still think we check behind the waterfall."

Julia let out a relieved little laugh and Martin felt the tension leaking out of him. It was easy to forget that Jericho was his friend, especially when he insisted on being antagonistic all the time, but that was just the way he communicated. Martin had a habit of shutting down, turning inward. Sometimes he needed a Jericho or a Lindsay to force him out of his shell.

"You know it's a trap, right?"

Jericho squatted down until they were face to face. "You know they hide good treasure behind traps for people who can beat traps, yes?"

Martin was forced to concede that point. "We need treasure less than we need progress."

Speckles was hopping up and down beside them. "You no want fight big monster. Me no want fight big monster!"

"Big monster, eh?" Jericho chuckled. He brought his forehead forward to bump against Martin's, much more gently than anyone could have expected. "Come on now," he murmured. "Treasure is progress. Have you seen any useless items down here?"

Martin knew he'd lost the argument, especially with Julia's close… relationship with Jericho. Still, he could win on the details.

"We should wait for Lindsay before we trigger whatever is waiting behind that waterfall," he said.

But Jericho had already set off for the central chamber. He called back over his shoulder, "I am thinking we surprise her with prizes after. We make her happy. You want her to be happy, yes?"

Julia was trying not to smirk. "She would be very pleased," she said.

Martin grumbled under his breath, but his choices were to follow them or stand around like a petulant child. This wasn't the time or the place.

Jericho strode up to the center of the waterfall, clapping his huge hands together and readying the little censer-weapon that he'd got from the last boss.

Julia was already preparing spells, blinking over and over to take in her full ability list and work out her timing. Martin would have to corner her for the details of exactly how hierophant magic worked and how that new staff interacted with it, because each time she cast something a new blossom opened up on the living wood.

A quick glance confirmed that they still had the chamber to themselves. Martin drew his sword, but there wasn't much else he could do to get ready. For his part, Speckles had found a sheared-off column and was cowering behind it like any sensible creature would when confronted with this level of idiocy.

Jericho charged right into the water with a roar, apparently trusting in Martin's prediction that he wasn't running into solid stone. He vanished completely behind the wall of water. The moments ticked by, each one of them with the weight of an hour.

Martin was just about to start in after him when the notification pinged.

[Jericho suffers 51 bludgeoning damage]

The furred mass of Jericho exploded out of the waterfall, shrouded for an instant in spray before he landed with a colossal splash in the central pool.

That could have been worse.

A tentacle lashed out of the waterfall after him. Massive, purple and ridged with lines of tiny spines, it was as thick around as Jericho. The first tentacle was soon joined by another, then another.

Celaphox, Harbinger of Catastrophe, The Year of Sorrow

When Martin tried to draw up more details it just flashed up, like a warning:

[Epic-level enemy]

TWENTY-TWO

The Falling Star

In a hushed whisper, Julia said a word so rude that Martin was surprised she knew it. The central tentacle reared up, ready to plunge into the pool and snuff Jericho out permanently.

There was no *real* danger here. The *real* Jericho would wake up in the real world unharmed if that blow fell.

Logically, Martin knew it, but nobody had informed his gut. He was already moving. His hand was already up.

He cast *Rebuke* as the blow fell, and while there was no way he could have pushed the whole beast back, it was powerful enough to turn the killing blow aside.

The tentacle mashed into the edge of the pool, shattering the stone and revealing a rim of silver beneath.

Jericho popped up out of the pool, gravel raining all around him. He gasped for air. "Big monster. Is a very big monster."

A glow spread from the end of Julia's staff and enveloped him, and the massive caved-in section of his bare chest pushed back out. A wash of blood tinted the pool pink in the process.

[Jericho recovers 36 health]

Martin started barking orders.

"Get out of range! Everyone back."

It wasn't immediately clear what the beast's range actually was; Martin couldn't even see where the tentacles were rooted behind the waterfall. But he would bet the little cash he had to his name that Celaphox' weak spot was on that central mass. Otherwise it wouldn't bother to hide it.

Pulling back and forcing it to expose itself was a sound strategy, and it gave Martin the time he needed to think.

Even the Night Ravager hadn't come with a flashing warning sign, so there had to be more to this big squid thing than just raw damage potential. It would be the full package, dealing a ton of damage and soaking it up too.

He lit his sword up with *Celestial Strike* and backed away slowly. Julia didn't have the health pool to survive a hit from this thing, so he didn't dare leave her closer to Celaphox than he was. It still felt like he was playing chicken with a truck.

The huge tentacles lashed around the room, thick as tree trunks and nimble as hair in the wind. Martin wasn't even sure how you fought something like this. Whether you tried to treat each tentacle as a separate foe or... His train of thought was derailed as the nearest tentacle seemed to notice him, coiling up and then lashing out, straight for him.

There was no hope of dodging – no point in blocking – the blow was going to fall. Martin thrust out his glowing sword and bent his knees, pretending his hands weren't shaking.

[Celaphox suffers 8 light damage]
[Celaphox suffers 8 piercing damage]

The blade bit deeply into the monster, driven deeper by the force of its own attack. The soft jelly flesh of the tentacle peeled away to the sides of the sword, leaving him standing in a hollow, surrounded by its wound. Martin let out a little bark of victory.

A shadow rushed back along his sword as the glow of *Celestial Strike* faded, leaping out to hit him square in the chest.

[VENGEANCE]
[Skaife suffers 8 piercing damage]

The tentacle withdrew, but it wasn't the pained jerk of an injured animal. It was languid. Like Celaphox was amused, buoyed in confidence by its *Vengeance* ability.

Martin needed time to think. He needed a moment when he wasn't under attack to work through this new development.

He wasn't going to get it.

Another massive tentacle slammed through the columns beside him, throwing a cloud of detritus into the air and pummeling him with shrapnel.

[Skaife suffers 1 bludgeoning damage]
[Skaife suffers 1 bludgeoning damage]
[Skaife suffers 1 bludgeoning damage]

Through the clouds of marble dust, the others became nothing but shadows. Julia was briefly visible as the impact of a tentacle slamming down into the ground sent out a gust of air, but it was only for a moment. Just long enough for Martin to see the panic on her face.

Martin tried to shout, but the dust set him to coughing instead. He pressed his sword hand to his guild crest and covered his mouth with the other.

"Don't try to fight it. Get clear."

Lindsay's voice whispered in his ear, "What the hell are you doing down there?"

Jericho was baying for blood somewhere beyond the clouds of dust and Martin could sense movement all around him, the disturbance of huge things moving just out of sight.

There was no way of knowing what the others were doing, not without charging out of the cloud that blinded him and protected him in equal measure. He had to trust them to do what he'd asked. He had to trust that they'd listen to sense instead of their instincts.

Martin cast *Healing Touch* on himself and then did what he did best. He worked it out.

[Skaife recovers 15 health]

The *Vengeance* mechanic returned whatever damage was dealt to Celaphox back on its attackers. That much was clear. Martin's head spun as he tried to work out a way to make it injure itself, but no bright ideas immediately presented themselves. If a group had enough healing, they could probably still whittle Celaphox down, but Martin knew without any doubt that the three of them weren't going to be up to the task.

He should have pushed back more when they wanted to leave Lindsay behind. He should have stood his ground. He never had any trouble fighting the endless hordes of enemies that games presented him with, so why did standing up to his friends seem so insurmountable?

As much as he tried to justify it to himself as managing relationships and emotional bolstering, the truth was that he was a lonely man and the fear of alienating his only friends made him weak.

A shadow fell over him. The tentacle came down like a tree falling in the forest, and *everyone* heard it. Martin flung himself beside one of the shattered stumps of marble in the hope that it might deflect some of the impact and maybe jab the thing back, but the stone crumbled to dust under the blow.

[Skaife suffers 24 bludgeoning damage]

He couldn't breathe. All the light was blocked out by the mass of spongy flesh, grinding him down into the tiles. Was it just going to lie there like an oversized lapdog until it had crushed all the life out of him?

The tentacle lifted, but the barbed hooks running the length of it had caught in Martin's fur and armor, sticky with blood. He rose out of the fog of war and looked out across the battlefield in utter dismay.

Jericho was surrounded by a nimbus of light, fending off four of the huge tentacles as they lashed at him, taking turns to spin him around and around. The only one to actually take Martin's advice and get to safety had been Julia, who was now cowering in the entrance to the tunnels.

As he rose higher and higher, the whole chamber came into sight. The central bulbous mass of Celaphox was now protruding out of the waterfall. Phosphorous green eyes seemed to cover that bloated body, staring out with the same blind malevolence as the Night Ravager's had.

Exactly the same malevolence. Like it was the same evil mind driving them both. That same whisper. *"Come to me."*

Martin shook off that thought, and his own shock. He wasn't here to see the sights; he was here to kill it.

The tentacle's tip was beneath his feet, and as it rose up, he was slowly being turned upside down. Lucky for him, it did not seem to notice he was there — or it could have smashed him to pulp.

A quick cut would free him, and he'd survive the *Vengeance* damage, but the fall would kill him just as surely as another whip of the tentacles. Martin had to bide his time for more reasons than one. He tore an arm free and pressed it against his sigil.

"You're doing great, guys," he said. "Just hold out a little bit longer. Help is coming."

Lindsay whispered directly into his brain a moment later. "Dude. What am I supposed to do?"

He concentrated hard on her name. Tesra. Slowly, the names of the others grayed out.

"Well, that depends," he said, trying to keep his voice calm and jovial. "How do you feel about glorious death in battle?"

He didn't feel good about asking her to die again. Not after the obvious trauma that she'd gone through last time. If it had been Julia or Jericho, he probably wouldn't have even made the suggestion, just accepted the inevitability of death and a two hour-long lockout.

He knew they had limitations; that if he pushed them too hard, they would just stop playing along. He'd never found that limit with Lindsay. They would find each other's limits and just keep on pushing until that invisible barrier moved.

That was how she had learned his name to start with. That was how they had gone from strangers who played a game together to being friends.

Martin held his breath.

"Again?" she groaned, reverberating in his skull. "I just got back in here!"

He couldn't keep the grin off his face. She was still Lindsay. "Hold that thought."

Martin's sword lit up with another *Celestial Strike* and he hacked haphazardly into the meat above him. Ichor sprayed out onto his face, bitter and salty as the sea, but it worked.

[Celaphox suffers 8 light damage]
[Celaphox suffers 8 slashing damage]
[VENGEANCE]
[Skaife suffers 8 slashing damage]

Shadows darted over him, opening long bloody scratches across his chest to match the wounds he'd inflicted on the tentacle. Martin didn't have time to care. With the tentacle tip severed, he was tumbling down, end over end, still hooked to the dead flesh.

It didn't matter; he had judged the momentum right. He hit the pool instead of the stone, and it absorbed the impact perfectly. A few frantic chops got him clear of the dead tissue and back up to his feet. No more drowning today.

At the side of the pool, he stopped just long enough to notice the thick silver rim that the damage had uncovered: unmistakably the outer edge of a Deep Gate, but covered in strange runes beneath the dust. A circle in the exact size of a gate, right there in plain sight all this time.

He'd have time to beat himself up over his mistakes later. He had bigger calamari to fry right now. He dragged his sword over his bracers and grit his teeth against the shriek it made.

Celaphox stared down at him with what could easily have been mistaken for curiosity. Martin must have seemed like an insect to something this huge, and about as threatening.

Jericho held a pair of tentacles at bay on the far side of the room. Julia was weaving in and out of the decimated pillars, keeping out of range but drawing the monster's attention.

"Lindsay, where are you?" he asked.

She sounded breathless. "Just about to hit the Crab Step. Hold on to your hats. I'll be down as fast as I can."

He froze. "No! Stop. You aren't taking the stairs. You're coming down the express."

"Oh. Hell, no."

A tentacle swept around, not even aimed for him, but Martin had to fling himself down to roll under it.

"Lindsay," he said, a pleading edge to his voice.

"No. Nope. No thanks."

"Lindsay, listen." Martin scrambled back to his feet, counting down the seconds until his *Trinity Strike* activated. "Back in the Murovan village, you did extra damage because you dropped down on the enemies."

"Dude, I know. That's what *Raptor Strike* does. It converts your fall damage into—" He could hear her muffling her beak with her own hands. "Oh, damn. Nope. No. Still not doing it."

One of the attacks made it through and Jericho was slapped off his feet. He smashed through a row of columns while Julia frantically poured more healing into him, crouched beside his fallen body.

[Jericho suffers 34 bludgeoning damage]

Martin couldn't stop to help, only stare at the pulsating mass of flesh up ahead. His voice dropped to an awed whisper.

"You are absolutely going to do it. Because I'm going to set you up to critically hit with your new knife."

""What?" Lindsay scoffed as she blinked through the menus and noticed her new item. "What new… ooh, shiny."

"Listen to me. Really listen. This is going to work. There is nowhere else in the whole dungeon where it might work, but in this one place, with this one vertical drop, we can still win this."

He didn't know where he found the confidence to speak like that, not when he was standing beneath a glowing green eye that was the same size as he was.

"I don't want to die again." Her voice dropped to a whisper. "It is… it is really not fun."

This close, Celaphox was too large to understand. It was an abstract image, just impossible shapes, unnatural colors, movement.

Martin still pressed in closer, so close that the few flailing tentacles heading his way couldn't quite bend far enough.

"You won't feel a thing. I promise. Just aim for the center; I'll be right underneath it."

She huffed. "Dude. You are asking me to jump off the top of a skyscraper. I'm going to feel something."

"Lindsay, there has never been a giant hole that you haven't wanted to jump into." Even Martin could hear the wheedling edge in his voice, and he hated it. "I am finally giving you permission."

"I am not jumping!"

Jericho coughed up a mouthful of blood and pushed himself unsteadily to his feet, just in time to catch Celaphox' next sweeping attack in his own massive brawny arms.

[BLOCKED]

He skidded along a few feet, but it had the intended effect: Julia was protected. Jericho's growl felt justified for once. "You will jump, or we will all die. Game will be over for the night. We will have wasted this whole time because you rushed off and got crabbed. You want this?"

Lindsay seemed genuinely surprised. "Dude, what the hell? Are you trying to guilt me into jumping to my death?"

"Did it work?" Jericho replied with a savage grin.

There was a long pause during which Jericho was dragged from his feet by the tentacle that he was still, inexplicably, wrestling. Finally, Lindsay sighed. "Kinda?"

Martin hoped she couldn't hear his grin. "Tell me when you're ready." Celaphox flicked Jericho into a wall, and this time he did not bounce back so readily.

[Jericho suffers 18 bludgeoning damage]

Julia took a halting step forwards, then another tentacle swept her away.

[Adriel suffers 21 bludgeoning damage]

It was safe to say that neither of them was going to be helping much from this point on. Martin scraped his sword over his bracers for one last tiny buff and then waited.

Then Lindsay bellowed at the top of her lungs, "Daddy's coming!"

Martin started to count it down. *Forty-four, forty-three, forty-two, forty-one.* When he got to twenty, he activated *Rite of Retribution.* When he got to ten, his sword lit up with his *Trinity Strike.*

It was a more vibrant light, less warm and more electrical. A purer, brighter white than anything he'd seen in the whole game.

He drowned that light in the flesh of Celaphox.

[Celaphox suffers 16 light damage]

There was no *Vengeance* from purely light damage. Jericho probably could have pounded this thing to bits eventually, if it could have been convinced to stay still the whole time.

One shot. That was all they had. If the random number generators of Strata went against them, if all that Martin had done didn't widen the critical range enough for Lindsay to slip through, then it was all for nothing. They were all dead.

He could hear her fall in those last few seconds, a scream of pure delight torn from her throat as she plowed right through terminal velocity.

When she hit, the immovable object of Celaphox rocked with the impact.

[CRITICAL HIT]
[Celaphox suffers 268 piercing damage]
[VENGEANCE]
[Tesra suffers 268 piercing damage]
Tesra has died.

There was a moment of silence, then the monstrous squid let out a jarring roar, so loud that Martin thought he'd gone deaf. He fell to his knees, gnashing his teeth in frustration.

How can it still be alive?

They'd dealt three hundred and sixty-four damage to it so far. More than anyone who'd made it as far as this deep could have ever hoped to do. It wasn't fair.

Celaphox's tentacles lifted up into the air, enough crushing blows to put an end to every one of them. Martin stared up at them hanging there and every moment stretched out like it was a year.

A year.

Celaphox was called the Year of Sorrow.

They were a day short. One more damage would make three hundred and sixty-five. A year.

He snatched up his sword from where it had fallen beside his limp hand and swiped it at Celaphox one last time.

[Celaphox suffers 10 slashing damage]
Celaphox has died
Skaife gains 4021 experience.
[LEVEL UP]

The tentacles that had been filled with murderous intent flopped uselessly to the cavern floor.

It was over. They'd actually won. Blessed silence fell over the cavern.

[ANNOUNCEMENT: *Iron Riot* have defeated **Celaphox, Harbinger of Catastrophe, The Year of Sorrow**]

TWENTY-THREE

The Burdens of Triumph

Yo! Congratulations broseph! That thing killed me twice before I gave up.

Nobody could have killed that thing. You liars.

Ayyyy I've been waiting for somebody to murk that squid for months, nice one! What did you do?

How the hell did you kill Celaphox? I thought that thing was meant to be unbeatable.

You taking new recruits? I'm on Deep Twenty-Two, but I'll come back to you. No questions asked.

Total bull, nobody can kill squidface. You're cheats. You're scum.

How did you do it? Didn't Vengeance get you?

Can I join your guild? I'm a level seven knight.

Good job buddy. Next round is on me.

The messages started almost immediately. First one or two, then dozens. Hundreds. A deafening chorus of voices. All of them begging. All of them demanding. A few of the more flattering ones were looking for membership in the guild, but the rest were aggressive.

How had they done it? How had they killed the unkillable boss?

Martin looked around at his guild, scattered around the corpse of the fallen boss. The monster was dead, but now they looked shell-shocked.

Julia kept opening and shutting her mouth, trying to answer one direct message before the next arrived and never getting a moment. Martin slapped his hand to his guild crest and bellowed, "Don't say a single word to any of them! Not to anyone. Not yet. Knowledge is our only advantage, and the game just slapped a big target right in the middle of our backs. We're the ones to beat now."

Just like the orders he barked during battle, this got the same immediate response. Jericho nodded firmly, Julia smiled nervously, and then they both barked out, "Iron Riot!"

It was something primal that bypassed all of the logic Martin usually prized. This was his tribe. This was their victory. He threw back his ratty little head and howled.

"Iron Riot!"

It wasn't easy to ignore the clamor of voices. The deniers and the parasites ranted and raved as Martin and the others attended to the practicality that followed their great victory: a *lot* of healing spells.

With that done, Martin left Jericho and Julia standing guard over their prize for a moment so he could go and inform their glorious leader of their victory.

He should have remembered to turn out the lights when he logged back into the game. The headache was sharp and immediate the moment his eyes opened in the real world. His phone was buzzing away frantically by his side, and to his absolute horror, not all of the messages were from Lindsay.

He had dozens of emails, mainly from auction sites and their representatives. According to the first message, typed all in caps, nobody had ever killed this boss before, which meant its loot was going to be completely unique. Even if it was useless, that uniqueness meant folks would pay a premium for it.

There were frankly staggering sums of money listed at the bottom of each email, bids to buy everything as a job-lot, but Martin just flicked them away until he found the tab with the two hundred and rising messages from Lindsay.

"*Come on dude, did we win?*"

"*Did we win?*"

"*We all died didn't we.*"

"*You killed me for nothing, you rat-faced rat.*"

"*Sorry that wasn't very imaginative. I'm a little stressed.*"

"*Because NOBODY IS TELLING ME WHAT IS HAPPENING.*"

"*I am now guessing that we did win, and you are too busy making out with the tentacles to answer me.*"

"*I hope you and sucker-pucker are very happy together.*"

"*Will you answer me???*"

"*Please tell me if we won or not. I'm so booooored.*"

"*Not bored. Annoyed. Because you aren't answering me.*"

"*How can you still be fighting? After my super-duper drop-kick suplex meteor strike nuke-it-from-orbit-it's-the-only-way-to-be-sure attack it is totally mush by now, right?*"

"*Mush! MUUUUUSH!*"

"*I regret to inform you that Lindsay is now dead. You killed her. With your failure to answer messages. I hope that you are proud of yourself. She was a beautiful genius with her whole life ahead of her, and now she is dead.*"

"*I regret to inform you that Lindsay is not dead, but you soon will be if you don't ANSWER ME.*"

"*I am not afraid to come over to your house and slap you. I have your address.*"

"Slappy slap slap."

"That's it, I'm calling a cab. I'm going to drive three states over, break into your apartment and slap the crap out of you while you're still in Strata."

"Dude that is a creepy thought. What if someone broke in while you were playing to rob you and found you all zombied out with the headband on."

"They could draw soooooo many dicks on your face."

"Forget slaps. This is the new plan."

Martin managed to type a reply through his tears of laughter.

"Put down your pens. We won."

There was a momentary lull in Lindsay's ceaseless tirade, then one last message came through.

"Yaaaaaaaaaaaaaasssssssssssss."

He tried to stay focused.

"People are going to try to contact you. This is a world-first kill. Don't tell them anything yet, okay? Let's get our story straight and decide how much we're willing to give away."

"YAAAAAAAAAAAAAAAAAAAAASSSSSSSSSSSSSSSS."

He snorted.

"I kind of feel like you might not be listening."

"We wooooooooooooon."

He grinned.

"Yeah we won. But don't tell anybody how we won. And don't sell any of the drops. We don't even know what it has got yet."

"Go loot the squid, dude! Save me something shiny! I'll be back in an hour."

"All right," he typed back, already lying down on the bed. *"Talk soon."*

"YAAAAAAASSSSSSSS."

The last thought going through his mind before he plummeted back into Strata was: that had better not become her new thing.

There were a lot more people around than Martin had expected when he logged back into the game.

None of them dared to approach the remains of Celaphox, whether out of residual fear of the thing, or a healthy respect for the colossal Wulvan standing on top of it.

Jericho turned his fierce grin towards Martin. "Call the exterminator. We have got a tourist infestation."

For once, Martin was glad to be an overlooked Murovan. He was able to scurry across to the body and loot it before anyone even noticed him.

Celaphox, Harbinger of Catastrophe, The Year of Sorrow
This horror was the firstborn of the Heart of Strata. Imbued with all the fecund evil of its creator, it turned the strength of the crusaders back against them, bringing all the power of the Heretic to bear.
Loot: 438 Silver, Bloodletter's Kris, Schisming Flagellant Ninetails, Defender of the Faith, Saintly Vestments.
Requires Leatherworking *to Harvest: Waterproof Hide, Grapple Suckers, Illuminating Eyes.*
Requires Herbalism *to Harvest: Blue Ring Venom, Red Ring Venom, Essence of Darkness, Darkling Ichor.*

The Kris was a wavy dagger that was destined for Lindsay, whenever she got back down here. As for the Ninetails, it was a short, multi-headed whip with a crackling mote of red light clinging to each of its tips.

That one was meant for martyrs, but Martin was going to have to get Jericho to read out the rest of the details to him so he could work out exactly how such a vicious looking thing fit with that class' whole aesthetic.

The Defender of the Faith was a gently glowing shield in the shape of an eagle with spread wings meant for knights only. That, they could sell.

The Vestments were probably the most interesting out of the set, usable by either hierophants or invokers. They seemed to have entirely different effects depending on which of the two was wearing them.

But most frustrating of all, there was nothing for him. Again.

It would be petty to be annoyed about something like that after they'd had a big victory and leveled up to boot. But he was only human, and he wanted shiny new toys just like the rest of them kept getting. The most interesting item he'd found in the whole dungeon so far were a couple of rocks that he'd strapped to his wrists. Even now, days later, the Master was screwing him over.

Martin sent each of the items to their new owners and kept that bitterness to himself.

He tried to be amused by Jericho, who was looking at the whip in utter puzzlement, and be pleased when Julia made a delighted noise and equipped her new dazzling white robes an instant later. At least they wouldn't lose her in a crowd.

With a wave, Jericho called him over.

"I don't understand this new item. It makes no sense. Doubles damage of all self-inflicted wounds and doubles effects of *Penance* and *Sufferance*."

Martin cocked his head to one side. "I mean, it obviously makes you into a better damage sponge for the group?"

"But why double damage to self?" Jericho leaned in closer. He'd always been a bit embarrassed about asking advice, and the crowd that had started to gather was not easing his self-doubt. "This makes no sense," the wolf-man growled. "Why would anyone want this?"

It was a puzzle to Martin too. As he tried to think it through, his eyes strayed to Celaphox. He stopped and stared at the monster. It was already starting to decay and melt.

The tooltip had said that Celaphox had all the powers of the heretic. What if that was another class?

"Do you know what your PvP class is called?"

Martin was almost whispering too. He really didn't want the second set of classes to become public knowledge if they hadn't been properly explored yet, although it seemed unlikely that the first thing people had done in the game wasn't trying to murder all their friends. "You know, the one that you switch to when your Sin gets too high?"

"This is first I am hearing." Jericho's brows furrowed.

"When you kill other players, it adds to your Sin score. Once it gets high enough, all of your abilities switch. They invert. My spells that make light make darkness instead."

Jericho started to race ahead himself. "You think that instead of absorbing damage for others, I deal damage when I'm hurt?"

Martin nodded. "Vengeance. The same mechanic that seafood here was using against us."

Jericho grinned. "Shame I will never get to use that part. Never been a fan of killing other players. Like you, I play for the game, no?"

Martin smiled at him, then headed over to where Julia was surrounded by a cluster of admirers, all cooing and offering her cash for her new robes.

"Sorry, they're not for sale," she crooned, reveling in the attention.

This close to the robes, Martin could make out a pearlescent sheen on the fabric, embroidery made from thread so close to white he hadn't even noticed it before. He sidled up to her.

"What do you want to do?" he whispered. "Start fresh when all of this attention has simmered down a bit?"

A Wulvan in the crowd shouted after him.

"Hey rat-boy, how did they kill Celaphox? Did anyone see them do it?"

Julia gave Martin a discreet nod then did her best to ignore the noise going on around her. There were more players in this deep than Martin would have suspected, but then, he supposed the game had been running for long enough now that most of the players had migrated deeper. It made sense that the higher levels had fewer people around.

Traffic from up above had started to trickle down too, a half-dozen players from up above descending the steps on the waterfall without a care in the world.

They weren't going to be able to get anything done with all these people around — they made Martin too uncomfortable to concentrate, and it was probably long past any sensible person's bedtime anyway.

He touched his guild-crest and spoke softly.

"I say we call it a night. Get some sleep, reconvene at midday tomorrow for a full day. That will give Lindsay time to catch up too. What do you think?"

Jericho nodded to him across the room, then vanished in a beam of light just a moment later. Julia was trying to be polite and say goodbye to each member of her new court of admirers before leaving, so Martin held off to make sure she got logged out safely.

The best plan seemed to be to emulate the other sightseers and hope that they continued to overlook him.

It was while he was doing a wide-eyed circuit of the gigantic decaying corpse that he noticed something that was actually interesting. The central pool of the chamber was still exposed on one side, and what looked like a Wulvan invoker in filigreed robes was crouched down beside it.

Martin sauntered closer. "What is it?"

She didn't even look up, just answered in a voice like a purring lion.

"Just a skip. Not the real Deep Gate. You probably don't know this, but when you beat the Archdukes, your respawn point shifts further down into the dungeon. There are more settlements deeper in, but a lot of the equipment and stuff for sale up in Beachhead is only available there, so there are these extra gates that we can use to move around faster. This will take you right down to ten. Carnifex's cave. We found the skip to twenty and thirty, but never this one. Nuts that they hid it from us. Even the shortcuts they've put in are hidden. It's crazy. It's like they really don't want anyone to win, yeah?"

Martin smiled. "Yeah. Crazy how they want to challenge us."

She glanced up at him and then rolled her eyes. "Eh, what do you know. Noob."

Martin rolled his eyes right back at her, but then caught sight of the tell-tale flare of Julia logging out in the periphery of his vision. He gave the Wulvan woman a big fake smile then logged out himself.

This time, he was ready for the lights. He kept his eyes shut and just lay still for a long moment as he settled back into his body.

Sleep probably would have taken him then and there if it wasn't for the persistent buzzing of his phone beside him. Vibrating closer to the edge of his bedside table, one inane message at a time.

"Dude, being dead is super boring. Why do people do it? I'm going to have to be immortal. It is the only way to keep from getting bored. Right? You're a smart guy. Make me immortal."

He fumbled for the phone with hands that were too big and clumsy for his purposes.

"Hey. We're going to stop for the night since it is 3 a.m. Reconvene by the pool at midday tomorrow. Don't tell anyone how we beat Celaphox."

"Ugh. But I want to stab things now. You promised me stabbings."

She had probably been bouncing up and down waiting to get back into the game — he felt a little bit bad.

"You'll get a new knife to stab things with tomorrow. Very rare. Very magical. Probably. Looks cool, don't know what it does. Knave only."

With the inevitability of the rising sun, she replied.

"Yaaaaaaaassssss."

"I beg you, please stop saying that."

It was probably just going to encourage her, but he had to try, for his own sanity as well as the sanity of others.

"Shan't."

He didn't know whether to sigh or to laugh.

"Goodnight."

"See you in, like, a few hours, dude."

With the phone finally falling silent, Martin moved as quickly as he could through his bedtime rituals, setting an alarm for 10 a.m. so he could get some reading in before gaming then moving his trash towards the can, even if he didn't quite get everything in it.

The lights went out and he finally started to feel at home again. He settled into the well-worn dip in the mattress and let the long overdue sleep take him over.

TWENTY-FOUR

The Dark Descent

First there was darkness. Then came the light.

Not dazzling, not even all that bright, but still more than the void that surrounded Martin now. He was dead, he had to be.

This was that dark place that you had to log out of, to wait out the timer before Strata brought you back. The shadowy backdrop on which all the structure and mechanics of Strata had been laid out.

The light was a dull green to begin with, but as time went on, it pulsed brighter and brighter, until Martin could see the great green phosphorescent eye down beneath him staring right up into the hollow where his body should have been.

He couldn't be seen. There was nothing for it to see. But still that great green eye stared up at him, full of sinister passion, crushing him with the weight of its attention. He tried to call up a menu, to log out, to get back into the real world where it could not reach him, but nothing responded to his thoughts. He was truly dead, suspended in this nothingness with no hope of salvation.

"Come to me."

It wasn't a voice, because that would have implied sound. It would have implied lips and air and vibrations, and none of those things could exist here.

All he had was the knowledge of what that great green eye told him. Words sprang fully formed into his mind, unbreakable and unshakeable knowledge lodged inside his skull, wherever he had left it.

"Come to me, Skaife. Come down into the deep, into the dark. You belong to me. You are mine. Born of my will. Born of my power. You belong at my side."

Martin had no voice of his own, but he wanted desperately to reply, to deny the words that were seared across every inch of his consciousness, driving all rational thought away with the sheer dark majesty of the one who put them there. He did not belong in the dark. He did not belong to Strata. He was there to conquer it. Not to be swallowed up.

"When the sun rises, you will come back down into the dark. You will face the least of my favored children and you shall be found wanting. You will fall at my executioner's feet with joy in your heart. With each rebirth you will become a little more mine. With every death, you will carry a little more of my life within you. This is not corruption, it is rejuvenation. Through me, you shall live forever. Through you, I shall be free of my shackles. We shall have eternity, my pet. My beloved."

Martin's eyes snapped open and he gasped for air.

What the hell was that?

Light filtered in through the frosted glass of his apartment's only tiny window. Dawn had arrived hours ago, but this was still long before his alarm was due to wake him.

He shuddered in the sudden cold and pulled his blankets tighter around him. Wherever he had been in that dream, it wasn't cold. It had been as warm and comfortable as the womb. Perfect body temperature, so perfect you couldn't feel a thing. Even the tiny tickle of air from under his ill-fitting door was enough to make him shudder now that he was out here in the real world again.

Lindsay had said something about the NIH, some warning

about strange dreams. He'd paid no attention at the time – why would he, when there was such a rich bounty of game spread out in front of him? – but now he wished he had listened a little closer.

Did that dream mean that the game was giving him some sort of brain damage? Was he going to end up going the same way Jezebel had?

He pushed that fear aside. This was hardly the first time he'd dreamed about a video game. It didn't matter that this dream had been a little bit intense or strange compared to the usual "whack-a-monster" dreams Dracolich used to give him. Strata was a strange game; of course it would prompt strange dreams. There was nothing wrong with him.

If anything, he was feeling better now than he had all week. Every session spent playing Strata felt like a much-needed rest, like a much-needed reward after years and years of misery in the rat-race of his everyday existence. He wasn't going to abandon that over one silly little dream that probably didn't mean anything.

The chill seemed to abate and he managed to fumble his way into some clothes that were probably clean. Everything felt awkward. He missed Skaife's nimble little fingers. After a moment of hunting around for his keys, he realized that he missed having an inventory system that worked at the speed of thought too.

He scooped up his phone and searched for a player called Jezebel on any of the Strata forums. Nothing came up. He did the same thing on the Dracolich character registries and had the opposite problem: hundreds upon hundreds of Jezebels as far as the eye could see.

There was no way he was going to find this particular one. And even if he did, the anonymity that protected players from real-life weirdos coming after them for what they did in the game also prevented him from sending any help her way.

The next time one of the Masters came by to dunk on him,

he'd have to ask them to look into it. Pride was one thing, but this was someone's life.

Out of curiosity, he flicked over to what seemed to be the biggest auction site for Strata goods, the only place where real life and the game really seemed to intersect. There were no Jezebel listings, but while he was there Martin tossed the useless shield that he got from Celaphox up for a 24-hour auction.

He had no details on what it did, just the name, origin and [Knight Only] but that seemed to be sufficient. As soon as that was done, he promptly forgot about it and turned his attention to food.

A quick run to the store gave him some fairly gross edible supplies to last out the day, and he still had a solid half an hour before meeting back up with the guild to start planning their next move. It wasn't a lot, but he'd made bigger decisions in far less time.

With as much preparation done as he could muster, he slipped on the NIH and let out a little sigh of relief as it stripped his senses away and he sank back down into the blessed darkness of Strata.

The crowds around the corpse of Celaphox seemed to have dispersed for the most part, but there were one or two players still lingering around. They were the competition to watch out for, in Martin's estimation; the ones who were willing to backtrack to try and decipher how an unbeatable boss had been beaten.

He could see them all separately trying to conduct a forensic investigation of the dead monster, to work out how it had been done.

Martin kept the smirk off his face and set out to do some investigation of his own. He had no intention of roaming the tunnels around here alone. Not when he was still out-leveled by practically every enemy. But in all the excitement last night, he had completely forgotten about Speckles.

First he worked his way around the ruined columns that

Celaphox brought down, hunting for a froggy little corpse. Then, when that proved fruitless, he tried shouting into the entrances to the tunnels, though he doubted a timid little frog-man would even consider running that way.

Eventually he gave up and wandered back to the waterfall, which was, almost inevitably, where Speckles had been hiding all along.

Speckles' mouth protruded from the water first. The bitching started before Martin could even see the little frog-man's eyes.

"Me no like waterfall. Bonk head real good. Why leave me?"

"Sorry, buddy. With all of those other pl – uh – crusaders around, it wasn't really safe to come find you. It's quietened down a bit now."

His lips flapped again. "Bad people make hurt?"

Martin couldn't help but smile. "That was my concern, yes."

There was a brief lull in the conversation, then Speckles asked, "I come out now?"

Martin sighed. "Just hang in there for a little bit longer. I think I've got a plan to get us out of here."

"Gods below," Speckles grumbled. But he went without any real protest back into the flood of water.

Martin's gamble could come to nothing if it didn't work, but it could also completely change the race to the bottom of Strata for them if it did, transforming the work of years into one thirty-day sprint.

He had weighed the odds himself and found that it was worth the risk, and he was convinced that Lindsay probably wouldn't let him get past the phrase "wild gamble" without saying yes.

With all his other loose ends attended to, and a plan in mind, there was nothing left to do except administration. He pulled up the menu and sent the knight-only shield off to the auction house's agent, then he turned his attention back to a more plea-surable activity. Leveling up.

[LEVEL UP]

Skaife Murovan Exorcist
Strength: 12 Agility: 8
Endurance: 9 Willpower: 7
LEVEL 6

You have 3 points to assign.

Before, his course had been clear: dumping everything into strength for a direct increase in damage. But with the new ability that popped up last time, willpower had become a viable way to push up his raw damage too, even if it didn't have the synergy of his *Celestial Strikes* yet.

More than that, he was finding himself using his spells more often the longer they played. Swinging a sword around was all well and good, but the class abilities were how you won fights, and all of his seemed to draw on willpower.

Beyond that, endurance and agility were tempting him too. There was always some perverse part of his brain that wanted to create a balanced character instead of hyper-specializing the way that RPGs rewarded, but in Strata there wasn't any one stat that didn't serve a purpose.

A bit more agility and Celaphox' attacks might have missed him entirely. A bit more endurance and he could have shrugged them off. He knew he'd been lucky and smart in equal measure up until this point, but eventually he was going to run head-on into a straight fight that he just couldn't think his way around.

Judging from the fuss that was made about the Archdukes, he suspected that they were going to be the gatekeepers for the lower deeps, the hard stat and skill tests that ensured none of the low-level dregs made it through to the high-level content.

It was classic game design, and it could completely wreck his plan to rush ahead through the deeps and backfill the leveling they had missed out on using a few clever wins.

Thinking on his team, it seemed likely that Lindsay was always going to be their go-to for damage. Jericho was always going to be the tank to soak up enemy punishment and Julia was always going to heal.

He didn't have a role in that triumvirate. He was left floating outside, adding a little healing here, a little damage there, taking the odd hit so it couldn't down someone softer.

The exorcist was a jack of all trades, master of none, and he had known that going in, but somehow it still grated having no clear path to progression.

To hell with it. He dumped it all in willpower.

Skaife *Murovan Exorcist*
Strength: 12 Agility: 8
*Endurance: 9 Willpower: **10***
Health: 45 Stamina: 58

You may select 1 new ability.

Smite – Your next successful melee attack deals an additional 10 light damage.
[20-second cooldown]

Lay on Hands – Restores 100% of an ally's health. Reduces your stamina and stamina regeneration by 7% for 5 minutes.
[60-minute cooldown]

Rite of Consecration – Increases all healing effects within the 11ft area of effect by 50% for 30 seconds. Increases all light damage within the area of effect by 25% for 15 seconds.
[60-minute cooldown]

The new ability was pretty juicy in a way that honestly might only appeal to statistic geeks like Martin. Just one or the other of those effects would have been spectacular, but the combination, and the utility of being able to apply it to two completely different situations, made it even tastier.

Nonetheless, he selected *Smite*. *Celestial Strike* was great, but it was costing him the benefit of his strength score on every hit. This ability combined the best of both worlds, and he could slot it into his rotation in between *Celestial Strikes* to keep his damage potential high, even against armored foes.

His only regret was that he hadn't been able to buff up his health. He didn't want to end up as a glass cannon; the game environment wasn't forgiving enough for that, and with one of the Masters gunning for him personally, Martin knew that the first sign of weakness in his build would be the moment a figurative truck full of alligators got dropped on his head.

With all of that busywork done, there was nothing left to do but wait as Lindsay came leaping and bounding down the waterfall stairs, shouting into the guild-chat.

"Give me the new stabby! My stabby stabby stabby!"

He knew her well enough to wait until she was actually down in the main chamber to turn the kris over to her. It wouldn't have been helpful if she'd stalled out on the stairs.

She danced around in a circle, kissing the sinister looking blade in between outbursts.

"Oh, my precious stabby. I shall love him and squeeze him and call him stabby."

"I hope the two of you will be very happy together," Martin deadpanned. He couldn't find it in his heart to actually be annoyed with her antics anymore. Not after everything that he'd put her through yesterday.

"Don't worry Martin, if it all falls apart, I will still come back to you. Keep looking for that rat tuxedo."

She was already taking practice slashes with the dagger, so she had to shout back over her shoulder.

"Hey, what did you get? Jericho said he got some weird whip that he can't really use, and Julia was all hyped about her new robes, but you never said what calamari grandé dropped for you."

He sighed. "Nothing. Vendor trash."

"Ah, don't worry, dude. There's always another boss. Another loot drop. At least you get to keep the cash. Cash is good, right?"

"Well, that depends if we ever get a chance to spend it. I don't know if you noticed, but we can't exactly backtrack to a city from here."

"Sure we can, dude." She pointed up into the dark in the vague direction of the last Deep Gate. "You can give me a boost, I'll throw down a rope... I really should have bought a rope before I came down, huh. Never mind."

Martin shrugged. "I'm trying to sell it online anyway. Maybe get some cash to pay you back."

"Dude, your money is no good here. You don't pay people back for gifts. You just slavishly worship them for the rest of your life. Maybe peel some grapes. Fan me a bit. You know the drill."

Martin chuckled. "All right. As soon as I find some grapes, I'll get right on that."

Julia and Jericho arrived within a moment of each other yet again. If they were trying to hide a relationship, they were doing a pretty poor job of it.

"Good afternoon, comrades," Jericho rumbled.

By his side, Julia gave a half-hearted wave, but this was not good enough for Jericho. He took a hold of her wrist and waggled her arm from side to side. Putting on a high-pitched, grating voice, he whined, "Good afternoon, everyone."

Julia retrieved her arm and scowled. "There is nothing good in the world until after I've had a coffee."

Lindsay couldn't help herself. "Maybe we'll find some of those deer-men I keep hearing about in the next deep. The ones sent from outer space to bring us coffee."

Jericho and Julia both looked confused, while Martin put his face into his hands.

"The star bucks?" he groaned.

The other two joined him in his groaning, while Lindsay cackled. Her dad jokes were getting too powerful. She had to be stopped.

Martin looked around at them – his guild, his people – then he tried to wet his lips and found that the mechanics of it didn't work right with a rat mouth.

"Last night was awesome. We did something that nobody else in this game has ever managed. That means that from this moment forward, we are the ones to beat. We are the ones who the Masters of Strata are going to be trying to trip. We are the ones every other guild is going to try to take down a peg."

Lindsay pretended to examine her pinfeathers. "Let them try. See what happens when you mess with the Riot!"

Jericho reflexively barked, "Iron Riot!"

It was loud enough that the lingering high-level players took notice. Martin had to act quickly.

"We don't know how much that fight is going to help us going forward, but our understanding of how we won, that is privileged information. If you share that with someone, you are giving away guild secrets. You are giving them the tools they need to beat the same mechanics and catch up to us. I don't want any of you sharing this story around."

Julia cocked her head. "Won't one of the developers leak it eventually?"

"Not a chance." Martin smirked. "The Masters can't keep track of everything in the game. They need player reports to understand everything that is happening. They've made a game so complex, they can't even read the back end. That was how I pissed them off to start with. I wouldn't share."

Julia frowned. "That doesn't make any sense."

"Tell me about it." He shrugged. "But it's the only explana-tion for how they've been behaving that makes sense."

One of the high-level players, a Sythvan knight wearing a

colorful, feather-trimmed set of plate, approached them. Lindsay cut him off at the pass.

"No autographs. No pictures. No exclusive. Jog on."

His eyes narrowed, but he moved away as if he'd never intended to speak to them at all. Martin sighed.

"There is going to be a lot of that, and most of it is going to be a bit more subtle. So let's just keep our heads down and press on, yeah?"

"Back to roaming tunnels?" Jericho groaned.

"Actually, I have an idea. It is a little bit risky, and the Masters might intervene to stop us, but if it works, it will change everything."

Lindsay patted him on the back. "You had me at risky."

With one last glance around to make sure nobody was listening, Martin explained his experiment.

"The ability that I unlocked, *Rite of Passage*, it lets me unlock a Gate."

"We know this. You explained." Jericho rolled his eyes. "Every three days, we get to skip a boss. Very boring. My new abilities are much more dramatic."

"And I can't wait to hear all about them," Martin pointed past Jericho's hairy bulk towards the pool. "But there is a Gate there. Not a Deep Gate. Something much better. They've built skips into the dungeon, so that once you've beaten one of the big bosses you can jump back and forth through the previous deeps more easily."

Julia smiled. "Metroidvania-style."

"Exactly." Martin grinned back. "So if we can pop this gate open…"

Lindsay was literally hopping up and down on the spot. "We can jump straight to the big boss and skip the next seven floors of boring!"

Martin held up a hand, and Lindsay managed to roll back her excitement to merely vibrating on the spot rather than jumping around.

"There is a real risk with this, though. If we skip too far ahead of the leveling curve, every monster that we face is going to—"

Lindsay interrupted. "Give us a ton of experience points!"

"They are going to out-level us to the point that we might not be able to beat them," Julia sighed.

Jericho seemed to be weighing all of this.

"I am thinking we will still crush them all. I am thinking nothing can stop the Riot, yes?"

Lindsay crowed with excitement. "That is three votes yes!"

Julia frowned. "Where did you get three? You and Jericho might want to rush ahead, but Martin—"

Lindsay butted in again. "Martin wouldn't have even come to us with it if he didn't think it was the best plan. You know Martin."

Martin had the good grace to look embarrassed about how transparent he was. "Three votes was all we needed. Let's go waste my biggest cooldown."

All their eyes were on him, and for some reason that was embarrassing now. In battle, their eyes turned his way constantly; it seemed strange that in these quiet moments he should get so awkward.

He held out a hand to the pool, the ring of silver barely visible beneath the crumbled stone. This was it. With one last press of effort, he cast *Rite of Passage*.

For one long awful moment, nothing happened. Then sparks started to dance around the edges of the pool. Arcs of purple lightning snapped back and forth, dancing around, coruscating across the surface of the water.

With a sudden thump that Martin felt in the pit of his stomach, the Gate opened; a glowing spiral of that same purple light, barely bound within the confines of the ring.

He couldn't see anything on the other side. Just that blinding light. They had no way of knowing what they would be jumping into. No way to plan for what was to come.

Lindsay cannonballed in. The lightning rippled for a moment, then returned to its entropic state. Jericho took Julia's hand and jumped too, before there was time for doubt.

Martin looked up into the stunned faces of the players around him with a fair amount of surprise showing on his own rodent features. Then, with a laugh, he dove in too.

He regretted everything. Beyond the eye of purple light, there was nothing but absolute darkness. Just the briefest glimpse of the hollow robes of a Master, hanging below the portal, an arm raised up in a mocking wave, then nothing at all.

He could feel himself falling, but after that first moment he couldn't see a thing. Tumbling end over end, he wondered if he should just log out. Get out of the game rather than suffer through whatever fresh hell he'd just delivered them all into.

Maybe the spiteful Master had come by with one final trick. He supposed it would be easy to whack a magical portal out of alignment. A couple of lines of code tweaked a little and instead of landing at the intended location he could be dumped outside of the game world in this awful primordial darkness.

Dread settled over him like a funereal shroud. This wouldn't kill him. He would never respawn. He would just fall forever and ever. It had all been for nothing. He would have to start over, with none of the advantages and tricks that they'd had the first time around. Lindsay would have to leave him behind, if she hadn't been dragged into the same void.

Tears of frustration pricked at the corners of his eyes. Why were people like this? Every time people got involved, everything good seemed to fall apart. His job. This game. If everyone would just leave him alone, he could be happy. Why did everyone want a piece of him?

For another long moment he fell. Trying to keep his fury under control. Trying to think of a solution. Then he caught a glimpse of something down below. A speck of green light. All his dread and anger flushed away in terror.

"Yes. Come to me."

"No. No. No."

He startled at the sound of his own voice.

"Come to me. Serve me. Come down into the dark."

Martin twisted with all of his strength, and just barely managed to break eye-contact with the green light. Pressing his own eyes shut. Trying to will this nightmare away.

He hit the ground and the numbness that Strata gave instead of honest pain spread across his back like ice-water. He opened his eyes and gasped up at the looming animal faces of Lindsay, Jericho and Julia, illuminated in the light of a ragged looking torch they'd fashioned from a well-chewed femur.

"What took you so long?" Lindsay asked.

A shaky laugh rattled life back into his body.

"Took a wrong turn."

Lindsay's cackle dumped warmth right back into his chest.

"And here we thought you'd just wimped out on us. Come on, dude. You've got to see this place."

TWENTY-FIVE

The Executioner of Strata

They were at the foot of a great basalt cliff, with the crackling purple portal only just visible within a great crack. The shadows lay thick and heavy over the bottom of the chasm, and the others kept tripping over one another as they crept along.

They were all being buoyed along by their own bravado, by their inflated sense of their own power and skill in the face of Strata. Martin was just as bad as any of the rest of them, still certain, despite all his suspicions, that somehow they would overcome the odds. That he could best the first Archduke of Strata with trickery and cunning the way they had beaten the impossible bosses before.

It was easier to focus on that than to consider any of the other things that had been happening down in this dungeon; the Master out to get him, the inexplicable qualities of the game, and – most pressingly – the voice in his head, echoing up from some unfathomably dark place beneath their feet.

Normally, he would backtrack through the lessons he had learned from the lesser bosses in the levels before; but in that regard, as with their character progression, they were lagging massively behind the curve.

Martin had no clue what they were about to walk in on,

whether it would be some big angry plant or a crab-man or anything else. All he had to work with were the whispers of that voice that should not have been in his head and the scraps and tatters he had managed to piece together.

Carnifex, First Archduke of Strata, had been defeated by other guilds while they were playing, so it was possible to defeat him. All they needed was to find some way around their statistical disadvantages.

In a normal game, Martin would have just dragged everyone back up to grind through some levels, but the race lay forever at the back of his mind, ticking away like a clock. They couldn't afford to waste the time. Not if there was a chance they could push right through this fight the way they had so many before.

The chasm gradually widened as they went along, the bare black stone fading out of sight as they walked ever forward into the echoing dark chamber up ahead.

Beneath their feet gravel gave way to flagstones, then to graven flagstones marked with the same complex symbols that Martin had been trying to decipher through the mud way back in the second deep. All clear as day here, each detail picked out in sharp relief as though blackened with soot.

Martin stared for a long moment, then sniffed at the air. There was something wrong. They had been strolling through the dark long enough for tension to build and abate.

The boss should have sprung out on them by now. There was some trap here that he just hadn't been able to put together yet. He sniffed again, and caught what he was searching for: a faint acrid aroma just a little like the breath of the Night Ravager.

"Oh no. Kill the torch. Kill the—"

There was a sudden rush of that same foul air from up ahead and the torch suddenly exploded into a fireball.

[Tesra suffers 6 fire damage]
[Adriel suffers 7 fire damage]
[Jericho suffers 6 fire damage]

Martin had taken a few precautionary steps away, but even still he could smell his fur sizzling off, flooding the room with its burnt-popcorn stench. The soot made sense at least. Where the flames had touched the flagstones, those strange familiar runes now took on an even more familiar glow.

An emerald-green light flickered up from beneath them, spreading out from where the flames had burst over the ground and rippling out until the whole chamber was up-lit.

It took him far too long to recognize what he was looking at and he reacted far too slowly to the movement up above them in the endless darkness. Martin was barely able to fling himself aside before the massive cleaver of bone hammered down onto the spot where he had stood and sent up flares of green light.

[MISS]

That flash was enough to furnish his overactive imagination with just enough details to go wild. The cleaver was not a weapon held in some creature's hand. Tendons clung to it further up. Patches of wiry black hair grew from the meatier parts.

It was the Archduke's arm. One great jagged length of bone, five times the length of Martin's whole body. A weapon from shoulder to tip.

Beyond the cleaver arm, up in the shadows beyond the immediate murderous swipe there was only the faintest sheen of bare wet bone reflecting back down. Just the hint of a horse-like skull exposed amidst more of that same bristling hair.

Carnifex, First Archduke of Strata, Executioner of the Heart

It was huge. The size of a building. Too big to be moving so quickly into another attack.

The next swing was far less precise, a ragged hacking thing

that swept across the whole room and sent the whole guild diving onto the ground to avoid being ripped in half.

[MISS]

There was no way that any one of them except Jericho could survive a single blow from a weapon like that, no matter how far game mechanics might differ from reality. For as long as Carnifex was alive, they were all just one mistake away from death.

The tip of the blade scraped along the far wall, marking the edge of their battlefield, leaving a jagged tear through the runic tiles and unleashing another sudden burst of that same sickly green light from each damaged symbol.

Martin dragged his eyes away from the horror-show of the patchwork beast and bellowed to be heard over the sound of the scraping bone.

"This is going to be a DPS race. We need to burst him down before he lands a hit. Don't just stare. Buff and move!"

He took his own advice, igniting his *Celestial Strike* and charging, wishing all the while that it didn't give off light marking his position and exposing him to more brief glimpses of the lumbering thing up ahead.

The body of Carnifex seemed centaur-like, with four legs and a torso jutting from its forequarters. That was good. He could work with that. A body like that came with a lot of blind spots. If he could get under the belly, he'd get a few free swings, and if he could get on its back he might be able to focus on churning out damage as fast as he could.

His sword burned like a rising star amidst the murk of the cavernous chamber. It was hardly surprising that he was the one Carnifex chose to attack again. He could feel the disturbance in the air before he saw the great ridge of bone coming for him out of the darkness.

There would be no ducking this swing. It came in at waist height and he had to fling himself up into the air and cast *Rebuke* just to deflect it low enough to have the pleasure of tumbling head over heels across the flat of the blade.

[MISS]

Every miss was another win for Iron Riot. But it had to miss every time, and they only had to make a mistake once before it was all over.

Martin didn't hesitate when he felt stone beneath his back once more; he just uncurled and half-ran, half-scrambled the rest of the distance to the great grotesque hoof that was closest to him.

[Carnifex suffers 16 slashing damage]
[Carnifex suffers 16 light damage]

Any hope of light doing extra damage was sunk, as was any hope that this monstrosity relied on armor to soak up damage. It must have had a health pool big enough to drown dragons in.

Martin nearly fell as a sudden impact hit him in the middle of his back, then again on his shoulder an instant later.

But to his relief, there was no blood or numbness. Lindsay had used him like a springboard for her *Raptor Strike*.

[Carnifex suffers 36 piercing damage]

"Nice," he called out.

Lindsay laughed as she kicked off the thick trunk of a leg to land back on her feet. "Glad you approve. I'll go on using you as a step-ladder in the future."

[Jericho BLOCKS 76 damage]

The impact rang out through the chamber, a concussive wave that rocked them where they stood. Jericho was trying to go toe to toe with the titan. He was trying to treat this like a fair fight that they could win by playing their roles.

Martin had no time for nicety, not now. "Get your ass out of there, you idiot."

"Julia tripped over new robes," Jericho grunted back.

Julia spoke at almost the same time. "My fault. My fault."

Lindsay rolled her eyes. "Just get Jericho back up and keep moving."

Martin had closed the distance with Lindsay and was holding his bracers up for her use. She swept her odd daggers over them with a shriek.

"All damage is good damage. Now get in the fight!"

There were flares of light in the distance, bright enough to illuminate Jericho and Julia for brief moments before darkness swept them away again. Martin could see her laying her hands on him, and Jericho jerking her aside as another massive sweep of the cleaver came too close.

[MISS]

Together, they were better than either one of them could have been alone. Together, they were more. Then the steady percussion of Jericho's flurry attack began, ticking off point after point of damage in brief bursts before he had to dive out of the way of yet another attack.

[Carnifex suffers 5 light damage]
[Carnifex suffers 6 light damage]
[Carnifex suffers 5 light damage]
[Carnifex suffers 4 light damage]

The hoof that they had been attacking lifted off the ground and sent Martin and Lindsay scampering away before it came hammering down.

They charged back in as one and he called on *Smite* as his

sword swung for the gleam of exposed bone amongst the thicket of fur and the stench of rot.

[Carnifex suffers 31 slashing damage]
[Carnifex suffers 10 light damage]

Martin was taken aback by how much damage he had actually done until he remembered that his attacks were finally benefitting from his strength. Smite was his new favorite thing. Lindsay's blades took on a purple flicker as she darted in and stabbed them both solidly into the meat beside Martin.

[Carnifex suffers 28 piercing damage]

She let out a cackle of delight that turned into a yelp as the leg lifted off with her still attached.

Martin was under no illusion about how much damage they were really dealing to this thing as a percentage. A hundred damage and change might have been enough to polish off a Night Ravager, but this was one of the game's raid bosses. If it didn't keep moving the same hoof, he would have said it probably wasn't even feeling their attacks.

They needed more. He ran for the back leg on the same side. If they could topple the thing then Lindsay could get at its head. An exposed skull probably meant a lot of those organs that people liked to keep on the inside could very well be on the outside too, and they needed some advantage if they were ever going to get this over with.

By the time he reached the back leg it was already sweeping towards him, but he didn't slow, just adjusted his aim, diving to one side and slashing at an exposed tendon. *Celestial Strike* came off cooldown and flared to life just before he made contact.

[Carnifex suffers 16 slashing damage]
[Carnifex suffers 16 light damage]

It was another drop in the bucket, but it meant that his *Trinity Strike* would be up next, and he could blow his other cooldowns to get their critical hit chances up enough to make it all worthwhile.

If this was going to be a meatgrinder, he was going to make it into the most efficient meatgrinder that any of them had ever been in.

Jericho was still diligently pounding away with the flurrying lights of his aura, ticking off damage points like the seconds off the clock. Julia must have been by his side, topping off his health and empowering him however hierophants did. They seemed to have worked out the synergy of their roles, and Martin trusted them enough to let them get on with it.

Martin slapped a hand to the guild-crest. "Save your big hits. I'm blowing a cooldown in ten seconds that should put your crit chance through the roof."

Lindsay's voice didn't come back through the same connection. It echoed in a shriek from somewhere up above them.

"I'm on a really wrinkly knee! It's like one of those bald cats. But corpsier!"

Martin couldn't help but laugh. "Keep climbing!"

That was when everything went to hell. The underside of Carnifex's long body split open, like two great doors of putrid skin flapping apart. A downpour of rancid liquid, tainted green by the rune-light, came gushing out a moment later to splash across the floor.

Martin was so taken aback that he just gawked up into the shadowed opening as the reek of the Archduke's innards washed over him.

Eggs began to rain down, each as big as his fist. Each leathery and spiked with bone fragments that made no sense to any egg-laying mammal, but awful sense to a creature that could drop them like bombs from its guts.

One egg hit Martin in the shoulder before he came to his

senses, but instead of bouncing right off, it latched there. The jagged bone hooked cruelly into his flesh.

[Skaife suffers 6 piercing damage]
[Skaife is poisoned]

This was the first hint at poison in the game – probably another of the many things that they had skipped past. Martin reached up to yank the egg free, then froze with a horrible realization.

The spines of bone on the egg's surface were rippling, adjusting their position as his fingers approached, ready to hook into them too, to pin his hand uselessly in place.

There was no blessed cold as the poison spread through his blood; only an ever-growing heat, and a horrific sensation of something scuttling around under his skin.

He fumbled his sword from the numb fingers of the hand on his injured side into the other and struck the egg. It popped like a cyst, spraying more of that rancid fluid everywhere. It blinded one eye with an acidic sizzle, the sound turning Martin's stomach.

[Skaife suffers 2 poison damage]

He scrubbed at his eye with a fumbling, half-dead hand, but it was no use; all vision had been burned away on that side. He had to swivel around to take it all in, then he had to dive backwards as Carnifex's great black hoof came slamming down where he'd stood just a moment before.

[MISS]

The eggs beneath that hoof popped, but a hundred or more of them still lay on the ground, quivering, just waiting for someone to be foolish enough to get close to them. He should have climbed the damned leg when he had a chance.

Lindsay's voice bursting out of the guild channel nearly made him jump out of his skin.

"*Raptor Strike* right in the eye, coming up fast. Pop those cooldowns!"

She had no idea what had happened beneath her. Martin dashed forward, popping *Rite of Retribution* as he went and willing *Trinity Strike* to light up his sword too. The back leg was still the closest, even if his feet were slipping in the foul ichor splattered across the floor all around it.

His feet smoked as the vicious chemicals began eating through his boots. It didn't matter. He had to help Lindsay.

[Carnifex suffers 24 light damage]

It was a clumsy blow, scraping across the hard surface of the hoof before finding purchase, but the magic of his special ability seemed to discharge all the same.

None of them could see Lindsay up on the Archduke's body, but when she hit, everyone knew it. The monster rocked on the spot.

[CRITICAL HIT]
[Carnifex suffers 56 piercing damage]

Martin took his chance, casting another *Rebuke* at Carnifex' rear leg in the vague hope that it might be toppled, but the nudge wasn't enough. It stumbled, but it didn't fall.

The air writhed around Carnifex as it twisted and turned, trying to fling Lindsay free, but wherever she had lodged herself with that last attack was where she meant to stay.

Light strobed from the front of the Archduke as Jericho's assault began anew. Each flicker of light was another point of damage, and every odd one was doubled.

[CRITICAL HIT]
[Carnifex suffers 16 light damage]

It still wasn't going to be enough. Martin could see the great gaping opening in Carnifex' gut starting to fold shut as it trudged toward Jericho and Julia's position.

The floor beneath it was impassible now, a minefield of lethal acids, hooks and poisons. They couldn't even see the danger coming as the Archduke pressed on and on, sweeping that great bone blade every few steps to drive them helplessly back.

The whole room would be flooded with noxious poisons, and eventually Lindsay would lose her grip or her footing and fall down to die with the rest of them. They just weren't doing enough damage fast enough.

Half blind and numb down his strong side, Martin ran for his friends. *Healing Touch* reversed the impact of the egg on his health pool, but it did nothing to ease the burning or to return sight to his eye. Poison must have had some separate cure that he hadn't unlocked.

The great bone cleaver swept by him, almost invisible in the dark even when he'd had both eyes. It was only luck that saved him.

[MISS]

As he passed underneath it, he stared up towards Carnifex's skull, hoping to catch some glimpse of Lindsay inside. Instead, he saw twin pinpricks of green light within those hollow black voids, lights burning as bright as the dead and distant stars.

"Come to me. Die for me. Live for me again."

He had to wrench himself away before it used this moment of hypnosis against him. Already the executioner's blade was being lifted once more. It didn't matter if it could get in his head. All it did was lie anyway. Martin spat out a bitter whisper. *"You will fall at my executioner's feet with joy in your heart."*

There wasn't a chance in hell that he would be happy when he died to this thing. Furious, maybe. Disappointed, almost certainly.

He could already feel the bitterness rising up inside him. They had come so far just to fall to this thing, for no better reason than the numbers on their character sheets being too low?

Jericho and Julia stood back to back, her reptilian tail coiled around one of Jericho's tree-trunk legs to keep them together. She cast healing spell after healing spell, topping off his health every moment. It made no sense until Martin remembered the class name: martyr.

Jericho was damaging himself with every attack, his stupid defensive powers turning against him as he tried to use them offensively.

When Jericho saw him approaching, he waved haphazardly with his whip, then returned to the task at hand, launching another flurry of lights off into the Archduke's chest, illuminating the patterns of patchy hair, rotten skin and the deep ritual lines of scarification.

[Carnifex suffers 4 light damage]
[Carnifex suffers 6 light damage]
[Carnifex suffers 5 light damage]
[Carnifex suffers 4 light damage]

"We lose this, yes?" Jericho said it so softly Martin didn't even register his words for a moment.

Martin took one look from Julia's fearful eyes to Jericho's jaw, set rigid in determination, and he made a decision. "We don't lose."

He pressed his eyes closed for a moment and was aghast. His health, usually a warm red color, had turned the same emerald green as the light that surrounded them and it had drained halfway in the time since he'd cast his *Healing Touch*. He was going to die. Nothing could prevent that now. All he could do was make it mean something.

"Kill me."

Jericho and Julia both snapped their heads around, distracted from their work at the most inopportune moment. The great blade swung down at them all over again and Martin had to bodily tackle them out of the way.

[MISS]

Martin rolled off the lovebirds with a laugh.

"Come on, big guy. You say you want to kill me about ten times a day. Now is your chance."

Julia already had a spell beginning to glow between her hands. "How would that help us?"

"The player-versus-player mechanics would kick in. He'd switch class to the one that can use that whip worth a damn. His burst damage would go through the roof."

They all flattened themselves as the blade swung by again at waist height, but Martin was so distracted that it caught his tail, snipping it neatly in half and sending a fresh splatter of blood over all three of them.

[Skaife suffers 19 slashing damage]

Jericho crawled over and dragged Martin back to his feet. "This is crazy. Will this even work?"

Martin didn't know. He really didn't. He couldn't even calculate how much health a raid boss like this might have. He had none of the usual context from surrounding enemies. His own clever solutions had seen to that. But a fighting chance was all Iron Riot had ever needed.

"You can turn the damage this thing churns out against it, just like Celaphox did to us. The two of you, working together. You can beat it."

Indecision was written all over Jericho's face until he felt Julia's scaly hand squeeze his forearm. "He is usually right, you know."

Up in the shrouded darkness, they heard Lindsay scream. They were too far away to see the notification of whatever damage she'd been dealt, but they weren't too far out to hear the sickening crack of impact as her body hit the flagstones.

Tesra has died.

Whatever hope they'd had was waning by the moment, and Martin refused to let Lindsay's suffering be for nothing. He dropped to his knees and Jericho hefted the whip in his hand.

"How should I—"

He closed his eyes. "Just do it."

Jericho let out a snort. Then he swung.

[Skaife suffers 18 slashing damage]
Skaife has died.

In the darkness on the other side of death, the Master was waiting. Hanging smugly in the air.

"It isn't going to work, you know," the Master hissed triumphantly. "Even with the whip, and the power of the heretic. It isn't going to be enough. You died for nothing."

Martin didn't rise to the bait. He just drifted around to watch the scene unfolding before him.

Jericho had turned the whip on himself in a zealous frenzy. The golden glow that had surrounded him before now burned red, as though he were enveloped in flames. With each crack of the whip, they rose higher and burned brighter. And with Julia pouring healing into him non-stop, that fire would not consume him any more than the lashes. The wounds that he opened on his own back were closed before the next blow fell.

There was nothing Martin could do now, only watch. Well… there was *something*. He turned to the Master.

"There was another player, a Sythvan called Jezebel. I wonder if you could check on her in the real world. She seemed to be seriously ill. It would probably be bad press if your players started dropping dead."

The empty hood jerked towards him for a split second. "What?" The Master was clearly invested in the fight unfolding beyond the veil of shadows.

"Jezebel. Snake lady. Lost her mind. You might want to check on her."

The Master flicked a sleeve at him. "Stop trying to distract me."

"Oh, I'm sorry," Martin scoffed. "I thought a real person in the real world might be more important than—"

"The real world. Hah." He was cut off with another wave. "Cease your pitiful deceptions. Do you think that by playing on my sympathies you might earn preferential treatment?"

"I mean, I wouldn't mind if you stopped being a dick to me. But I am genuinely concerned that—"

Another wave and this time Martin's voice was literally cut off, like someone had turned off his microphone.

"She shall be given all due consideration. Now be silent and watch as your sacrifice is proven worthless."

Carnifex was so much clearer now that Martin was dead. Its massive looming form was clearly painted in contrast and shadows. Ugly didn't even begin to describe it. It was like a half-dozen nightmares all stitched together.

Deep in the bare skull, one of the flickering pinpricks of green light still glowed. Lindsay had done her bloody work on the other, and done it well, even if it cost her life.

Martin was careful not to meet that stare. He had a nasty suspicion that it would find him here just as readily as it had in the real world.

Exposed muscles contracted beneath tattered skin that

seemed more of a sheath than an attachment, and the great cleaver blade rose up. This time Jericho did not dodge, or flinch or block. He spread his great arms out wide and welcomed the blow like a long-lost lover.

Being dead was infuriating, because Martin could only see what was in front of him, not all of the complex mathematics behind it.

He saw the blow fall against the red aura around Jericho. He saw the massive Wulvan driven to his knees by the force of it despite all of his mystical protections. Then he saw a great shadow leap up the length of the bone blade to hammer into the Archduke's chest and set it reeling.

Martin's vision was starting to dim, the shadows of death encroaching on his vision, but he was certain that Jericho rose again, bathed in the light of Julia's healing. He was almost certain that he saw the heretic charge, each whipcrack sending out another blast of destructive power at the Archduke as it flinched away.

Darkness fell over Martin entirely before the fight was over. All that was left in his whole world was the Master, hanging like the Grim Reaper beside him. That, and the hourglass warning him that he had 119 minutes until rebirth.

When he tried to ask what was happening, no sound came out. He was still muted by whatever the Master had done before. So, he studied the hooded form of the Master in silence.

What had he done to earn this stranger's hatred? The grudge went well beyond him being insufficiently subservient when they'd first met.

Something deeper was going on here. Something to do with whatever secret was so important that Klimpt, the game designers and everyone else had to be vanished from the internet.

Martin was going to get to the bottom of it. Just as surely as he was going to get to the bottom of Strata.

"No."

Martin attention snapped back on the Master again. Had they won?

"Impossible."

He wished he could speak. Wished he could see. Wished he could do anything but just linger here. Leaving the game didn't even cross his mind. Not when all around him, the most important battle of his life was being fought.

[ANNOUNCEMENT: *Iron Riot* have defeated **Carnifex, Tenth Archduke of Strata**]

The Master spun on him. There was a trace of a snarl in the voice that came out of the hollow hood.

"How are you doing this?"

"Did we win?" Martin asked. He was pleased to hear his own voice again.

"Answer my questions and you will be allowed to leave with your new levels intact."

"So we won?"

"The First Archduke of Strata has been defeated. Is that what you wanted to hear?"

Martin had no body to express his excitement with; no legs to jump around and no fist to pump. But some part of his delight must have radiated, because the Master's tone turned even more vicious.

"This means nothing. You have bested the weakest of ten Archdukes. You have traversed ten deeps. You have barely broken the surface. There are ninety more, each more dangerous and harrowing than the last. Nobody has defeated the fourth Archduke. Nobody has taken a step beyond the fiftieth deep."

"Then why are you freaking out? If this doesn't matter then—"

"Because you should not be winning," the Master snapped. "You have not worked for it. You do not deserve it. Others have spent months pouring their efforts into this great crucible, their very lifeblood. And you? You just waltzed in!"

"Gods below, are you *that* scared I'm going to beat your game?"

An even deeper silence fell. The Master hung frozen again. When they finally spoke, all emotion had been sapped from their voice all over again.

"You know nothing."

Martin growled through his teeth. "I know you're so scared that you tried to throw me right off the side of the damned dungeon when I went through that portal. I know you are breaking all your own rules to try to slow me down."

"Take your little victory and get out."

"Not without an answer. Why are you hounding me?"

The Master seemed to freeze. "Because you… you might be the one to kill us all."

With those words, the Master blinked out in a sudden flare of light, one so blinding that it persisted in Martin's vision even after it was long over.

He didn't even know what to think of that random and ominous statement. How was he going to kill anyone by playing a game? Did the Master mean that they'd lose their jobs if the game was over?

None of it made sense.

TWENTY-SIX

The Spoils

He logged out, fearful of more ominous voices in the oppressive darkness, and opened his eyes to the last of the afternoon's sunshine. That, and the ceaseless buzzing of his phone. All from Lindsay.

"Did we win? Did we all die?"

"If you died, why haven't you sent me a message yet?"

"Yo, corpse-boy! Tell me how you lost!"

"That thing was huuuuuuge."

"Dude, don't sit and sulk about it. We'll get back in a couple hours."

"J+J just messaged me. We won! You died! Why aren't you telling me things?"

"All right, that is it, I'm booking a flight and getting my pens. Prepare for the face of a million dicks."

"Dude! TALK."

Martin fumbled for the thing.

"We won. Had to die to beat it."

"Duderino, I already know all that. Jericho logged out to tell me. They're looting now. Going to take a break and get back to it in 2 hours. Big J says: thanks for dying. You okay?"

Martin stopped for a moment to ask himself the same question. In all of the chaos, he hadn't really had time to think about it at all.

"Poison isn't a lot of fun, but I'm all right now. We won, you know?"

"Winning is good. Cool. Eyeball acid sucked too."

His fingers hovered over the screen for a little too long.

"Sorry I keep sending you to your death."

"Dude, it is fine. We all got to go sometime."

He could almost see the shrug in the words.

"Yeah, but we don't have to go all *the time."*

She fell silent after that. But soon, Jericho was blowing up his phone. He was polite enough to rattle off a list of all the loot they had discovered.

"Knight Battleaxe. Armor for you. Invoker robe. Cloak for me. Craft stuff. Silver."

Some decent armor would be helpful, so he wasn't going to complain about that. He sent a brusque *"Thanks,"* back and then pulled the NIH off his head with a groan.

When he got back in the game, there would probably be a heap of new levels waiting for them to apply. He'd have to dive right into another complex set of puzzles and statistics, help the others divide up all the equipment equitably, strategize their next move and lay out their immediate course. Normally, he relished every moment of all that, but after all the weird crap that had happened in the last few days it was starting to feel less like fun and more like a second job.

He pressed his eyes shut, half expecting to see a health and stamina bar when he pressed the heels of his hands into them. He needed to stop. He needed to get out of his head. It was just a game. It was all just a game.

More importantly, it was a game they were winning. Two raid bosses in two days. One of them a world-first victory, the other grossly out-leveling the guild.

These were the sort of achievements he would have pinned to his heart like medals just a few days ago. He had to remember why he was doing all this.

The Masters of Strata were against him. Well, that wasn't technically news. They had set themselves against him the moment they turned their game into a challenge. The moment they decided to make Strata into a competition, they set themselves up as his enemy.

It didn't matter if they interfered with his progress. It didn't matter if they clipped a level from him here and there, because in the end he would overcome it, the same way he'd overcome every other challenge they'd thrown at him. He was getting special treatment and attention because they recognized that he was a threat to them. Excellence always bred contempt.

His belief that they would win Strata had not always been unshakeable. He was just as human as Lindsay and all the rest, even if he refused to show that weakness. But now more than ever, he felt certainty in the outcome.

They would be the first to defeat the Heart of Strata, and they would be immortalized as a result.

Fear and doubt dropped away from him in the light of that certainty. Nightmares and petty designers and the feeling of poison writhing under his skin all got washed off. He had two hours to spend, and he was going to make every moment count.

Edwin Klimpt might have been invisible, but that didn't mean his whole family was too. Martin worked his way methodically through every Klimpt in the registry, narrowing down options and taking meticulous notes of everything – he was not going to be caught out by some clever little filter a second time.

By the end of his two hours, he had every one of them listed out and pinned to a map in his mind.

People moved around, especially people in the tech industry, so there was no way of knowing which, if any, of these Klimpts were related to his one: Edwin.

But this list was still someplace to start. As in Strata, he had a plan now. It wouldn't be easy to track the creators down and it wouldn't be easy to find out every secret that they were trying to hide away from the world, but the Masters had set themselves against him, and that meant total war.

Though the last hours had given him more leads than answers, it had passed the time. Now the game was waiting for him.

He logged back in and fell head over tail all the way down through the dark, to land with a crunch in the chasm. Trembling with anticipation, he waited for the numbness to spread over his back and his health points to deplete, but instead that same, awful burning filled in for it.

It wasn't pain, not yet, but the heat of it was so close to pain that he nearly logged right back out again. He blinked to pull up his menu. The poisoning had been cleared by death, but when he reached up, he found his eye socket was still a mass of scar tissue and his fur was pocked with long-healed burns.

[LEVEL UP X 3]

That was something nice to come back to, at least. There certainly wasn't a welcome party. He limped his way along the basalt chasm, awkward in his body with these scars tugging at him with each step. He was so stiff that he fumbled his sword when a monster suddenly leapt out of the shadows at him.

"You leave me behind!"

Speckles. He had completely forgotten about Speckles.

"You followed us?"

"Me wait until cave empty. Jump through purple hole, fall here. You gone. You leave me behind!"

"I am so sorry, Speckles. We had the Archduke to fight, and I didn't know if I'd be able to protect you."

"Words less."

It took Martin a moment to filter everything he was trying to say into the Anurvan's limited vocabulary. "We fight scary bad. Very sorry?"

Speckles leaned in closer. "You beat scary bad?"

Martin grinned. "Yep."

"Good. No leave Speckles again."

It was only when he stepped into the dim chamber and saw the rapidly putrefying corpse of the Archduke that Martin found some rhythm in his steps. Up ahead, looking down on their broken foe, was the unmistakable iceberg bulk of Jericho. Lindsay was standing beside him, looking strangely solemn for a woman who had just gotten one of the biggest wins of her life.

Jericho's red aura had faded away and a quick glance revealed that killing the Archduke had been sufficient to reset his Sin to normal, but his whole attitude and posture seemed to have changed. There was a predatory gleam in his eyes as he looked around at Martin, and his fingers kept tickling over the whip strapped to his hip. Apparently, the taste of power had agreed with him.

They both stared at Martin with open disgust.

"Dude, what the hell happened to your face?" Lindsay asked, unabashed.

"Demon-egg acid. What's your excuse?"

She snorted half-heartedly, but it was enough to break the tension. Jericho rumbled. "Armor, here."

Solarium Mail

[+24 armor. Celestial Strike damage increased by 13%]

After so long with nothing resembling exorcist gear, Martin was stunned at how good that was. No wonder he'd been lagging behind the others with their specialized gear.

As he equipped the armor, he grinned, scar tissue tugging at his cheek as he showed his teeth. "Nice."

The others were not smiling when he looked up. "What happened?"

Lindsay and Jericho met each other's eyes but wouldn't meet his. Eventually, Jericho spoke. "Julia is not coming back."

Lindsay already had her hands up and fluttering.

"It isn't the end of the world. She'll be back tomorrow. She got called in for some work emergency. Don't get mad. Please don't get mad."

Martin blew out a breath and started quietly recalculating his plans. "Do you think I'm some sort of ogre? Real life happens. Don't worry about it."

They visibly relaxed. Jericho rolled his eyes at Lindsay.

"I said this to you."

She squawked. "He doesn't like it when plans change!"

Martin couldn't help but smile. "Thank you for being... sensitive. But it's really all right. We need to stop and make some plans anyway."

Where the Archduke's acid had spread over the runed flagstones, it had pitted and reshaped their meaning, but one circle of the stones in particular had been eaten away to nothing. The Deep Gate. The iris opened at Lindsay's touch.

Beneath the opening there was a tangle of green roots, wound together into something like the Anurvan village walkways; a basket to catch them when they fell. Jericho hopped down with fresh confidence guiding his footing, then caught Lindsay and Martin in his huge arms when they dropped. Martin grinned. "My hero."

Speckles landed beside them with a splat.

They crept along the tops of the woven surface, winding through low arches before finally the cavern opened out ahead of them and they realized that they were actually right up beside the ceiling.

"Wow," Martin breathed.

There was greenery, the same living wood that had comprised the monsters in the deeps above, hacked apart and woven back together into a tangle of walkways and wicker-looking buildings.

The lower half of this cavern was given over to pitch darkness so deep that even Martin's *Night Vision* couldn't penetrate it, and the whole town hung suspended from the massive stalactites that covered the roof.

They had considered Beachhead to be populous compared to

the desolation of the rest of the dungeon, but this place wasn't just bustling with life; it was bursting with it.

The local population seemed to be predominantly Corvan, and they leapt from one walkway to the next with utter abandon. There were painted signs dangling out over the abyss, hinting at wares and services that Martin couldn't even believe were being offered in a dungeon, and hanging over all of them were the banners of trading companies from far and wide.

With that last bit of information in mind, he looked back down onto the city and realized that the whole thing was a marketplace. Every Corvan hawking wares was roosted over a stall of their own. Every building had goods bristling out through the gaps in its weaving. Capitalism was alive and well in Strata.

He turned to tell Speckles that he'd need to hide and found the Anurvan already gone. With puzzlement, he looked askance to Lindsay. "Invisibility cloak," she explained. "Not like I need it in town."

As Iron Riot walked into the bustling market, a silence descended over the crowds. All eyes were on them. Two raid bosses in as many days, one impossible to beat and one way ahead of their level curve. No wonder people were staring. In real life this kind of attention would have made Martin shrink, but here he felt as tall as Jericho. He smiled, and some, if not all, of the people in the crowd smiled right back at him.

It had never been like this in Dracolich. They had been known and respected, but they had never received this reverence. *Because Dracolich was only a game.* The crowds parted before them and Martin wondered if this was what it was like way back in history in the real world, when heroes walked the earth.

One knot of bodies in the central square did not move aside at Iron Riot's approach. Among them were the familiar faces of Dmitri Blackpaw and Snekboi, but it was neither of them that spoke. It was a Sythvan martyr named Virgil that pushed back his shoulders and sneered, "What took you so long?"

That voice was all too familiar. Lindsay yelped. "Dante?"

Dante, their old, slightly useless shaman, scoffed. "You didn't think that the four of you could sneak off and abandon your whole guild with no consequences? You didn't think you were the only ones who'd made the jump over to Strata?"

Lindsay grinned. "It's awesome to see you! If I'd known you were here I would have invited you the minute I arrived."

"I've got my own guild. Thanks. The Brotherhood in Exile. Maybe you've heard of us?"

They'd cleared Carnifex while Iron Riot had still been dawdling in the upper levels. How long had they been playing?

"Oh, cool. Cool." Lindsay blustered on. "So, what's up? Do you guys want to work together?"

Snekboi spat on the ground, and Dante grinned. "Nah, we don't want to work together. We want to kick you back to Dracolich. This is our game. Go home."

Whatever the fight with Carnifex had awoken in Jericho was straining beneath the surface. He surged forward with a roar, and while the other four members of the Brotherhood in Exile didn't run for their lives the way Snekboi had, they all flinched.

Martin took a deep breath. "I'm pretty sure there is plenty of dungeon to go around. No need for any unpleasantness. I'm sure our paths won't even cross again."

Dante's sneer was looking a little strained in the face of Jericho's snarling maw, and he seemed pretty eager to latch onto any excuse to leave. "Yeah. Right. Because you'll be left behind. In our dust."

Jericho barked, and the Brotherhood scampered off with their tails between their legs, literally and figuratively. The rest of the town went on staring at Iron Riot for a moment, then decided that the street theater was over and went back to their business.

There was no shortage of inns in the town known as Reach-root, but the one they settled on in the end was as close to the basket-elevator down to the cavern floor as it was possible to get. They got themselves drinks, settled into a corner and laid out all of their intentions.

"There are ninety more deeps and nine more Archdukes to get through," Martin said, thinking aloud. "I think we can keep going as we have been, using the first three deeps after each Archduke to grind up the levels that we're lagging, then using my *Rite* to pop the skip-gate and head straight on into the next big boss. It means we'll be running blind a lot of the time, but we'll also close the distance on the front-runners in nine days, provided we can keep up the same pace."

Jericho nodded along, but his mind was clearly still on the Brotherhood in Exile. Lindsay was so intent on everything Martin was saying that she was nearly leaning over the table.

"If we're ever down to the next gate before my ability unlocks, I propose we spend our time developing craft skills. You've seen how expensive gear is. Nobody is making anything because they're in too much of a rush, and it is messing with the equipment curve."

Lindsay groaned. "Sounds boring, but fine. Whatever."

"For today, I think we level up, split up, explore the town a little and get whatever supplies we think we will need for the next few deeps. I think there's going to be more water, but that's about as far as my predictions go."

All it took was another shrug from Jericho and another nod from Lindsay and Martin evenly split the silver they'd collected and sent them off to do some shopping. He had more pressing matters to attend to.

Skaife *Murovan Exorcist*
Strength: 12 Agility: 8
Endurance: 9 Willpower: 10
LEVEL 9

You have 9 points to assign.

Nine points was enough to completely reshape his character. Enough to make any given stat his new area of expertise. He didn't have to think twice.

Strength: 12 Agility: 8
Endurance: 9 Willpower: 19
Health: 45 Stamina: 58

You may select 3 new abilities.

Celestial Chorus – All nearby allies' next physical attacks deal 50% physical and 50% light damage. These attacks count as activators for Trinity Strike. [60-second cooldown]

Javelin of Faith – Deals 19 light damage to a target within 30ft range. [20-second cooldown]

Purify – Removes a curse effect from an ally. Touch range. [60-second cooldown]

Lay on Hands – Restores 100% of an ally's health. Reduces your stamina and stamina regeneration by 5% for 4 minutes. [60-minute cooldown]

Rite of Consecration – Increases all healing effects within the 20ft area of effect by 50% for 30 seconds. Increases all light damage within the area of effect by 25% for 15 seconds. [60-minute cooldown]

Rite of Revival – Restores one deceased ally back to 1% health. Reduces your stamina and stamina regeneration by 15% for 60 minutes. [24-hour cooldown]

Curses hadn't featured too heavily into their journey so far, so Martin discounted *Purify* out of hand, at least for the moment.

Javelin of Faith had too much utility to gloss over. He selected that one the moment he'd finished browsing the list. In the confines of the usual tunnels there wasn't much use for ranged attacks, but in fights with monsters so huge you couldn't even see all of them, being able to hit a weak point from a distance seemed mandatory.

He'd have to ask Lindsay to look into some ranged weapons too, if she didn't want to keep on mashing directly into raid bosses' faces.

Consecration and *Lay on Hands* were both still nice, and he could see a lot of situations where they'd come in useful, but with Julia present, his healing abilities had been used almost entirely on himself up until this point, and the very specific "ally's health" in the description made him suspect it wouldn't serve that purpose.

Likewise, *Consecration* would probably have been more helpful in a group with more players to benefit from it. Just the four of them made it seem slightly underpowered compared to the other offerings.

The other new abilities had his attention and his heart almost immediately. *Revival* was a must. He had been wondering if resurrection by the players was ever going to show up in this game, and there was no way he was going to let that opportunity slip him by.

Celestial Chorus was another must. If he timed it properly, he would be able to churn out *Trinity Strikes* so often that they never lost the buff to critical hit chance. At 33%, that was too good to ignore.

With that done, there was really only one more item of business for Martin.

All of the contempt that he had met up in Beachhead had transformed down here, under pressure, where the coal of humanity was crushed into diamonds. The few folk that recognized his name or his guild gave a respectful nod before turning to whisper to their friends. Even the native NPCs seemed to recognize him as a person of value now. They didn't exactly defer to him, but some switch must have been flipped by his defeat of Carnifex to provide him with the same respect as other players. It didn't take long before he found the town's healer, a self-proclaimed alchemist affectionately known as Greenfeather.

She didn't look up from the big wooden bowl where she was grinding some herbs that looked suspiciously like they'd come out of a Swamproot. Another of the settlement's predominant Corvan, she lived up to her name thanks to the various smears that covered her gray feathers.

"Be with you in a moment, my lover. Don't want this stuff going to brown just because I'm lost clapping my beak."

Martin explored the store slowly but methodically, taking in all of the different labels, noting which ones were behind iron gratings and which were free to be manhandled and shoplifted.

There were only a few ingredients locked away due to their value and he was careful to remember them all. The appraise skill was all well and good, but there was no reason he couldn't use his brain to find the valuable loot too.

"What seems to be the bother?" Greenfeather finally asked. "Aren't many folk seek out a doctor when there's Aten's magical glow-stuff on the go."

She finally looked up from her work and let out a little gasp. "Oh, I'm sorry, sir. Most terribly sorry."

"I died fighting against the Archduke, but when I came back my injuries were still here." Martin paused, then looked away from her mournful stare. "I mean, the wounds were closed, but they... they scarred."

Greenfeather carefully set down the vial of odious goop she had been harvesting from the bowl and sighed.

"I am truly sorry, sir, but I cannot help you. Strata itself remakes you when you die, and if it chooses to remake you with some small adjustments, there isn't much we can do about it."

Martin took a deep breath. "I've lost an eye. I don't mind paying to get it back."

"You misunderstand me, sir. There's a few folk that Strata seems to take a personal interest in. It leaves its marks on them, sir, so that all who know what to look for know they're chosen."

Still that horrible pity.

Martin was incredulous. "Chosen?"

"Aye, sir. Summoned by the will of the dark, not some crusader's call."

Martin suppressed a shiver and a memory. "So there is no fixing this?"

"Not unless Strata wants it fixing, sir."

He blew out his breath and went through his usual polite script. "All right. Thanks for your help."

He was almost out the door when she replied.

"I know I didn't help you none, sir. But there is nobody who can now."

Suddenly the bustle of town seemed claustrophobic, and it was all Martin could do to barge his way through the press of bodies to a quiet corner near the elevator apparatus. He needed to get out. He needed to get out of this body. He needed to get out of Strata.

He pressed his hand to his guild crest and tried to force normalcy into his voice.

"Listen guys, I'm pretty beat after everything. I think I'll call it an early night if Julia isn't coming back. Meet you back here tomorrow night?"

Lindsay seemed genuinely startled.

"Uh, yeah, no problem dude. Sleep well and junk."

He had his eyes shut and the menu open to escape when he froze. There was a slimy little hand clasped around his wrist. Speckles was lurking between him and the side of the apothecary, almost invisible within the Pearlfeather Cloak. "No afraid. Gods below good. Gods below love you."

That was the icing on the cake. Martin logged out as fast as he could. Night had actually fallen by the time he pried the NIH from his forehead. He didn't bother to look at the time on his phone.

For once, he was relieved to be back in his own body. He blinked both eyes slowly, really appreciating them for the first time in his life.

In a few seconds, his usual misery would catch up to him. He would realize that his life out here wasn't any more within his control than his life in Strata and he would sink into a depression nap that would last until dawn if he was lucky.

But for that one glorious moment, he was relieved to be home.

TWENTY-SEVEN

The Final Boss

The nightmares never came.

Or if they did, they were so weak he was able to shrug them off and go about his usual dream business.

Did he hear a whisper? Was there a flicker of green light beneath him everywhere he went? Both were quite possible, but neither encroached on whatever else had happened enough for Martin to recall them upon waking. That was good.

Strata was his freedom and it had started to feel far too much like a whole new cage. The dream, that had been a big part of that. If his brain was going to calm down and let him get on with things as usual then Strata could go back to being fun, rather than harrowing.

With no long night of gaming behind him, Martin was up and active a lot earlier than he would have expected on a Monday morning.

"Well rested" wasn't usually a status effect that he managed to achieve in real life, relying far more often on "Over-caffeinated."

There was a strange ache in his muscles as he walked down to get the early train, not painful exactly, but tense in a way that he wasn't used to.

He didn't have a mirror at home, but some poking and prodding in the shower made him suspicious that he might actually be growing muscles instead of rubber bands. Whatever cycle the NIH ran on him while he was playing was actually making him fitter. Video games that made you healthier; that was a confusing thought. He wondered why something like that wouldn't have shown up in the news, then realized that his exposure to the game might have been a bit more intense than the average user's. That, or news about the game was being suppressed.

The press of bodies on the train was less intrusive than usual. He was getting barged into and bothered less frequently too, which he eventually realized was because he wasn't staring down at his phone.

He had things that he could be doing, websites to scour and leads to chase, but right now he felt oddly at peace. He just had to get through the day and he could slip back into Strata.

Something felt wrong the moment he stepped into the office. There were eyes on him from the very first moment, and not just Gillian's usual prying stare. He very carefully did not make eye contact and headed to his desk to log in well ahead of time.

The work here wasn't exciting, but after dealing with the complexities of Strata, the minor challenges of untangling orders in the system, pulling extra details from the database when they were missing and feeding everything back into the almighty algorithm... he could lose himself in it, if they'd let him.

It was only an hour into the day when he looked up from the screen to see Gillian hovering by the open door of his cubicle. She looked flushed. There was a little line between her eyebrows; she was worried about something. Upset.

It was strange that this person he could barely stand had the face that he knew best in all the world.

"Good morning, Martin. I need to talk to you in my office, please."

There was no way this was good news. He supposed it was possible that she was giving him some sort of formal reprimand for being tardy last week, even if that was a break from procedure, but she didn't have that usual satisfied gleam in her eyes that she got when she was about to tell him off.

In her office, one of her usual lackeys was sitting waiting. A witness. That was even more concerning. They all sat in their respective seats, and then she began.

"Martin, we are all very worried about you."

He blinked. "I beg your pardon?"

"You've... you've never been the most positive person on the team, but these last few weeks, you have changed so dramatically and... I just want you to know that I am here if you want to talk."

"What would I want to talk about?" He glanced nervously at his coworker, who looked genuinely bored.

Gillian let out a weary sigh. "It's drugs, isn't it?"

Martin gawked at her. "What?"

"You've been irritable. Your concentration has been faltering. These are all symptoms of addiction, Martin. Listen to me: you are not alone in this. The company has an instant dismissal policy about drugs, but I am still here to support you. I am your friend, Martin, and I will help you to get the help you need."

He had to raise his voice to be heard over all the mealy-mouthed platitudes. "I am not on drugs!"

It was Gillian's turn to look dubious. "Martin, you have to admit that you have a problem or nobody can help you."

His mouth drew into a thin line. "I don't have any problems! Everything is fine."

Gillian steepled her fingers. "I saw your tattoo, Martin. I know what things like that mean. It's a gang sign, isn't it? Have you gotten involved in crime?"

"Are you kidding me? My tattoo is..." How did he explain this to someone so obnoxiously normal? "I play a video game with some friends. That is the logo of our group."

"A video game? You expect me to believe that a video game is so important you got it branded onto your skin?"

She looked so painfully serious that Martin was worried she was going to sprain something.

He sighed. "Gillian, it doesn't matter what you believe. My personal life is none of your business."

"You aren't part of the team, Martin. Everyone else socializes. Everyone else has friends. You just come to work, do everything that you have to and then leave."

Just a hint of whine was creeping into her voice. But whining was not going to help her case.

"That is all you pay me to do," he said flatly.

"But it isn't enough to just be a machine, Martin. You have to work with others. You have to—"

He cut her off with ever increasing volume.

"I work with the rest of the team constantly. Whenever one of them is having a problem I am happy to—"

She returned the favor, cutting him off mid-sentence. "To take it away and fix it yourself instead of helping them to learn how to solve problems themselves. It's like you don't even understand why we are concerned about you."

He had to calm down or he was going to start screaming.

"Gillian, I don't understand the problem. I show up on time. I do more work than everyone else put together and I go home. That is a model employee."

"Martin." She looked so heartbroken that he just wanted to shake her. "There is more to life than just doing what needs to be done."

He took a deep breath.

"There… there is. And that is what my life outside of work is for. I have people who care about me. I have a whole life that you know nothing about. A life that matters."

His phone buzzed in his pocket and he instinctively reached for it. Gillian rolled her eyes but made no move to stop him so he pulled it out anyway. Not having to look at her for a second might help with the urge to strangle her.

"This is exactly what I'm talking about. You are so distracted all the time. I have called you in here to try and help you with your problems and you would rather check your email than actually engage in meaningful—"

His eyes darted over the screen as she rambled on, but he had already read the important part of the message.

He glanced up at Gillian and said the two words he had been dying to scream at her from the moment he met her.

"Shut up."

That was enough to take the wind out of her sails.

"What?"

His mind rushed ahead, making the calculations. The useless shield from Celaphox had sold for just a little over three months' wages. If he cut back on his living expenses, he could stretch it to four. That would be enough of a margin for error to finish Strata comfortably.

"Just be quiet for one second. Let me think."

The flush came back over Gillian. Not embarrassment, but anger. It was almost cute when she puffed up and turned red.

"I will not tolerate being spoken to in this manner. Martin, you are an employee, and you cannot—"

"Not any more I'm not." He smiled up at her. "I quit."

Her mouth hung open.

"What?"

He stood up and gave his ex-coworker a pat on the shoulder.

"I quit. I'm done. Goodbye."

Gillian shouted after him, desperate to keep his attention as he headed for the door. "You can't just quit. What are you going to do with your life?"

He rolled up his sleeves and grinned. "Believe it or not, I'm going to play video games."

"What?"

She was standing too now. When had that happened?

"Martin, don't throw your life away."

That touched a nerve.

"I'm done throwing my life away. Day after day. Coming here

and pushing buttons, years of my life just pushing buttons, all to change some numbers I don't care about on some screens. This isn't real. This... this is the life that doesn't matter. Why am I wasting my time on it?"

He walked out into the deathly silent office with a bounce in his step. It felt like a victory as he strolled back to his desk to gather up his meagre belongings.

He might have walked out there and then had inspiration not struck at the last moment.

Perhaps this place would be of some use after all.

He clicked over to the telecoms database and typed in the words "Edwin Klimpt." It wasn't like they could sack him for improper use of company property now.

There was only one entry, and it looked like someone was in the process of scrambling it from the moment the data appeared on the screen.

He was too late for a phone number, but he scribbled down the address, one state over, before they could finish. He slipped the post-it note away and turned to leave, only to be confronted with a security guard.

"Turn out your pockets please, sir."

Gillian was hovering behind the guard, tears in her eyes. Martin rolled his eyes.

"Really?"

The guard must have been on standby in the stairwell to get here so quickly. Maybe Gillian had better organizational skills than he'd thought.

"Standard procedure when escorting downsized employees out of the building."

Martin looked him up and down. "You aren't touching me, and you have no right to search me."

"Sir."

Well, that was informative.

Martin let his eyes flick away from the security guard for a moment.

"Gillian, call the cops. They'll tell you the same thing."

She just shook her head. "I called him, Martin."

The guard had about a foot on Martin, weighed about half as much again in muscle and he had pepper spray too. Martin found himself reaching for a sword that wasn't at his hip.

"I'm warning you, if you touch me, I'm going to treat you the same way I'd treat anyone else trying to lay hands on me without permission. Now stand aside."

The guard went for him and instincts that Martin didn't know he had kicked in.

He vaulted clear over the cubicle wall without even thinking. A single leap. Just like that.

He didn't look back. He just ran for the exit. In fact, he didn't stop running until he was on the train, and by then his brain was already rattling through the glorious days ahead of him.

All that money. He didn't need to work for three months, and all that extra time would let him explore Strata more thoroughly, level up, even manufacture gear.

It would also give him all the time he needed to get stuck into the mystery of the invisible developers, starting with a daytrip to visit his new best friend Mr. Klimpt.

There was no way that the company would send anyone after him or warn Klimpt that he was coming. That would involve admitting their culpability in the breach of his privacy. He only had to hope whatever algorithm scrambled Klimpt's data didn't notify its owner each time it did so.

Even if his accelerated plans to delve through Strata were derailed, there was no way that in the next three months of exploring Strata he wouldn't come across a single item that could go to auction. If he got far enough into the crafting systems then he could just make that a part-time job.

His hands started to shake as the adrenaline wore off. How the hell had he been able to jump that high? What was the NIH shaping him into while he played? With habitual movements he pulled up the newsfeeds about Strata on his phone, expecting to see some stupid think piece somewhere in the mix about a game that made you healthier, but that wasn't the front-page news. Somebody had died.

Some girl called Jessie Beldrum, three states north, had been playing the game without a break for over a fortnight and dehydration had finally finished her off. The body had been discovered today, though it looked like she'd been dead a week, and whatever algorithm the Masters of Strata had been using to keep their game out of the news hadn't been able to stand up to the swathe of reports.

Jessie Beldrum. Jezebel?

The dates didn't add up. He'd seen Jezebel after this Jessie girl died. She couldn't have still been playing. That made no sense.

He pushed that momentary spike of fear aside, turned off the news and focused on his excitement. It was all over. The dead-end jobs and the grind. He was finally free. Even years from now, when the last boss was slain a dozen times over and people abandoned Strata, there would always be a new game. There would always be somewhere that Martin belonged, and could use his own excellence to pay his way.

Back in his apartment, Martin stripped the bed, tossed out all of his trash and even ran the little handheld vacuum over the place; everything he could think of doing before logging back into Strata and getting started on his grand plans. This was more than a fresh start for him. It was a whole new life. He felt like he needed to do something, other than checking his newly healthy bank account, to mark the occasion.

He picked up his phone and tapped the only number he seemed to use.

"Hey Lindsay. Want to start early tonight?"

There wasn't even a moment's hesitation.

"Can do, can do, how early are you finishing work?"

"I'm finished now," he tapped back. *"I quit."*

There was a momentary pause, then:

"Dude. What? That is crazy. Talk in Strata. Give me like 20 minutes to duck out."

He smiled down at the message, already reaching for the NIH.

"I'll be waiting for you down there."

This time, as the numbers counted down and he closed his eyes to blissful darkness, Martin didn't feel like he was falling; he felt like he was coming home. It might have been a dark place, but it was his.

And he wouldn't give it up for anything.

To be concluded in **Masters of Strata.**

More LitRPG from Portal Books

Portal Books is a LitRPG publisher, and our team are passionate about the genre.

If you'd like to try out stories from the other fantastic Portal Books authors, you can sign up to our mailing list for 60,000 words of LitRPG stories. Whenever we add more, you'll get the update, absolutely free.

https://portal-books.com/sign-up

Below are some of our titles, which you can read right now!

Occultist (Saga Online #1)
Welcome to the world of Saga Online, the newest fantasy VRMMORPG. Join Damien as he discovers the rare Occultist class and summons an army of demons to save his mother's life.

It's available on Kindle Unlimited and on Audio.

Bone Dungeon (Elemental Dungeon #1)
Reborn as a dark dungeon, Ryan was happy defeating

adventurers with undead minions. Then a necromancer arrived, and un-life got a whole lot harder...

It's available on Kindle Unlimited and coming soon to Audio.

God of Gnomes (God Core #1)
Deep beneath the earth, Corey finds himself reborn as a God Core – a sentient crystal with unusual powers. His new worshipers? A colony of incompetent gnomes, scratching out an existence in their underground grotto.
If that wasn't bad enough, Corey soon realizes that his gnome denizens are about to become extinct. They are threatened by groups of blundering adventurers, and abducted by raiding kobolds to be sacrificed to their own dark god: an ancient, mysterious foe who does not take kindly to Corey's arrival.
With the aid of his helper sprite and a menagerie of newly evolved creatures, Corey must protect and guide his gnomes until they can stand on their own two feet. But the kobold army is on the march, led by his new rival's powerful avatar.

It's available on Kindle Unlimited and Audio.

Warden: Nova Online.
Imprisoned for a murder he didn't commit, Kaiden's only hope of early release is in serving as a Warden in the game-world of Nova Online.

It's available on Kindle Unlimited and on Audio.

Mastermind (Titan Online #1) - A Superhero LitRPG
Karna was just like any other comic book fan. He dreamed of fighting alongside colorful heroes and taking down dastardly villains. In Titan Online, the most popular VR MMORPG going, he finally got the chance to live out his cape-donning fantasies.

It's available on Kindle Unlimited and Audio.

Battle Spire: A Crafting LitRPG Book.
Battle Spire is a meeting of *World of Warcraft* and *Die Hard*, using crunchy LitRPG mechanics with a heavy focus on crafting. Readers can expect to find in depth item and spell descriptions, along with stat tables and profession recipes.

It's available on Kindle Unlimited and Audio.

For more general discussions about the genre, these groups may be useful to you.

www.facebook.com/groups/LitRPGsociety/

www.facebook.com/groups/LitRPG.books/

www.facebook.com/groups/LitRPGGroup/

Join the Group

To learn more about LitRPG, talk to authors including myself, and just have an awesome time, please join the LitRPG Group.

Made in United States
Troutdale, OR
05/09/2024